DIAMONDS AND PEARL

ALSO BY K'WAN

Street Dreams

Hoodlum

Hood Rat

Still Hood

Gutter

Section 8

Welfare Wifeys

Eviction Notice

DIAMONDS AND PEARL

K'WAN

St. Martin's Griffin
New York

This is a work of fiction. All of the characters, organizations, and events portrayed in this novel are either products of the author's imagination or are used fictitiously.

DIAMONDS AND PEARL. Copyright © 2016 by K'Wan. All rights reserved. Printed in the United States of America. For information, address St. Martin's Press, 175 Fifth Avenue, New York, N.Y. 10010.

www.stmartins.com

Designed by Omar Chapa

Library of Congress Cataloging-in-Publication Data

Names: K'wan, author.
Title: Diamonds and Pearl / K'wan.
Description: First edition. | New York : St. Martin's Griffin, 2016.
Identifiers: LCCN 2016021589 | ISBN 978-1-250-10261-4 (trade paperback) |
     ISBN 978-1-250-10262-1 (e-book)
Subjects: LCSH: Man-woman relationships—Fiction. | African
     Americans—Fiction. | Street life—Fiction. | Urban fiction. | BISAC:
     FICTION / African American / Urban Life. | FICTION / Urban Life.
Classification: LCC PS3606.O96 D53 2016 | DDC 813/.6—dc23
LC record available at https://lccn.loc.gov/2016021589

Our books may be purchased in bulk for promotional, educational, or business use. Please contact your local bookseller or the Macmillan Corporate and Premium Sales Department at 1-800-221-7945, extension 5442, or by e-mail at MacmillanSpecialMarkets@macmillan.com.

First Edition: October 2016

10 9 8 7 6 5 4 3 2 1

ACKNOWLEDGMENTS

Thank you:

It's been years since I've done acknowledgments, so if I miss anyone, blame it on my head and not my heart.

First and foremost, God. All things are possible through the creator. If you don't believe me, you simply have to look at what I come from and see where I'm going.

My mother, Brenda M. Foye. You gave me three great gifts: life, the ability to write, and the courage to dream. Writing was your passion, and I reluctantly inherited the fire that burned in your heart. I didn't understand at first, but I see it with great clarity now. I will continue to honor your memory by living your dream and respecting the craft. I do this for YOU!

My wife and children who endure the long months when I'm locked away in my head working on a project. I'm sure it can be incredibly frustrating, yet they patiently wait for me to return from wherever my mind drifts to during the creative process.

My agent, Marc Gerald, who continues to fight the good fight for me to be recognized and respected as more than just a "street" writer and still thugs it out with me when I give in to frustration and go through short bouts of insanity.

A HUGE thank-you to Monique Patterson and the entire St. Martin's Press family. I credit Monique with helping me to become a better writer by not only being a bomb editor but also making sure I had a clear understanding of the process. Great editor, greater person.

Roughly thirteen years ago St. Martin's took a chance on an underground writer with more than a few rough edges and helped me to grow as a person and a writer. I can still remember showing up to meet Matthew Shear (RIP) for the first time wearing a Dickey suit and Chuck Taylors, stinking of weed. I can only imagine what must've been running through his mind, yet he embraced me and was always there when I needed him. You are missed.

Even during the short period when I decided to go off and explore the world, St. Martin's continued to be supportive of me. It's only "write" that the journey has come full circle and the wayward son has returned home, older and wiser, to continue what we started with *Street Dreams*.

Last but certainly not least, my readers. The lifespan of an author is short yet you guys have stuck with me through the good and the bad for nearly two decades. For this I am EXTREMELY thankful.

Now on with the show.

Enjoy the story.

PART

I

WHEN THE LEVEES BROKE

CHAPTER ONE

"It looks bad out there, man," Larry said, staring out the rain-slicked window of the second-floor bedroom. It was the only level of the house that hadn't been completely flooded yet, or soaked to shit. Looking at the rapidly rising floodwaters, that was likely to change soon. Larry doubted if the house would last through the night before being washed away like everything else. In his thirty-five years of life he had never seen anything like it. It was a storm of biblical proportions that made him think back to his grandma reading passages of the bible about God washing sin from the earth in a merciless tide of judgment. The city he had grown to love so much was being cleansed.

It was fitting that this particular hurricane had been named after a woman, Katrina, because she had come through and unleashed the wrath of a woman scorned on the city of New Orleans. Just about everyone who was able to had already fled the area, and those who couldn't scrambled for higher ground and prayed for help that was in no rush to get there.

"This shit has got the white man's stink all over it." Big Aaron came into the bedroom. He had a ham sandwich in one hand and a can of beer in the other. He took a huge bite of the sandwich and continued his theory. "As strong as them levees was supposed to be, how the hell are damn near all of them gonna fail at one time? If you ask me, this shit was all a government plot to get all the niggers out of New Orleans so they can turn this into a tourist trap."

"I don't recall asking you about no damn conspiracy theories, but I do recall asking you to help them young boys finish loading my dope onto that truck before the water gets too high to drive out. Most of the roads have already flooded, so we only got a small window of time to get gone. Turn that sandwich loose and tend my business, hear?" Slim barked in a heavy Southern drawl. He was sitting on the bed, stuffing money into a duffel bag. It was one of several that now littered the bedroom floor. Having his money outside the safety of his vault rattled him, but there was no way they'd be able to move the massive thing.

He'd acquired the name Slim as a boy, when playing the harmonica and picking the pockets of tourists in the red-light district had been his means of living. As his reputation and wealth grew, so did he, currently tipping the scales at just nearly four hundred pounds. Slim used memories of starvation to motivate him in his climb up the underworld ladder, devouring food and territory alike. It was whispered in some circles that Slim enjoyed the touch of a greasy cheeseburger and his money over that of a woman.

"Slim, them young boys got it under control," Aaron said as if it were nothing. "What you need to be worried about is how the police is gonna be looking at your ass driving down the street in a big-ass rig!"

Slim looked at Aaron as if he were crazy. "Nigga, what you talking? Brah, people floating down the damn streets in bathtubs, and nobody give 'em a second look. Police was amongst the first to get their families outta here when the water came. Between the storm and these larcenous muthafuckas out there tripping the city, ain't got time to stunt no truck. The government is gonna wait this shit out and come clean up whatever's left. Hell, they'll probably be happy to see us going and out of their way."

"Don't trip, Slim; I'll make sure they're finished. The sooner they get that dope stashed in them hidden panels, the sooner we can get outta this damn soup bowl," Larry said disgustedly. He loved his city more than any of them, but even he knew that New Orleans wouldn't be the same after Hurricane Katrina.

"You buy into that shit that everybody saying, Slim?" Aaron asked after Larry had left the room.

"And what shit would that be?" Slim had resumed his counting.

"About it being the end of New Orleans?"

"You can't put an end to something that has always been here. New Orleans might be more notorious for shit like Mardi Gras and the murder rate than anything else, but our city has a far richer history that it's given credit for. It won't be the end of New Orleans, but it'll sure as hell be the end of an era when them army dogs finally come in to clean this shit up. The dope game down here is dead, and they'll build a newer, more tourist-friendly New Orleans over its corpse."

"So you think we'll have better luck in Texas?" Aaron asked.

"I sure hope so, because it's the best chance we got at surviving this freakish shit. An old buddy of mine is gonna set us up in a spot we can operate out of until we're strong enough to stand on our own again," Slim said, zipping the last duffel bag.

"That shouldn't be too hard, since most of the people who bought drugs from us here are gonna be scattered around Texas in those fake-ass concentration camps," Aaron joked, referring to the temporary shelters that were being erected for the evacuees. "Between the poor conditions and the mingling of all them rival gangs and crews, those camps ain't shit but a powder keg waiting for somebody with the match that's gonna blow it smooth to hell."

Their conversation was broken up by a loud thump coming from the hallway. Aaron was about to go and investigate when Larry came into the room. He wore a worried expression on his face, and beads of sweat rolled down his forehead.

"Larry, please don't tell me them young boys done fucked up and let my dope get wet?" Slim asked in an irritated tone. He had lost enough money and drugs due to the flood, and couldn't stand another hit.

"That dope plenty fine where it is, boss. It's you who got the issue," a voice called from behind Larry. Two men wearing ski masks materialized in the doorway. Both of them were armed with assault rifles: an AK-47 and an M16. Slim went to reach for his gun, but the one holding the M16 was in on him. His face was hidden behind his mask, but Slim could see his dead black eyes through the holes. When he spoke again, Slim caught a glimpse of his shiny diamond covered teeth. "You can keep reaching if you got a mind to, fat man, but I'd bet this here chopper against whatever you got that can fit in that drawer any day." When the gunman spoke, there was something about him that tugged at Slim's brain. Most of the children of New Orleans spoke with Southern accents, but his was closer to French.

"Man, you nigga know who the fuck you're trying to rob?" Aaron barked. The second gunman, the one with the AK-47, closed the distance between them. A short, fat dude, he moved swiftly for a man his size. He raised the AK and slammed the butt into Aaron's mouth, knocking his two front teeth out.

"See, this is what being funny amongst serious men will get you." The diamond-toothed robber pointed to Aaron, who was curled up in the corner, holding his bloody mouth. "*Souple,* no more games. Just go along with the program and nobody else gets hurt, Slim."

Slim let out a weak chuckle. "Ain't this about a bitch? Man, y'all petty muthafuckas in here pressing me over some dope when we might very well be living in our last days."

"And as it was written, the last shall be first. Y'all are the last of the old regime, and we're the first of the new," the diamond-toothed man said, matching Slim's tone. "Now, I don't plan to keep repeating myself, so hand that shit over before I start feeling like I got something to prove." He adjusted his grip on the M16.

"All right, man. Just be easy with them guns." Slim used his foot to push one of the duffel bags over.

Keeping his M16 trained on Slim, the man with the diamond covered teeth made a quick check of the bag. He looked back at his partner and nodded in approval before scooping up the bag and slinging it over his shoulder.

"A'ight, y'all got what you came for, so you can split," Slim continued.

"Not just yet." The fat gunmen with the AK moved over to Slim. His eyes were on the gaudy diamond pinky ring on Slim's left hand. "Run that, too."

"Man, this old ring ain't worth nothing to nobody but me. It was a gift from my wife. I lost her last year, and this is how I keep her close to me," Slim said sincerely.

The diamond-toothed man saw the situation about to take a turn in the wrong direction, so he intervened. "Fat man, my own grief already heavier than my shoulders can take. I don't need to add yours to it, so keep the ring." All he wanted was to get what they'd come for and get out, but his partner had other ideas.

"Fuck that! We came for everything," the fat robber insisted. Behind his mask, his eyes flashed a hatred toward Slim that few understood. For his partner, it was business; but for him, it was personal.

"Kid, why don't y'all just get the fuck outta here before some-body gets hurt?" Larry said in an easy tone. He knew he'd fucked up by letting the masked men get the drop on him, and he was trying to make up for it by getting to his gun, which was hidden under the newspaper he'd been reading.

"Fuck that!" the fat robber snapped. "Y'all niggaz ain't the kings of the hill no more, so don't tell me what to do!"

"Kings of the hill? Young boy, in case you ain't noticed, the hill is turning into a damn mudslide," Slim said with a chuckle.

"You laughing at me?" The fat robber turned to Slim, eyes blaz-ing. Before his partner could stop him, he clubbed Slim in the head with his machine gun, knocking him off the bed and onto the floor.

"Boy, you lost your senses?" The diamond-toothed robber shoved the fat one away from Slim. He'd seen his partner in his rages before and wanted to prevent what he knew would happen if he let it go too far. "Check yo muthafucking feelings and stay focused on this paper."

"I wouldn't have cracked him if he hadn't been laughing at me," the fat robber argued.

"Wasn't nobody laughing at you; I was just trying to ease the ten-sion a little." Slim hauled himself back onto the bed. His lip was bleeding and his jaw felt cracked, but the blow had also helped to jog his memory. "You know, I done met plenty of cats in my day weren't big on humor, but there's only one who comes to mind who gets to crying like a bitch when he thinks he's being laughed at. What's up, John-Boy?"

"Greasy little nigga!" Aaron hissed. When he spoke, it made a funny whistling sound, because he was now missing his front teeth. They had known John-Boy since he was a fat little kid stealing snacks out of the corner store.

"And if that's John-Boy, I'm guessing you're Diamonds," Slim addressed the diamond-toothed robber as the pieces began falling into place. "This fat piece of shit ain't got the brains or the balls to walk into this one without somebody putting the battery in him."

"Since all the cards on the table, I guess ain't no need for these." Diamonds pulled his mask off and shook his dreads lose from the stocking cap that'd been holding them down. His face was smooth and golden, with high cheekbones and slanted eyes. Diamonds had always been a hit with the ladies, but his heart belonged to the streets.

"After all I've done for your little asses, this is how you come at me?" Slim was genuinely offended.

"Manti," Diamonds accused. "Slim, feed your lies to someone who don't have eyes and ears, because ain't no sane man gonna believe a lunatic. You sat back and watched while we fought like dogs for the scraps that fell off your plate. How long you think you can deny hungry dogs proper meals before they learn to hunt on their own?" He hoisted the duffel bag full of Slim's cash for emphasis.

"You think y'all can come in here and take our shit like we soft?" Larry snapped, not able to hold his tongue with the disrespectful youths.

"Funny, because that's exactly what was happening," Diamonds said sarcastically.

Slim shook his head. "You know, from the first time I seen you and your brother crawl up outta the swamp and into my city, I knew you were going to be trouble. I tried to nurture you little niggas and teach you about loyalty and how to get paper, but I should've cut you down like the dogs you were."

"And therein lies the problem, fat man. You see a young nigga from the mud and don't see nothing but a servant . . . somebody to do the shit you ain't got the balls to do on your own. All risks and no reward. If you had it your way, I'd have been eating out of your hand until the end of my days, but this is not to be. I ain't gonna die no soldier, brah. I gots to be the king or nothing! *Bonswa*, fat man." Diamonds scooped up an additional duffel bag and began backing out of the room, leaving John-Boy to collect the other ones.

John-Boy scooped up two bags and carried a third in his free hand. He swept the AK back and forth, in case anybody had any ideas, and followed his partner. Seeing the furious look on Slim's face, he decided to add insult to injury. "Don't feel bad, Slim. We're doing you a favor by robbing you. Your fat ass looks like you could stand to miss a meal or three," he taunted. He had just turned to leave when pain exploded in his back. He staggered forward, nearly crashing into Diamonds when he fell at his feet.

Seeing his childhood friend fallen, Diamonds didn't even think; he just reacted. Shrugging off the duffel bags, he brought the M16 into play. The assault rifle swung up, expelling shell casings the size of ink pens and ejaculating vengeful fire from the muzzle. With a sweep of his arm, he tore the furniture in the bedroom to pieces en route to cutting Larry in half. Aaron threw his hands up in surrender as if to signal that it hadn't been him, but it didn't make him exempt from Diamonds's rage. The grief-stricken man got close up on Aaron before burring the barrel of the M16 into Aaron's chest, pulling the trigger and turning him into meat. When he turned the gun on where Slim had been sitting, all he found was an empty bed.

The hulk of a man had rolled over the bed and was making a mad dash to the other side of the room. Diamonds tried to cut him down, but Slim was more evasive than Diamonds had given him credit for. He was well over three hundred pounds, but the fear of death gave him the speed of a man one-quarter his size. The M16 rattled to life one last time before clicking empty, and Diamonds heard Slim cry out just as his huge frame crashed through the window. Diamonds wasn't sure how many times he'd hit him, but if the bullets didn't kill him, the headfirst fall would.

Diamonds turned his attention back to John-Boy, who was down but still breathing. Diamonds knelt beside him to assess the damage. "How bad?" He pulled the ski mask from John-Boy's face to help him breathe a little easier. It was a redundant question. The blood pooling from beneath the fallen soldier and soaking the knees of Diamonds's jeans already answered it.

"I'm fucked up," John-Boy said, and coughed, sending a trickle of blood down his chin. He was grabbing for his sweat shirt, trying to lift it, but his fingers didn't seem to want to cooperate.

Cautiously, Diamonds lifted the front of the sweat shirt. It was soaked, and it clung to John-Boy's portly stomach. When Diamonds spotted the leaking wound in John-Boy's chest, he had to swallow the gasp that had almost escaped him. It was a mortal wound. "Damn, what happened to the vest I gave you?"

John-Boy managed to muster a weak smile and showcased his bloodstained teeth. "It was fucking with my aim." He winced as if he was in pain, but then his face was calm again. "Don't tell Buda that I got caught slipping. I know he's gonna be pissed at me, and I don't wanna hear his mouth. After the last time, he told me that if I fucked up again, then y'all was gonna cut me out."

"Buda was just talking shit. We'd never cut you out. The four of us is brothers—don't you go forgetting that." Diamonds had known John-Boy and Buda as long as he'd known anybody in New Orleans. They were the first kids he and Goldie had met when the department of child services had found them being raised by their aunt in a backwater shack and forced her to enroll the two boys in a regular school with other kids their ages. With Diamonds and his brother spending most of their lives in seclusion in the woods of rural Louisiana and speaking more Creole than the Queen's English, the transition hadn't been an easy one, but Buda and John-Boy had helped them through it. They were amongst the rare few who didn't tease them for their ragged clothes and bare feet, or Diamonds for his thick accent.

The sound of footsteps behind him caused Diamonds to spin, drawing the backup .45 he had shoved into his pants. He was angry and in a shoot-first mood, but his trigger finger was stayed when he saw his brother, Goldie, round the corner with Hank.

Goldie was three years Diamonds's junior, but hard living and a thick black goatee made him appear slightly older. He stood at a wiry six foot three, with deep olive-toned skin and eyes that had seen too much too soon. On his cheek, just below his left eye, were tattooed the numbers 187, so there was no mistaking exactly what he was about. His signature black bandanna hung loosely around his neck, and you could see the tips of his cornrows hanging from the black beanie on his head. Something was just about to roll off his tongue, but when he spotted his brother hunched over his best friend, the words died on his tongue. He and John-Boy were closer in age, so they often found themselves spending a great deal of time in each other's company, trailing their older brothers as they found creative ways to break the law.

"From the way you're looking at me, you'd think I was dead already," John-Boy tried to joke.

"You ain't gonna die." Hank knelt beside Diamonds over John-Boy. "If you kick the bucket on us, we'll have to burry you here, because there's no way we'll be able to haul your fat ass out," he joked while checking John-Boy's wounds. Hank had some medical experience from his time in the army. He was by no means licensed to practice medicine, but he had done a better than average job patching up the homies after battles over the years. The solemn look on Hank's face confirmed what Diamonds had already suspected.

"You ain't gotta say it, Hank. I know I'm a goner." John-Boy read the old head's eyes.

"I ain't lost a man in the field since ninety-eight, and I ain't gonna have you fucking up my streak. Somebody, help me get him up." Hank tugged at one of John-Boy's arms, trying to get him to his feet. It took the combined efforts of himself and Diamonds to get him up.

"Damn, this shit hurt!" John-Boy cried out.

"I ain't never known a gunshot that felt good," Diamonds capped, looping John-Boy's arm around his neck to help support his weight, which was no easy feat. Diamonds scooped up one of the duffel bags, slinging it over his free shoulder before helping Hank get John-Boy to the door. "Goldie, grab as many of them bags as you can carry, and follow us downstairs. You and Dip can come back for the rest once we get him clear."

"Solid," Goldie replied, and stated grabbing bags.

With Diamonds and Hank half carrying, half dragging John-Boy between them, they were able to struggle downstairs, only to find themselves knee-deep in water. The tide was rising faster now, and it was only a matter of time before the house and the corpses inside were washed away with everything else.

"This is some bullshit here. I'm a gangster, not no damn fish!" Goldie said, trying futilely not to get the money wet. He was nervous that the heavy bags would pull him under the water, but he was too greedy to let any of them go.

"Shut yo ass up and keep that money dry!" Hank shouted. He tripped over something he couldn't see, and nearly dropped John-Boy into the water.

"First ol' boy upstairs shot me, and now your old ass is trying to drown me," John-Boy joked.

"Better this then letting them patch you up in the prison hospital," Diamonds told him. "Now, quit wasting your energy bumping your gums, and try get them legs moving. Hank, how'd everything go with them boys Slim had out back?" He'd assigned Hank and

Goldie with the tasks of taking out the guards around the house and rounding up the dope, while Buda and Dip were responsible for their exits.

"They was like cats in the freezer—cold pussies!" Hank said in an amused tone. "When Goldie laid the first two out, the rest took off running. Do you know Slim's crazy ass was actually trying to get the dope out of here in a truck?"

"Ain't nothing with wheels moving out there," Goldie added. "Old Slim must've forgotten that damn near the whole city is underwater."

"It's a good thing we didn't," Diamonds said with a knowing smirk. He pulled out his Nextel and hit the chirp button on the side. It was the signal to let Buda know they were ready to go.

They had just cleared the front door with John-Boy and the money in tow when two airboats eased to stops in what used to be the front yard. Buda and Dip thought Diamonds was crazy when he suggested using the boats to make their escapes, but in light of all the streets unexpectedly flooding, Diamonds's foresight had worked in their favor.

Buda stood at the helm of the lead boat, bald head slick with rain, his thick Santa-like beard completely waterlogged. Like John-Boy, Buda was short and thick, but his body was composed almost entirely of muscle. He jumped down into the waist-deep water to help Goldie, who was struggling to load the duffel bags onto the deck. When he saw Diamonds and Hank carrying his brother out, he abandoned the money and waded through the water to them.

"I know that ain't my baby brother." Buda's voice trembled at the sight of the boy he'd promised his grandmother on her deathbed that he'd always look out for. John-Boy dangled like a wet noodle between Diamonds and Hank, bloody and pale.

"They caught me slipping," John-Boy said, offering a weak explanation.

Buda reached for his baby brother, but his hands stopped short as if touching him would make his condition worse. There were no words he could find that would be adequate for the situation, so he responded in a way that would best convey what he was feeling and pulled his gun. Buda stormed toward the house, but Diamonds blocked his path.

"They shot my little brother," Buda said, as if he expected Diamonds of all people to understand.

"And I shot them. Ain't nothing in there but work for the coroner. We gonna get baby brother to Auntie and have her fix up one of them potions, and he'll be strong as an ox again in no time. You'll see." Diamonds tugged at his arm. Buda lingered for a few more seconds, as if he were weighing the decision. Reluctantly, he allowed Diamonds to pull him away from the house.

After getting John-Boy onto one of the airboats, the men finished ransacking the house. It took them three trips to collect all that they could carry. They were able to take all the money and most of the dope, but they had to leave a good chunk of it behind. The two airboats were already stacked over capacity, and they feared adding any more weight would sink them.

"So what we gonna do now? These airboats are good for the heist, but they ain't gonna get us outta New Orleans," Dip said from his perch behind the wheel of the second airboat. He was a short, skinny youth with shifty eyes and lips that always seemed chapped.

"You know me better than to insult my intelligence. Just because I didn't share the plan with you, doesn't mean there isn't one," Diamonds said, checking him. "The boats are to get us to higher ground where we can repack the dope and prepare it for proper transport. I got some things in motion, and once we wrap our business up here, it's the open road for these outlaws. I got some people in Florida who we can lie low with until we get straight."

"Diamonds!" John-Boy cried out unexpectedly.

"I'm here, little bro." Diamonds rushed to John-Boy's side and clutched his hand. It was cold, and his eyes were now glazed over as if he were having trouble focusing.

"You hear that?" John-Boy asked. His voice now sounded flat and tired.

"Hear what?"

"Hooves . . . they say that death rides a horse. He's coming for me, but I don't wanna go."

"Don't talk crazy. You ain't going nowhere but to Florida with the rest of us. The Horseman is an old wives' tale Auntie used to tell us to scare us. He ain't real," Diamonds assured him.

"Then how do you explain that black steed marching alongside us?" John-Boy's eyes drifted to something just beyond Diamonds.

Diamonds looked in the direction of John-Boy's gaze but saw nothing but the murky waves caused by their airboat and the drowned New Orleans streets. The loss of blood must've been making him delirious. "There's nothing there," he tried to tell him, but John-Boy continued to stare at whatever phantom he alone could see.

John-Boy began to chuckle softly.

"What's so funny?" Diamonds asked, taking his hand in his. It was clammy.

"I was just wondering how the Horseman plans to get me to hell, since he only brought one horse? My fat ass is liable to sink us both." He pushed out one last giggle before going still. John-Boy had pulled his last caper.

Buda leaned in and kissed John-Boy's forehead before gently brushing his eyes closed. "Travel safe, little brother."

"I'm sorry, man," Dip offered.

Buda nodded but didn't speak. He stood turned to Diamonds. "I don't suppose Auntie's got a tonic that can bring back the dead." His tone was light, as if he were making a joke out of it, but there was a hint of desperation in his eyes.

Diamonds gave him a sad look. "Even if she did, he wouldn't be your brother anymore. Best to let the dead rest."

Buda nodded.

"Listen," Diamonds continued, "we can put the move on hold if need be, to give you some time to grieve. My heart's heavy over this too, so maybe we should all take a minute."

Buda shook his head. "Nah, we stick with the plan and get the fuck out of Dodge while we still can. We ain't doing John-Boy's memory no justice if we dead or in jail. All I ask is that we give him a proper send-off before we pull out. I'll always carry my brother's spirit with me, but Louisiana soil is welcome to his body."

Diamonds nodded. "So be it."

CHAPTER TWO

It was well into the night by the time the rain had decided to show them a bit of mercy. It was still falling but had scaled back from a monsoon to a consistent spray. The floodwaters had stopped rising, but they hadn't begun to recede yet either. The city was in bad shape, the rural areas ever worse, especially along the banks of the Mississippi. Diamonds could remember hot summer days when he and Goldie called a shack in the backwoods *home,* and they'd go for cooling afternoon swims in the murky waters. The storm had swollen the river to the point where it was nearly unapproachable, and it looked like they were going to have to break a time-honored tradition, but luckily they were able to find a high patch of land along the river that hadn't been swallowed yet. It was little more than a patch of mud and rock, but it allowed them to get close enough to the river to do what they'd come for.

A darkness lingered between Diamonds and his assembled team. He had just orchestrated and executed the biggest score of his life, and it should've been cause for celebration, but there was no joy in Diamonds's heart, only twisting sadness. He had lost friends before, and even family members, but this was the first time he had lost a member of his crew and it hurt. Though Hank was the oldest of them, the entire team looked to Diamonds for guidance. He was their leader and supposed to be their protector, but he had failed to save John-Boy. Everyone knew it wasn't Diamonds's fault and nobody held him accountable, but his heart was still heavy with guilt.

Standing just behind Diamonds was roughly three-quarters of what remained of his crew. The small fire they had managed to erect on the patch of mud sputtered as drops of rain fell to their deaths in the heat. They'd created a small tent of sticks and leaves over it to keep the fire lit, but it was waning, as was their time in the Big Easy.

Buda stood closest to the river, whispering softly to his brother's corpse. Every so often he'd take a deep swig from the bottle of whiskey clutched in his hand. Buda had never been much of a drinker, because he couldn't hold his liquor, but he had been making slow love to the bottle for the better part of an hour. He hadn't said much since they'd left the stash house, but he wore his feelings on his face. It looked like somebody had ripped his heart out. John-Boy was the last of his blood kin, and being that neither one of them had any children, Buda represented the last of their bloodline.

Vita sat alone on a rock, polishing a dented gold horn with an oil rag. It was what she did when she was nervous, or angry. For as long as any of them had known her, the horn had been an extension of her heart, and you could always tell what was in it by what she chose to play. If you asked Vita about her relationship with the horn, she'd tell you that she could articulate herself through music in a far better way than she could through words. Every so often her gaze would drift to John-Boy's body and she would start crying again. Vita and John-Boy had fought like cats and dogs in life, but next to Buda, she took his death the hardest. They'd had a nasty argument that morning over the fact that Diamonds didn't want her going with them when they took off Slim. Vita was a down-ass solider, and her gun went off when called on, but she was still young and somewhat green. This was the reason Diamonds gave for not wanting her along, but others suggested different.

There were mixed feelings amongst the team, so they put it to a vote; John-Boy had sided with Diamonds and voted against Vita. He, too, claimed it was for her own safety, but Vita accused him of wanting to cut her out so he could get a bigger split of the pie for putting in the work, which led to words being exchanged. The two of them arguing was hardly unusual, but Vita had said some hurtful things to John-Boy, and now that he was dead, she'd never be able to take them back.

Goldie paced back and forth while mumbling under his breath. Every so often he'd look down at his watch and shake his head so hard that Diamonds feared it would fall off his shoulders. John-Boy's death had affected Goldie, too, but he processed grief differently than most. Instead of being sad, Goldie channeled his grief into balls of rage. When he was hurt, he wanted to hurt people. Diamonds had to be sure to keep an extra eye on his little brother, because Goldie could be a wild card when he was in his feelings, and his temper could derail their whole plan.

Diamonds couldn't say he didn't understand why Goldie was so irritated. In addition to everything else they had going on, Dip had gone missing. After the robbery they had all split up with plans to meet on the riverbank at ten o'clock to see John-Boy off. From there they would head to Texas, where Diamonds had a deal in place to sell off some of the dope they'd stolen, before heading to Florida. It was nearly eleven, but there was still no sign of Dip.

"Where the fuck are these niggas?" Goldie asked for what felt like the hundredth time in the last fifteen minutes. He was incredibly impatient.

"You gonna wear a hole in them Timberlands if you don't stay still," Diamonds warned.

"Fuck these boots. I can buy twenty more pairs when we get to Florida . . . *If* we get to Florida. These niggas are holding up progress, bruh."

"Have patience, little brother," Diamonds said, motioning toward the glare of a set of headlights coming in their direction.

Hank's dark-blue pickup truck pulled to a stop about a yard or so from the patch of land they huddled on. The mud-covered road was too slick for the truck to bring him any closer, so he'd have to go the rest of the way on foot, much to his dismay. Hank jumped from the cab and immediately sank ankle-deep into the mud. He moved awkwardly through the sludge toward the clearing, cursing with each step. As he drew closer to the fire, Diamonds noticed a newspaper folded under his arm.

"Everything straight?" Diamonds asked, once Hank had reached the clearing.

"Other than the fact that my feet are soaked to the bone for the second time today, everything is peachy fucking keen," Hank said sarcastically while trying to shake some of the excess mud from his boots. "Why couldn't we do this indoors like normal people?"

"Because we ain't normal," Diamonds shot back. "Did you handle what needed handling?" he asked, changing the subject.

"Yeah, we good. The dope is all repackaged and tucked safely into an RV on its way west on I-10. It should be there by the time we arrive tomorrow," Hank told him.

"It better be," Goldie interjected. "I still don't like the idea of letting them white boys drive our shit instead of taking it ourselves."

"Because driving it ourselves would've been too big of a risk. Something goes wrong, we go down and lose the dope. Can't put all our eggs in one basket," Diamonds explained.

"I feel you, bruh, but how we know we can trust them?" Goldie asked.

"We don't, which is why I got the names and addresses of their next of kin." Hank handed Diamonds the folded newspaper.

Diamonds peeked inside to examine the contents and nodded in approval. "Any sign of Dip?"

Hank shrugged. "Swung by his pad twice and even checked with his baby mama, but ain't nobody seen him."

"You think the police got him?" Vita asked. She had been so quiet, none of them even noticed her standing there. She was a cute girl, but not sexy, with smallish breasts and just enough ass to make you take a second look but not stare. Behind her rose-colored, pouty lips, she sported a mouth full of gold teeth. Instead of her usual wardrobe of loud-colored clothes and even louder weaves, she was dressed down in a simple black skirt set and black wig. The expensive flat shoes on her feet had been ruined by the mud, but she didn't seem to notice. Vita was clearly overdressed to be standing on the banks of the Mississippi at a Viking funeral, but she insisted on showing John-Boy the same respect as she would someone being laid to rest in a funeral home.

"More like larceny got him," Hank said in a disgusted tone. "I didn't want to say anything until I was absolutely sure, but when I was loading the dope, the bird count came back shorter than it should've been. Looks like he got us for two."

"I knew we shouldn't have took that closet dope-head with us on this run!" Goldie fumed, angry at Dip's betrayal. Dip had never been part of their inner circle, but besides Buda, he was the only other person they knew who could operate an airboat. "I say we ride by that nigga's house and spray it."

"I told you he ain't home," Hank repeated.

"So what? Maybe his mama home. I'll bet if I put the screw to that bitch, she'll tell us where her ol' fuck-ass son hiding," Goldie suggested.

Diamonds gave his brother a cold look. *"Etes vous fou?"* he asked, questioning Goldie's sanity. "After all we've already sacrificed, you willing to throw it all away to go after a piece of shit like Dip? Them two bricks ain't shit compared to what we took off from Slim. Let that thirsty nigga have them two birds. Whatever he think he gonna make off what he swiped, he'd have made ten times that by keeping it trill with us. Niggas who big on greed are small on brains, and it'll only be a matter of time before his karma settle up with him and save us the trouble."

"You think it's gonna be backlash from what we did, bruh?" Goldie asked.

"It always backlash from death and money, tadpole," Diamonds told him. "Wrongs always got a way of righting themselves, but I think I'll owe on this here debt for a while."

"Well, if y'all killed Slim, we ain't got too much to worry about in the way of retaliation. He is dead, isn't he?" Vita asked.

Diamonds didn't answer at first. He knew he'd hit Slim, but he'd lost sight of him after he went out the window. As he thought on it, he couldn't recall seeing the body outside when they cleared out. In all likelihood his body had been washed away by the flood, but Diamonds wasn't certain. He thought about expressing his concerns to the team, but there was no sense in adding to their already dismal moods.

"Slim dead as a wounded dog lying on the riverbank, waiting for the gators to come for him." Diamonds hugged Vita to him. "Get your mind off them ghosts and on this money, baby girl. Our lives are gonna change big-time when we finally pull up in New York City."

"New York? I thought we were going to Florida after we pass through Texas?" Buda asked, clearly not feeling the sudden, and un-expected, change in plans.

"That part of the plan hasn't changed. We grab this quick paper in Houston and then push on to Florida to set up shop, but we'll only be in Miami for as long as it takes us to get strong enough to start broadening our horizons," Diamonds said. Seeing that his crew still didn't look totally sold on his new plan, he decided to elaborate. "We've been hustling and killing in the South for so long that our names are starting to ring like church bells on a Sunday. Everybody know what we about, so they'll know what to expect. That's going to make it harder to stretch our legs, but on the East Coast they'll never see us coming."

Goldie frowned. "Bruh, I'm down for expanding, but why the fuck we gotta go all the way to New York to do it? Just off what we could make in Miami alone is enough for us to live like kings."

Diamonds clasped his hand behind his brother's neck and gave him a serious look. "Why settle for being *kings* when we can be *gods*?"

"I don't care where we go, so long as we leave this place," Vita added. Her clothes were now soaked, and the cold settling into her bones made her shiver.

Diamonds looked at the faces of the rest of his team and saw no objections. "Then let's see our little one off and be done."

Tied to the shore was a raft they'd constructed from an old door and some loose wooden planks. The rickety flotation device was piled high with branches and whatever dry leaves they could find. When the wind blew, you could smell the pungent stench of kerosene. Resting atop the mound was John-Boy, decked out in a black pinstripe gangster suit and a pair of black Stacy Adams polished to a high shine. Clutched in his dead hands were a bottle of Crown Royal and his favorite gun. They were two of the things he had loved most in life, so it was only fitting that he carried them with him in death.

The funeral pyre was how ancient cultures honored warriors who had fallen on the field of battle. Instead of committing them to the earth, they burned them. Most civilizations had abandoned it in favor of traditional funerals, but it was still one of the most time-honored traditions in Diamonds's family. He once asked his grandmother why they burned the bodies of their dead instead of burying them, and she replied: "So they won't be tempted to come back."

Buda approached almost timidly. The blunt between his lips bobbed when he spoke. "Rest easy, little brother." He splashed whisky onto the pyre. "Get as twisted in heaven as you did on earth."

Once by one they came and said their farewells to John-Boy, each offering up some personal artifacts of theirs for John-Boy to carry with him into the afterlife: Buda, the book he had used to teach John-Boy to read when he was little; Hank, an expensive cigar; Goldie, the bandanna around his neck; and Vita gave up the oil cloth she used to polish her horn. The offering of things they held dear to them were so that they would all be able to find one another on the other side when their times came.

Diamonds was the last to approach. His face was dark, his eyes darker. He stared silently at John-Boy for a long while, trying to organize the dozens of jumbled thoughts bouncing around in his head. Seeing his comrade laid out in his Sunday's best and bound for greener pastures made Diamonds contemplate not only his own mortality, but also of those in his charge. He had promised them a better life in exchange for their loyalty, and it was time he made good on that promise. He removed a knife from his pocket and sawed off one of his locks, which he placed on the raft with John-Boy. "See you on the other side, *mon amie.*"

Once the last good-byes were said, the pyre was ignited and cut loose from the shore. The fire ate up the leaves and branches before slowly consuming John-Boy's earthly shell. The flames cast an eerie

glow on the saddened faces of the five friends standing on the riverbank. They watched in silence as the raft floated down the river,
carrying John-Boy to his final reward.

The silence was broken by Goldie slowly clapping his hands in
a rhythm. Buda came to stand next to him and began softly humming
a tune they had become familiar with on the streets of New Orleans.
Vita joined in, blowing softly through her horn in tune with their
rhythm. Then quite unexpectedly, Hank's voice boomed soulfully.

"Don't shed no tears for me when I die, but bet yo ass you better
Second Line!"

Under the soft glow of the moonlight, Goldie, Buda, and Hank
danced and sang their farewells to their fallen brother while Vita
played her horn like she was single-handedly trying to call all the
angels home. Diamonds watched them from a distance.

Kneeling, he scooped up a handful of the moist soil and rubbed
it between his palms. He listened closely and thought he could almost
hear the whispers of all the souls they'd lost during the storm. He
savored the sensation of the cold, wet mud, knowing it would be the
last time he would ever feel it. It would be concrete and steel from
there on out. It saddened him to be leaving the only home he'd ever
known, but he wasn't as attached to New Orleans as the others were.
The Big Easy held too many dark memories, and he was ready to put
them behind him. It was time for him to move on, but first he had
one more soul to offer back to the soil.

CHAPTER THREE

Dip sat on the edge of his sister's couch, drifting in and out of a nod. White powder was dried and caked around his nostrils, but he made no attempt to clean himself up. He was so gone that the cigarette between his fingers had burned down past the filter and was threatening to burn him, but he hardly noticed. Dip was on such a beautiful ride, nothing seemed to matter. Resting on the table was an open package of heroin.

The crew was so twisted over what had happened to John-Boy that it was almost too easy for Dip to cuff two bricks of the dope when they'd robbed Slim. Dip hadn't set out to pull a grease move, but when he'd laid eyes on their haul, larceny had gotten the best of him. He had never seen that much product in his life, and it made him dizzy. The next thing he knew, he was filching the two birds and planning his exit strategy. They could have their dreams of setting up elsewhere, but Dip had no plans on leaving Louisiana. The streets of New Orleans were all he knew or ever cared to know, and his brain couldn't fathom a life beyond them.

Considering the fact that Diamonds and the others had always treated Dip like family, what he was doing was a scumbag move, but Dip reasoned that since he'd only taken two bricks from the entire haul, it wasn't that bad. In contrast to all they had made off with, the dope he'd stolen wouldn't hurt them one way or another, but it was enough to change Dip's life. With all the competition in New Orleans being wiped out by either Diamonds's bullets or Hurricane Katrina, when the market finally opened back up, Dip would be the only game in town.

A knock at the front door snapped him out of his nod. Dip managed to force his eyes open, but he was still having trouble focusing. He tried to push himself to his feet, but it was a wasted effort, so he fell back into his nod and ignored the door. When the knocking turned into a loud banging, it drew Dip's sister Pauletta into the living room. She was dressed in a floral housecoat and slippers, colorful rollers in her hair.

"Nigga, don't you hear the fucking door?" Pauletta stopped in front of her nodding brother, arms folded over her large, saggy breasts.

"Nah, I ain't heard it," Dip lied, scratching at his neck. He looked every bit the dope fiend he was turning into.

"See, this pitiful shit is why you need to be out trying to sell the dope instead of snorting it all up!" Pauletta scolded him. For as long as she could remember, her brother had always been a fuckup. The only reason she let him stay with her is because she wanted a cut off his dope money. "Get your shit together, Dip, and get this dope to moving or get the fuck out of my house," she said before shuffling off to answer the door. With an attitude, she snatched it open, a barrage of curses pursed on her lips and ready to fire off at whoever was behind the banging. Instead she received the business end of a shotgun that opened her chest.

Hearing the roar of the shotgun brought Dip back to sobriety. He got to his feet in time to see his sister's body fly across the living room. Two men stormed in, both wearing black, both heavily armed. Dip managed to dive behind the sofa just before the shotgun kicked again, dismantling the chair he'd been sitting in. Dip crawled on all fours, trying to make for the kitchen, where he hoped to slip out the back door. He'd nearly made it when a strong hand snatched him up by the back of his shirt.

Dip knew that the only chance he had was to fight, and fight he did; it was just too bad he wasn't very good at it. The man holding Dip by the shirt swatted off his punches and delivered one of his own to the gut, which landed with so much force that Dip shit himself. He lay on the ground, his body racked with pain, the rank smell coming from his pants assaulting his nose. As the two men who stormed the house yanked him roughly to his feet, Dip couldn't help but think how his situation couldn't possibly get any worse. But when he saw who else had entered the house, he realized that they could and they had.

He was in a wheelchair now, a result of his two broken legs. His arm was in a sling, his head heavily wrapped in gauze. A gnarled cigar was clinched between his teeth as he sneered down at Dip. "So, this is one of the rats who made off with my cheese?" Slim asked in a sinister tone.

"Big Slim, what you talking, man? I don't know nothing about no cheese," Dip lied. One of the men who was holding him slapped Dip so hard that blood and spit flew from his mouth.

"So you mean to say that the *dope fairy* dropped that off to you?" Slim nodded at the package on the table.

"I can explain that—" Dip began.

"You can't explain shit to me except where to find that hillbilly Diamonds and the shit he took from me!" Slim cut him off. "Now, I know you were part of the crew that robbed me, killed two of my closest friends, and contributed to breaking both my legs. Best believe you got something coming to you for that, but how severe the punishment that comes down on your head is entirely up to you. You're gonna talk or you're gonna die."

Quite unexpectedly, Dip broke free of the two men who were holding him. Everyone in the room tensed, thinking he was about to attack or, at the very least, flee. Instead Dip threw himself at the foot of Slim's wheelchair and clawed at his pant legs, sniveling. "Slim, I swear on my mama, this wasn't on me. Diamonds gave me a stack to drive one of the airboats, but he never said it was you he was planning to rob! It was all on him!" he insisted.

Slim backhanded Dip with his good hand and sent him skidding on his rear. "Pussy, don't give me them crocodile tears. Was you crying when you and that hillbilly crew were making off with my bag? Get this nigga on his feet," he ordered his men.

Dip continued his sobbing while he was jerked back upright. "Slim, man, all I got is what you see; Diamonds and them got the rest of the work and the money."

"And where is Diamonds?" Slim asked.

"Slim, I don't know. I was supposed to meet them tonight to figure out where we were moving to next, but as you can see, I missed that meeting." He motioned toward the dope. Dip intended to keep up his lie for as long as he needed to, because as fearful as he was of what Slim could do to his body, he was more terrified of what Diamonds could do to his soul. Though Dip had only been working for Diamonds a short time, he was well aware of the rumors about him trafficking in things Dip dared not speak of aloud.

Slim shook his head in disappointment before tossing the gnarled cigar out and plucking a fresh one from his jacket pocket. He fished around in the satchel hanging from his wheelchair and produced a small butane torch. "I guess you fancy yourself a real ride-or-die nigga, huh, Dip?" He sparked the flame and lit his cigar. "I could almost respect the act if I didn't know you were a chickenhearted son of a bitch. But fuck all that—let's talk turkey. If I know Diamonds, as I'm sure I do, this wasn't some random jacking. Sneaky bastard has probably been planning it for months. Right now he's probably in the wind with my cash and my dope, having a good laugh at my expense. You know, had it been about what he stole, I may have been able to overlook it and spare myself the trouble of having to chase him down, but when he put a bullet in me, that made it personal." Slim adjusted the flame on the torch to its highest setting and began wheeling himself toward Dip.

"Big Slim . . ." Dip pleaded while struggling against Slim's men, who were holding him again.

"It might take me a few days, weeks, or even years, but I'll never stop chasing him. I'm going to be nipping at that piece of shit's heels until the day comes when I see the life drain from his eyes. I will find Diamonds, and you're going to tell me where to start looking." He turned his attention to his men. "Get his pants down."

CHAPTER FOUR

For a long while Diamonds didn't move. He just stood there, in the shadows of an old willow tree, while misty rain soaked his face and hair. His eyes stared out into darkened thicket of seemingly endless woods as if he were looking at something only he could see. Overhead, something squawked from a tree before flapping off into the night, followed by a roll of thunder. It was like nature was speaking to him, letting him know it was a bad place and he had no business there. Diamonds ignored the warning and moved toward the darkened thicket.

The closer he got, the more manageable the path became, the mud and grass giving way to a small stone road that had been all but completely washed away by nature and the passing of time. Just ahead he could begin to make out the shape of the small building that had been almost completely hidden under the dense foliage. On either side of the black hole that served as the entrance were two large toads, carved from wood and painted over. Their red eyes seemed to stare accusingly at Diamonds as he approached the entrance. The thunder rolled again, and it began to rain harder than it had all that night, giving Diamonds a final warning before he stepped inside.

It was dark, save for the fire burning at the far end of the hut.

The air inside was thick, warm, and smelled of dead things. People who ventured there for the first time were often overwhelmed by the smell and opted to wait outside, but Diamonds had long ago become numb to it. He wandered to a table that was cluttered with small jars, pieces of parchment, and other things that Diamonds couldn't quite identify. In the center of the clutter was something that he had become quite familiar with over the years, a dagger that was as black as night. Diamonds picked it up and ran his fingers over the handle, which had been carved from human bone. Though it was humid inside the shack, the knife was cold to the touch, as if it had just come out of the freezer. The handcrafted dagger had more ghost stories attached to it than the old woman who had first shown it to him. When he closed his eyes, it was almost as if he could hear the souls the knife had snuffed out whispering to him from the great beyond.

After a few blissful moments, he was able to break the hold the dagger was trying to get over him, and he remembered why he had come. He moved toward the rear of the hut, boots making a wet sound on the rickety floor as he drew near the fire burning inside the small pit. In a shadowed corner, the red ember of a cigarette burned in the darkness. Diamonds wasn't alone, but of course he hadn't expected to be.

After a few dramatic seconds, he heard movement, followed by the squeaky sounds of wheels that hadn't been oiled in a while. An old woman in a wheelchair rolled out into view. The skin of her sagging jowls was the color of midnight and seemed to be one sharp movement away from falling completely from her bones. A patchwork blanket was slung over her gnarled legs, dragging slightly on the floor when the chair moved. Milk-white eyes that had long ago failed her scanned the room before coming to rest on where Diamonds was standing. A smile spread across her thin lips, showing off the four

remaining teeth in her mouth. "So, the conquering hero returns." She
lifted her bony hands in his direction.

Diamonds took her hands and kissed the back of each lovingly.
"Hello, Auntie. How are you?"

"As well as can be expected, considering these dark times we've
fallen into. 'For behold, I will bring a flood of waters upon the earth to
destroy all flesh in which is the breath of life under heaven. Everything
that is on the earth shall die.' Genesis told it, and if they'd listened,
they'd have been better prepared," Auntie preached.

"These ain't the end of days for the world, Auntie—just New
Orleans," Diamonds told her.

Auntie shrugged her frail shoulders. "Same difference, depending on who you ask. New Orleans is the only world some of us have
ever known. What care we got for anything going on anywhere else?
You being a child of these lands, I'd expect you to understand better
than most."

"I do understand, Auntie, but I also know there's a great big world
out there just waiting to be conquered."

"And you plan to take it all for yourself, huh?"

"As much of it as I can," Diamonds said honestly.

Auntie shook her head. "Your eyes always were bigger than you
belly. Even as a kid, when the others were done eating, you would sit
and keep going until you damn near popped. You have always been
a glutton."

"Not a glutton, just not as easily satisfied as some. I believe
children born with nothing are owed a debt by the world, and I intend to collect what I got coming," Diamonds said.

"Be mindful that in your pursuit of what you feel you're owed,
you don't end up with what you got coming. You can't keep taking
from the cycle of life without giving something back. Nothing is without a price, and you, my little glutton, are racking up quite a tab."

"Fuck the cycle! Tonight I paid a debt so heavy that me and the cycle should be square for a while," he said, thinking of John-Boy.

"My arrogant little prince. After all these years you still think you're above the laws of nature?"

"The only law I know is that of the jungle: the strong live and the weak die," Diamonds said arrogantly. "Me and my team got big plans, and we intend to execute them by any means necessary."

"Is that what you're calling them? Your *team*?" Auntie asked in amusement. "Poor fools bound to your insane quests by love, enchantment, and plain stupidity. What happens when the mask slips and they see you for who you really are?"

"By the time I have to worry about that, I'll have already set myself and those around me up with nice enough lives that it won't matter. And what does any of that matter to someone who, by your own power, has been made immortal?" He removed a braided piece of leather from around his neck and brandished the pouch hanging from the end of it.

Auntie's hands reached out for the pouch as if drawn to it by whatever power was emitting from it. She ran her fingers along the finely stitched edges and recalled the day she had sewn it together and filled it with soil from her private garden.

" 'For so long as I keep home close to my heart, no harm will ever befall me,' " Diamonds said, reminding Auntie of her words on the day she'd given it to him.

Auntie laughed, and it sounded like a small car sputtering to life. "There's a difference between immortality and being harder to kill than most, and you're determined to find that out the hard way. Diamonds, I love you too much to watch you go down this road. I wish you well in your travels, but I'm afraid there's no more help I can offer you."

Now it was Diamonds's turn to laugh. "Auntie, I haven't come here for your help. I've come for your blessings." He snatched the blanket from her lap and used it to tie her arms to the wheelchair.

"What are you doing?" Auntie struggled feebly against her restraints.

"Using the past to ensure my future," Diamonds told her, drawing the black dagger.

Auntie didn't have to be able to see the dagger to know it was near. She could feel its sinister presence taunting her. "Dirty dog! I invite you into my home and teach you my secrets, and this is how you do me?"

"Yes, Auntie. You did teach me all your secrets, and this is why I know I'll need more than a few loyal souls and some bullets to accomplish what I'm setting out to do. If I am to conquer this world, then I'll need a blessing from the other side." He moved behind her, placing the knife under her chin. "Trust me, I take no pleasure in this, Auntie. If there was some other way, I'd gladly explore it, but there's too much at stake. What you got ain't gonna do the world no good, festering out here in this swamp."

"Thieving bastard!" she hissed. "You always look to take what don't belong, and that is gonna be the thing that lays you low! You think you can snatch my power and bury me in the swamp like you do all your secrets, but some things ain't meant to stay buried. The same power you crave so desperately is going to rise up and swallow everything you hold dear to your heart before dragging your wicked ass to where it needs to be. And when that time comes, old Auntie will be waiting for you. Be it in heaven, hell, or the between, I will have my revenge!" she vowed.

"Of this I have no doubt, but by then I'll have lived like a king in this life, so I could give a shit about what happens to me in the next," Diamonds said before slitting the old woman's throat.

PART

KINGDOM OF STONE

CHAPTER FIVE

NEW YORK, NEW YORK / MAY 2008

Devonte could feel his eyes involuntarily rolling back in his head. He'd kept his game face on for as long as he could, but eventually he succumbed to the waves of pleasure that were rolling over his body. He was traveling through a beautiful place, the young thing riding his stiff cock like she was his tour guide.

The first rays of the rising sun were just crawling through the window of the hotel room, painting her brown body in a soft orange glow. She had a near perfect shape, slim waist, plump rear, and slightly over a handful of breasts. She ran her fingers through her long black hair, letting it rise and fall playfully. Soft-brown eyes looked down at him from under hooded lids as she bit her lip, letting Devonte know he was hitting her sweet spot. It was such a perfect picture that he almost shed a tear, but he was too much of a G to let her see him cry.

"Right there, baby . . . right there," she said, panting, and gyrated her hips to push him deeper inside her.

Devonte felt himself about to cum, so he decided to change positions. "Let me hit it from the back," he suggested, gently sliding her off him. She was only too happy to oblige, getting on her knees and resting on her elbows, giving him a full view of her shaved, dripping box. He smacked his lips like a starved man about to sit down to a meal. Unable to help himself, he leaned in and lapped at her moist pussy. He had never been a fan of going down on women, because some tasted sour or carried a hint of sweat, but she always tasted like honeysuckle. Munching her box made his dick swell. He was ready to enter her again. As he stared at her heart-shaped ass, hiked up and ready for him, he couldn't help but imagine how much better her pussy would feel if the layer of rubber from the condom wasn't between them. Taking a quick peek to make sure she wasn't paying attention, he used his thumb to pop off the rubber. When he stuck his dick back inside her, it was like a whole different experience. She was so wet and so warm that he lasted all of ten strokes before exploding inside her womb.

"No, the fuck you didn't!" she cursed, sliding off of his dick. Thick cum ran down her inner thigh and dripped onto the bed. She grabbed the sheet and began wiping the semen from her vagina and legs.

"My fault, baby. It must've broke and I didn't feel it," Devonte lied.

When she looked up at him, the passion was gone from her eyes and had been replaced by rage. "That's bullshit and you know it! This was some real lame shit, Devonte." She got up and stormed into the bathroom to clean herself up properly.

Devonte leaned against the bathroom door for a long while, thinking about what he'd just done and listening to the shower running on the other side. He knew he had fucked up. He had been seeing the girl for a few months now, and from the first time they'd had sex, he had been dreaming about what hitting it raw would feel like. It was a thirsty move and a lapse in judgment on his part. "I'm sorry," he finally said. "Look, I know you're worried about getting pregnant and all, but don't be. It was only one time. Even if you did end up getting pregnant, I'd step up and handle my business."

She snatched the door open and came out wrapped in a towel. She wasn't as mad as she had been when she went in, but anger still lingered in her eyes. "First of all, it only takes one time . . . or didn't you learn that in school like everyone else? And pregnancy isn't my only concern. I'm more worried about my life than anything."

"What do you mean by that?" Devonte didn't understand.

"I mean STDs," she explained while putting her bra back on. "A wayward dick is just as dangerous as a loaded gun." She slipped her white shirt on and began buttoning it.

"You ain't gotta worry about that. I'm clean," Devonte assured her.

She paused her buttoning and gave him a serious look. "And how do I know that? Because you told me? Let's keep it real, Devonte. I know you're out there sticking your dick in all these hood bitches, and I'm okay with that because we're not exclusive. But the minute your dick puts my life in jeopardy, it's a problem."

He wanted to argue, but she had a valid point. Devonte had a roster of chicks he was sleeping with, and he didn't use protection with all of them. "Listen, I feel fucked up about this. Let me make it up to you."

"You should feel fucked up, because it was a greasy move. The only thing you can do for me right now is drop me off so I'm not late," she told him while wiggling into her plaid skirt and mumbling obscenities to herself.

Devonte had seen her upset before, but never like this. He suddenly started thinking of all the bad things that could come of falling out of her good graces. Before they left that room, he needed to know where her head was at. "I know you're pissed and all, but I hope this ain't gonna create a problem between us."

She turned to him with a look that was somewhere between playful and dangerous. "What kind of problems? You mean like my father finding out you tried to knock up his only daughter and killing you, or the fact that you've been fucking a seventeen-year-old girl?" When she saw him bristle uncomfortably, she cracked a smile. "Don't worry, Devonte. I'm not the type to kiss and tell. Besides, our little secret going public would probably hurt my reputation more than yours." She moved closer to him and ran her hand tenderly down the side of his face. "The daughter of a boss sleeping with the help would make me look like a woman of small principles, and we can't have that." She patted his cheek playfully before sashaying toward the door.

Devonte stood there, still in his birthday suit, trying to decide if he was angrier at her insult or turned on by the audacity of the young girl. "You're a cold piece of work, Pearl Stone."

"Not cold enough to keep your thirsty ass away," she shot back. "Now, hurry and put your clothes on. I've got homeroom in an hour, and I don't want to be late."

Pearl sat in the back of her global studies class, trying her best to stay awake. Her eyelids felt like they had sandbags tied to them, and it was a struggle to keep them open. Devonte had kept her awake half the night, plowing into her like he was trying to use his dick to dig his way to China. He wasn't the most savory fella she'd ever met, but he fucked like a rock star and could reach places inside her that Pearl had only recently discovered existed. She had always enjoyed her escapades with Devonte until recently. Over the last couple of weeks had had started to become clingy, and the stunt he'd pulled with the condom confirmed what she had already been thinking: it was time to put some space between them. Being the baby mama of a drug dealer was not something she saw in her future. Pearl had bigger plans for her life.

At the front of the class her teacher, Mr. Gaines, continued to talk. He was going on and on about the trouble down South as a result of the hurricane and the government's mishandling of the aftermath. The storm and the havoc it wreaked were more than three years old by then, but Mr. Gaines continued to speak about the events as if they had just happened. He was new to New York, originally from Baton Rouge. When Katrina had hit, he'd gotten to witness her fury firsthand. When he spoke about the people and things that he'd lost, it was in a tone so passionate that there wasn't a dry eye in the room, except Pearl's. Her mind was elsewhere.

To Pearl, school was a necessary evil that she endured for the sole purpose of appeasing her father. Pearl was by no means a bad student. In fact, she was in the top tenth percentile of her school and had made the honor roll every year since the seventh grade. She was good in school, just not very motivated by it. Other than math and reading, you never used the things you learned, so she figured if she just focused on those two areas, the rest would be a breeze. Pearl had learned to add, subtract, and multiply before she got to kindergarten, and those were the only life skills she would ever need as far as she was concerned. The only reason she was so hell-bent on graduating was because her dad had promised to buy her a Mercedes. Daddy always knew how to motivate her.

Her father was somewhat of a local celebrity, which made Pearl famous in her own right. Wherever she went, people treated her with respect. That was one of the perks of being the daughter of one of the most feared men in the city. Having a father who was a boss is what often got Pearl noticed, but it was her beauty that kept all eyes on her. She stood at a statuesque five nine with a body that curved in all the right places. In addition to being physically beautiful, she exuded a confidence that you couldn't help but notice when she walked into a room. With money, looks, and charisma . . . Pearl had it all but still wanted more.

The bell finally rang, signaling the end of the class and the beginning of *social hour,* as she liked to call it. It was lunch, which meant it was time to meet up with her girls. They mostly congregated in the lunch room, where they played cards and exchanged gossip, but every so often they would sneak off school grounds and walk the five blocks to the pizza shop near Bowman High. Bowman was an alternative school that catered mostly to teenage parents and knuckleheads who'd gotten booted from other schools and were on their last chances. But there were also students who were victims of various circumstances that wouldn't allow them to attended regular high schools, and they were determined to finish their educations. Most of the girls at St. Francis shied away from the hard-nosed guys at Bowman, but Pearl and her crew embraced them. They loved dancing on the razor's edge.

When Pearl stepped out of Mr. Gaines's class, she was met by her friend Marisa. Marisa was a Cuban girl with rich chocolate skin, pink lips, and thick black hair that she sometimes wore in a puffy Afro. At first glance most people assumed Marisa was Black, but when she got to rattling off in Spanish, her true colors came out. She was pretty fly and down for whatever, same as Pearl. The two of them were as thick as thieves.

"What's popping, mommy?" Marisa greeted Pearl with a high-five.

"Chilling, glad to finally be outta that boring class. Who gives a fuck what's going on in Louisiana when we live all the way up in New York? That shit ain't got nothing to do with us," Pearl said, dismissing the tragedy.

Marisa shook her head. "It would be a coldhearted bitch to say something like that. You know a lot of people lost their lives and their homes in that storm. New Orleans looks like a disaster area, and to make things worse, Uncle Sam is taking his sweet fucking time in trying to help them clean it up. It's been almost three years since it happened, and I hear that families are still displaced. That's no joke, Pearl."

"You're right—it's not funny. It's fucked up, but that doesn't mean I wanna listen to Mr. Gaines talk about it for forty-five minutes."

"If you're that sour on it, why don't you just ditch the stupid class?" Marisa asked.

Pearl gave her a serious look. "And have my father break my neck when the school calls about me cutting?"

"Stop acting like that. It's the last day of school before spring break. I don't think anybody will even notice if we cut out early."

"Big Stone would know," she assured her. Her father seemed to have a crystal ball that gave him a glimpse at anything and everything that went on with his family.

The two girls headed down the hall together, exchanging gossip and ignoring the envious glances they were getting from some of the other girls as they passed. Marisa wasn't on anyone's Christmas list, but most of the shade was directed toward Pearl. The girls who attended St. Francis either hated Pearl and her crew or wanted to be down with them. Either way, they were usually the topic of conversation.

About halfway to the lunch room, they were joined by Ruby. She was the oddball of their crew. Ruby was a short, plump Jewish girl with fiery red hair and a pointed nose. She was kind of on the weird side, but nobody fucked with her because she was Pearl's friend. For a white girl, Ruby had a lot of soul and was cool people. She also served as the minister of information for their gang. There wasn't much that went on at St. Francis that Ruby didn't get the scoop on first. From the mischievous look on her face, Pearl knew she had something juicy to spill.

"What's the word?" Marisa asked, beating Pearl to the punch.

"Girls, let me tell y'all . . . ," Ruby began in her heavy New York accent. "I just heard from Carla, who heard from Jane, that Kate is talking shit about you," she told Pearl.

Pearl rolled her eyes. "What else is new? These bitches hate me cuz they ain't me!"

"They don't wanna see us!" Marisa cosigned.

"I know they ain't trying to do nothing. All mouth and no action, but you know I had to tell my girl what's up," Ruby said.

"And that's why I fucks with you." Pearl gave her dap. Pearl knew that Kate was all bark and no bite, and could've let it go, but she was feeling petty that day. "Still, these broads need to recognize who the *real* queen is. Let's go down to the lunch room and see what's good," Pearl suggested.

"Pearl, don't go down there starting no shit with that girl. Remember what Father Price said after the last incident you were involved in," Marisa reminded Pearl, referring to the small riot she'd almost caused in the auditorium.

"Marisa, I ain't stupid enough to get into a fight with my birthday coming," Pearl assured her.

"Somebody is about to turn the big one-eight." Marisa smiled broadly.

"Eighteen and finally grown." Pearl rested her fists on her hips.

"So, what's up? I haven't heard any talk of a party yet. Aren't you gonna have one this year? You know your dad throws you the best parties," Marisa said.

"Oddly, he hasn't mentioned a party to me, which leads me to believe he's planning some type of surprise," Pearl speculated. Every year since she could remember, her dad always threw her an epic birthday party, but that year the subject hadn't come up, which was odd.

"I sure hope so, because I know it's going to be popping!" Marisa exclaimed. "If it goes down, you know I'm in there. How about you, Ruby?"

"I wish. My grades weren't so good last marking period, so they've been extra-strict on me. Besides, you know my mom and dad think everyone darker than a paper bag is trouble." Ruby said it as a joke but couldn't mask the hint of embarrassment in her voice.

"You'd think that after all these years, she'd be cool with you hanging out with the Blacks and Hispanics. I guess some people just can't get with jungle fever," Marisa joked.

Ruby rolled her eyes. "Judith gets on my nerves sometimes with her old-world mentality," she said, referring to her mother. "And don't even get me started on my father and his constant ranting about how a proper Jewish girl is supposed to behave."

"That's just code for 'Stop fucking Black guys.' " Pearl snickered.

"Well, she can forget that. You know how I love my chocolate," Ruby joked. She was making light of the whole thing, but it was only to hide her embarrassment over her parents' views. Ruby's parents were older, having had her late in their lives. They were Russian immigrants who had only come to the States shortly before Ruby was born, so they were behind the curve on a lot of things. They weren't necessarily racists, but felt strongly about intermingling the gene pool.

"Don't worry about it, ma. If it does happen and you can't make it, you know you'll be there with us in spirit," Pearl said, trying to make her feel better.

"Spirit my ass. Pearl, you've known me long enough to know that what my parents expect and what I do are two different things. I'll just wait until they go to sleep and sneak out. I'll probably be grounded until I leave for college, but for one of your parties, it'd be worth it." Ruby laughed.

CHAPTER SIX

St. Francis had two lunch rooms, the North and South. The North Side was supposed to be for the juniors and seniors while the South was designated for freshmen and sophomores, but what it really translated to was that the North was for the cool kids, and the South was for everyone else. One of the advantages of hanging in the North lunch room was that it had an exit in the back that opened up into the faculty parking lot—and freedom. If you had enough juice with security, you could slip on and off school grounds without worrying about being written up.

There were always two guards at that back door during lunch periods, Jones and Melrose. Melrose was an ugly, heavyweight wrestler–looking muthafucka who looked like he had been carved from a block of onyx. Jones was much easier on the eyes, short with wide hips and nice tits, with hair that was so rich and thick that it made her the envy of some women. Judging by looks, you'd have thought Melrose was the more vicious of the two, but it was Jones you had to watch out for. Unlike some of the staff, she treated all the girls in the school with equal respect, no matter what class of financial standing. All she asked in return was that you showed her the same. The smart ones did, but the ones who foolishly tested the waters learned the hard way that Security Officer Jones wasn't to be fucked with. She had been written up on multiple occasions for laying hands on students. The only reason she hadn't been fired is because her mother worked for the school superintendent. To her credit, Jones never whipped an ass in the school that didn't deserve it.

"Little Stone, what the deal?" Melrose gave Pearl dap when she and her crew strolled into the North cafeteria.

"Little Stone is my brother; I'm just Pearl," she corrected him.

"My bad, my bad," Melrose said apologetically. "How's Stoney doing anyhow? He managing to stay out of trouble?"

"Hell no." Pearl rolled her eyes at the thought of her troublesome little brother. "He got written up in school again the other day for fighting."

"A chip off the old block." Jones laughed.

"Only blocks he's gonna know are cellblocks if he doesn't slow his ass down," Pearl said.

"You'd think for as strict as Big Stone is, that boy wouldn't be so wild," Marisa chimed in.

"My father is only strict when it comes to me. He lets Stoney run wild."

"Speaking of Big Stone, how is he?" Melrose asked. He'd worked for Pearl's dad back in the day, and had even taken a drug charge for the crew. The whole three and a half years he'd sat in prison, he never once mentioned Big Stone or the organization. When he touched down, Stone blessed Melrose with a few dollars and plugged him in with the board of ed so he landed the security job.

"He's good."

"Tell him, Joey said what's up."

"I got you, Melrose," Pearl promised before leading her crew deeper into the cafeteria.

Pearl's whole demeanor seemed to change when they entered the lunch room proper. The smile faded from her face, and her eyes got hard and serious. She had slipped into what Ruby called *boss mode*. She strolled casually, her crew in tow, nodding and shaking hands with girls who'd break their necks to speak to her. Pearl was like a local celebrity, partially because of who her father was, but mostly because her name carried weight with staff and students alike. Her status gave her access to things most people couldn't get within the walls of St. Francis, such as contraband. That was her side hustle. If you needed something, be it pot, school supplies, or treats they didn't sell on school grounds, you went to see Pearl.

It took them nearly ten minutes to make it to what they dubbed as their section of the lunch room. It consisted of a long table near the back entrance that was always on reserve for Pearl and her team. This was where they ate, played cards, and brokered deals. It was an unspoken rule that you didn't sit there if you weren't part of that circle . . . a rule that if you broke, Pearl or one of her minions would make sure you didn't break again. Standing around, waiting for them, were several underclassmen who Pearl liked to refer to as *stragglers*. They were her foot soldiers, girls who were vying for membership to her inner circle. Most of them would never make it, but a few showed promise.

Pearl's ass had barely touched the seat before other girls started drifting over, inquiring about this or that. Depending on who they were and what they wanted, Pearl approved or denied their requests. Ruby collected the money while the stragglers were assigned to retrieve whatever was needed. She had learned from her father that bosses never touched product, so if the shit ever hit the fan, she and her inner circle's hands were always clean.

Pearl was just about to send one of the stragglers to fill their lunch orders when she was approached by a girl named Drea. She and Drea weren't necessarily friends, but they'd done business in the past. Drea was one of the smartest girls in the school, and for a few dollars, she would knock out class projects for you.

"Hey, Pearl." Drea took a seat on the bench, which got her a stink look from Marisa, as she hadn't been invited to sit.

"Sup, ma?" Pearl replied.

"So listen, I know it's about that time of year again, so me and a few of my girls wanted to know what's going on with your annual birthday party?" Drea asked.

"I don't know if I'm having one this year," Pearl told her.

Drea frowned. "C'mon, Pearl. Don't be like that. Every year you have a dope party, and every year I get snubbed. I need to be in there this year."

"Even if she does have one, it'll be invite only," Ruby said, adding her two cents.

"Hush, white girl. I wasn't talking to you," Drea told her. She meant it as a joke, trying to act like she belonged with their group, but it caused an awkward moment.

"Drea, I know I don't have to tell you that dissing my homegirl is one of the quickest ways to get you touched. You don't really know her to be playing like that," Pearl said seriously.

"My bad, Pearl. I didn't mean anything by it. So like I was saying, how can I go about getting an invitation for me and a few of my friends? We don't mind paying if we have to," Drea said, hoping to sweeten the pot.

"Drea, you know I ain't pressed for no cash, but I respect the fact that you even offered. Most bitches want shit for free. Tell you what: I don't know your friends to have them up in my shit, but since me and you got history, if I do happen to have a party, I'll consider you for an invitation. But in exchange, I'm going to need you to knock out this class assignment for me. I'm supposed to do a report on *To Kill a Mockingbird* over spring break, but a bitch got better shit to do than to be all up in some book when I'm supposed to be chilling. Hook me up and you're in, but I don't know about your friends."

"I don't mind doing the project for you, Pearl, but I think it'd be kind of foul if I left my girls out. There's only three of us. Don't you think you could look out this one time?" Drea asked.

"Nope, take it or leave it," Pearl said flatly.

Drea weighed it. "Damn, I really wanna come, but I can't do them like that. Thanks anyway, Pearl." She stood to leave, but Pearl motioned for her to stay.

"Loyalty is a rare trait in people these days, Drea, and I admire the fact that you ain't willing to shit on your friends. *If* by chance I happen to have a party, you and your friends can come, but since it's more than just you, I'm going to need more than one class assignment done. From now until the end of the year, you will be on retainer for me and my whole crew. Whenever we get an assignment we don't wanna do, you'll knock it out."

Drea frowned. "Pearl, between my own schoolwork and what I take on from you guys, I won't have any type of social life. Let's be reasonable about this."

"First of all, you don't have a social life to begin with, so stop it, Drea. And second, I am being reasonable. It's like you said: my parties are always over-the-top and you always get snubbed. This is your opportunity to stop being on the outside looking in. Think about how jealous the rest of the chicks in this school are gonna be when they find out that you got in and they didn't. It'll send your credibility through the roof."

Drea knew Pearl was getting over on her, but she desperately wanted to go to the party and finally feel like one of the in crowd. "Deal." She shook Pearl's hand to seal it.

"You ain't shit, Pearl," Ruby said, and snickered when Drea had gone.

"You might be right about that, Ruby, but I just guaranteed your remedial ass will make it out of high school," Pearl teased her.

The girls continued to chat and crack jokes while they waited on the stragglers to come back with their lunches.

"Peep game." Marisa nudged Pearl under the table.

Three tables over, Kate sat with her ragtag bunch, who were all staring venomously at Pearl and her friends. Kate was a pretty blond white girl who came from a wealthy family and acted like she owned the world, much like Pearl did. The two had so much in common that some found it strange that they were bitter rivals instead of friends. Both Pearl and Kate believed there was only enough room in the pride for one lioness. Kate was so engrossed in the game of cards she was playing that she didn't notice Pearl until one of her cronies nudged her and nodded in Pearl's direction. Kate gave her a dirty look and then went back to her card game.

"Bitch," Pearl mumbled, and gave Kate her back.

A few minutes into the period they were joined by their fourth member. Sheila was dark-skinned, with short hair, thick lips, and a button nose. She wasn't an ugly girl, but hardly anything to write home about, especially when measured against Pearl. Whereas Pearl was naturally beautiful, Sheila needed a bit of help from time to time, which is why her gear was always on point and she had damn near professional skills at applying makeup. What Sheila lacked in looks she more than made up for in body. She was only slightly older than the other girls but already had the body of a woman in the full bloom of her life.

Like Ruby, Sheila was also the child of immigrant parents who had had to pull themselves up by their bootstraps to provide a better life for their family. They had come to the United States from Haiti, her father finding work as a janitor, her mother as a schoolteacher. They pumped every dime they made into providing their children with top-flight educations. Sheila was the oldest, so they were harder on her than her siblings. They heaped an almost unfair amount of pressure on her to excel in school and set what they thought was a proper example for her brothers and sister, but it had an adverse effect. Sheila coped with the strain of being the reluctant savior of her family by embracing her inner alcoholic. All the girls in the clique enjoyed an occasional sip to get a good buzz, but Sheila drank to get drunk. It wasn't unusual to smell the faintest hints of vodka coming out of her pores in the middle of a school day.

"Why are those hos looking over here like they got problems or something?" Sheila asked once she was seated. Kate and her friends still were staring at Pearl and her crew, whispering and snickering.

Marisa sucked her teeth. "Them chicks is *soft* with a capital *T*."

"Don't pay them no mind." Pearl waved them off. "Now that we've got a fourth, we can get a proper game of spades going. Ruby, did you bring the cards?"

"You know I did." Ruby pulled out a fresh pack of Bicycle cards. She handed the cards to Pearl, who began to shuffle them. They were halfway into the second hand when Pearl felt someone lingering behind her. She peered over her shoulder to see Kate and a girl she only knew by face and not name hovering over her.

"I've got next," Kate said. It was more of a statement than a request.

"Sorry, private game." Pearl turned her attention back to the card game.

"How you gonna have a *private* game in a *public* cafeteria?" Kate challenged.

"What I think she meant is, *no,* you can't play," Ruby capped sarcastically.

"I wasn't talking to you, Oreo," Kate snapped. "Like I said"— she turned back to Pearl—"I got next."

"Pwoblèm?" Sheila asked, reverting to her native tongue. She had worked for many years to drop her accent, but it tended to peek out when she was upset or drunk. Judging by the glassy look in her eyes, she was probably a bit of both.

"This is America, where we speak English." Kate's friend gave Sheila a disapproving look. She was a short, fat white girl who wore her hair in a bob.

"Well, this is the North Cafeteria, where we whip bitches out for popping shit," Marisa chimed in.

"What, am I supposed to be afraid of you because they say you cut a girl's face in your last school?" The girl puffed up.

"No," Sheila answered for her. She rose to her feet, cracking her knuckles. "You should be afraid of her because she has a best friend who will gladly smash you the fuck out if you keep wolfin'." All the girls were capable of defending themselves, but Sheila was the resident bruiser. They'd seen her knock boys out with her powerful mitts.

Kate knew this about Sheila, but her friend didn't, so Kate interceded before things got out of control. "No, Sheila, I don't have a problem with you. What I do have a problem with is hood bitches walking through my lunch room, sending me dirty looks." She looked at Pearl.

The gauntlet had been laid. The tensions that had been building between the two crews were finally coming to a head, and though no one in the cafeteria came over, all eyes turned to the confrontation.

Kate had been running the social circle in school since she was a sophomore, and if she'd had it her way, she'd have continued running it until she graduated. But Pearl's ever-growing popularity had started to threaten her position during senior year. It was like a presidential race to see who could garner the most votes by June. Kate had worked too hard and her family's money ran too deep for her to accept being prematurely unseated by a girl from the ghetto.

Pearl calmly placed her cards facedown on the table and stood. She was an inch or two taller than Kate, and could see the brown roots spilling out into bleached strands on the top of her head. "You might've happened to fall into my line of view, but as far as looking at you"— she gave her the once-over—"I seriously doubt it. You ain't nowhere on my radar, ma."

Laughter erupted from the girls who had tried to act like they weren't paying attention to the Pearl and Kate's exchange. Kate's face reddened from embarrassment. "I am so sick of your shit, Pearl. You act like I should respect you because your father is a gangster!"

Pearl laughed. "Silly little girl, my father ain't got nothing to do with why muthafuckas recognize. They respect me because I demand nothing less."

"Fucking bitch," Kate's friend mumbled.

"That's *Queen* Bitch to you, chubby," Pearl shot back. By now everyone was standing. Marisa, Sheila, and even Ruby stood at Pearl's flank, ready to pop off, while Kate's friends stood at her back. It was about to go down.

"I know y'all know better than to start shit in my cafeteria." Jones walked up and stood between the girls. She was tugging on a pair of black leather gloves and wearing a look that dared either one of them to buck.

Kate continued to glare at Pearl, contemplating whether to swing or not. If they'd had numbers on their side, she might've gone for it, but their ranks were near even. She wasn't afraid of Pearl, but she wasn't exactly thrilled at the prospect of fighting her either. Kate could scrap, but she didn't have the advantage of the combat training Pearl had probably had growing up in the hood. Besides, she knew Pearl had the security guards in her back pocket and that most of the blame would be heaped on her if they scuffled. The last thing she wanted was a suspension marring her near perfect academic record so close to graduation. Reluctantly, she backed away. "See you soon, Pearl," she promised.

"Bitch, you know where to find me anytime you feel like you want it," Pearl boasted.

"That's enough, Pearl," Jones said. She and Pearl were cool, but not cool enough for Pearl to cause trouble on Jones's watch. "And, the rest of you, get back to your lunches or your next classes. The show is over!" she barked at the gawking students, making her way back to her post.

"I've never met such a big hater," Sheila said, once they were all seated again. She was looking over at Kate, who was shooting daggers at their table.

"For a minute I thought she was going to actually get up the courage to take a swing at you," Marisa said.

"Nah, you know that punk bitch ain't trying to get into nothing on school grounds. The only reason she was talking shit was because she knew security would break it up before it got out of hand," Pearl said.

"You think she's gonna try something after school?" Ruby asked.

"If she's smart, no. If she's dumb, then she'll come looking for this ass-whipping."

Sheila sucked her teeth. "Fuck that white cunt—no offense, Ruby. I got something better for us to talk about. I know where there's a party going on tonight if y'all are down to roll?"

"I dunno. You know how my parents get." Ruby said.

Sheila sucked her teeth. "But there's no school tomorrow. Why would they trip? Don't be a wet blanket, Ruby. I'm talking about a party, with real liquor, real music, and real niggas."

"You don't even have to say any more. You had me at party," Marisa said. "I'm down to roll. Whose party is it?"

"This Jamaican nigga I know named Boom put me up on it. It's his man's birthday, so they're doing something for him uptown at that little spot on One Hundred and Forty-Fifth and Lenox."

"Isn't that a bar?" Ruby asked.

"Of course it is, silly white girl," Sheila teased her. "We ain't gotta worry about them asking for ID, 'cause we're rolling in with Boom and his peoples."

"Ah shit, I'm bout to get my swerve on." Marisa danced in her seat. "Pearl, I know you rolling with us?"

"I don't know." Pearl bit her bottom lip. She had a project due the next morning, and she hadn't even started it. Then there was also her father to consider. Big Stone frowned on Pearl going out on school nights.

"What do you mean *you don't know*?" Sheila asked in disbelief. "Pearl, these ain't some high school boys I'm taking you to hang out with; these are grown men with grown paper. And Boom's whole crew is fine as hell!"

"It ain't that, Sheila. My dad is supposed to be coming back from his trip, and you know how that dude is when it comes to me hanging out on weekdays," Pearl explained. "Marisa, you should be worried too, since they're together."

Marisa's dad, Tito, and Big Stone had known each other as long as Pearl and Marisa had. They'd actually met because of them. Both of their daughters were enrolled in the same junior high school, and with both of their dads being so heavily involved in their daughters' educations, they would often see each other at school functions and on field trips. Eventually they developed a friendship. Tito was a square, working at a brokerage firm downtown, but he was from the hood, so it didn't take him long to figure out what Big Stone did for a living. Tito didn't condone it, but he didn't judge Stone for it either. So long as Stone's relationship with the streets didn't overlap his relationship with Tito and his family, they were good. Tito had even helped Big Stone with some investments when he wanted to legitimize some of his holdings.

"Yeah, but they're not coming back anytime soon. My mom is supposed to be picking my dad up from their airport around midnight," Marisa informed her.

"See, that'll be more than enough time for us to go in, have a quick drink, and get you guys back home before your parents find out. Stop acting like that, Pearl," Sheila urged. "If it'll make you feel better, look at this little outing as a prequel to your bash."

Pearl felt like she was under a hot lamp at the police station, with three sets of eyes pinned to her, waiting to see which way she would decide. Pearl knew that if her father came home and found her missing, he'd shit a brick right before he killed her. Still, peer pressure was a muthafucka. "Okay, one drink and then we're gone."

By the end of the period, they had their plan all mapped out. They would meet at about nine thirty, hit the party for an hour or so, then leave. Marisa wanted to meet in front of Pearl's building, but Pearl quickly shot that idea down. She didn't want anybody to see her, especially her father's pet watchdog, Knowledge. He was always skulking somewhere in the shadows, watching, especially when her father was away from home. Knowledge was the only man he trusted enough to watch over his family when he wasn't around. To avoid getting busted, the girls would meet on 125th Street and head to the party from there.

When lunch period was over, the girls headed to their respective classes. Sheila and Marisa had fifth-period algebra together, so they headed up to the fourth floor while Pearl and Ruby walked downstairs to the first. They didn't have class together, but their classes were on the same floor that period, so they always walked together. As usual, Pearl was slow, dragging down the stairs while she spoke to people she knew. By the time they'd made it downstairs, everyone was in their classes and the halls were empty, except for Kate and three of her home girls. They were posted up at the end of the hall near where Pearl's next class was. It seemed that Pearl had underestimated Kate's level of stupidity. Never one to run from a fight, Pearl started in their direction.

"I knew they weren't gonna let it go. I just knew it," Ruby said nervously, walking beside Pearl. She would fight if she had to, but it was always her very last resort.

"Just be cool, Ruby. None of us want trouble in school. I got this under control," Pearl said in a very calm tone.

For once, Ruby thought Pearl would take the high road and avoid confrontation. That thought died when she saw Pearl take the combination lock from the strap of her knapsack and loop it over her middle finger.

Kate started toward Pearl, two of the three girls behind her while the other one manned the end of the hall to watch for security or teachers. To Kate, the confrontation with Pearl was no different than any other time they'd butted heads, except this time it had happened on the big stage: the North Cafeteria. The fact that the black girl had slighted her in front of all those people didn't go unnoticed by Kate's crew, and they had been on her for the remainder of the period about what she was going to do about it. If she didn't handle it, she would look weak. Fighting in school was a risky idea, but catching Pearl between classes was her best chance to act without having to worry about her friends getting in it.

They were mere feet away now, both combatants' eyes locked on each other. "What's up now, bi—" Kate never got a chance to finish her sentence.

Pearl's fist shot out like a missile, hitting Kate square in the mouth, busting her lip, and knocking one of her bottom teeth out.

Seeing their leader broken and bloodied gave the other girls pause, and it cost them. Taking full advantage of the situation, Pearl tore into another one of them with the lock. It was the thick girl from earlier who Pearl had referred to as chubby. Her chin was stronger than Kate's, so it took a few good pops in the face to steal the fight from her. Pearl was whipping on the bigger girl when she felt a flash of needlelike fire. The third girl had a fistful of her hair, trying to rip it from the roots, and with her free hand she was trying to reach around and scratch Pearl's face. Pearl was about to redirect her attention to the third girl and give her the business, but Ruby beat her to the punch.

Ruby brought the thick math book she was carrying down across the back of the third girl's head like the hammer of judgment. The first blow dazed her, but the second swing put her on her ass. The remaining girl, who had been playing lookout, saw what was happening and wanted no part of it, so she took off and left her friends to the savage beating being placed upon them by Pearl and Ruby. By the time security showed up, all they found at the scene were the three wounded girls and a mess of blood to clean off the walls.

CHAPTER SEVEN

When Big Stone had first purchased the three-story dilapidated building smack in the middle of Harlem, everyone told him that it was a bad investment. The building was damn near falling in on itself, and to make matters worse, it was located on a block infested with drug addicts. If you'd asked the opinions of ten people, nine of them would've told you that he had completely wasted his money. That was why it was fortunate that Big Stone never gave too much of a damn about the opinions of other people. They could only see the present, but Big Stone had his eyes on the future. With this in mind, he purchased the building and, six months later, purchased two more like it in other high-risk Harlem neighborhoods. Just over a decade later Big Stone's properties were worth more than ten times what he had paid for them. He was always a few steps ahead of everyone else, which was why he was the boss.

Pearl opened the front door on the main floor of the brownstone and descended the three stairs into what her father referred to as the receiving room. Aside from the massive bookshelf, which covered an entire wall, the room wasn't much to look at. It was sparsely furnished with a sofa, love seat, and two recliners. Big Stone didn't allow many people into his home, and fewer still ever made it passed the sitting room, so there was no need to deck it out.

Pearl removed her shoes and crossed the sitting room into the living room, which was fully furnished, but even less inviting than the sitting room. The reason being that Big Stone had done that room in all white. Everything from the furniture to the carpet and even the entertainment system was devoid of color. Something about white soothed her father, and he would often sit in this room when he was deep in thought.

Off to the side, there was a small entryway that allowed access to the kitchen. Pearl could hear the water running, so she knew she wasn't alone. She doubted that her little brother had taken time from his busy schedule of menacing to do the dishes, so it had to be Sandra. Stealthily, Pearl crept to the entryway and peered inside.

A middle-aged woman hovered over the stainless-steel island, chopping onions on a wooden board and watching *Law and Order* on the small television mounted above the refrigerator. Her black hair was pulled back into a pony, and every so often she would pause her chopping to dab her eyes with the apron tied around her waist. Beneath the apron, she wore a simple white shirt and dark slacks, which hugged her enough for you to see that even at her age, she still had her curves. Sandra had been with the family for as long as Pearl could remember, and she was the only one besides her who could argue with Big Stone and keep all her teeth intact. She was a real spitfire who always spoke her mind, and some whispered that the only reason Big Stone hadn't fired her was because he was sleeping with her. Anyone with eyes could see there was something between them, but neither would ever admit it.

Seeing that Sandra was preoccupied with her cooking and her

television show, Pearl tried to ease by the kitchen unnoticed, but she was unsuccessful.

"Hey, Pearl," Sandra said without looking up from her cutting board.

Fuck! Pearl cursed in her head. It always amazed her how Sandra seemed able to feel her presence when they were in proximity of each other. Pearl knew how she looked, and she wanted a chance to clean up before Sandra saw her and started asking a bunch of questions. "Hi," she said flatly, and stepped into the kitchen.

"How was school?" Sandra asked.

"Long and boring." Pearl perched herself onto one of the stools across from Sandra. "It almost seems like a waste of time to break my beauty sleep five days per week to go learn a bunch of stuff I'll probably never have any use for."

"You don't know what you'll have a use for until you need to use it," Sandra replied. "This is your last year, and in a little over a month you'll be all done with high school."

"I know, but a month seems so far away." Pearl sighed. "I wanna be done with it *now.*"

Sandra shook her head. "I swear, you young kids today have no patience at all. You want all the glory but aren't willing to put in the work. An education is important, Pearl, not just because there ain't much you can do without having at least a high school education, but more important, it'll add to your character." Sandra wiped her hands on her apron. "Think about it like this: no man who's about something wants a girl who ain't about nothing. And if they do, it's just sex. Pearl, don't ever put yourself in a position where you have to depend on a man to take care of you. Some of these young girls got it twisted and think our pussies are our greatest weapons, but it's really our independence that will serve us best when all else fails."

One of the things Pearl loved most about Sandra was her seemingly infinite wisdom. Pearl would often come to Sandra when she needed advice on something, and no matter what the topic was, she seemed to have some insight on it. Pearl felt comfortable talking to Sandra because she didn't treat her like a kid and, no matter what it was, Sandra would always keep Pearl's secrets. Over the years she had become Pearl's caretaker, confidant, and, when necessary, her disciplinarian. She did all this without ever once making Pearl feel like she was trying to take her mother's place. They were as thick as thieves, but it had always been like that.

Because Pearl's mother had died, she had been the only woman in Big Stone's life for many years, and anybody who had tried to get close to him, she had treated like an enemy. It had been the same when Sandra had come into the picture. Big Stone had introduced her as an old friend he was helping out by hiring her to keep the house and help her attend to his daughter, but from the moment Pearl saw the way they looked at each other, she knew it was far deeper than just a job situation. Pearl wasted no time digging into her bag of cruel and petty tricks to try to run Sandra off like she had the others, but what she would learn was that Sandra was *nothing* like the others.

Before becoming Big Stone's housekeeper, Sandra had been one of his street lieutenants. She first landed on his radar back when she was working as a drug mule, transporting his product from state to state. She'd taken a pinch over nine ounces of heroin on her way to DC. She was a nobody in the organization, and the police knew it. They really wanted Big Stone. Sandra could've snitched and been released, but she never uttered a word. In fact, she actually spent more than a year in Baltimore County Jail while fighting the case. When she came back to New York, Big Stone blessed her and brought her in off the streets. She had proven herself loyal, so he bumped her up from mule and gave her domain over three of his stash houses.

Sandra's new position put her in close proximity with Big Stone, and it didn't take long for their business relationship to evolve into something more intimate. Anyone who saw them together could tell they were sweet on each other, but they dared not go public with their indiscretions because they were both involved with other people. Big Stone was married to Pearl's mother, and Sandra had a long-time boyfriend who she shared a child with. Around the time Pearl was just a baby, Sandra found herself incarcerated a second time. She had been tried and convicted with manslaughter for the killing of her child's father. He had mistaken her face for a punching bag one time too many, and she'd shot him. The whole time Sandra did her bid, Big Stone made sure she and her son were taken care of, and he kept in constant contact.

When Sandra was released from prison, Big Stone was right there waiting for her. By then Pearl's mother had passed, and he was raising his little girl alone. He offered Sandra her old spot back, but she was done with the streets. Her last prison stint and being away from her son for more than five years had killed her taste for the fast life, and she was ready to square up. Big Stone saw an opportunity in this to kill two birds with one stone and offered her a position as governess to his daughter. This would allow him to have someone he trusted and respected watch over Pearl, as well as keep Sandra close to him.

Looking back, Pearl could only imagine how hard it must've been for Sandra to endure the things that Big Stone and his unruly children had put her through over the years. From their house being raided, to attempted assassinations, to Big Stone leaving the kids with her while he had to go away for a while, Sandra handled it all and never complained. Everyone thought the tipping point would have been when a young stripper Big Stone had been fucking dropped a baby boy off on his doorstep, naming him the father. He and Sandra weren't officially a couple, but it didn't make it hurt any less. Still, she accepted baby Stoney with open arms and raised him with the same love she showed Pearl. Some would've called her a fool for this, but Sandra understood the position she'd chosen by dealing with a man like Big Stone, and she played it accordingly. Her choices in life were the reason she was so adamant about Pearl never settling when it came to a man, because she knew she had.

"Girl, what the hell happened to you?" Sandra finally noticed the blood on Pearl's shirt. She rushed around the kitchen island and checked her for injuries.

"I'm fine. It isn't my blood." Pearl went on to give Sandra the short version of her fight with Kate and her friends.

"Pearl, why is it that every time I turn around, you're in the streets, fighting like a damn hoodlum?" Sandra folded her arms.

Pearl sucked her teeth. "Because these bitches are always hating."

"Watch your mouth, young lady! We're cool, but we ain't friends," Sandra checked her.

"Sorry. I know I can be troublesome, but lately I've been trying to do better, and it seems like people take that for weakness. These chicks walk around sour for no reason, trying to start with me. It's like they hate me for being fly." Pearl absently twirled a lock of her silky hair around her finger.

"You know how it can be, Pearl. Whether you're up or down, haters are gonna come, but when you're up, it makes it twice as hard. You were blessed because you were not only born to money, but love, too. Not everybody can say that. Some people look at you and the things you have in your life and develop resentment because their lives are lacking in it. Shit, with these kids nowadays, you're likely to find more madness in their homes than love."

"Well, it ain't my fault that their parents are fucked up or just not around," Pearl tried to reason.

Sandra looked at her sadly because she knew that Pearl just wasn't getting it. "Baby, it ain't their faults either. Children are born innocent;

it's the adults that program the bullshit into them. A lot of young girls you see out there with their legs thrown open are looking for the love they were denied at home. Just like some of the guys you see up on them corners are really just kids who got tired of coming home to empty refrigerators. Sometimes you have to look beneath the surface of what's going on to really get the picture. I know that when you look out that big picture window in your bedroom, you see the world as all roses, but it ain't. It's a cruel and nasty place that will swallow you if you let it. You just thank your lucky stars that your father was one of the rare few who were willing to go above and beyond to ensure that his kids could have better."

"Yeah, everybody knows how far Daddy is willing to go over what he's laid claim to," Pearl quipped.

"And what do you mean by that?"

"Come on. I'm not eight years old anymore, Sandra. I know what time it is with my father, and even if I didn't, you know the streets are always talking," Pearl told her. "Just the other day we were talking at school, and Daddy's name came up. This girl was saying—"

"Stop right there," Sandra cut her off. "Whatever you're about to say, I don't want to hear it, and especially not in this house," Sandra leaned in closer to whisper to Pearl.

"I was only about to tell you what I'd heard," Pearl tried to explain.

"Only a fool entertains rumors, and it's an even a bigger fool who discusses family business with people who ain't family. I'm pretty sure I didn't raise you to be no fool, did I?"

"No, ma'am."

"That's what I thought. Let me tell you something: regardless of what people say, you need to remember that there has never been a move your father has made without having you and your brother in mind. Good, bad, or indifferent, anything Lenox does is for the good of this family, do you understand me?"

Pearl nodded.

"Good. Now go upstairs and tell your brother that dinner will be ready in about an hour. Then Knowledge wants to see you. He's downstairs in the game room."

"Damn, as much time as he spends here, he needs to be paying rent," Pearl remarked.

"Knowledge is just as much a part of this family as anyone else under this roof. Now cut that sass and do like I asked," Sandra said, and went back to her cutting board.

"Okay." Pearl sighed and slid off the stool. "Did he say what he wanted?"

"Nope, and I didn't ask."

Somehow Pearl didn't believe her. Not too much went on under their roof that she didn't know about. Seeing that she wasn't going to get any more answers from Sandra, Pearl turned to leave. But before she exited the kitchen, Sandra called after her.

"If I were you, I'd change out of that bloody shirt before going to talk to Knowledge. You know he's your father's eyes and ears, and Big Stone will be far less understanding than I am about you being in the streets, fighting again."

CHAPTER EIGHT

Pearl bounced up the stairs to the second floor, where her room was located. She hated having her room on the same floor as her brother's and Sandra's rooms, and she'd pleaded with her father to let her have the larger bedroom downstairs, but he wouldn't hear of it. He needed to be aware of her comings and goings at all times, and there was no easier way than to put her upstairs near Sandra. That woman didn't miss a trick.

As soon as Pearl stepped off to the second floor, she caught the distinct smell of one of her scented candles, which was odd because she had been in school all day. She knew Sandra wouldn't touch her stuff without asking, so that meant her little brother had been snooping around in her room again. Nostrils flared in anger, she marched down the hall to Stoney's room. She didn't bother to knock, instead twisting the knob, intent on barging in, but it was locked. Big Stone had a strict policy about no doors but his being locked in his house, so that meant Stoney was up to no good.

"Open up!" Pearl banged on his door like the police. On the other side she could hear panicked movements as Stoney tried to hide whatever he was doing. Pearl continued to bang until he finally snatched the door open.

Stoney was two years Pearl's junior, but he was already taller than she was and seemed to be growing more each day. He was a beanpole of a young man, with his mother's high yellow skin and pink ducklike lips and his father's dark, heartless eyes. His body language was tense, as if he had just been caught with his hand in the proverbial cookie jar. When he saw that it was only Pearl and not Sandra, he relaxed and regressed to the adolescent asshole that he was.

"Why you banging on my door like the *po-lice*?" Stoney asked in a cracking tone. He was at the age where his voice was changing, so its pitch danced between high and low.

"Why you got the door locked, knowing how Daddy feels about that?" Pearl shot back.

"Oh . . . we was just in here playing video games for money, and I didn't want Sandra busting in. You know how she feels about gambling," Stoney said as if it were that simple. It was clearly a lie, and Pearl knew it.

"Then how come it smells like chocolate Thai in here?" Pearl pushed passed him and stepped in the room. Stoney wasn't alone.

Sitting on the floor at the foot of his bed, trying futilely not to look suspicious, were Stoney's two cohorts, Raheem and Domo. They were two kids from Newark who he had met when he'd gone away to basketball camp, and they'd ended up developing a friendship out side of sports. If you looked up the phrase *Project Nigga* in a dictionary, you'd likely find a picture of Raheem. He was a pudgy kid who wore his hair in thick, neglected dreads. Hygiene had never been one of Raheem's strong suits, and even when he was wearing clean clothes, he still looked like he could stand a good bath. Pearl didn't too much care for him because he was always begging. Raheem was the type of nigga who never brought anything to the table but always wanted a taste of whatever was being served.

Domonique, aka Domo, was only a step or two up the ladder as far as Pearl was concerned. He was a dark-skinned youth who didn't say much but watched everything. He carried himself a little neater than Raheem, but he still had that same hood nigga mentality and was always looking for a come-up. Domo was only a year or so older than Stoney, but the way Pearl heard it, he was involved in some very *adult* things. Like the rest, he was a degenerate and more likely to catch a lengthy prison bid than finish high school, but Pearl rocked with him because he looked out for her little brother. No matter what type of gangster shit he was into on the other side of the Hudson, he never brought it with him when he came to hang out with Stoney.

Pearl looked around the room at the faces of all three of the youngsters and shook her head when she noticed how red all their eyes were. "Now I know y'all know better than to be getting high in Big Stone's crib."

"That ain't weed. Domo was smoking a Black & Mild," Stoney lied.

Pearl looked at Domo, who happened to be the poorest liar of the trio. When he averted his eyes, she knew she had them. "Bullshit. Y'all are high as hell. I know you've been in here smoking, and if y'all don't cut me in, I'm telling Sandra."

Stoney and his older sister stood there, eyes locked in a battle of wills. He was weighing whether or not he should come clean or continue to try to bluff her. Pearl was generally supercool as far as big sisters went, but he also knew how cutthroat she could be when it came to getting what she wanted. There was no doubt in his mind that Pearl would make good on her threat and tell Sandra, and that was the last thing he wanted. He was already in the doghouse for getting suspended from school, but Sandra hadn't told his father yet. If she found out about the weed, she likely would, and he could expect an epic beatdown when his father arrived back in the States. Stoney gave Raheem the nod, and he reluctantly produced their weed stash and broke Pearl off a few buds.

"Why you gotta be in here trying to extort us?" Stoney asked with an attitude.

"You need to be glad I'm just banging you for a few buds and not convincing Daddy to check your ass into a treatment program," Pearl shot back. "Since when did you start smoking weed, Stoney?"

"I don't . . . not really. This is only my second time trying it," Stoney lied.

"Well, don't let there be a third time." She wrapped her buds in a piece of loose-leaf paper and tucked it into her bra. "Stoney, all you ever talk about is how you want to play pro basketball one day. How do you think it's going to affect your draft stock if you can't pass the urine test?"

"As long as Stoney keeps scoring the way he does, he won't have to worry about it," Raheem answered for him. "When you're a star player on a team, they always tell you before you gotta drop a piss sample."

"Nigga, you sound stupid. You're the oldest one out of this little crew, but you got the least amount of sense!" Pearl snapped. "Stoney"— she turned her attention back to her little brother—"I'm going to let it slide this time, but if I catch you getting high again, I'm telling on you."

Stoney sucked his teeth. "Dang, Pearl, why you riding me like that?"

"Because I want you to have a future and not end up like some bum-ass corner nigga." She cut her eyes at Raheem and Domo.

"A'ight, you got it," Stoney agreed. He just wanted her out of his face and his room.

Pearl had barely cleared the room before Stoney slammed the door shut and locked it again. She shook her head sadly, thinking about the menace her brother was growing up to be. Big Stone paid top dollar for them to have the best of everything, from clothes to education. She was no angel and got into her fair share of mischief, but the things Stoney did were borderline criminal. Big Stone or Sandra would jump in his ass whenever he got it trouble, but it still didn't seem to deter him. He had an unhealthy fascination with the streets, and Pearl couldn't say she blamed him, considering who their father was.

Pearl hated to come down on Stoney, but from time to time he needed it. Everything from school to sports had always come naturally to him, so he sometimes took them for granted. Stoney was not only a great athlete, but he was also a genius. He tested so high, normal private schools were no longer challenging enough, and Big Stone was paying a ton of money for him to attend a specialized school for the gifted. He was a kid who literally had the whole world at his fingertips, and all he to do was reach out and grab it.

Pearl went into her bedroom and peeled off her uniform. She held up her white shirt and examined the bloodstains. It was ruined, and she'd likely have to throw it out. She had a good mind to kick Kate's ass again because of it. On the bright side, the school hadn't called about the incident, which meant Kate hadn't told on her, and that kind of surprised Pearl. She thought for sure the prissy white girl was going to snitch, but apparently she misjudged her. She almost respected Kate for keeping her mouth shut. She was still a royal bitch, but at least she wasn't a rat.

After tossing her skirt into the laundry hamper and trashing her shirt, she went across the hall into the bathroom and took a hot shower. When she had scrubbed the day's grit off her, she went back into her bedroom to put on some comfortable clothes. She grabbed her favorite sweat pants and was about to slip them on when she remembered that Knowledge was downstairs, waiting to see her. A devilish grin crossed her face, and she tossed the sweats back onto the bed and put on something more *appropriate.*

The game room was located in the basement of the brownstone. This was where Big Stone and his boys went to unwind or watch sporting events. There was a ridiculously large plasma television dominating nearly an entire wall, a pool table, and a bunch of old-school arcade games set up throughout the basement. Pearl had spent many hours down there, trying to conquer the prehistoric games, but she hadn't had much luck on anything other than Ms. Pac-Man.

As she neared the bottom of the stairs, she could hear the soft whispers of Maxwell coming through the surround-sound speakers. When she stepped into the basement, she could smell the sweet aroma of chronic floating in the air. In the center of the room, leaning over the pool table, a blunt dangling from his mouth, was the man her father trusted like a son, Knowledge.

Knowledge was a wiry youth, with skin so black that it sometimes looked blue in certain lights. He wore his hair in a low Caesar that was almost always covered by a crispy fitted cap. That day he was sporting a red St. Louis Cardinals cap turned to the back. As usual he was wearing a fresh white T-shirt that looked like he'd starched and pressed it before he came out of the house. The muscles in his tattooed forearm bulged as he stretched the length of the pool table, trying to get just the right angle for his shot.

Pearl stood there watching him, trying to keep her thoughts pure. Knowledge was gorgeous, but also off-limits. Even if there wasn't an age difference between them, Pearl doubted if she could get him to bite. Big Stone's dog only bit at his command.

Knowledge had been under Big Stone since he was about twelve years old. He was a neighborhood kid with no father and a mother who smoked up every dollar they got. His mom, Genie, had been a dime back in the day, so it wasn't uncommon to see her keeping time with whoever was on top at the moment. Then the eighties rolled and crack hit, and it was all downhill from there. Like so many others, Genie had fallen victim to the pipe and in under a year had gone from a diva to a dud.

Being that Genie spent the majority of her time high, Knowledge was free to run wild from an early age. From the time he had gotten his hands on his first gun, he'd proven he was a hungry dog and nobody's food was off-limits. It was his wild-ass antics that had brought him to the attention of one of Big Stone's lieutenants—he robbed one of their stash spots. He was local, so it wasn't hard for Big Stone's people to find him and snatch his ass up. Big Stone expected him to be afraid or at the very least apologetic, but he was neither. The boy was either too stupid to be afraid or he just didn't give a fuck. Most likely the latter.

The kid had balls, and Big Stone admired that, but it didn't change the fact that he had touched what belonged to him; an example had to be set. He found himself with two choices: break the little bastard's legs or kill him. Neither appealed to Big Stone. He didn't have a problem dealing death or punishment to adults, but he had a strict policy about harming children. Still, if he didn't do something, he ran the risk of looking weak, and he couldn't have that. After much contemplation, Big Stone came up with a third option. He would make Knowledge work off his debt. Until he had repaid him for the drugs he'd stolen, Knowledge belonged to Big Stone.

Knowledge started out small, running errands for Big Stone and some of the other guys. In time he would come to earn Big Stone's trust enough for him to let him hit the block and start making money. Knowledge took to the game like a fish to water and soon became one of Big Stone's most promising young stars. He was a hard worker, never came up short, and would do things without Big Stone having to ask. His natural leadership abilities allowed him to quickly climb the ladder of the organization and become one of Big Stone's must trusted lieutenants. Knowledge was as loyal as a dog and would kill or die for Big Stone without even thinking about it, and Stone knew it, which is why he kept him so close.

"You know Daddy doesn't like nobody to smoke weed in the house." Pearl leaned against banister of the stairs.

Knowledge blew smoke into the air and dropped what was left of the weed in a near-empty Corona bottle. "He doesn't allow *you* to smoke in the house."

Pearl rolled her eyes. "Whatever. Sandra said you wanted to see me, so what's up?"

"Yeah." Knowledge bounced the cue ball off the nine but missed the shot. "What happened in school today?"

"What do you mean?" Pearl faked ignorance.

"Don't play stupid, Pearl. You know what I'm talking about. You know you fucked that girl's face up, right?"

"I knew that bitch was a fucking rat!" Pearl fumed.

"Calm your little ass down. When they pressed shorty, she played it off like some girl who didn't go to the school snuck in and jumped her. It was a weak story, but she's sticking to it, so there ain't too much the school can do about it."

This surprised Pearl. "Why would she go through all that instead of just telling on me?"

"Because it was in her best interest, which is the only reason you're not kicked out of school and sitting in a police precinct, looking at a charge." He rested the pool stick on the table and came to stand in front of Pearl. "Why is it that every time I turn around, you caught up in some chicken-head shit? Your father is paying a lot of money for you to go to that school. I don't think he'd be too thrilled if you got kicked out for fighting."

"If Kate and her friends hadn't tried to jump me, I wouldn't have had to clown."

"That doesn't make it right. If you have learned anything growing up in this house, you should've learned how to do dirt without getting caught. I understand the need to defend yourself, but you could've caught her off school grounds and done it to her. You're just lucky this didn't blow up in your face."

"Like I said, they tried to jump me. If somebody fronts on me, they're gonna get it where they stand," she said defiantly.

"A hard head makes a soft ass."

"My head ain't got nothing to do with my ass feeling like a cloud. I get that from my mama." She slapped herself on the buttocks and sent a ripple over her plump booty. Pearl made Knowledge look, but she couldn't get him to stare. This was an old game she played with him, dating back to when she'd first discovered the differences between girls and boys. Pearl got a kick out of making Knowledge as uncomfortable as she could whenever she could.

"You need to go somewhere with that bullshit, Pearl." Knowledge tugged at the brim of his fitted cap.

Pearl rested her elbows on the pool table and leaned over enough so that he could see her cleavage beneath her tank top. "Whatever do you mean?" she asked playfully.

Knowledge ignored her advances and walked over to the bar, where he poured himself a finger of Hennessey. He tossed it back and then poured another. "Your father is coming home tonight," he said, putting things back into prospective.

"I heard. What time is he getting in?" Pearl asked, trying to coordinate her night.

"*Soon,* which is all your sneaky ass needs to know. It'd be in your best interest to be here when he arrives. Your dad has been under a lot of stress lately, and y'all kids need to be mindful that you don't add to it."

"Is he bringing me something back?"

Knowledge gave her a disapproving look. "I tell you that your father is dealing with something, and that's your response?" He shook his head. "Sometimes you can be extremely shallow."

"I'm just kidding," Pearl lied. "But you can't blame a girl for wondering. You know I got a birthday coming up, so I just thought maybe I should be looking forward to a little something," she said suggestively.

"The only thing you should be expecting is to make it through another year of life. There are people in the world who won't be that fortunate. What do you have planned for your birthday anyhow?"

"I was hoping you could tell me. I know Daddy is planning on throwing me a surprise party, so you might as well spill it," Pearl told him.

"Big Stone hasn't said anything to me about a party."

"Stop acting like that, Knowledge. My dad has thrown me a party every year since I came into this world, so I know he's got something cooking this year," Pearl insisted.

"Like I said, he hasn't mentioned it to me. Maybe he's decided you're getting too old for birthday cakes and pony rides," Knowledge teased her.

Pearl sucked her teeth. "Now I know you must've fallen and bumped your damn head. If I don't get a party, I'm going to be mad."

"You know, sometimes you can be one ungrateful-ass little girl." Knowledge shook his head again sadly. "Your dad showers you with gifts all year-round, not just on your birthday. I don't know about a party, but I'm sure he's going to get you something nice. You could at least pretend to be grateful from time to time. I never had a birthday cake that wasn't homemade until I was, like, sixteen, and I don't think I ever had a *real* party until when I turned twenty-one? Nobody ever gave enough of a shit about me to make a big deal over my birthday."

"Sucks to be you," Pearl joked, but he didn't laugh. "For the sake of argument, if he is throwing me a party, are you gonna come through with some of your boys?"

"For what? So one of you young-ass broads can try to slap a statutory charge on us?" He laughed. "But seriously, you know if something goes down, I'm going to come through and show you some love, but I doubt if I'll linger. That's not really my scene," Knowledge said.

"Yeah, I know. You're Daddy's good soldier, always on duty," Pearl mocked him.

"It ain't about being a good soldier, Pearl. It's about being selective about what kind of people you choose to entertain. One day when you're a little older and a little wiser, you'll dig where I'm coming from." He playfully plucked her top lip with his finger and headed for the stairs. "I've got some moves to make before I pick your dad up from the airport. Try to keep your ass out of trouble while I'm gone, and for the love of God, please stay in the house tonight."

"Yes, Daddy," Perl teased. "Knowledge, one question before you go. How did you know what happened at school with Kate?"

Knowledge paused and looked at her. "All you need to know is that I got eyes and ears everywhere, which is why you and your family can sleep good at night."

After Knowledge had gone, Pearl stayed in the basement for a while longer, basking in the lingering scents of chronic and his cologne. She could've sat and listened to Knowledge scold her for hours just to be around him. Pearl had had a major crush on Knowledge since she was little, and now that she was getting older, it was evolving into something more. She sighed, knowing they were just the pipe dreams of a little girl smitten. Even if it weren't for the age difference between them, Big Stone would kill any man he caught sniffing around his baby girl, even one he claimed to love like a son.

CHAPTER NINE

Knowledge had to stop and take a breath when he emerged from the basement. Pearl loved to play him close because she knew it made him uneasy. She was definitely a stunning young woman, and as a man, it was only natural that he noticed, but she was a baby. More important, she was Big Stone's daughter. He was well aware of the standing execution order for anyone caught trying to deflower the Stone family prize, because he was charged to execute it in the event that it happened. Knowledge didn't have the heart to tell Big Stone that his daughter hadn't been a virgin for quite some time. If Big Stone wanted to live that dream, he'd let him.

Before heading for the door, he made a quick stop by the kitchen to tell Sandra he was leaving. When he went outside, he bumped into Stoney and his two friends on the stoop. They were speaking in hushed tones about something but got quiet when they spotted Knowledge. "What up?" he greeted the youths, dapping each of their fists. "Y'all staying out of trouble?"

"Yeah, man. You know I'm on probation," Domo told him.

"What about you?" Knowledge looked at Stoney.

"I'm just chilling," Stoney said, trying not to sound guilty.

"What's this I hear about you getting into a dustup? You're just as bad as your sister with this fighting-in-school shit," Knowledge scolded him.

"Wait, Pearl was fighting in school, too? How come she didn't get suspended?" Stoney asked.

"Don't make this about Pearl; we're talking about you right now. What the fuck is your deal, little man?"

"It was a situation that couldn't be helped," Stoney said simply. He sounded like a man far beyond his years.

Knowledge looked at him. "And what's that supposed to mean?"

Stoney looked at Domo and Raheem, but they turned their eyes away, letting him know they wanted no part of that discussion. Stoney cast his eyes up at Knowledge, who was glaring down at him impatiently. "If I tell you, you gotta promise you won't tell my father."

"That all depends on what it is. Now start talking," Knowledge demanded.

"Okay, they bet some money with me on a football game and lost, but they acted like they wasn't gonna pay me."

That one caught Knowledge off guard. "Stoney, you gambling in school?"

"You can't get no action if it don't run through Stoney," Raheem capped.

"Shut up, nigga!" Stoney snapped. "Knowledge, before you even get on my back about why I shouldn't be gambling in school, I wasn't. I had a little something going with the guys at the community center. The only reason I put my hands on him in school was because that's the only place I've been able to catch him. He's been ducking me for days," he explained.

"You too fucking young and too wet behind the ears to be out here gambling and shit, Stoney. You got a cushy life, but you insist upon playing gutter games that can get you hurt. That gambling shit stops now, and if I find out you're still at it, I'm fucking you up and then telling your father why I did it," Knowledge threatened.

"You got it, Knowledge," Stoney said shamefully. He looked up to Knowledge and took it personally whenever he got on him. He felt slighted and his face showed it.

When he heard Raheem snicker, Knowledge realized he'd gone too far. He was mad at Stoney, but it was a conversation he should've had with him in private and not in front of his friends. No man, no matter how young or old, wanted to be castrated in front of his peers. "Lil bro," Knowledge said, softening his tone. He threw his arm around Stoney affectionately. "I don't condone what you did, but I understand. You was wrong for gambling, but you were right to go see sun over ass-betting you. Never let a man take anything from you without taking double in return. That's what'll make muthafuckas respect you. No matter who your family is or how much money you got, there will be nothing more valuable to you in life than respect, you feel me?"

"Yeah," Stoney said, feeling a little better now.

"Okay, I'm about to get out of here to go handle a few things before I have to pick your dad up from the airport. Tell your friends good night, and go get yourself ready for dinner. Sandra is waiting."

"I swear, we gotta be the only family in the hood who eats dinner at five P.M.," Stoney complained.

"Whatever, just take your little ass into the house," Knowledge told him before descending the steps and heading to his car.

Parked at the curb was a booger-green 1993 Acura Legend that looked like it had seen better days. Aside from the stereo system and the tints, there was nothing in or about the car that was under ten years old. He had another whip, but you hardly ever saw him in it. The Acura was his everyday vehicle. Whenever Knowledge pulled up on the block in the clunker, he always found himself the butt of a joke. All his people he had come up with in the game with now drove whips more fitting for men in their positions, but Knowledge was good with the same car that had been holding him down for years. They were welcome to their flash and shine, while he was content to lurk in the shadows.

He sat behind the wheel, the car idling, watching as Stoney and his crew said their good-byes. He smirked as he thought of how odd of a group they seemed. They were from different cities, different upbringings, and different places in society, but they had seen something in one another than no one else had, which was the glue that bound them. Knowledge respected their childhood friendship and hoped that it held up into adulthood.

Raheem and Domo were passing Knowledge's car on their way to the train station when he rolled the window down. "Domo, let me holla at you for a second." Knowledge popped the automatic locks. Without questioning it, Domo pulled the passenger door open and climbed in. Raheem opened the back door and was about to slide inside when Knowledge stopped him. "Your man will get back with you in two seconds," he told Raheem, letting him know that whatever he had to say wasn't for Raheem's ears.

"A'ight," Raheem said with a hint of an attitude. He closed the door a little harder than he needed to and stood on the curb to wait for his friend.

"That kid has got a real attitude problem," Knowledge said, looking at Raheem in the passenger-side mirror. "If I were you, I'd watch him."

Domo glanced over his shoulder at Raheem. "I ain't gotta watch him. He's from what I'm from, so I know what he's about. It's the niggas who ain't from what we're from who I gotta keep my third eye on," he said, sounding like someone ten years his elder. Domo didn't talk much, but whenever he did, his words were always measured and thought-out.

"Must be a Jersey thing," Knowledge half joked. "How's Understanding these days?" he said, changing the subject. Understanding was Domo's big brother and an acquaintance of Knowledge. They had never been part of the same crew, but their paths had crossed in their respective hustles, and they'd done the occasional side business.

"He's as well as can be expected, considering the circumstances," Domo said.

"Yeah, that shit is wild how they did him—five years over some bullshit." Knowledge shook his head sadly, thinking about how they'd done Understanding dirty over a parole violation and an ounce of cocaine.

Domo shrugged. "The game gives and the game takes."

"Yo, if you need anything for him, just let me know and I'll take care of it. Un was a good soldier and a good dude."

"Appreciate it, but we straight. Me and my mom been holding him down all this time, so I think we can manage until when he comes home next year," Domo said respectfully. In truth, whatever Knowledge was trying to lay on him would've been helpful. It hadn't been easy for him and his mom to struggle to keep themselves above the poverty line while also taking care of the things Understanding needed while he was away. Some of his people would drop money off here and there. It was a burden that sometimes got too heavy to carry, but their family had too much pride to reach out to his street affiliates like beggars. They hadn't been offered anything before, so they wouldn't take it now.

"I hear that. Well, if you ever change your mind, just know that it's a standing offer," Knowledge told him. "On another note, you still be fucking with them cats from off Prince Street?"

"I don't be over there like that no more, but I'm still cool with niggas from that side," Domo replied.

"I need to have a word with one of your comrades from over that way. He calls himself Montega. You know him?"

"Yeah, I know him. We ain't friends, but I know who he is and he knows me. We're cordial," Domo answered.

"Are you two cordial enough that if I hit you with some bread you could get me close to him?" Knowledge asked.

Domo weighed the question. "I probably could, but I wouldn't."

"Why not?" Knowledge asked, curious as to why a hungry young dude would turn down cash.

"Because I know you don't mean Montega no good. If you did, I'm sure you could get in touch with him on your own instead of going through me," Domo said, calling Knowledge on his bullshit.

"If you don't know him like that, then why does it matter to you if I mean him good or bad?" Knowledge quizzed him.

"Because he Blood, same as I am," Domo said simply. "I'm not sure what your problem is with Montega or whether or not he deserves whatever you got in store for him, but so long as he's riding that *five,* I can't play a part in you doing him harm. I don't know how the Bs move in New York, but in the Bricks, that ain't how we're brought up."

Knowledge stifled the smile that tried to spring to his lips at Domo's answer. "I can respect that." He gave him dap. "I trust this conversation will never leave this car, right?"

"Like I said, I can't cosign whatever you got cooking, but I won't stand in your way, either."

Knowledge nodded. "Spoken like an honorable young cat."

"I don't know if I'd say all that, but I try to stay true to what I believe. We done? Me and Raheem gotta shoot downtown and catch the PATH train, and I don't wanna get caught in that rush-hour crowd."

"Yeah, we done," Knowledge said, dismissing him. Then he continued to sit there, contemplating the exchange long after Domo had gone. It was true that Knowledge did need to get at Montega over some business that hadn't been handled properly, but it wasn't as serious of a situation as he had led Domo to believe. It was a test of his morality. Knowledge always liked Domo and had been considering recruiting him, but he wasn't sure Domo had the nuts to play at that level. But in showing that he wouldn't compromise his integrity in the name of a dollar, Domo had proven that he may indeed be ready to take the next step.

CHAPTER TEN

"What'd that nigga want?" Raheem asked once they were off the block.

Domo shrugged. "Just asking me if I knew some dude from out of East Orange," he lied.

"We from Newark. Why would he be asking you about somebody from way over in EO?" Raheem asked suspiciously.

"You know New York niggas assume everybody in Jersey knows everybody else," Domo said, downplaying it. He didn't like being dishonest with his friend, but Raheem had a tendency to be chatty sometimes, and Domo never wanted it to get back to Knowledge and have him think he couldn't hold water.

"Word, they wouldn't know the difference between East Orange and Atlantic City. It's all the same to them." Raheem laughed. "Yo, one thing I can never figure out is with all the money Knowledge is making working for Big Stone, why the fuck does he still drive that old-ass car? If I was getting it like that, I'd be pushing a fly-ass Benz!"

"Niggas who flash are the first ones to go to prison," Domo warned.

Raheem sucked his teeth. "Fuck that! What's the good of having money if nobody knows? I'd have a fly ride, nice crib, and a bad-ass bitch like Pearl. Yo, did you see her giving me the eye when we were at her crib?"

"Nigga, you know Pearl wasn't looking at you."

"That's on the hood she was checking for me!" Raheem insisted. "She be playing hard to get, but I'm gonna wear her down and she's gonna be my girl. Once me and Pearl start fucking, I'll get her to hook you up with her Spanish homegirl, because I know you be liking them yellow bitches. Once niggas in the hood see us with them, everybody gonna be on our dicks!"

Domo chuckled. "Bro, I love you, but you sound crazy. That's Big Stone's golden princess. Ain't no way her or anybody of her caliber is stunting no broke-ass niggas from the other side of the water."

"We ain't gonna be broke forever, Domo. Our time is coming, and I can feel it," Raheem proclaimed.

"Well, if it is coming, I wish it would hurry up," Domo half joked, wishing he shared his friend's confidence.

"Have you given any thought to what we talked about?" Raheem asked.

"Yeah, and I'm not so sure it's a good idea. Stoney is our friend, and I'd never want him to think we were using him," Domo told him.

"We ain't using him—just asking for a favor. It's like you said: Stoney is our friend and his dad is the plug, so who better than to get us a formal meeting?"

"We been around them long enough to know that Big Stone don't let his kids anywhere near his business. He'd probably beat the black off Stoney for asking, and us killed for putting him up to it. Nah, I'm gonna pass on that."

Raheem sucked his teeth. "C'mon, Domo. If we keep sitting around waiting for someone to hand us an opportunity, we're never gonna get to where we need to be. We gotta step up and claim it.

Sometimes to get where you need to be in life, you have to be willing to take risks."

"I'm cool with risks. I just got a problem with dying," Domo said, and ended the conversation.

The entire ride home, Raheem continued to chatter on about his dreams of becoming a crack lord, but Domo was only half listening. His mind was elsewhere. Sometimes when he visited Stoney and his family, it put him in what he could only describe as a funk. It wasn't that he didn't enjoy visiting with the Stone family; to the contrary, the visits were sometimes the high points of his weeks. Stoney had everything and was always generous with his friends, sharing money, food, and even clothes. During those visits, if only for a short time, Domo was able to forget that he was a poor kid from the Bricks, but then reality would set back in and he would remember that's exactly what he was. Every visit to the Stone residence was a reminder of how desperately he needed to get his weight up.

This brought him back to the conversation he was having with Raheem about asking Stoney for an introduction. He agreed with him that they needed a way in so they could start making some real money, but he wasn't about to go through Stoney to do it. Unlike Raheem, he valued Stoney's friendship too much to taint it by looking for a handout. Be it in Big Stone's organization or someone else's, Domo would earn what he got or he wouldn't have it.

They got off the PATH train at Newark Penn Station in Downtown Newark. Raheem wanted to jump on the bus and ride into Union to see if they could come up on a lick, but Domo wasn't up to it. It wasn't that he couldn't use the money, but he just wasn't up to it. He had too much on his mind, and going on a mission when your head wasn't in the game was a surefire way to get yourself caught. He suggested they put it off for another day, but Raheem's mind was set, so he went alone.

Instead of waiting for the bus to take him to his block, Domo decided to walk. He only lived a mile or so from the station, and the fresh air would help him to think. He sparked a Black & Mild and strolled down Market Street, navigating through the clusters of people who were roaming in and out of the various stores that seemed to be springing up like weeds. With the way new stores were popping up every other week, Market Street was starting to look like a miniature version of 125th Street in Harlem. The city was calling it *gentrification*—creating a beautified Newark—and it went over well with those not in the know, but to those who did, it was putting a Band-Aid over an already infected wound and hoping it didn't get any worse.

By the time the fire had eaten its way down to the filter of the Black, Domo was approaching his neighborhood. He was originally from South Fourteenth Street off Eighteenth Avenue, but his current residence was the second-floor apartment of a two-family house near Lincoln Park. The block he lived on was relatively quiet, but you could go two streets in either direction and find yourself in the middle of some shit. His mother had moved them out of the old neighborhood right around the time Domo had come of recruiting age for the local set. She thought that if she got him out of the neighborhood that she could save Domo from going down the same path his brother had, but unbeknownst to her, Domo had already been on the hood for a year. When you grew up in certain hoods, you either claimed whatever gang controlled that area or you moved. Everybody who was part of his set he had either grown up with or played ball with, so making it *official* only solidified the bond they already shared. Unlike some kids who joined gangs for protection or to fit in, Domo got down because it felt like the natural thing to do.

To get to his block, he had to pass the corner liquor store, which was a popular hangout spot for the locals. You could always find homies posted up, but on that afternoon the corner seemed a little more crowded than usual. As he got closer to the small crowd, he noticed they were huddled around a shiny red BMW. Domo had never seen the car in the hood before, and it had New York plates. The crowd parted momentarily, and Domo was able to catch a glimpse of the two people in the car. Behind the wheel was a chick he had never seen before. She was a slim brown-skinned cutie who wore a green wig to match the green dress she was wearing. Leaning in the driver-side window, chopping it up with her, was a kid by the name of LA. LA was a career criminal who was responsible for damn near 80 percent of the crime that went on in the neighborhood. From jacking cars to selling dope, LA was with all that. He and Domo were cool and would sometimes hang out and smoke weed, but Domo kept his interactions with LA to a minimum. LA had done so much shit to so many people that you could never be sure when someone was going to come along and try to blow his head off.

Domo slapped the palms of a few of the guys standing out front before slipping inside the liquor store. He had ten dollars to his name, so he grabbed a forty-ounce of St. Ides and two loose Black & Milds and saved a few dollars for later in case he needed something. When he came out of the store, the BMW and the girl were gone, but LA was still there. He was posted up outside the door like he had been waiting for Domo to come out.

"What the deal, Blood?" LA greeted him.

"Ain't shit." Domo gave him dap. "About to go in the crib and kick back for a while."

"A'ight, well, I'll walk with you. I need to holla at you about something," LA told him. From the tone of his voice, Domo knew LA was up to something, which was nothing new. "So what you been up to?" LA asked once they were out of earshot of the rest of the homies.

"Not too much. Chasing this paper like everybody else," Domo told him.

"Well, are you ready to stop chasing it and finally catch it?" LA asked.

"All depending on what I gotta do to get it."

"Check it: a friend of a friend plugged me in with some cats from out of town that could use a little extra muscle for a job they got lined up. Nothing too serious," LA said casually.

Domo gave him a look. "Me and you got two different definitions of serious."

"C'mon, man, you think I'd let Understanding's little bother get caught up in some bullshit? Like I told you, these niggas just need some extra muscle to watch their backs while they hit this spot in Harlem. Me an' them would handle all the heavy shit, and all you'd really have to do is hold down the door so nobody can get the drop while we're robbing this joint. You'd be making a few grand for less than five minutes of easy work."

The thought of making a few thousand dollars was definitely tempting, considering Domo was ass-broke, but he was still suspicious. LA was making it sound too easy. "Why'd you come to me? I'm sure there're at least ten more niggas on the block who are way more qualified than me to do this with you."

"Fo sho, I can think of ten niggas off the top of my head who'd be down to shoot a bunch of shit up over the promise of a few dollars, but them niggas ain't got no common sense. So that's why I come to you." He looked around cautiously to make sure no one could hear what he was going to say next. "I ain't gonna bullshit you, Domo. These country niggas I got turned on to are supposed to be real heavy, and according to the streets, they have some real promising futures. I'm trying to get in good with them so maybe I can finally stop fucking around out here with this chump change and get some real money. I need to make a strong presentation, and I can't do that rolling in with a bunch of hardhead-ass niggas with 'blast first' mentalities. I need someone who I know ain't gonna fold and do some dumb shit if things heat up, and you're one of the most level-headed dudes I know."

LA sounded sincere enough, but Domo wasn't completely sold. "Let me think on it and get back to you."

"Don't think on it too long. This shit is going down in a few hours. Blood, I ain't gonna twist your arm, because whether you go or not, I'm still mobbing. This is too good to pass up. If you decide you're tired of risking your freedom on petty shit and ready to step up, you know how to reach me," LA capped, and then ambled back down the street.

For the rest of his walk home, Domo examined LA's offer from every possible angle. Knowing LA, it was likely that he was keeping it G and it would be easy work, but it was just as likely that Domo might find himself in over his head. Domo was no choirboy—he did more than his fair share of dirt in the streets and would even blast on a nigga if his hand were forced—but LA was a straight-up killer. Unlike some, Domo wasn't a man who believed in swimming out of his depth unless he was absolutely sure how deep the water was. If he had learned anything, he knew that all money wasn't good money.

A few minutes later, Domo was walking into the apartment he shared with his mother. Her car wasn't in the driveway, so he knew she wasn't home. She was most likely at work, which was where she spent the majority of her time. Domo's mother worked two jobs to keep the bills paid, and on weekends she did hair on the side just so they could have a little extra change. Domo kicked in when he could, but the few ends he gave her from his various hustles weren't much. Domo wanted to drop out of school so he could focus more on making money, but his mother wasn't having it. She told him the best way for him to help the family out was by finishing school so that he could find a legitimate way to get them out of the hood. Domo didn't like it, but she had made him promise he would at least finish high school before exploring any other options.

Domo plopped onto the couch and sat his forty-ounce on a pile of mail on the coffee table. He grabbed the remote control to cut the television on, but when he hit the button, nothing happened. Confused, he got up and went to check the wires. Everything was plugged in and properly connected. Perplexed, he grabbed his forty-ounce from the table. As he was chugging, he noticed one of the papers from the table was stuck to the bottom. When he peeled it free and read it, he found out why the television wasn't working. It was an electric bill dated two weeks ago, the words FINAL NOTICE stamped on it in red letters.

Frustrated, Domo tossed the bill back onto the table and headed for the door. If he hurried, he could catch LA before he left the block.

CHAPTER ELEVEN

Knowledge pushed his Acura through Harlem in no particular rush, windows cracked and chronic smoke billowing out. He was deep in thought about the dilemma Big Stone had asked him to deal with before he left for his trip. He was on the fence about the best way to handle it because it hit so close to home, but he suspected that was the reason Big Stone had insisted that Knowledge take care of it instead of passing it off to someone else. It seemed that the older his mentor got, the more paranoid he became. He was constantly testing the loyalties of those he kept close, including Knowledge.

You would think that for as much blood as he'd spilled and the secrets he'd buried in Big Stone's name, the old head would be a bit more trusting, but he wasn't. It irritated Knowledge, but he understood. In his decade of hustling, he had seen best friends become enemies and kingpins become star witnesses for the prosecution, so to an extent he could understand Big Stone's paranoia. But that still didn't make him feel any better about what he was being forced to do.

Knowledge had to go out to Queens. . . . He hated going to Queens. He didn't have anything personal against the borough or the people in it, but whenever he went out there, he always felt like he was cut off from the rest of the city. It was like being out of town without leaving the city. That didn't change the fact that he had to go. He needed to pay a call to a man he had once called a friend, but in light of the current set of circumstances, he wasn't sure where they stood. He could've rolled in with his usual shooters, but it was an already delicate situation that he didn't want to force one way or another, so he needed someone who was nonthreatening yet would lay something down without hesitation if the situation went left and they needed to get out of Dodge in a hurry. This is what brought him to the barbershop on 132nd and Lenox.

He left his car double-parked and hopped out, stepping onto the curb. He gave a quick nod in greeting to the two dreads who sold weed on the stoop next door, and went inside the shop. It was alive with the sounds of buzzing hair clippers and banter about everything from world politics to who the nicest rappers of the time were. Barbershops could be a wealth of information and sometimes foolishness, spewed from the mouths of everyone from the well-educated brothers who had no common sense to men who had little to no formal education but could've held their own with some of the deepest philosophers. Knowledge would sometimes sit in the shop for hours, soaking up game or trading laughs, but he didn't have that kind of time that afternoon. He planned to get in and out.

At his usual post, in the first chair, the one closest to the door, was the shop owner, Mr. Davis. All the guys in the neighborhood called him Cap, which was short for his street name that had at one time been Red Cap, but the fuzzy red afro that he had been notorious for had long ago thinned out and all but abandoned him. He now wore his head clean-shaven. He was locked into a heated debate with one of the other barbers. Cap loved to argue almost as much as he loved to cut hair, and no matter what, you could never convince him that he was wrong.

"What's shaking, Cap?" Knowledge greeted him.

"Not too much. How you today, Knowledge? You in for a cut?"

"Nah, just need to holla at P. Is he working today?"

"Yeah, he in the back. Listen, don't be coming in here, trying to take him off on no missions either, Knowledge. Today is the first, and there's gonna be a lot of little nappy heads coming through here that need cutting when they mamas cash their checks. I need all my barbers on deck."

"Whatever you say, Cap," Knowledge said halfheartedly, and started toward the back.

"I'm serious, Knowledge!" Cap called after him. "Ol' baby Scarface muthafucka," he mumbled once he was out of earshot.

Knowledge bumped through the crowded barbershop, giving dap to the people he rocked with and ignoring the ones he didn't. He was a man of few words and fewer friends, but that didn't change the fact that everybody wanted to stand next to him. They knew that standing next to Knowledge would put you one step closer to standing next to Big Stone.

Power was at his usual post, hovering over the last chair in the rear of the shop and administering a haircut to one of his regular clients. If you had only heard about his exploits in the streets before ever meeting him personally, you'd be caught totally by surprise by Power. He was a brutishly built man with skin so pale that it looked like it had never been touched by the sun. Over the last few years he had let his hair grow out and now wore it in cornrows that were such a rich shade of blond that they looked gold. He didn't see Knowledge at first, but he must've felt him standing behind him because his clear blue eyes glanced up at the mirror.

"Peace, God," Power greeted Knowledge in a tone that hardly matched his appearance. "Gimme a sec to finish up." He went back to grooming his client.

The friendship between Knowledge and Power went back to a time when they were both snot-nosed kids getting into mischief in the streets. Power had always had it rougher than most. He looked white but spoke just like everyone else in their neighborhood. Kids used to call him nasty names like Oreo or Wigger, accusing him of pretending to be Black, but he was African-American, at least in part. His father had been a fair-skinned Puerto Rican with blond hair and blue eyes, and his mother was as dark as Knowledge. It was just a strange twist of the gene pool that had given him most of his father's features and hardly any of hers.

When Power finished with his client, he cleaned him up and stepped off to deal with Knowledge. "What's the science?"

"Came by to see if I could convince you to take a ride with me," Knowledge said.

"What kind of ride?" Power asked suspiciously.

"I gotta make a move for Big Stone, and I need somebody I can trust to watch my back," Knowledge told him.

"Yo, God, you know I'm still on parole," Power said. He hated his parole officer, and the feeling was mutual.

"I know, I know. It ain't nothing like that. In fact, I hate to even ask this favor of you because I know how hard you been working to stay straight, but it's a delicate situation and I can't roll up with some knucklehead who can turn this whole thing into a worse mess than it already is."

"Sounds serious. Who is it?"

"Born," Knowledge told him.

This caught Power by surprise, because he was well aware of the relationship between Knowledge and Born. "Damn, sorry to hear it. Big Stone want you to take him for a walk?"

"Nah, just a chat . . . at least for now. I would go by myself and speak with him, but shit been different since he's started surrounding himself with them young project niggas."

"I heard. Word on the street is one of them dudes cut Little Paul's face up pretty bad the other night." Power recalled the story he'd heard from one of his clients in the barbershop.

Knowledge shook his head. "Fucking savages. These young boys don't respect nothing out here."

"And that's just why Born keeps them so close. That old nigga is slicker than a pig in shit. Fuck it. I'll roll with you. Let me just grab my culture-cipher," Power said, speaking of his trusty .45.

"I told you I was just going to chat with him," Knowledge reminded his friend.

"Yeah, and I heard you, but not everybody speaks the same language. It never hurts to have a translator."

An hour or so later Knowledge and Power were pulling up in front of Astoria Houses. Knowledge had purposely arrived fifteen minutes earlier than he'd told Born he would meet him, but he arrived to find him already on the avenue, waiting for him, and he wasn't alone. Four men were with him, two of which Knowledge knew well—Freedom and Lakim—and one he only knew in passing, a kid named Daou. They were all associates of Born, so it wasn't unusual for them to be with him, but the fourth man he did not expect. Judging by the way he was looking over at Knowledge, he was just as surprised and not in a good way.

"Yo, ain't that . . . ," Power began.

"Yup," Knowledge said, and got out of the car. Power followed a few feet behind. "Peace, peace, peace." Knowledge dapped, Daou, Freedom, and Lakim, respectively.

"Knowledge, what's good, sun?" Lakim greeted him with a warm smile. He was a short, pudgy dude with a goatee and gold caps covering his bucked top teeth.

"Out here trying to get a dollar like everyone else." He was speaking to Lakim, but his eyes were on the man standing next to him. Born was older than Knowledge and the others, but the man with him was older still. Wearing a do-rag, baggy hoody, jeans, Timbs, and a gold chain that was probably fake or stolen, he looked like a washed-up rapper trying to rediscover his youth. From the guilty expression on his face, he was clearly up to no good, but that was nothing new when it came to Rolling.

"Peace, youngster," Born spoke up, drawing his attention away from Rolling. He was wearing a tracksuit and a Yankees fitted cap turned backward.

"What up, OG?" Knowledge embraced him. He didn't miss the fact that during their hug, Born let his hand casually run down his back, checking him for a weapon. No doubt he felt the 9mm tucked in the rear of his belt and would think twice if he had been pondering some funny shit. "How you be?"

"I'm good, just out here shooting the shit with a few friends. Y'all two know each other, don't you?" Born patted Rolling on the back sarcastically.

Rolland Stone aka Rolling was the older brother of Big Stone and the black sheep of the family. He wasn't as heavy as Big Stone was on the streets, but he was a player in the game. In fact, Rolling played every game. From drugs to heist to murder, his paper chase knew no limitations and he wasn't above crossing you in the process. This was why Big Stone didn't fuck with Rolling like that. He was a man with no honor who would step over his own mother in the name of a dollar.

Rolling gave Born a sour look for being funny, before mustering his best plastic smile for Knowledge. "Sup, nephew?"

"Neither one of my parents had any brothers," Knowledge replied, not bothering to hide his contempt for Rolling. "Your brother know you back in New York?"

"No, I just got back a few days ago and haven't had a chance to reach out. I was gonna come by the house later on today to check him," Rolling lied. He had no intentions of going by the house. In fact, he didn't even want Big Stone to know he was back in the city, but he was sure Knowledge would blow his spot the first chance he got.

"Who's your friend?" Born's eyes were on something just beyond Knowledge.

Knowledge looked back at Power, who was standing just beyond the group. "That's Power. You remember him, right?"

Born studied him for a minute as if he were trying to place his face. He had put on nearly sixty pounds since the last time he'd seen him, but he remembered Power. He had been the little white boy with the big heart. Power would throw hands with anybody, anywhere, no matter their size, but Born really knew who Power was. He remembered him as the pale firecracker from the old neighborhood who was always throwing down to prove himself. He would fight anybody anywhere. "Yeah, I see you two are still hanging tough."

"You know mind detects mind," Power replied, letting him know he and Knowledge were of the same types of thinking. "The gods gotta hold each other down."

The statement drew muffled snickers from those who had heard it.

"Something funny?" Power asked.

No one spoke up at first, but when Born saw Power's face turn angry, he interjected to keep the peace. "Don't take it like that, Power. It's just that it ain't too often you hear a white man refer to himself as a god," he explained.

"Yeah, that title is an honor deserved by the true and living, not a genetic experiment," Daou spat.

Knowledge saw what no one else did: the change in Power's demeanor when Daou insulted him. It was subtle, the tightening of his jaw and his blue eyes turning a dull gray. As easily as someone pulling on a coat, Power had slipped into his old skin. This usually meant violence would follow. But as tempted as he was to let Power smash Daou, it would make an already bad situation worse. "Power."

Power turned his head slowly in Knowledge's direction. His eyes burned with rage pleading to be let loose. Knowledge shook his head, letting him know it wasn't the time or place. Reluctantly, Power stood down. "You got it, Knowledge. . . . You got it." He backed away. Power walked off and sat on the hood of the car, fuming.

"I see your boy still has that hot-ass temper," Born said.

"Nah, Power just doesn't tolerate disrespect, and he's not the only one." Knowledge's tone turned serious. "I need a word with you, Born. In private." He cut his eyes at Rolling.

"I gotta get out of here anyway. I need to go check my baby mama," Rolling said, taking the hint and the opportunity to get out of there.

"Which one? You got about ten of them," Knowledge said sarcastically, but there was some truth to it. Rolling had kids by at least five women who he knew of and didn't take care of any of them. This added to his legacy of being a world-class piece of shit.

Rolling ignored his insult and made a quick exit.

"Since when did you and Rolling become so friendly?" Knowledge asked Born.

"Rolling is just a means to an end, same as everybody else." Then Born cut to the chase. "Now, what was so important that you couldn't talk to me about it on the phone?"

"Stacey," Knowledge said.

Born chuckled. "I figured this subject would come up sooner or later. I just didn't expect to be having this conversation with you."

"Born, if it were up to me, I wouldn't have come, but Big Stone insisted." He shrugged. "So here I am."

Born shook his head in disappointment. "Knowledge, how long have we known each other?"

"I've known you for what feels like forever. You were my enlightener and the man who gave me the lessons," Knowledge said respectfully.

"That's right. When you were a running around here like a savage, it was me who opened your eyes to the world and its endless possibilities. I taught you how to use your brains rather than your pistols, but more important, I always taught you to be your own man, which is why this is kind of disappointing to me."

"I'm always my own man," Knowledge said confidently.

"Then why are you out here stepping to me for the next nigga, over a bitch who none of us has papers on?" Born challenged.

"It ain't like that, Born. It's just that Big Stone feels like it ain't a good look for the both of you to be fucking the same broad. Me, I could care less, but you know how Stone is," Knowledge explained.

"Indeed I do. That greedy-ass old nigga think that the world and everything in it belongs to him," Born spat.

"Born, I know what with all the money you getting, you ain't pressed for no pussy. There're a million chicks out here you could be fucking, so you ain't gonna miss out on nothing by leaving Stacey alone," Knowledge said, stroking Born's ego.

"You're only saying that because Stacey ain't never put her mouth on you. I swear that broad is top three when it comes to giving head. I can kinda understand why Big Stone is salty," Born joked. "But seriously, it ain't even about Stacy. That little bitch is a slut and willing to set it out to whoever got a few dollars to offer her. This is about Big Stone always overplaying his stroke. When I came home and found out he gave my turf to some other nigga and banished me out here to Queens, I didn't complain. I sucked it up and made the best of it. But now he's not only telling me where I can hustle, but trying to tell me who I can fuck?" He shook his head. "C'mon, Knowledge, I gotta draw the line somewhere."

"I feel you on that," Knowledge said honestly. He hated to admit it, but Born was right. The way Big Stone was carrying it over Stacey was beyond petty, and he felt like a fool for even stepping to Born over it. He didn't really care if they resolved it or not, so long as he could tell Big Stone he had done what he'd asked. "So what do you want me to tell Big Stone?"

"Honestly? I don't really care what you tell him. I ain't gonna pursue Stacey, but I ain't gonna turn her away either if she comes sniffing around for some more of this dick."

"Fair enough. A'ight, I'm gonna get outta here."

"Bet, I'm gonna walk you to your car," Born said.

They two of them were walking back to Knowledge's car, making small talk when Daou said something that gave Knowledge pause.

"Yo, next time you come through Queens, leave that devil back in Harlem," Daou called after him.

Knowledge stopped and turned around. "What did you just call him?"

"I called him what he is, a fucking devil!" Daou repeated.

Without warning, Knowledge slapped blood out of Daou. He didn't go down with the first one, so he gave him two more and put him on his ass. Freedom and Lakim looked like they wanted to flex, but before they could, Power was on them with his .45.

"Don't make me do it to you," Power warned them. There was no doubt in any of their minds that the white boy would make good on his threat, so they wisely fell back.

"What the fuck is wrong with y'all?" Born stepped between them. "Y'all be cool," he told Lakim and Freedom before turning back to Knowledge. "Man, you know better than to be coming around here, making my spot hot with this gunplay shit. Get in your car before these dudes decide to do something stupid. And take that crazy fucking white boy with you!"

"I'm not white!" Power corrected him.

"What-the-fuck-ever—just go!" Born snapped. Knowledge was walking around to get behind the wheel when Born had some parting words for him. "Knowledge, I know you ain't a kid no more, but you always gonna be my lil man, so I'm gonna drop a jewel on you: While your boss is out here worrying about who a nigga is fucking, he might wanna pay a bit more attention to the real problem that's developing right under his nose."

"What you mean by that?" Knowledge asked defensively. Born's words almost sounded like a threat.

Born raised his hands in surrender. "Calm down, Knowledge. All I'm saying is that I'm not the enemy. I got love for you and Big Stone, but that doesn't mean everybody feels the same way. Look, man, I'm telling you this out of love: the streets are talking, and I hear something is brewing in Harlem. I'm not sure what it is, but it's big enough to have all the top dogs moving real careful lately. Maybe you should convince Big Stone to follow suit."

Knowledge laughed. "Appreciate the advice, old head, but we ain't never run into a problem we couldn't handle. Big Stone got Harlem under control; you worry about Queens," he capped, and then peeled off.

Born stood there, watching the smoke from Knowledge's tires. He really did have love for the youngster, but Knowledge's head was too far up Big Stone's ass to see it. A sad look crossed Born's face as he reflected on what was to come. "That's the problem with some niggas. You can tell them it's about to rain, but they gotta get wet to believe it."

PART

A SWARM OF LOCUSTS

CHAPTER TWELVE

TJ had always been big and tall for his age. By the time he turned twelve, he was already five ten, and now, at twenty-two, he was six foot three and built like a professional athlete. Whenever he went out, he was usually the biggest amongst his friends, but in the presence of Eddie Costas, TJ felt very small.

"I don't know, TJ. This shit all sounds a little too sweet," Eddie said, picking the dirt from under fingernails with a large hunting knife. Eddie was a portly man with a soft voice and a vicious nature. He was an old-school Puerto Rican and a holdover from the old regime of the late eighties. Eddie and his crew had managed to lock down several key drug blocks over the years and were flooding the streets with heroin. He controlled a large slice of Washington Heights, but that wasn't enough for Eddie. He envisioned himself being the next Pablo Escobar and controlling the Latino drug market in New York City. There was only one thing standing in his way . . . Pana Suarez.

Pana Suarez was a wild-ass dude who the Mexican government had exiled to America so they didn't have to deal with him anymore. When he arrived in the United States, he got even worse. Pana had assembled a team of young killers who were just as crazy as he was, and he'd been wreaking havoc on the streets of New York for the last few years. He primarily operated out on several blocks that were just south of the Heights, which is part of the reason why Eddie hadn't been able to expand.

"Eddie, I'm telling you: this shit is official," TJ assured him. "Pana and his whole clique will be out of the way, and you'll be free to distribute heroin in the territory he once controlled, provided my people are taken care of for the work they're gonna put in. I think a discounted rate on the wholesale prices would be fair and still keep money in your pocket."

"I'll finally be rid of Pana and make a few dollars in the process." Eddie scratched his chin, weighing the offer. "TJ, this is very tempting, but I think you're forgetting one thing: Pana ain't so easy to kill. Trust me—I've been trying for years. There was even talk of some Haitians who sent a whole crew of shooters after Pana, and none of them came back."

"These aren't just shooters I'm talking about—they're a death squad," TJ said seriously.

"Sounds like some bad-ass muthafuckas," Blanco said sarcastically. He was a tall, pale albino with white hair that he wore in a buzz cut. Blanco had been leery of the plan since TJ had presented it. He didn't like working with new people, especially Blacks.

"I wouldn't disrespect Eddie by bringing anyone to the table who was less than official," TJ capped. "These people lost their whole city and damn near everyone and everything they loved. They got nothing else to lose or to live for except profit. All we need from you is to make sure that Michael turns the other cheek when they lace this nigga's boots."

Michael was the plug. He provided Eddie as well as several other prominent hustlers with dope and coke. There weren't many drug transactions that went on in the five boroughs that Michael didn't see a few coins off of. In addition to being his supplier, he was Eddie's uncle.

"See, this changes the playing field. My uncle might not like that arrogant son of a bitch Pana any more than I do, but he knows playing a part in Pana's execution will cause a major headache. Pana is a piece of shit, but he's a well-connected piece of shit. Some of our friends who owe him favors south of the border might be offended if he turns up dead. I don't see my uncle risking that type of headache, unless of course there was some compensation offered."

TJ smiled. "My people thought you might feel that way, so I've got it on good authority that if your uncle looks the other way on this, his pockets will be seventy-five grand heavier." TJ saw the twitch in Eddie's right eye at the mention of the money.

"TJ, you know my uncle; his money is longer than both ours and Pana's." Eddie watched TJ to see how he would respond.

"We know that, Eddie. But we also know that with a nigga like Michael, it's more about the nobility of the gesture. For even offering, he'll recognize us as stand-up guys."

"And what do I get for my part?"

TJ smiled broadly. "Eddie, you win all the way around the board. Look, when Pana is dust, the lane is gonna be wide open for you. All they want in return for eliminating your problem is free reign over Pana's territory and a nice discount on the dope and cocaine we'll be buying exclusively from you and your people. All you gotta do is fall back and collect your money."

Eddie regarded him. "TJ, I can get anybody to move drugs for me. What makes your people so special that I should give them Pana's blocks?"

"Because these ain't your everyday hustlers. Eddie, these guys are like locusts on crank. When my cousin and his crew hit a town, they swarm in like locusts and devour everything in sight."

"And what you say the ring leader's name was again?" Blanco asked suspiciously.

"They call him Diamonds," TJ said proudly.

"Yeah, I think I've heard of him," Blanco said in a less-than-thrilled tone. "He's supposed to be some kind of witch doctor."

"Diamonds is what you would call a spiritual man," TJ said modestly.

Blanco snorted. "I hear he's more than that. There are some who say he's protected by the devil and can't be killed." He recalled some of the stories he'd heard about the young upstart from the swamps.

"*Anyone* can be killed," Eddie said confidently. "Now, for the sake of argument, let's say your people are successful in taking Pana down. There will still be those who are loyal to him, even if only in memory. That could cause some nasty fallout."

TJ couldn't stifle his laugh. "Eddie, with all due respect, you obviously haven't been listening to anything I've said. When these muthafuckas hit a town, it's like a swarm of locusts, gobbling up everything in their path. Alexandria, Houston, Fort Worth, and several cities in Florida are still trying to heal from the wet bites they took out of their asses. By now I'm sure you've spoken to our mutual friend in Orlando, and he's confirmed everything I'm telling you about these cats."

Indeed, Eddie had spoken to the man in Orlando, who'd told him a story so gruesome that thinking about it made him shiver. Just as TJ claimed, Diamonds and his crew had been eating a path through cities out West and now up the East Coast. They'd established themselves in Miami and had started branching off into neighboring cities, including Orlando. Most rolled over and got out of their way, but there was a man in Orlando who decided he wouldn't be muscled by the roving bandits. He sent Diamonds a message by putting a price on Diamonds's head, but when the assassination attempt failed,

Diamonds sent a response to his message that was heard in the underworld circles throughout the country. Days after the botched assassination attempt, the police found the mauled remains of not only the man who had put the price on Diamonds but his family as well. They had been cut open and tied to trees for the gators to finish off. The youngest victim was a child of nine years old. Word got out, and it was clear that any man who would feed an entire family to alligators wasn't someone you wanted to fuck with.

Eddie thought long and hard on it. He was skeptical, but he couldn't resist the opportunity to have such savage killers as allies. They would instantly make him a power player in the New York City drug trade. Michael wouldn't be happy about it, but so long as it was quick and clean, he would get over it. "Okay, TJ. Do what you gotta do, but if this comes back on me, I'm going to deny any knowledge of what you were up to and put a bullet in your head personally."

"Don't worry, Eddie. My boys are professionals. You don't have anything to worry about," TJ promised. He took out his phone and began composing a text message.

"So how long do you think you'll need to pull this off?" Eddie asked, still unsure if he had made the right decision.

"Not long." TJ hit send on the text. "Not long at all."

CHAPTER THIRTEEN

Bonita's was a very nondescript-looking place that sat on 161st Street between Amsterdam and Broadway. It wasn't very big and its furniture was out-of-date, but Bonita's boasted some of the best Mexican food in the five boroughs. During the day it was a place where you could bring your family to get a good meal with an ethnic feel, but when the sun went down, they rolled out their makeshift bar and let the good times roll.

It was still fairly early in the evening, so the dinner crowd was only just starting to filter in. There were a few people eating at the counter and a few more sprinkled in the booths on the floor, but there weren't many people there yet besides some of the regulars.

At a table in the rear, hunched over a large steak, was a squarely built Mexican man. Between bites of the steak, he was saying something to the two men sitting with him and raining food all over the table. The two men listened intently, as if he were revealing to them the theory of relativity. Two waitresses and a manager moved in rotation, constantly checking with the man to see if he needed anything else. Pana Suarez was an important man, and everyone north of 135th Street knew it.

Bonita's was only one of many establishments where he received that kind of love. Pana had his hands in everywhere from restaurants to corner bodegas. For a small taste, Pana would make sure your business ran smoothly and keep the wolves off your back. Probably because when the wolves came, he was likely the one who sent them. There was no doubt that Pana received more than his share of love, but he prided himself on being feared.

As usual, he was dressed in a sharkskin suit, his shoes polished to a high shine, and no socks. Beneath it he sported a horrid banana-yellow shirt, unbuttoned at the top so you could see the multiple gold chains lying over his nappy chest hair. He looked like an extra in the movie *Scarface,* and fancied himself just as wild a cowboy as the infamous Tony Montana.

Bonita, the owner of the spot, came out from the kitchen and strolled over to Pana's table. She was an older Spanish chick who still had a body to rival those of a lot of girls much younger than she. Her golden-brown hair was pulled up into a messy bun that leaned to one side. The gold hot pants she wore made a swooshing sound when she walked and her thick thighs rubbed together.

"Pana, baby, you need anything else?" Bonita asked in a heavy accent.

He paused from chastising his men, his face softening when he replied. "No, thank you, I gotta get outta here in a few."

"Okay, papi. I'm going in the back to watch my soaps. If you need something, Miguel will get it for you." She nodded at a teenage boy who was lounging behind the counter. After giving Miguel some last-minute instructions, Bonita swished to the door marked PRIVATE and disappeared inside.

"Mommy still got it," remarked the man sitting closest to Pana. He was thin and sported a five-o'clock shadow along his tanned jaw.

"And the pussy is as sweet as a spring bloom." Pana smirked, remembering the last time he'd bedded Bonita.

"You hit that?" the second man with Pana asked in surprise. He was a chubby pale fellow and new to the crew.

"We do a little something from time to time," Pana said, as if it were no big deal.

"You the man, boss!" the chubby man praised him.

Across the room, a cell phone blared so loud that it got Pana's attention. He looked up and saw an older black man sitting at the counter and eating a bowl of soup. He was dressed in an off-the-rack brown suit and shoes of the same color, their heels worn. At his feet rested a black briefcase. He paused his slurping and retrieved a cell phone from his pocket, and then spoke for a few seconds with whoever was on the other end before hanging up and slipping the phone back into his pocket.

Pana watched curiously as the man with the loud cell phone dabbed his mouth with a napkin and slid off the stool. When he turned, he could see his face clearly. He was an older gentleman with hard eyes. He walked calmly in Pana's direction, but before he could get too close, the men who had been sitting with Pana were on their feet, guns drawn and ready.

"Something you need?" the tall one with the five-o'clock shadow asked in a hostile tone.

The man was clearly frightened but managed to find his voice. "I was just going to the bathroom." He pointed to the restrooms, which were just beyond Pana's table.

Pana looked over his shoulder at the doors to the restrooms, then turned back to the man and glared at him for a long moment. When he was satisfied that the man posed no immediate threat, he waved his men off. "You guys, relax. You're too fucking tense."

The two men stared at the stranger for a while longer before doing as they were told and backing off.

On shaky legs, the man skirted between the two men past

Pana's table. He kept looking back over his shoulder like he was afraid they might renege on their pass and jump on him. He was so shook that he decided to skip the bathroom and leave the restaurant altogether.

"Fucking pussy." The chubby one laughed at the fleeing black man.

"Some guys have no balls." Pana chuckled, digging into his pants pocket for his bank roll. He peeled off fifty dollars and dropped the bills onto the table. Pana's meal was free, but the tip was for Miguel. He liked the young boy and always made sure he had a few dollars in his pocket. In another year or so he would be ripe for recruiting, and Pana planned to add him to his ranks.

The money had barely touched the table before Miguel swooped in and took it. He wanted to get to it before one of the other staff members stole it. He thanked Pana for the money before clearing the abandoned dishes off the table. The dinner rush would be in full swing soon, and Bonita liked for them to be prepared.

"Let's get out of here. I got some shit I need to handle later on," Pana told his men, and started for the door. He stopped short when heard Miguel's voice. He was walking toward them, holding a brief-case.

"Señor Pana, that *negro* forgot his briefcase!" Miguel announced.

Pana's brain froze for a half second, as if he were trying to decipher what Miguel was saying, but when he hit the play button again, panic clutched his heart. Without saying a word, Pana turned and bolted for the exit.

Pana had barely cleared the door before there was a loud boom, followed by a fireball engulfing Bonita's. Miguel was lucky—he died instantly from the blast—but the chubby man who had been with Pana wasn't as fortunate. He stumbled from the rubble of the ruined doorway, screaming as fire ate away at his skin and clothes.

Pana laid facedown in the street, dizzy from the force of the blast and trying to regain his wits. A shadow fell over him, causing him to look up. Much to his surprise, he found the stranger from the restaurant standing over him. He was no longer cowering, but grinning triumphantly and pointing a .45 at him.

A split second before the bullet struck the ground where Pana's head had been, he rolled to his left and was on his feet, drawing his 9mm from his waist. He was getting on in years, but he was still a seasoned killer and moved as such when he needed to. Pana blasted away with the 9mm while running for cover. Pana dashed toward an alley, but he found that route cut off when a second man stepped from the shadows. He was wearing a ski mask over his face, but Pana could see, behind the man's sneering lips, what looked like diamonds in his mouth. Pana scurried in the other direction, trying to dip across the street, but he found that exit cut off by two more men wearing masks. He was trapped between a quartet of killers.

Pana's head whipped back and forth nervously as the four men closed in on him. He figured he could take two of them out, three if he were lucky, but his chances of surviving the ambush were slim to none. Just then fate threw him a bone, and there was an additional gun added to the skirmish.

The tall man with the five-o'clock shadow came staggering down the street, firing his pistol. His face was badly burned and smoke rose from his clothes, but he still had some fight left in him. He fired shot after shot, but his wounds made his aim unsteady, and most of the slugs missed their targets by a wide berth.

With an amused smirk on his lips, the man with the diamond teeth strolled casually toward the tall man with the five-o'clock shadow, ignoring the bullets whizzing by him as if they were little more than passing flies buzzing around him. The wounded man's gun clicked empty just as the man in the ski mask closed the distance between them. Calmly, he placed his gun to the man's head and cocked the hammer back with his thumb. A look between sadness and disappointment settled in his eyes before he blew the other man's brains out.

CHAPTER FOURTEEN

Domo sat in the back of the minivan, wringing his hands nervously. For the millionth time since he'd gotten into the van, he wondered if he had made the right decision.

Him finding the electricity shut off in his apartment was the last straw. He knew he had made a promise to his mother to try to fly straight and focus on school, but he could no longer sit idle and watch her struggle. He was a man and men took action. With this in mind, he went and found LA to let him know that he was in. LA didn't appear at all surprised when Domo came looking for him. He knew Domo's family and their struggles and was just biding his time until the young man decided to come out of his shell and get into some real gangster shit, which is exactly what they were about to do.

Next to him on the backseat was LA's sidekick Rafik. He was a wild young dude who sometimes talked too much, but Rafik lived his life like an outlaw and was always down for whatever, so long as it put a few dollars in his pocket. Rafik was a live wire and way too reckless for Domo's tastes. Had he known prior that Rafik would be rolling with them, Domo would've probably changed his mind again, but by that point it was too late to turn back.

LA was slunk low in the passenger seat, smoking a blunt of something that smelled like horseshit. He and Rafik had been ping-ponging the blunt back and forth and hadn't attempted to pass it. Not that Domo would've taken it anyway. There were rumors in the hood about LA sometimes dabbling in things heavier than weed, but Domo believed to each his own and didn't judge him for it. So long as he never tried to lace Domo when they smoked together, he didn't have a problem with it. LA's thumb clicked the safety of his gun on and off in a rhythm, and he seemed jittery. Domo wasn't sure if it was his nerves or the effects of whatever they were smoking.

Behind the wheel of the minivan was the girl he had seen earlier in the BMW. She had changed out of her green wig and dress, and now wore a black wig and black hoodie. Domo had learned that her name was Vita. She hadn't said much, but from the few words she did speak, he picked up on an accent that placed her origins somewhere in the Deep South. From where exactly that was, he wasn't sure and he dared not ask. There was something about Vita that gave him the creeps. As if she could feel his thoughts, she glanced up at the rear-view mirror and looked at him.

As they crossed the George Washington Bridge and rolled into the section of New York known as Washington Heights, Domo's heart beat a little faster. They had almost arrived at their destination. It was time to put up or shut up.

Vita turned to LA. "Everybody know what they're supposed to be doing?" she asked as she pulled the minivan to a stop next to a fire hydrant in front of a tenement building.

"Sho nuff." LA chambered a round into his gun.

Vita turned around and addressed the two youngsters in the back-seat. "Remember, no cowboy shit. Y'all follow my lead, and we all walk out of there in one piece, get it?"

"No doubt. These muthafuckas ain't gonna know what hit 'em!" Rafik boasted.

"You sure you up for this, pretty boy?" Vita asked Domo, seeing the worry on his face.

"I'm gonna hold up my end." Domo patted the .22 on his lap. It wasn't the most intimidating pistol, but it was all he had.

Vita laughed when her eyes landed on the small gun. "Nigga, not with that piece of shit you won't. Reach up under the seat."

Domo fished around under the seat until his hand brushed against something metal. He came up holding a small yet powerful-looking handgun.

"Glock .45," Vita informed him. "You only got ten shots, but when that bitch spits, it makes a statement, just like me. It's from my personal stash, so make sure you return the muthafucka when the job is done." Then she jumped out of the van.

LA and Rafik followed closely behind Vita into the building. She warned them that no matter what happened, they were to keep their guns hidden until she said otherwise, which bothered Domo. If they were going to rob the spot, then it'd be best for them to already have their guns out so no one could get the drop on them. From the looks on LA's and Rafik's faces, that didn't sit too well with them, either, but Vita was calling the shots and so they did what they were told. She bounced up the steps and then motioned for them to wait on the second-floor landing until she gave the signal.

On the floor just above them they could hear Vita speaking to a man in the hallway. Domo tried to eavesdrop, but he couldn't understand what they were saying because Vita was speaking to the man in Spanish. The conversation started off in a soft tone; then they heard the man yelp, followed by two quick chirping sounds. A split second later there was the sound of something heavy hitting the floor. Assuming that was the signal, they rushed up the stairs. Vita was standing in the middle of the hallway, holding a 9mm, smoke coming from the silencer screwed onto the end of the barrel.

"Damn, how you gonna start the party without us?" Rafik asked in disappointment.

"Shut the fuck up before these niggas hear you and you get us killed," Vita hissed as she fished through the dead man's pants pocket. She came out holding a single key at the end of a leather strip. "Now look, we gonna go in here and bag these niggas for all their shit and get gone. She addressed Domo. "Pretty boy, you play the top of the stairs and cover our backs. Anybody come up these bitches, you drop their asses. You got it?"

Domo nodded. Too nervous to speak.

"Good." She eased the key into the lock. "Now let's go in here and relieve these pussies of their shit."

Vita and the others had barely been in the apartment thirty seconds before the shooting started. They had left the door open, so it gave Domo a clear view down the long hallway that ran the length of the apartment into the living room. The people inside the apartment scrambled back and forth, some returning fire while others were just trying to get out of the way. LA and Rafik were like two cowboys, going from room to room and shooting anything moving. Vita was more poised, taking her time and measuring every shot before she took it. Watching her was like watching a professional figure skater going for Olympic gold. A woman came darting out of one of the rooms and was running down the hallway toward the open front door. She had almost cleared it when something slammed into the back of her head and she pitched forward. A few feet behind her, Vita stood. She put one more bullet into the woman's body for good measure. They had invited Domo to participate in a robbery, but what was going on inside the apartment wasn't a robbery; it was an extermination.

Rafik and LA were in one of the rooms, doing only God knew what, while Vita crouched down on the living room floor, scooping up scattered money into a garbage bag. Just beyond her, Domo caught a flicker of motion across the behind the shade of the living room window. He thought his mind was playing tricks on him until he saw a pair of hands just below the bottom of the drawn shade, lifting the window up. Vita was so focused on the money that she didn't see the two men slip in behind her. Without thinking about it, Domo abandoned his post at the top of the stairs and rushed down the hallway.

Vita looked up with a start when she heard the heavy footfalls coming down the hall. When she saw Domo rushing toward her, she thought the hired guns from New Jersey were attempting to cross her, so she raised her gun, ready to fire. Just before she squeezed the trigger, Domo let off a barrage of shots that sailed over her head. She heard a scream, followed by the sounds of breaking glass. She turned around in time to see one of her would-be killers falling backward out the window. She rolled to her right just as Domo cut loose again and made the second killer, sending him flying into the big-screen television. She watched in shock as a cool and collected Domo continued to advance, pumping round after round into the already downed man. Long after the gun had clicked empty, he continued to squeeze the trigger, as if there might have been another bullet hidden somewhere in the chamber.

"I think he's dead," Vita said, bringing Domo back from wherever his brain had retreated to.

Domo blinked as if he were waking from a dream. When he glanced down at the body at his feet, a look of sadness crossed his face. He had shot at a few people before, but to his knowledge, he'd never hit anyone. He had started his night out as a thief and would end it as a murderer.

"It was either him or me, kid. You did the right thing," Vita said, trying to ease some of his guilt.

The commotion in the living room brought LA and Rafik running, guns drawn and looking for someone to shoot. When they saw the bodies in the living room, they were disappointed to have missed out on the action.

"Damn, what happened out here?" LA asked.

"I almost got my fucking head blown off, no thanks to y'all," Vita spat. "What the fuck were you two doing so long anyway?"

"I was in the back room, collecting this." LA proudly hoisted the trash bag he was carrying. "Came up on at least ten keys under the bed."

"And what about you?" She looked to Rafik.

"I was in the bathroom, making sure we didn't miss none of their stashes. I didn't find shit, though," Rafik told her.

Vita let her gaze linger on Rafik for a while longer, as if she were trying to read his face. "Fuck it—let's get this shit and get gone before the police come." She slung her trash bag over her shoulder and started for the door.

LA looked from the bodies on the floor to Domo and patted him on the back. "Looks like you finally busted your cherry!" he said proudly.

By the time Domo and the others had come out of the building, Vita was already behind the wheel and putting the minivan in gear. LA and Rafik got into the back while Domo jumped into the passenger seat. He barely had time to close the door before Vita peeled out.

The ride back to New Jersey was a tense one, at least for Domo. LA and Rafik sat in the back, arguing about who had dropped the most bodies that afternoon, but Domo hadn't uttered so much as a word since they had left the apartment. He was reflecting on what he had done and what it would mean for him going forward. He'd heard guys tell stories about what it was like to catch a body, but nothing compared to actually being behind a the gun when you snuffed a life. Domo had taken two.

"Your first?" Vita asked, snapping him out of his daze.

"Huh?" Domo didn't understand the question.

"I asked if it was your first time dropping somebody?"

Domo nodded.

"First time is always the hardest. It'll get easier." Vita cracked a half smile. It was the simplest of gestures, but it somehow managed to sooth Domo's nerves. He didn't know Vita very well, but something in her eyes told him that he could trust her.

They exited the Turnpike in the industrial section of Newark. It was an isolated area lined with old warehouses and factories that hadn't been used in some time. Vita turned the minivan off the main road and onto a gravel path that lead to the abandoned building where they'd stashed a switch car and fresh clothes. She pulled behind the building and killed the engine. The all filed out of the car and stretched their legs, while Vita busied herself rummaging through one of the trash bags.

"That was some good work back there." Vita came from around the rear of the minivan, carrying stacks of money. "A little rough around the edges, but you boys have got potential." She tossed each man a stack of bound bills.

Domo did a quick thumb through the money. "This is, like, five grand!" he said excitedly. He had never seen that much money at one time in his life.

"It's actually seven thousand. I put a little something extra on top for them niggas you dropped." She gave him a wink.

"We got our hands dirty too, but I don't see nothing extra on top of ours," Rafik complained.

Vita ignored him. "I'm sure I don't have to tell you guys to keep your mouths shut about this?"

"Nah, we know the game. Hear no evil, speak no evil. You ain't gotta worry about us Vita," LA assured her.

"Good, I'm gonna drop you guys off, but I'll call you in a few days for some more work. That is, if you're up to it?" She was speaking to all of them, but she was looking at Domo.

"Hell yeah, we're up to it!" LA answered for them.

"Good." Vita nodded in approval. "Now, there's just one more piece of business we need to wrap up." Without warning, Vita whipped out her 9mm and shot Rafik in the face.

"What the fuck?" LA jumped back to avoid the blood splatter. Domo just stood there, too stunned to speak or move.

"Shut up," Vita commanded, turning the 9mm on LA, her pistol sweeping back and forth between LA and Domo. She knelt and patted Rafik's corpse down. "Bingo," she said when she felt the bulge under his shirt. When she stood up, she was holding the parcel of cocaine Rafik had found in the bathroom and lied about. "This nigga was a fucking thief." She held the coke up for both of them to see. "Two things we don't tolerate in our organization are snitching and stealing from our own. A man who would take food out of his own family's mouth ain't worth shit. "Now, we can get into some gangster shit over what I did to your homeboy or we can charge this shit to the game and I bring you two in to make some real paper. Either way, I don't give a fuck, so pick your poison."

Domo and LA exchanged nervous glances. It really wasn't a hard decision to make, considering the choices placed in front of them. Get rich or die.

"Fuck it. We wasn't that cool anyway," LA said, trying to hide the fear in his voice.

Vita studied them both for a moment that felt like a lifetime before finally putting her gun away. "Glad we're on the same page. Welcome to the flock."

And just like that, Domo and LA were recruited into Diamonds's pirate crew.

CHAPTER FIFTEEN

Pana watched as the man with the diamond teeth stalked back in his direction, smoking gun in hand. With his crew gone and trapped, most men would've given up hope, but Pana wasn't most men. He was a survivor. Pana caught the taller of the masked men more focused on his partner than his quarry, and busted out a desperation move. He slammed the butt of his gun into his chin, stumbling him and creating a hole in the circle they'd formed around Pana. The opening was all the Mexican needed, and he took off like a bat out of hell. Pana had made it nearly to the corner before he heard the familiar retort of a gun being fired. He knew what would come next, but he still wasn't ready for the searing pain that exploded in the back of his thigh when the slug hit it. He was able to stumble a few more feet before pitching face first to the concrete. He wasn't even on the ground long enough to process the extent of the damage before a pair of powerful hands grabbed the back of his suit jacket and yanked him up.

"On your feet, bitch nigga!" The stranger from Bonita's pulled him off the ground. He and the taller masked man grabbed Pana by the arms and forced him against a wall.

Pana struggled against the men, but it was futile. Between being shot and the loss of blood, he was so dizzy that he had a hard time focusing. He watched helplessly as the masked man with the diamond teeth stalked toward him. He stopped just short of Pana, removing his ski mask and shaking his long dreadlocks loose. He was looking at Pana as if he were waiting for him to recognize him, but to Pana's recollection, he'd never seen him before.

"You know, I never expected to come out here and cause all this mess." He holstered his gun. "I'd hoped the bomb could've ended things quickly. Maybe not clean, but quick." His tone was almost apologetic.

"You know who the fuck I am? I'm Pana Suarez, muthafuckas! You and everybody you love are gonna die for this!" Pana threatened.

The taller masked man who was holding Pana hauled off and slapped him so hard that blood shot from his lips. "Watch your fucking mouth!"

"Ain't no need to be a brute about it," said the man with the diamond teeth. "No need to kick him when he's already down. Now, we know who you are, but do you know who I am?"

Pana shrugged as if he didn't know or care.

"The name is Diamonds—maybe you've heard of me?"

It took a few seconds, but the name finally clicked in Pana's head and he remembered where he'd heard it. During one of his excursions to Miami, he had heard stories about a newcomer who was making major noise by single-handedly raising the murder rate in Florida. The street cats called him Diamonds, but the old-timers had another name for him: *el hombre de fuga*, "the vanishing man." In hushed tones they told stories about men who ran afoul of him, vanishing from their homes in the night, as if by magic, never to be heard from again. The color drained from Pana's face.

"Noticing your sudden change in complexion, I'll take that as a yes," Diamonds said with a smirk.

"Look, if it's money or drugs you want, I've got plenty of both. Just name your price, cut me loose, and we'll forget any of this ever happened."

Diamonds patted him on the cheek playfully. "I thank you for your generosity, but we've got plenty of money, boss. As far as the drugs, several of my associates have already cleaned out your main stash house. I hear they made quite the mess, and for that, you have my sincere apologies. Robbery was never our intention, but it'd be a shame to have all them good drugs go to waste, seeing how you no longer have a need for them. What I want from you is worth more than anything you can give me, at least not willingly."

"If you've already taken my money and my drugs, what the fuck do you want?" Pana asked nervously.

Diamonds reached into the back of his pants and produced a sleek black knife. Its handle was made from what looked like a human bone. "Your soul," he told him before burying the blade into Pana's heart.

"You see the way my brother did that boy? Now that's how you murder a nigga!" Goldie said excitedly from the backseat. He, Diamonds, Hank, and Buda were in a dark-colored SUV, fleeing the crime scene.

"From the way he was shaking, I thought he'd die from a heart attack before anybody had a chance to shoot him," Buda added. He was sitting next to Goldie, working on his second bottle of whiskey for the day.

"If all these niggas in New York are as easy to knock off as that Pana character, we're gonna be running this whole city before long," Goldie said.

"Don't go getting ahead of yourself," Hank said over his shoulder. He was behind the wheel of the SUV. "Pana was as tough as nails, and had we not had the element of surprise on our side, that whole situation could've played out differently. No matter how big or how small, never underestimate an enemy. Remember that, and you're likely to live to be as old as I am."

"Listen to this old *Art of War*–ass nigga," Goldie said, mocking him.

"Hank is right," Diamonds spoke up. Until then he'd been riding silently in the passenger seat, staring out the window. "We got lucky with Pana, but that doesn't mean everybody else is going to fold that easy. We've got to be smart and careful."

"Speaking of careful, what was that shit back there about?" Hank asked.

Diamonds turned to him. "What you mean?"

"You know what I mean, Diamonds. I'm talking about you walking into those bullets like you're the damn Terminator or something."

"The bomb blast had that boy's brains so scrambled that he probably couldn't have hit me if I'd been standing right in front of him," Diamonds said as if it were nothing.

"But what if he had?" Hank challenged.

Diamonds waved him off. "Stop talking to me about possibilities and let's look at the facts. We went in there to get rid of Pana and we did. That was our goal. I don't know why you in here stressing me like an old hen over shit that's not important."

"Yeah, stop stressing, Hank," Goldie added from the backseat.

"Goldie, shut the fuck when you hear grown folks talking," Hank snapped. "Fuck, with you and your slipping ass, Pana almost got away. How many times do I have to tell you not to take your eye off the damn ball?"

Goldie was silent because he knew he had messed up by letting Pana steal off on him and run. Had Pana gotten away, they wouldn't have had a second chance to pull off the job.

"Diamonds," Hank continued, "you ain't never been the most cautious guy, but it seems like ever since we buried John-Boy, you're becoming more and more reckless with your life. You act like you wanna die."

Diamonds laughed at the statement. "OG, one thing you ain't never gotta question is my love of this world and the things in it. I got plenty more living to do before I die, and so long as I keep home close to my heart, it won't be a concern of mine anytime soon." He ran his finger along the cord around his neck. It held the soil-filled pouch.

Hank cut his eyes at him. He knew the pouch and the story behind it. "You can bet your life on the word of that crazy swamp woman if you want, but I'd rather you just got the fuck out the way when niggas are shooting at you."

"Man, I sure do miss that old bird," Goldie said, thinking of Auntie. He and his brother had spent many a night sleeping in her hut when they had nowhere else to go. "Say, Diamonds, I was thinking now that we've got a little paper squirreled away, maybe we could send for her. How do you think Auntie would like New York?"

"Ain't no way we could ever get that lady to leave New Orleans. She's as much a part of the land as it is of her," Diamonds told him, cutting dangerously close to the truth. Before he'd left New Orleans, he'd buried her body deep in the swamp.

"I guess you're right," Goldie said, slightly disappointed. "Maybe once we handle our business up here, we can take a trip back home and visit her?"

"We'll see," Diamonds said, and went back to staring out the window. He hated misleading his little brother, but he didn't have the heart to tell him that he had snuffed out the life of a woman who had treated them better than any of their biological family had. Goldie loved Auntie, and he'd never understand that her death was necessary for their survival. "Anybody hear from Vita?" Diamonds said, changing the subject.

"Yeah, she checked in a few minutes ago. Everything is cool," Hank told him.

"That's my girl." Diamonds smiled proudly. "So I guess things worked out with them kids from Jersey who TJ plugged her with, huh?"

"Depends on who you ask," Hank answered. "She had to lay one of them to rest, but the other two stood tall."

Diamonds shrugged. "There will be casualties in every war. On the upside, we only lost one out of three recruits."

"Diamonds, I don't know how to feel about you bringing all these new niggas into our thing," Buda spoke up. "TJ is your cousin, so I can dig it, but do we really need to be fucking with more outsiders?"

"I can appreciate your concern, Buda, but I think an infusion of fresh blood is a necessary evil at this point. Our troops are already spread thin between what we got going on in Texas and Florida. New York is a big city, and it's going to take more than just the six of us to hold on to what we're taking."

Buda frowned. "I feel you, but I'm just feeling a little funny about all the new faces."

"Rest easy, Buda. I trust Vita's judgment, but we ain't gonna give them the keys to the front door just yet. Every newcomer, including TJ, will have to earn their way into our inner circle," Diamonds promised, which seemed to put Buda at ease for the moment. "I had a thought. We should go out tonight," he suggested, catching everyone in the SUV by surprise.

"Am I hearing this correct? Mr. *All Business* is actually down to have some fun for once?" Goldie didn't try to hide his shock. They had been in New York for more than a month, and Diamonds had never once shown any interest in going out with them.

"I'm thinking I probably ain't been the easiest muthafucka to deal with as of late. I got a lot on my mind, and maybe I need a good night of drinking to even me out," Diamonds told him.

"I don't really care what his reasons are, so long as I get to jump in some New York pussy tonight!" Buda downed the remainder of his bottle in one swig. At the mention of having a good time, his sour mood picked up. "Maybe me and you can even double down on something like we used to, Diamonds. It'll be just like old times, right?"

"Sho ya right, Buda. Just like old times." Diamonds smiled, but inside he was frowning. Buda had been drinking heavily since John-Boy had been killed. Lately he was always drunk or on his way to being drunk, and it was starting to concern him. It would have to be addressed eventually, but this wasn't the night for it. "Hank, get TJ on the line and tell him to pass the word to his people that the deed is done. Goldie, I want you to raise Vita and tell her to go home and get pretty. I think it's high time that us country niggas see what this New York nightlife really be bout."

CHAPTER SIXTEEN

Pearl stood on the corner of 125th and Lenox, trying her best not to freeze her ass off. The short black leather miniskirt and thigh-high boots were cute to death but hardly appropriate for the weather. She looked like she was out there selling pussy, and she wanted desperately to get off that corner before she was either arrested or abducted.

It had been no easy task for her to slip out of the house dressed the way she was. After eating dinner, she had expected Sandra to do her usual and go to bed early, but as dumb luck would have it, *The Ten Commandments* was coming on television that night, and Sandra planned to stay awake to watch it. There was no way Pearl was going to wait three and a half hours until it was over, so she had to take matters into her own hands. She offered to make Sandra a cup of tea, and then spiked it with Benadryl. An hour into the movie, Sandra was fast asleep and Pearl was in the wind.

The plan was for Marisa and Sheila to swing by and pick her up in a cab, but it was fifteen minutes past their meet time and there was still no sign of the girls. This is why Pearl hated moving on other people's time. It was bad enough she only had about an hour or two to chill, and their being late was cutting into that. She would give them five more minutes and then she was taking her ass home.

Before she could make good on her threat, a red Jeep with big gold rims came bending around the corner. Reggae music blasted from the speakers, and even though all the tinted windows were rolled up, you could still smell the weed smoke seeping from it. When it stopped on the corner where Pearl was standing, she wisely backed away from the curb. Her father had always taught her never to get too close to a car if she couldn't see who was in it. With all the dirt her family was into, death or being kidnapped were constant threats. Her hand had just slid inside her purse when the passenger window rolled down and she saw Sheila's face smiling out at her.

"What's good, Pearl?" Sheila yelled louder than she needed to. She was tipsy already.

"Sheila, you know better than to be rolling up on me, all suspect. We almost had a situation out here." Pearl patted her bag.

"Stop fronting." Marisa rolled down the back window. "You nice with ya hands, but you ain't killing nothing."

Pearl took the small .22 from her bag and brandished it. "Like Pac said: *I ain't a killer, but don't push me.*"

"She listen to Pac and carry iron. Me thinks me like her already," someone with a heavy Jamaican accent said from the recesses of the backseat.

Pearl peeked inside the car and, for the first time, noticed there were two dudes in the back with Marisa. One of them was staring at her like she was well-cooked steak. He was light-skinned and rocking a Blue Jays fitted cap that was cocked to one side.

"I thought y'all were coming to pick me up in a taxi?" Pearl looked at the Jeep suspiciously.

"We were, but we figured, why waste the money if Boom was already in the area and could pick us up?" Sheila touched the arm of the dude behind the wheel, marking her territory. Boom was cute, handsome with a wavy fade and rocking large diamonds in both ears.

"Come on, mami. Jump in so we can go." Marisa pushed the back door open. In addition to the dude with the Blue Jays cap, there was another young man wedged into the backseat, closest to the opposite door. He was dark, rocking a freshly tapered cut and a thick gold rope chain around his neck.

"Looks like y'all are already full. I can't fit back there," Pearl said.

"Come, baby girl. Me got plenty of room for you to ride." The dude with the Blue Jays cap patted his lap, offering Pearl a seat.

Pearl rolled her eyes. "Nigga, what do I look like to you?"

"It's cool. I'll take one for the team. Let's just go," Marisa said, scooting onto his lap, much to his disappointment.

Pearl wasn't feeling her friend's display of thirst, but she kept it to herself. Holding her short skirt down with one hand so her entire ass didn't show, she climbed into the back of the Jeep. The first thing she noticed was how soft the cream leather seats were. They felt like butter. The interior was fully loaded, with a crisp sound system and three television screens, one in the dash and two on the headrests. On all three screens, the movie *Paid in Full* played with no sound. As she was admiring the car, she happened to look up and notice the driver, Boom, watching her through the rearview mirror. Pearl turned away and occupied herself by looking out the window.

During the ride to the spot, they passed around a bottle of Jamaican rum and two spliffs. Pearl only took one shot of the rum, but she hit every blunt they passed to her. Boom and his crew had some good-ass weed, and it had Pearl extremely relaxed and way less defensive than when she'd gotten into the car. She learned that the two guys riding in the back with them were called Ricky and Franz, Ricky being the one with the baseball cap. Ricky was the more talkative of the two. He kept going on and on about how much money he was getting in Brooklyn and how many bottles he was gonna pop at the club. Pearl hated dudes who always talked about what they had, because it usually meant they didn't have anything. Even if he hadn't been finger-banging Marisa for damn near the whole ride, Pearl couldn't deal with him.

Franz was different. He didn't talk much, other than to say a few words into his cell phone, which seemed to ring every five minutes. She read in his eyes that the constant calls from whoever was on the other end were getting on his nerves, but he never raised his voice or showed any kind of emotion. He was very composed for a dude that young, and it intrigued her.

"So, whose birthday is it?" Pearl asked curiously. She didn't really care, but the weed had her feeling chatty.

"My homie Doodles," Boom answered over his shoulder. His voice was thick and heavy like the bass from a speaker.

"Doodles—what kind of a name is that?" Pearl laughed.

"The kind of name you don't want to let him hear you laughing over," Franz spoke up. Pearl noticed now that his voice also held a hint of an accent, but not as heavy as Ricky's or Boom's.

"Chill out, Franz. You gonna spook her," Ricky teased.

"Shit, I doubt it. Pearl is used to being around gangsters. She comes from a whole family of them," Sheila volunteered.

"Oh, so your people in the game?" Franz asked, suddenly quite interested in Pearl.

"Pay that drunk-ass girl no mind. My daddy did some time back in the day. Nothing special," Pearl said, downplaying it. She was secretly fuming at Sheila and her drunk-ass mouth. Pearl hated her family's business to be put in the streets, especially in front of strangers. Thankfully Franz picked up on her mood shift and let the subject drop.

A few minutes later Boom was parking the Jeep in front of the spot. Pearl had expected them to be hitting up a club, but it was more like a lounge . . . a bar, to be exact. She had ridden past the neighbor-hood wateringhole on the corner of 145th and Lenox plenty of times, but had never gone inside. The way she'd heard it, it was a den for thieves, killers, and hustlers. She would be surprised if she didn't run into one of her father's associates inside the place. Pearl was pissed that she had put on a good outfit to kick it at a local spot, and made a note to herself to have a conversation with Sheila about being more diligent in her reconnaissance before inviting her anywhere.

The girls spilled out of the Jeep, looking like eye candy. Sheila was wearing a smoke-gray faux fur coat with a one-piece white cat-suit that threatened to burst at the seams trying to contain her huge ass. Marisa was wearing an off-the-shoulder red dress that hugged her hips tight enough to show off her shape, but not so tight that she looked slutty. From their heavily made-up faces and their choices in outfits, they looked more like grown-ass women than schoolgirls.

There were a surprising number of nice cars lining the block in front of the bar/lounge. Congregating on the sidewalk were small pockets of people, talking amongst themselves or smoking. Some of the faces Pearl recognized, but for the most part she didn't know any of them. They likely weren't from Harlem, which told her that this Doodles person had to have been a man of some type of stature to bring them out like that.

Boom led their way toward the spot, Sheila clinging to his arm as if he might fly away if she let it go. At the entrance there was a doorman checking the IDs of the people going inside. Pearl became nervous because she knew none of them were old enough to be in there. She looked at Sheila as if to say, *What's the deal?* Sheila gave her a wink and signaled for her to be cool. Boom greeted the bouncer with a firm handshake when they got to the door. He whispered some-thing in his ear and motioned toward Pearl and her friends. The doorman looked out at them before smiling and giving Boom the nod.

With just a few words, he had thrown the gates open to the start of their night.

The inside of the spot wasn't as sleazy as Pearl had expected. It was far more spacious than it looked from the outside, with a wide dance floor and fully stocked bar. It was dark, but the fluorescent bulbs that framed the bar mirror illuminated the room enough for them to navigate their way across it without breaking their necks. They picked their way across the dance floor, with occasional stops for Boom to shake hands with someone or offer a word of greeting. Pearl noticed that there were a lot of Jamaicans, Haitians, and West Indians in the spot, and most of them seemed to know Boom and his friends.

There was a small crowd gathered on the dance floor, watching the spectacle of a man and woman dancing suggestively. Pearl watched in fascination as they gyrated and ground against each other, lips locked and swapping breath. If not for the fact that they were both fully dressed, you would've thought they were fucking right there on the dance floor. Something stirred low in Pearl, and her face flushed a bit in embarrassment. She pulled her eyes away from the couple in time to see that her friends had moved on.

A quick scan of the crowd and she found them on the other side of the bar. They were approaching the roped-off area in the back, where about a dozen people were partying privately. In the center of them was a brown-skinned man with a shaggy beard. He towered over the crowd, probably standing on a couch or table, waving a bottle of champagne over his head and unapologetically spilling it on whoever was standing close enough to him to get wet. He seemed to be having more fun than anyone else in the joint. Pearl needed some of whatever he was drinking to get to that point, and she wouldn't get it standing there like a lame duck.

The crowd seemed to have doubled in the short time since they'd first entered the bar, making it hard for her to move without bumping into somebody or somebody bumping into her. Ahead, a word exchanged between two girls got things heated. A well-placed drink tossed in one girl's face was the match that lit the fuse of the brawl that ensued. Pearl tried to sidestep the fight and ended up slipping on a wet spot on the floor. The tall heels of her boots made it hard to catch her balance, and the next thing she knew, she was stumbling on her way to a face-plant on the floor. She closed her eyes and braced for the impact, but it never came. When she opened them, she found that it was a muscular brown arm wrapped around her waist that had stopped her fall.

A soft breath tickled her ear. "You okay, miss?"

Once Pearl had gotten over the shock of almost falling, she pulled free and spun to find herself confronted with a man who she could only describe as beautiful. He was tall and athletically built, like he might've played ball at somebody's university. His long dreads were pulled into a thick ponytail that hung down his back. He didn't wear much in the way of jewelry, just a gold chain and a nice bracelet, but she couldn't help but notice the brilliant assortment of diamonds covering his top and bottom teeth.

"I asked if you were okay?" he repeated, snapping Pearl out of her daze.

"I'm fine. Thank you." Pearl busied herself smoothing her skirt so that she could avoid looking into his eyes. There was something in them that made the hairs on her neck stand up, and she wasn't sure if that was a good or bad thing.

"Looks like you spilled your drink." He motioned to the liquid on the floor she had slipped in. "Let me replace it for you."

"Oh, that wasn't mine."

"An empty hand in a bar is a sin," he said playfully. "Have a drink with me, love." He touched her wrist.

The simple gesture sent a chill up Pearl's arm. "I'm good. I'm here with my people for the private party in the back." She motioned toward Marisa, who was watching the exchange from across the room.

Diamonds glanced over at the crowd in the VIP area. "There're a million people back there. I don't think the party will grind to a halt if you slip off for a few ticks. Besides, it'd be rude of you to turn down the hospitalities of the man who just saved your life."

"You're persistent, aren't you?" Pearl looked him up and down.

"Nah, just focused." He openly admired her.

"But I don't even know you."

"*Padonnen m'.*" He gave an apologetic half bow. "My name is Diamonds." He extended his hand.

"Pearl." She went to shake it but was surprised when instead he lifted her hand and softly kissed the back of her knuckles. His lips felt like fine silk on her skin.

"Diamonds and Pearl," he said aloud, letting it hang in the air. "It's catchy."

"We sound like an R&B duet," Pearl joked.

"I'm sure we'd make some beautiful music," Diamonds said. "Now that the pleasantries are out of the way, how about that drink?"

Pearl took one last glance over her shoulder at Marisa, who was now occupied with some young hustler pressing her to dance. "Fuck it. But just one. I don't wanna keep my people waiting."

Diamonds flashed his brilliantly jeweled smile. "Fair enough. I'll have you back before they even notice you're gone."

CHAPTER SEVENTEEN

The crowd parted like the Red Sea for Diamonds as he led Pearl by the hand to the bar. There were two dudes occupying the stools directly in front of them. Pearl recognized them from the streets, but she couldn't remember their names. They worked for one of her father's associates and had reputations as tough guys around the neighborhood. Pearl was about to suggest that they move to the less crowded end of the bar to place their drink orders, but Diamonds was already heading in the direction of the men. She watched as he tapped them on the shoulders and whispered something to them. Pearl's heart leaped into her throat when one of the men jumped to his feet and squared off with Diamonds. The man outweighed Pearl's rescuer by nearly fifty pounds, but Diamonds was hardly fazed. Before anything could pop off, the man's partner jumped between them and made an apologetic gesture to Diamonds before pulling his friend by the arm through the crowd.

"Here you are." Diamonds pulled out one of the now vacant stools for Pearl.

"A gangster and a gentleman, huh?" She perched herself on the seat.

"Now, what would make you go and say a nasty thing like that?"

Diamonds took the other stool. He waved the bartender over and placed their drink orders while waiting for Pearl to answer.

"Because I just watched you put two known killers on time-out without having to raise your hand," Pearl observed. "What did you say to them?"

Diamonds shrugged. "Only that I had met an angel of mercy with an injured wing, who needed to take a load off for a spell."

"Aren't you a smooth devil?" Pearl teased.

"Baby, you have no idea how accurate of an assessment that is." He laughed, giving her another glimpse of his jeweled teeth.

"So why do they call you Diamonds? Is it because of that shiny grill of yours?" Pearl asked.

"No, they call me Diamonds because it's actually my name. I can even show you my driver's license if you don't believe me," he offered.

"Nah, it ain't that serious. That's just a strange name for a guy to have."

"So I've been hearing all my life. See, when I was in my mama's stomach, the doctors told her that I would be a girl, so she decided to name me Diamonds, after my granny. Imagine her surprise when the little girl she had been preparing for all those months came out with a dick." He chuckled. "She was already committed to the name, so she never changed it."

"Now that's an interesting story."

"My life is full of interesting stories. I'd love to tell you a few of them, if you'd but permit me the time."

Just then the bartender came back over and placed two glasses in front of them: one was a Hennessy on the rocks, and the other was a rum and Coke. Diamonds tossed a hundred-dollar bill on the table and told the bartender to keep the change.

"What made you order me rum instead of Hennessy too?" Pearl asked, sipping the rum and Coke.

"Because I didn't want you mixing liquors. I smelled a tinge of rum on your breath when we were first talking, so I took a stab in the dark." Diamonds winked.

Pearl covered her mouth in embarrassment, thinking her breath stunk.

"Easy, love." He gently pulled her hand away. "Your breath is fine. My nose is just a little more sensitive than most."

"You part bloodhound or something?"

Diamonds laughed. "No, I'm one hundred percent wolf, *amoure.*"

"What is that, French?" Pearl asked.

"Close—Creole. Where I come from, we speak just as much of it as we do English," he told her.

"And where is that?"

"Da Boot, but you might know it as New Orleans. I grew up in a small parish just outside the city."

"So what brings you to New York?" she asked.

"Same thing that brings everybody else this way. I'm looking for the pot of gold at the end of that concrete rainbow."

"Good luck with that. New York can be a hard place to survive, especially for out-of-towners," Pearl told him.

"So I keep hearing, but I've been getting along famously during my stay here. From what I can see, New York is just right for a sporting young man like me. I might even take up permanent residence so I can see more of you, Ms. Pearl . . . lots more."

"Don't get your hopes up. This is just a drink—not a date," Pearl said, checking him.

"But of course. Besides, when I take you on an official date, it won't be to no bar," Diamonds said confidently.

Pearl raised an eyebrow. "Okay, Mr. Presumptuous. Hypothetically speaking, if we did go on an official date, where would you take me?"

Diamonds pulled her stool closer so that they were eye to eye. "Anywhere your heart desired."

Pearl gazed into his inky-black pools and found her own reflection staring back. His gaze was almost hypnotic, and she found that she could look nowhere but at the beautiful creature sitting across from her. They say that the eyes are the windows to the soul, but Diamonds's were looking glasses, and Pearl was ready to play Alice and tumble as far down the rabbit hole as he was willing to pull her. Her mouth went dry to the point where she could feel her tongue thickening, and Diamonds's thick lips were the only things that could quench the all-consuming thirst that had just overcome her. She leaned in to sip from the well of Diamonds, but before she could take a sip, their connection was broken.

"Should've known all I had to do was look up a random skirt to find you." A woman slithered up beside him. She was wearing a tight black-and-white-striped dress that frayed just above her knees. On her head she wore a black wig that had white highlights running through it. She ran her zebra-print acrylic nails down the back of Diamonds's neck while giving Pearl a challenging look. She was marking her territory.

"Quit cock-blocking, Vita." A taller, slightly lighter-skinned version of Diamonds joined them. He was wearing baggy jeans and crisp Jordans, and at least five gold chains lay on the chest of his white T-shirt. Tied snugly around his neck was a black bandanna.

"You tend to your dick and I'll tend to *mine*, Goldie!" Vita hissed and then turned to Pearl to give her a dismissive look.

"You need to tuck them fangs and remember your place," Diamonds told her. His voice remained even, but no one missed the threat in his words.

"And you need to tuck that wayward dick of yours and remember what we're here to do," Vita spat. She made sure to shoot Pearl one last dirty look before storming off through the crowd.

"I'll go see about her," Goldie offered, and went after the zebra.

"Sorry, didn't mean to cause any problems between you and your lady." Pearl eased her stool back to put some distance between her and Diamonds.

Diamonds glanced back in the direction Vita had gone in and shrugged. "I got no more claim on Vita than a man hustling on the same corner every day. He's on that corner so often that he knows it better than anyone else, but he can't produce a deed to prove ownership."

"Is that a nice way of saying you're just fuck buddies?" Pearl accused. "Look, I'm digging you and all that, but I don't do side-bitch drama."

"Call it what you need to, Pearl. Me and Vita got history, but nobody got claim to this heart. I'm a free agent who does what he wants, and what I want is to get to know you."

An older man wearing a sour scowl on his face slid up behind Diamonds, shadowed by a brute sporting a thick beard and a bald head. The brute eyeballed Pearl like he was praying rape was legal, while the older man whispered something into Diamonds's ear. Whatever he said seemed to darken Diamonds's mood.

"Pearl, as much as I would like to spend the rest of this night and the next convincing you that I'm a genuine soul, I got something I need to attend to. Before I go, let me leave you with this: I've never been good at games, so I don't play them. You can either come out with me and see for yourself how sincere I am about what I say, or you can write me off and I'll grow to be that old man who tells his grandkids stories of the one who got away."

"I ain't no home-wrecker," Pearl said seriously. Diamonds was talking a good game, but hers had to be better.

"And I ain't no fraud," he shot back.

The older man cleared his throat, reminding Diamonds that they had something to do.

"Duty calls," he continued, "but you go on and wrap your brain around what I said, and we'll take this conversation up at another time."

"So is this the part where you ask me for my phone number?" Pearl asked, thinking she was two steps ahead of him.

Diamonds cracked a sly smile. "Pretty lady, there's a difference between being pressed and being sincere. I fall into the latter category. If it's meant to be, it'll be, and our paths will cross again soon," he capped, and walked off.

Pearl stood there for a few minutes, trying to figure out exactly what had just happened. She had always considered herself a smart girl and able to run game with the best of them, but Diamonds had successfully screwed her head on backward. As she watched him strut cockily away, she couldn't decide if she wanted to run up on him and say all the things she would've had he not turned the tables, or take him into the bathroom and fuck him. He was cocky and borderline arrogant, but there was also a magnetic quality about him that drew her like a bee to honey. Had it not been for the bitter bitch Vita, there was no telling what would've gone down between them. He thought he was saying something slick when he spat his little game and pimped off with his boys, but what Diamonds didn't know about Pearl was that she always had the last word.

CHAPTER EIGHTEEN

"That's a dangerous game you're playing," Hank told Diamonds as they moved through the club.

"What you mean?" Diamonds asked.

"Poking a hornet's nest with a stick. You know you ain't right for pressing up on that broad while Vita's in eyeball's distance."

Diamonds waved him off. "I'm free to do me, and Vita's free to do her. I'm not her man and she ain't none of my girl."

"Then maybe you should stop making her feel like she is," Hank said slyly.

Diamonds stopped and turned to face Hank. "Since when did who I'm fucking become your business?"

"Since who you're fucking started affecting *our* business," Hank shot back. "You been dicking that girl down since she was old enough to take a grown cock, so don't act like you don't see that same starry look in her eyes that everyone else does. The difference is, we also see the evil looks: that glint in her eyes that says that every time she catches you dirty, she inches just a wee bit closer to getting up the courage to kill you. Diamonds, you know I know how the game goes, but that's a young girl with a fragile heart. The last time she went off the rails over you fucking that girl in Dallas, her head was so scrambled that she almost blew the whole damn job!"

Diamonds cringed, thinking back on the incident. Vita had caught him fucking some broad he'd met in the club, and it ended up being a bad situation. She didn't say anything when she initially found out. She waited on it, and during a siege they were laying to a trap house in Dallas, she decided to take her revenge and try to blow Diamonds's head off in the middle of a job. Buda managed to wrestle the gun from her hand before she killed Diamonds, but her bullshit allowed the dudes they were moving against a chance to regroup, and they ran Diamonds and his crew off. That was one of only three jobs that had gone bad. It was Vita who blew it, but Diamonds who had pushed her to it. "I'll talk to her. Everything gonna be cool," he promised.

"You'd better. The next time, she may slit your throat in your sleep instead of trying to shoot you while we're on a job. If you know like I know, you'll either stop parading your bullshit in front of Vita or let her go," Hank warned.

Diamonds understood Hank's point of view, and the old-timer was right, but it was Diamonds's ego that wouldn't allow him to completely cut Vita loose. He had started quietly sleeping with Vita since right before she'd graduated high school, and by the time she'd blossomed into womanhood, he had molded her in his image. He was smart about it, never officially committing to her but constantly dangling the possibility. So long as she had hope, she would always be loyal.

"What's up with you and brown skin anyhow?" Hank nodded in the direction they'd just come from.

Diamonds looked over his shoulder at Pearl, who was just entering the VIP with her friend. He caught her looking back at him. "Her." He smiled. "I don't know, but I got a serious hankering to find out. She feels special."

Hank shook his head. "Man, you got a serious weakness for pretty bitches. It seems like you fall in love with a different one in every city we mob through."

"Those other times weren't love, but a need to get my dick wet. This is a different kind of situation," Diamonds told him. "I ain't gonna front like I wouldn't dick her down if I had the chance, but I wouldn't mind getting to know her either. She feels right."

"You got all that from spending a few minutes with the broad?" Hank didn't believe it.

"Sometimes that's all it takes. You ain't never heard of love at first sight?" Diamonds questioned.

"Of course I have. How do you think I met my ex-wife?" Hank questioned. "I knew I loved her from the first time we said hello, which is why it hurt all that much more when I found out she was a scandalous bitch. I spent a whole week wallowing in my own piss and self-pity before I was able to crawl out of that funk, and trust me when I say, you don't want no part of that kind of heartache."

"So you mean because of one bad experience, you've closed your heart to the possibility of love?" Diamonds asked.

"That's exactly what I mean," Hank confirmed. "In this life we live, the only things we can afford to love are this paper and this power. Anybody who tries to stretch his heart beyond that is inviting disaster."

"With that kind of attitude, you'll likely never know the endless possibilities of true love. What good is having the finer things if you don't have anyone to share them with? I know most of these broads ain't got nothing but larceny and ambition in their hearts, but that don't mean there aren't some good ones out there. Who's to say Pearl might not be the one for me?"

"Vita," Hank replied. "Regardless of what you think you might be feeling toward this young chippie, Vita ain't gonna never sit idle and watch you give some random chick what she's been working to earn for all these years, especially some bitch who looks young enough for you to get locked up over."

"Hank, you act like I'm a long time removed from high school just because I didn't graduate. I figure I probably got her by a few years, but how young can she be if she's up in a gangster bar, hanging out with gangsters? Big homie, I ain't saying I'm trying to jump her bones fresh out the gate, but that's somebody I think I need to know. When you get a minute, I want you to find out all you can about Ms. Pearl. Now, on to more pressing business. You have any luck getting us that meeting with the owner of this hole-in-the-wall?"

"I stepped to the manager twice, and he keeps saying he ain't in yet. Quiet as kept, me and Goldie spotted his car when we cased the block. I think they playing games."

"I might hide too if I knew a king cobra had just slithered into my place," Diamonds said. "We new faces, so I expected him to be suspicious, which is why I called TJ."

Hank frowned. "What you call him down here for? His vote don't count in this collective."

"No, it doesn't, at least until I say otherwise. TJ is local and familiar with the natives, so they might be less suspicious of him. Either way, this conversation is going to happen tonight."

"Whatever you say, *boss.*" Hank's tone was laced with sarcasm.

Diamonds cocked his head and glared at Hank. "OG, we known each other too long to hold our tongues. You got something you feel like you need to get off your chest, go on and spit it out."

Hank glanced around to make sure no one was listening before speaking his piece. "Dawg, what the fuck are we doing here?"

"Exploring a business opportunity—what else?" Diamonds said as if his motives were pure.

"Don't be funny. You know what I mean. You promised the team a night out to unwind, yet we find ourselves in here trying to make a move, a move I advised you against, I might add."

"We always on the clock, Hank. Money don't take days off and neither do we," Diamonds said as if it were that simple.

"Need I remind you of our current position in all this? We just wiped out an associate of the Mexican cartel, a big-time player in Harlem, and took damn near his whole crew along for the ride. We did all this on the word of your cousin and with a suspect green light from a guy we don't even know if we can trust yet. And now, less than twelve hours later, you wanna try to put the squeeze on another power player who was never in the plans to begin with? Why do you even need me to tell you this isn't a good idea?"

"Where's your sense of adventure, Hank?" Diamonds laughed as if the whole thing were funny. "Nah, but I see what you're saying, and under normal circumstances, I'd agree, but what I've found during our stay in New York is that it's anything but normal. Things in this city move fast, and sometimes you gotta improvise. Right now we got the element of surprise on our side, and we need to use it to our advantage. Some parties we'll get invited to, and others we just gotta show up unannounced and convince them to let us in."

Hank frowned. "I hear that shit, but what if this gate-crashing mission goes to the left and we're called to task for our bullshit because you wanted to jump the gun? You know every member of the crew is ten toes down for whatever you need us to do, but we don't have enough friends in New York yet to go to war over a piece of property that probably ain't worth the blood that'll be spilled to take it."

Diamonds shrugged. "Fuck it. We been playing with the odds against us all our lives. What makes this any different? We came to this city to bleed it, and that's what we're gonna do. If you got cold feet and wanna step off, I can respect that. You've put in enough work to where nobody would question it if you wanted to retire early, Hank."

"Lil nigga, you know better than that. I been with you since the beginning, and I'm gonna be with you until the end. All I'm saying is, we need to pace ourselves and not jump too far out the window too soon. You've come in here with this ol' great offer to make, assuming he's going to go for it, but what if he doesn't? Pops is very well liked in these notorious circles, and people may not turn a blind eye to him going missing like we *hope* they'll do with Pana. We ain't got nobody's blessing on this one."

"Blessing? Since when we start lining up to take communion for the sins we commit in the name of survival?" Diamonds hissed. "New York ain't like Texas, or even Miami. The only thing niggas up here understand is persistence and violence. I'm damn good at both, so I plan to capitalize on them. This old man has something I need, and I intend to make my play for it. Anybody who got a problem with that, you tell them to go get a pistol and step to me properly," Diamonds capped, and walked off, leaving Hank standing there.

CHAPTER NINETEEN

They called it the VIP area, but it was more like a section of the bar that had been roped off from the main area. There was a sectional couch, two standing tables, and just enough room in the center for a few people to dance if they liked.

From the way Sheila had made it seem, they would be the main attraction, but there were at least a half dozen girls lingering in the VIP already, with easily that same number waiting outside the rope, hoping they could gain access. Not that Pearl was worried, but none of the girls she saw looked like they posed much of a threat. She could tell from the low-end gear, synthetic hair, and the heavy stench of cheap body spray that they were bottom-feeders and hardly in the same weight class as Pearl, or even her friends, but they were thirsty, and that would give them a leg up if guys started choosing.

Sheila was standing just beyond the rope, a drink in her hand, and staring over at Boom while he whispered into the ear of some girl with too much stomach for her halter top. The longer Boom talked to her, the tighter Sheila's face got. She looked ready to blow a gasket at any second and looked fit to lose it when someone called Boom's name and drew his attention away from the girl he was talking to.

Boom's posture seemed to straighten at the sight of whoever was calling him, so Pearl followed his line of vision to see who it was.

Much to her surprise, it was the guy she had spotted earlier, popping bottles and carrying on. When Pearl had initially seen him, she assumed that he had been standing on a chair or possibly a table, but now that she was in proximity of him, she realized he was just that tall. He had to be at least six foot six, and he sported a mess of thick dreadlocks and a beard that looked like it had never seen comb or shear. One of his eyes seemed to drift, making it hard to see where he was looking. He was by no means a handsome man, but he draped himself in high-end fashion to compensate for it. The heavy jewels and head-to-toe Louis Vuitton outfit screamed money, and it was all authentic. Pearl had been bathed in designer since she'd come into the world, so she knew quality when she saw it.

Pearl watched intently as the tall dread crossed the small space and greeted Boom with a handshake before pulling him in and patting his back. They spoke briefly amongst themselves before Sheila interjected herself into their conversation. Boom gave her a disapproving look, but if she noticed, she didn't seem to care. The Jamaican rum they'd had on the way over had her on her gangster shit. Sheila went back and forth between the two men, batting her eyes and spitting game. Every so often she would glance over to the corner Pearl and Marisa had settled into. Whatever she was saying drew a mischievous smile from the tall dread, and the next thing Pearl knew, she and Marisa were being waved over.

"Marisa, Pearl, this is Doodles." Sheila made the introduction as if she and Doodles were old friends and she hadn't just met him a few minutes prior.

"A pleasure to be acquainted," Doodles said in a heavy Jamaican accent, and extended his hand in greeting. He gave Marisa's hand a polite shake, but when it came to Pearl, he turned her hand over and kissed the back of her knuckles.

"Fuck is that about?" Sheila asked, feeling slighted that she hadn't gotten more than a nod.

"A man know how to greet a queen when him see one," Doodles told her. "When Boom tell me he was bringing the *entertainment,* I had no idea him meant Hollywood headliners." He sized them all up, paying special attention to Pearl.

"I don't know about no *entertainment.* My girl said she knew some cool dudes we could hang out and have some drinks with. Beyond that, I don't know if I can help you," Pearl told him, letting him know she peeped the slick shit. The way Doodles was talking and looking at them, you'd have thought they were circus monkeys he couldn't wait to throw peanuts at to see what kind of tricks they would do. She had a sick feeling in the pit of her gut. She glanced at Sheila, but she was trying her best to look everywhere except in Pearl's direction. The setup didn't feel right, and it made Pearl raise her guard.

"Chill out, gangster. I didn't mean to offend," Doodles told her.

"So, why do they call you Doodles? You an artist or something?" Marisa asked. She picked up on the tension and was trying to change the mood.

Doodles looked to Boom first, who shrugged as if to say he hadn't put her up to asking. He then turned to Marisa to see if it was a serious question or whether she was making sport at his expense. "If ya must know, it's a moniker that come from my day back home. It's a long story, but in short, some men try fe test me, and I doodle me name in them chest with a knife." He said this seriously and then made a slashing motion in the air with his finger, Then he let the dumb look of embarrassment settle in on Marisa's face over the all-too-personal-too-soon question, before breaking out into a smile. "I'm joking. They call me Doodles because I had skill with the pencil as a boy."

"For a second I thought we were hanging out with some killers," Pearl mumbled.

"Who says you aren't?" Franz whispered in her ear as he suddenly brushed past on his way to the other side of the section.

"We can make small talk about job occupations later," Doodles continued. "Today Jah blessed me to see another year and we're here to give thanks for it. I'm trying to get fucked up. Who's with me?"

Doodles invited to share the couch he had reserved for the night. He shooed away some of the girls who were already sitting there to make room for his new guests, which the girls didn't seem to be happy about, but Doodles wasn't a man who you argued with. Boom sat to Doodles's right, Sheila damn near breaking her neck to take up the space next to Boom. Pearl made to sit to Doodles's left when Marisa damn near shoulder-tackled her to get to the seat first. She let it be known she was shooting for the stars that night, so Pearl let her have it, and sat at the end of the couch.

At some point a large curtain was drawn, cutting off the VIP section from the view of the rest of the bar, and that was when the real party started. Doodles wasn't as bad as Pearl had expected him to be. He was loud and uncouth, but the man knew how to have a good time. Drinks were flowing and weed was being rolled nonstop, but never once did he allow any of them to dig into their pockets to pay for anything. He was indeed a gracious host. The fact that everything was free meant that most did their best to overindulge, and the party really got loose . . . too loose in some cases. Pearl spent half the night rejecting the advances of Doodles's people, who kept trying to push up on her. Some of them were okay-looking, but they were far too aggressive.

Needing some space, she got up from the couch and moved to a less crowded spot near the edge of the curtain. A few feet away Franz sat alone on a chair, sipping from a bottle of vodka. He wore a very uninterested look on his face, as if he had a million other places he'd rather have been but there. Franz hadn't been the most engaging fellow since she'd met him, but he started acting downright funny once they'd gotten inside. When Pearl made eye contact, she flashed him a smile, to which he replied by shaking his head before getting up and walking to the other side of the room.

"Well, fuck you too then," Pearl mumbled, slightly dumbfounded by the brush-off. She had thought Franz to be a cool dude, but apparently he was just as much of a dick as the rest of his friends. Whatever his problem was, it was obviously beyond her understanding or care, for that matter. She looked down at her watch and realized that time had gotten away from her; she'd stayed at the bar for more than an hour longer than she had intended to. It was time for her to find her friends and bounce.

Pearl noticed a small commotion brewing near the entrance as another guest was escorted into the VIP area. She was a tall drink of water with high yellow skin, blond hair, and thick thighs that strained against the fabric of her tight leather shorts. She strolled confidently across the room, large sunglasses covering her face, and swished hard enough to throw her hips out of place. Pearl expected the men to swarm her, as they had every other woman in the room, but surprisingly they kept a safe distance. From the respect they showed her, Pearl knew she had to be someone of importance.

Pearl looked on curiously as the woman approached Doodles and planted a kiss on each of his cheeks. They exchanged a few words before Doodles handed her a rolled-up knot of money, which she dropped into her purse without bothering to count it. The whole time Pearl watched the blonde, she couldn't help but feel like she had seen her somewhere before. She wasn't sure if it was her posture, or the way she flipped her wig every time she laughed, but there was definitely something familiar about her. It wasn't until she removed her sunglasses that she realized why.

The last time Pearl had seen Zonnie, she had been tugging at Big Stone's pant leg and pleading for him to accept her back into his life. It was the most pitiful thing Pearl had ever seen. She could tell by the way her father's body trembled that he was mad, but she didn't understand how much so until the back of his hand graced Zonnie's face. It was the first time she had ever seen him raise his hand. Had Pearl not just walked into the room, it was very likely that Big Stone would've killed Zonnie right there in the middle of their living room. Instead he banished her from the lifestyle he'd allowed her to be part of and the son she showed no interest in raising when she dropped him off on their doorstep a year prior . . . Stoney. The last Pearl had heard, Zonnie had relocated to LA and was shaking her ass in rap videos under the guise of pursuing an acting career.

Zonnie must've felt like she was being watched, because she started looking around. It was like she had radar, because her eyes zeroed right in on Pearl. Since it had been years since Pearl had last seen Zonnie, she hoped she didn't recognize her, but when the blonde headed in her direction, Pearl knew she had no such luck.

Pearl stood there like a deer in headlights as Zonnie crossed the room. She stopped just short of Pearl and let her weed-slanted eyes travel the length of Pearl's body. The younger girl tensed, not really sure what to expect, considering Zonnie's history with her father. For a minute Pearl thought it was about to go down between them, but a smile formed on Zonnie's heavily glossed lips.

"Is that little Pearl?" Zonnie asked, while continuing to give her the once-over. Seeing how nicely Pearl had filled out, she let a smile touch the corners of her mouth. "Well, I can't call you *little* anymore." She glanced at Pearl's ass.

"Hey," Pearl said dryly, tugging at her skirt to make sure her ass wasn't showing. The predatory look Zonnie was giving her made Pearl uncomfortable.

"I haven't seen you in years, and that's the greeting I get?" A look of fake hurt crossed Zonnie's face. "Shit, we was almost family—give me some love." She damn near forced Pearl into an embrace. Zonnie stank of liquor, cigarettes, and a hint of sex.

"So what you doing here?" Pearl broke their embrace. "I heard you was living the life of the rich and famous on the West Coast."

"California was good to me, but ain't no place like home. I got a crib in Jersey now, but my business brings me to New York from time to time," Zonnie told her.

"And what kind of business is that?" Pearl asked suspiciously.

"As if you didn't know." Zonnie gave her a wink. "I'm a little surprised to bump into you in a place like this, considering I'm pretty sure you ain't twenty-one yet."

"I'm here with some friends for the birthday party," Pearl told her.

Zonnie spared a glance over her shoulder. Doodles was leaning against a wall, whispering into Marisa's ear. "I've been knowing Doodles for a while. He's loads of fun, but that man has got a mean streak a mile long. That's some dangerous company you're keeping, suga. Watch yourself."

"Thanks for the warning, but I think I'm more than capable of handling myself," Pearl said confidently.

"I don't doubt that, considering who your daddy is," Zonnie replied.

"No doubt. My father and *Sandra* made sure me and Stoney were built Ford tough," Pearl shot back.

The words sliced Zonnie like a knife, and for the first time her confident smirk wavered. Pearl had struck a nerve. "How is he? How's my son doing?"

"You mean *my* brother?" Pearl corrected her. "Stoney is doing fine. He plays for the basketball team now and he's pretty damn good."

"I've seen. I went to one of his games about a month ago and saw him play for the first time."

"Really?" Pearl asked suspiciously. "That's funny, because me and Sandra go to all Stoney's games, and I don't remember ever seeing you at one."

"It was the game they played against Brandeis. My baby hung thirty-two on them boys!" Zonnie beamed with pride.

Pearl remembered that game, so she knew Zonnie wasn't lying. Stoney had played like a man possessed and had led his team in a twenty-point rout over the rival school. "If you were there, why didn't you say anything?"

"I thought about it, even waited around until the end of the game, but then I saw your daddy pull up outside the school. You and I both know what his reaction would've been if he'd seen me anywhere near his little prince."

Zonnie might've had a point. Just the mention of her name was enough to get Big Stone angry, so there was no telling how he would've reacted if he'd bumped into her at the game. Pearl saw the pained look in Zonnie's eyes as she spoke about Stoney, and for a second she almost felt sorry for her, but then she remembered how Zonnie had dropped baby Stoney off for what was supposed to be a few hours and then never came back. Pearl had never been able to wrap her mind around how a mother could abandon their child. Zonnie was foul, and Big Stone's justice was beyond fair.

"It was good seeing you, Zonnie, but I gotta make moves." Pearl excused herself and got up.

"Hold on. I was hoping we could talk for a minute. Maybe we can grab a drink and you can tell me some more about Stoney?" Zonnie fell in step beside her.

Pearl stopped short and turned serious eyes to Zonnie. "Listen, if you were that worried about my brother, you'd have checked up on him over the years."

"Wait a minute—that ain't fair. I wanted to be a better mother, but your father wouldn't let me. It was him who kept me out of Stoney's life," Zonnie explained.

"My father is powerful, but he ain't God. I wanna feel sorry for you, Zonnie, but I can't. If you really wanted to see your kid, you'd have found a way." Pearl tried to walk off again, but Zonnie grabbed her arm and spun her around.

"Little girl, how dare you try to stand here and judge me before you've walked a mile in my stilettoes. Now, I was wrong for leaving Stoney the way I did, but it's not like I left him with no damn stranger; I left him with his father! A father who could provide him with a life that I couldn't even dream of. I was a young dumb girl who thought letting a rich nigga get me pregnant would be my ticket out of the ghetto, and when the bottom fell out and reality set in, I did what was natural and ran away. For as fucked up as it looks on the outside, you can't tell me shit until you've been nineteen and pregnant with nothing to offer your child but the crumbs you get off somebody else's table."

"Whatever." Pearl folded her arms and rolled her eyes. She didn't have time for Zonnie's bullshit.

"Roll your eyes all you want, but this is some real shit I'm kicking to you. You in here looking at me like I'm less than a person because your family sitting on a few coins. Hmph, life can't be all that good in the kingdom of Stone if the princess is out here making herself available. Your daddy know you out here testing the waters or is this another one of them family secrets y'all keep so well hidden?"

"Fuck is you talking about?" Pearl was confused.

"I mean us being at this party for the same reasons." Zonnie smiled slyly.

"What reasons? Look, I don't know what your ass is high on, but I ain't got time for this shit," Pearl declared.

Zonnie studied Pearl's face to see if she was joking, and when she realized she wasn't, she doubled over laughing. "Didn't you read the fine print on your invitation? Did you think you and your young-ass friends got invited to a private party for one of the biggest gangsters in Brooklyn because you and that rat pack you run with are so damn popular? Little girl, you're either extremely naïve or further out of your league than I thought. Every bitch in here is on the clock. Shit, half of them work for me, and the half that don't probably will after they see all the bank Doodles is gonna shell out for their time. If you were down with me, I'd likely get you paid double." She looked Pearl up and down. "Doodles is especially fond of young dumb bitches who think they got life figured out, and you certainly fit the bill. What do you say, Pearl? Let's make this a family business!"

It took Pearl a few seconds to process what Zonnie was implying, but when she did, the revelation hit her like a slap. She looked around the room, and it was like she was seeing it for the first time. People had begun to get loose, in some cases too loose. Some of the girls had even started to come out of their clothes while men threw money while freely placing hands and fingers in places where they didn't belong. She now understood why Doodles had referred to them as the *entertainment* earlier that night. Pearl's chest suddenly constricted, cutting off the air in her lungs, and she knew if she didn't get away from Zonnie, she would pass out or punch her in the face.

As she moved through the crowd, she heard Zonnie's mocking voice calling after her. "Tell yo daddy I said hello!"

All Pearl could see was red as she plucked her way through the VIP in search of her friends. The lights had been dimmed, which made it hard for her to see more than a few feet ahead of her at a time. She searched high and low but couldn't find any signs of Marisa, or Doodles for that matter. It didn't take a rock scientist to figure out what that was about. If Marisa wanted to whore herself out, she was welcome to do so, but Pearl was out of there with or without her. While she couldn't find Marisa, Sheila was easy enough to spot. She was on her knees in the middle of the floor, popping her ass like she was auditioning for a 2 Live Crew video. She was clearly drunk out of her mind, but it didn't seem to bother the small crowd that had gathered to watch her little show. She danced and laughed as strange men slapped her on the ass and tossed crumpled dollar bills at her. She was playing herself and making them all look bad. Pearl was so mad that she was about to say fuck it and leave her to it when she saw two dudes try to lead Sheila off toward the bathroom. She was too twisted to even realize what they were doing, let alone stop it, so Pearl stepped in.

"I got it from here." Pearl took Sheila by the arm, much to the displeasure of the two men.

"Easy, baby, you can join the party too if you want," one of the men offered. He was an older dude wearing a velvet blazer and baggy jeans.

Pearl looked him up and down. "Not on my worse day." She shoved Sheila ahead and out of the VIP.

"Where we going? I'm trying to party," Sheila protested.

"Girl, shut your drunk ass up. You need some air and some

water." Pearl continued to shove her forward toward the exit. Sheila was so drunk that she almost fell twice before they even made it outside. No sooner than the night air hit her, Sheila threw up all over the sidewalk, barely missing Pearl's boots.

"Mama always told me about mixing my liquor." Sheila laughed, wiping her mouth with the back of her hand.

A few people who had seen it pointed and laughed. One of them even took out a camera phone and was trying to snap a picture. This all added to Pearl's already mounting frustration.

"I'm glad you find the fact that you're playing yourself out here funny," Pearl said in an irritated tone.

"C'mon, Pearl. Stop acting like you ain't never been tipsy in public," Sheila said as if it were no big deal.

"Sheila, tipsy I could understand, but you're fucking wasted!" Pearl pointed out.

"Nah, I'm good. Now that I've gotten rid of the old liquor, I can make room for the new." Sheila started back toward the bar, but Pearl grabbed her arm.

"The last thing you need right now is more liquor. That shit has got you making poor decisions," Pearl said.

"C'mon, Pearl, I know you ain't still mad about me throwing up. It happens sometimes."

"Fuck you throwing up! Let's talk about why people think we're in there selling pussy!" Pearl snapped.

"Huh?" Sheila faked dumb.

The minute Pearl saw the dumb look on Sheila's face, she knew what Zonnie had said was true. "Aw, damn, Sheila!" Pearl threw her hands up in frustration.

"I'm sorry, Pearl. Don't be mad at me. Boom told me about these old heads he knew who liked to blow money just to be seen with pretty young girls, so I figured it was a way to pick up a few extra dollars. I never told them that any of y'all were going to do anything though," Sheila explained.

Pearl looked at Sheila as if she had taken leave of her senses. "Yo, I don't know if I'm more pissed that you were dumb enough to let your so-called man talk you into renting your pussy out or the fact that you tried to drag me to the bottom of the barrel with you. Sheila, you know I'd never judge you for however you decide to chase paper, but my name carries too much weight in these streets to have mud on it behind some shit like this."

Sheila snorted. "I don't even know why I'm surprised that you flipped this situation to make it about you."

"How am I making it about me if I'm trying to put your silly ass up on game? Sheila, I know that even with both of your parents working, things can get tight, but there should never come a point when you're so hard up for money that you're whoring yourself out to second-rate hustlers in neighborhood bars. That's hood-booger shit, and I expect better from anybody I move around with." Pearl hadn't meant to go so hard on her, but Sheila's attempt to justify the situation only made her angrier.

Sheila rolled her liquor-glazed eyes at Pearl and sucked her teeth. "Why it gotta be who you move around with, instead of us moving together? You always screaming that we're a team, but it's more like you call the plays and we get in where we fit in."

"That's bullshit and you know it. We're a crew; everybody is the same."

"Nah, we ain't all the same. Since we first met, you've always had everything handed to you. While the rest of us bust our asses to make it in the world," Sheila spat.

"You act like we don't get money together. What about all the rackets we all see paper off in school?" Pearl reminded her.

"Yeah, but the difference is: we're hustling because we have to;

you hustle because you want to. You and I both know that you really don't have to do shit but kick back and live off your family's money!" Sheila said emotionally. The liquor had ahold of her, and she was speaking from her secret place of envy.

"Sheila, you're drunk and talking out your ass so I'm gonna let you have that, but don't push me," Peal warned. Sheila was one of her best friends, so to hear such sharp words come out of her mouth hurt, but Pearl wouldn't give her the satisfaction of showing it.

"There you go again, trying to tell me what to do!" Sheila yelled. She was causing a scene now, so people were looking.

"Sheila, you need to shut your mouth," Pearl said through clenched teeth.

"And what if I don't? You gonna tell your daddy and have one of his flunkies come and kill me?"

Pearl wasn't clear on what happened, but at some point she must've snapped. By the time she caught herself, she had already viciously slapped Sheila across the face twice, busting her nose and knocking her to the ground. Sheila looked like she wanted to get up and fight, but she thought better of it and stayed down. "That's the second time tonight you've said some funny shit about my family, and there won't be a third, bitch!" Pearl spat before storming off, leaving Sheila on the ground to nurse her bloody nose.

Pearl hadn't made it a half block before the tears came. She wasn't big on public displays of emotion, but Sheila had hurt her. Their crew was supposed to be tight, more like sisters than friends, but sisters didn't air family laundry in the streets to hurt one another. She knew Sheila was twisted, but a drunken mind often spoke a sober tongue. From the things she'd said, it made Pearl wonder if the other girls had felt the same way. One thing was for sure, there was no apology Sheila could offer to make this right. Their friendship was over.

Pearl knew there was no way she would be able to catch a taxi with all the people crowding the block of the bar, so she decided to cross the street. She had been standing out there for nearly ten minutes, but so far hadn't gotten anyone to stop, except old perverts mistaking her for a working girl. She needed to get out of there before she made the morning news.

Across the street she saw a sleek Lincoln Town Car idling and waiting for the light to change. When the car lurched forward, Pearl stepped off the curb, waving her hands frantically and hoping the livery cab would stop. As it neared her, she couldn't help but notice that instead of the normal factory hubcaps, this town car had deep-dish chrome rims on it. It brought back a memory from several years prior, when her father had pulled up, driving a similar-looking monstrosity. Only, that Lincoln had been green, but it, too, had big ugly rims. The running joke in the house was that Pearl would inherit it when she was old enough to drive. When her eyes drifted from the rims to the man driving the car, her heart came to a full stop.

CHAPTER TWENTY

Knowledge crawled along the BQE, drumming his fingers on the steering wheel in irritation. At that time of night it should've been smooth sailing, but he hadn't accounted for the five-car pileup that would shut down two lanes for miles. Knowledge was someone who prided himself on his punctuality, among other things, and this was unlike him. He had tried to do too much in one day, and being late for his most important appointment was the cost.

The incident with Born earlier had him off his square. He knew it would be an awkward, and potentially hostile, conversation, but he had never expected it to get physical. Truth be told, it didn't have to, and it shouldn't have. Daou was out of pocket, but Knowledge could've handled it differently. He'd walked into their circle as a friend delivering a message, but laying hands on a member of their crew had changed the dynamics of their relationship. Instead solving a small problem, he'd created a bigger one.

Born had set the bait, and Knowledge had foolishly bit. He was the only person, other than Big Stone, who knew him well enough to push his buttons. By making the remark about *being his own man,* it played on Knowledge's insecurities just enough to make his focus slip, and it was all downhill from there. Knowledge knew he couldn't take his frustrations out on Born because of repercussions neither of them wanted, so when Daou opened his mouth, he made himself the perfect consolation prize. Power was more than capable of handling himself, and it would've raised less of a stink, but Knowledge needed the wreck. . . . He craved the feeling of soft flesh under his sharp knuckles, and Daou satisfied had it, but the satisfaction would hardly be worth the cost when it came back around.

After leaving Queens, he'd headed back to Harlem to drop Power off at his crib. He hadn't said much during the ride back, but then again he didn't need to. His eyes told the whole story of what his mind was thinking. Power wasn't someone who let go of grudges easily. He might not do it that night, on the strength of Knowledge's and his connection to the situation, but sometime in the near future he would return to the place he'd been disrespected and address it. Knowledge would attempt to speak with him on the pros and cons of retaliation, but he doubted there was anything short of an act of God that would change the outcome.

He dropped Power off, making him promise not to make a move until he got back with him, and then zipped off to his next destination, which would further eat into his time. He pulled into a Midtown garage, where he would swap his Acura for one of Big Stone's rides. It would've saved him time to just pick him up in the Acura, but Big Stone had made it clear that he *wouldn't be caught dead riding in that piece of shit.* . . . Those were his exact words.

Even with the pit stops, Knowledge would've had time to do what he needed to do had Big Stone not changed plans on him at the last minute. He wasn't supposed to land until around midnight, but he'd called Knowledge that afternoon to tell him that he was catching an earlier flight. He could tell from his tone and the fact that he was in such a rush to get back that something had happened, but Big Stone wouldn't talk about it over the phone.

There was a break in the logjam of cars, and Knowledge went for it, nearly getting sideswiped by a truck as he broke for the exit. Thankfully there wasn't much traffic at the international terminal, and Knowledge was able to reach his gate without further delay. Considering all he'd gone through, Knowledge had made pretty good time, but it wasn't good enough. Big Stone was standing at the curb with all his luggage, and looking like he was mad enough to kill.

Big Stone was as imposing physically as he was by reputation: standing at a muscular six foot six with a skull and jawline that looked like they had been carved from the side of a mountain. A high black turtleneck clung to him like a second skin, while his long tan overcoat flapped in the wind like he was posing for a *GQ* cover. When his deep black gaze landed on Knowledge, who was just pulling to a stop, time seemed to stand still.

"Sorry I'm late. Got stuck in traffic," Knowledge said apologetically, getting out of the car to grab Big Stone's bags.

"I've been standing out here long enough for a nigga to kill me twice and be long gone before anyone who could do anything about it heard about it," Big Stone said. His voice was heavy yet smooth, like an Isaac Hayes interlude. "You know how I feel about punctuality," he said as he slid into the backseat.

Knowledge ignored his comment and went to retrieve the bags from the curb. When they were secured, he slid behind the wheel and pulled out into traffic. "So, how was your flight?"

"Cramped and uncomfortable," Big Stone said with an attitude. "Because I switched it at the last minute, I had to fly economy. First class was full. I ended up sandwiched between a fat guy who sweat a lot and an old woman whose breath smelled like onion bagels. It was a real stink fest. Then I come back, and you picking me up in this bucket was the icing on the cake. Out of all the cars in my collection, you pick this shit to come pick me up in?" Big Stone said in disapproval as he tried to get comfortable in the back of the Lincoln Town Car.

"You said you wanted to keep your arrival quiet and that I should pick you up in something inconspicuous," Knowledge replied.

"I know, nigga, but damn . . . this car screams country dope boy." Big Stone toyed with the knobs on one of the screens mounted in the headrests.

"It should, since it was a country dope boy who you took it from," Knowledge reminded him.

Big Stone chuckled, sounding like soft beats on a bass drum, as he recalled the circumstances under which he had acquired the car. Big Stone had been a guest at a high-stakes poker game thrown by a friend of his when one of the players made a wager that he couldn't cover, and instead of Big Stone taking his life, he took his ride. "I never liked this car, and goodness knows I don't need another vehicle, so I don't know why I didn't just let him keep it."

"Because had you let him keep it, there wouldn't have been a lesson learned," Knowledge said. "The act wasn't about the money—you've got plenty of that—but stripping him of something dear to him. To take a man's car is like taking his nuts. That loss is gonna stick with him longer than any other."

"Smart man," Stone confirmed. "Now get me the hell out of this airport, and please tell me you've got some weed on you. For the day I've been having, I need to blaze something."

Halfway through his joint, Big Stone seemed to loosen up. Knowledge decided that while he had him in a good mood, it was the perfect time to ask him about the prospect Knowledge had his eyes on. "Big Stone, what do you think about that kid Domo?"

Big Stone took a drag off the joint, searching his mental Rolodex to place the name. "You mean the Jersey kid who plays ball with Stoney? A little too quiet for my tastes. That tells me he's either sneaky as hell or plotting to take over the world. I don't know too much about him, other than what I get from Stoney, but I hear he's making a little name for himself in Newark. Why the sudden interest?"

"I was thinking about bringing him in," Knowledge told him. "I've been watching the kid for a while, and I like how he moves. Just earlier I laid the bait for some bullshit, but he didn't bite. He chose his honor over a dollar."

"Niggas like that are like unicorns in the hood; you hear stories but can't say you've ever laid eyes on one. He's going to make a good soldier in someone's army, but not ours."

"Why not? I know you see the potential in him, same as I do," Knowledge insisted.

"Oh yeah. There's no doubt in my mind that with the right guidance, he could be something special, but he's just a kid," Big Stone said.

"He's about the same age I was when you recruited me," Knowledge reminded him.

Big Stone shook his head. "Still, he's one of my son's friends. I don't give a shit what he does on the other side of the Hudson, so long as he doesn't bring it around my son or my home."

"I can understand that, but I don't plan on having him on the corners. That would be a waste of his talents. I wanna keep him close to me and show him the ropes. Maybe not right away, but Domo could be a real asset."

Big Stone smiled. "So the student wants to become the teacher, huh?"

"Pay it forward—isn't that what you always taught me to do?"

"Let me think on it for a while and see how I feel about it. For now just keep an eye on him, but don't pull him too close just yet.

He's Stoney's best friend but still an outsider. We need to see where his heart is at before we even consider letting him in."

"You got that," Knowledge said, happy for the small victory.

"While we're talking business, did you go see Born like I told you to?" Big Stone asked.

Knowledge flinched at the question. He knew eventually Big Stone would bring it up, but he still wasn't looking forward to having to answer it. "Yeah."

"Well, don't keep an asshole in suspense. What did he say?"

"He said okay."

Big Stone frowned. "That's it? Just okay?"

"I told Born to fall back from shorty, and he promised he wouldn't pursue her," Knowledge said, omitting the part about her pursuing Born.

"Damn well better had! He was out of bounds for sticking his dick in what's mine. I got a good mind to still have him touched over it, just on general purposes."

"So things are that deep with you and this chick?" Knowledge questioned. What he really wanted to ask was: *Are you seriously thinking about starting a civil war within your crew over a whore?*

"She sucks a mean cock and looks good on my arm, but she ain't nobody I'd roll through the presidential inauguration with. This ain't about feeling, Knowledge. It's about class and status. How would a boss nigga like me look, sticking his dick in the same bitch as a nigga I feed?"

"You'd look like two niggas fucking the same hood rat." Knowledge chuckled.

"Laugh now, but see how funny it'll be when you're sitting in the big chair, and the pups are trying to help themselves to your leftovers. Niggas will always try to steal your joy, especially those you've welcomed as family!"

"Speaking of relations, Rolling is back in town," Knowledge said, putting it out there to sidetrack Big Stone from the tirade he was about to go on.

Big Stone's teeth gritted, and a thick vein appeared down his forehead. "I thought I smelled trash when I got off the plane. Where'd you step into that pile of shit?"

"He was with Born in Queens. From his reaction, I don't think he had counted on running into someone who could blow his spot up. Born seemed amused by the whole thing though."

"I don't know why I'm surprised." Big Stone snorted. "Them two low-key dopeheads always been thick as thieves, and Rolling still ain't got the scruples to know he's always gonna wind up the scapegoat for whatever Born is into. After that last stunt Rolling pulled, getting me crossed in with one of his baby mamas, I told his fuck-ass I didn't want to see him in New York again. I wonder what the hell he's got going on that's worth him risking getting his shit split?"

"Can't be nothing good for us."

"Yeah, nine times outta ten anything that jealous-hearted nigga is cooking up will either come at my expense or I'll have to clean it up later." Big Stone shook his head.

"Had it been anybody else, I'd have taken care of it without bothering you with it, but he's your brother, so I figured it'd be best to get your take on how I should proceed. I can run him out or I can run him *down*," Knowledge offered.

Big Stone thought on it. "Nah, man. I promised my mama on her deathbed that no more of her kids would die before their parents. My daddy is still alive, so Rolling is too . . . at least for now. But I still want eyes on him. I wanna know what that sneaky muthafucka is up to."

"You got it," Knowledge agreed. "So, you gonna tell me why you were in such a rush to get back, or are you going to make me guess?" Knowledge said, changing the subject.

Big Stone pulled himself forward on the back of the driver's seat. He was so close that Knowledge could feel the heat from his breath when he spoke. "I'm glad you asked that question, considering it's partially your fault."

This took Knowledge by surprise. "What you mean?"

"When I made you my right hand, do you remember why it was that I did so?" Big Stone asked.

Knowledge thought on it, trying to recall Big Stone's exact words from all those years ago. "You said because in me you saw a young man who understood the importance of never taking your eye off the ball."

"Right, you've always been a sharp kid. At your age, you've got an eye and ear for these streets that most wouldn't develop until they're further on in years and years and have suffered more. I brag all the time that so long as you are the eyes in the back of my head, nothing will ever get past me. So can you imagine my embarrassment when someone other than you delivered the news about Pana Suarez being killed?"

Knowledge couldn't hide the shock on his face. "What? Where? When?"

"Those the questions I should be asking you!" Big Stone shot back. "It happened uptown on the West Side. They not only took out Pana and his both his top captains, but they managed to level an entire building in the process. Even if the streets weren't talking, it was on the news. How the hell did you manage to miss it?"

"I was caught up," Knowledge said, thinking about the dummy-mission Big Stone had him on earlier. "Anybody know who did it?"

"A lot of speculation, but nothing concrete yet. This whole thing has got Eddie's stink all over it, if you ask me. Eddie and Pana been at it for years, so it was evitable one got the drop on the other. The only problem with that theory is that neither party involved would want any part of the consequences that would come from a move that serious. Eddie is Michael's nephew, and Pana still has ties to some cartels south of the border. A war between the two would likely shut half the city down and fuck up everybody's money. Pana might not care about the losses, but Eddie is far too greedy to risk a work stoppage."

Knowledge processed the facts, and then an idea formed in his head. "Maybe Eddie was behind it, but used somebody else to do the deed. Eddie isn't a man who discriminates when it comes to who he does business with, so long as it's a guaranteed profit in it for him. I'm sure those loose circles he moves in have given him access to some good freelance killers."

"That was my initial thought and the reason I jumped on the first thing smoking back to New York," Big Stone admitted. "For nearly a decade the Mexican government couldn't do shit with Pana Suarez, yet in under five minutes an unknown party was able to take him out and cripple his whole operation. I don't have to tell you how tall of an order that is. The way I see it is, don't much matter if it was Eddie behind this or someone else looking to make a statement. Anybody with access to killers of this caliber is cause for concern for anybody who doesn't, including us."

CHAPTER TWENTY-ONE

The rest of the ride in Manhattan was spent in relative silence. Big Stone busied himself with his phone, likely trying to get a line on who backed the hit, while Knowledge focused on the road ahead. Every so often he'd look in the rearview mirror at Big Stone to gauge his mood. Big Stone was a man who didn't rattle easily, but hearing about Pana getting killed clearly unnerved him. Knowledge couldn't say that he blamed him. Pana was one of the biggest gangsters in the city, and he'd gotten rocked in his own hood. If it could happen to him, it could happen to any of them.

More troubling to Knowledge was that the assassination had gone down right under his nose and he'd missed it. It could've very well been Big Stone on the slab instead Pana, and the blood would've been on Knowledge's hands . . . all because he'd slipped. It was a mistake he wouldn't make again. As soon as he dropped Big Stone off at his house, he was getting in the streets to see what he could dig up about Pana's killers.

They were stopped at a red light on 145th Street and Lenox when Knowledge noticed a large gathering in front of a bar he frequented from time to time. It was owned by an associate of Big Stone's and usually catered to the local crowd, but there were a lot of unfamiliar faces out there. There was some kind of celebration taking place, and the timing and sudden presence of strangers felt suspect considering what had happened to Pana earlier and the mysterious circumstances surrounding it.

When the light turned green, he eased his foot off the brake and coasted slowly through the light, scanning the faces in front of the bar. He'd been so focused on the crowd that he nearly hit a girl who had just stepped out into the street. She was waving her hands, trying to get him to stop, likely mistaking him for a taxi, as most people did when they saw the Lincoln. She was a sexy, brown-skinned woman who was dressed like she was outside grabbing her wares. Knowledge was about to point the girl out to Big Stone and make a slick comment about the scantily clad girl, but when his eyes landed on her face, the words died in his throat.

For a long while all Pearl could do was stand there, stuck like a deer in headlights. If Knowledge was behind the wheel, she knew who was riding in the back. When Knowledge looked up and their eyes met, she knew there would be no way she could talk or lie herself out of it. She was stone-cold busted!

She waited for Knowledge to snitch and her father to jump out and drag her into the car, embarrassing her in front of anyone who was watching. Franz and everybody else who was standing outside. Her eyes pleaded with him not to do it, and for a second it looked like he was considering it, but then his eyes turned hard and a sinister smile spread across his face. Suddenly the engine gunned and the Lincoln shot passed her. She couldn't believe it, but he was giving her a sporting chance to beat them back to the house!

"Boy, what the hell is wrong with you?" Big Stone barked, once he was able to compose himself. When the car had lurched, he had damn near crashed into the back door.

"Sorry, Stone. I'm just trying to get through some of this traffic. I know you're anxious to get home," Knowledge lied.

"Yeah, I wanna get home, but in one piece. Slow the hell down!"

Knowledge ignored him and kept pushing the Lincoln. He couldn't believe the balls on that kid. Not only did she sneak out, but she was dressed like a streetwalker and hanging around a nest of vipers. He started to blow the whistle on her and tell Big Stone, but the man already had a lot on his mind and would likely break her neck if he caught her out dressed like that. He wasn't going to rat on her, but he would make her earn the pass. If she couldn't get home before Big Stone, then she was shit out of luck.

Pearl waited until she had made it around the corner, and out of sight of anyone who might recognize her, to go into full-panic mode. She knew she should've stayed in the house like she was supposed to, but she had let peer pressure get the best of her, and now she was about to pay the price for it.

She stumbled through the block, trying not to break her ankles in the heels. She would never beat the car on foot, especially in those boots. She leaned against a building and slipped out of them. She always called girls who walked around barefoot after the club tacky, but she didn't have a choice. Pearl hiked up her skirt and took off into a dead run.

Having run track all through high school, she was no stranger to long-distance running, but after three or four blocks, all the alcohol and weed she'd consumed that night started catching up with her, and she found herself getting winded. At the rate she was going, nothing short of a miracle was going to enable her to beat her father home.

God must've been listening, though, because he sent her just that: a miracle.

A Chinese delivery guy was dropping some food off at an apartment building, and he made the mistake of not chaining his bike up properly. Pearl waited until he disappeared inside before jumping on his bike and riding off. She could only imagine how she must've looked, barefoot, her skirt hiked up so high that her entire ass was exposed, riding the rickety bike, but she was more worried about her father skinning her alive than keeping up appearances.

She crossed over the blocks like she was being carried on the wind, pumping her legs faster and faster. Her heart thudded in her chest as if it would burst, but she dared not stop. In the distance she saw her block looming and became hopeful. Pearl hit the corner a little sharper than she expected and lost control of the bike, spilling over the handlebars and scraping her hands and knees on the concrete. Ignoring the pain, she picked herself up and limped the rest of the way to their brownstone. Her heart sank when she saw that the Lincoln was already there, idling at the curb.

Pearl watched from her hiding place, behind a parked truck across the street, as Knowledge got out of the car and went around to open the door for Big Stone. They exchanged a few words before Big Stone headed for the entrance while Knowledge retrieved her father's luggage. Knowledge must've felt like he was being watched because he stopped and looked around. His eyes landed on the spot where Pearl was hiding, and a triumphant grin spread across his face. He thought he had her beaten, but little did he know Pearl had one last card to play.

Big Stone breathed a sigh of relief when he crossed his threshold. It was one of the few places he felt safe and the only place he could find any type of peace of mind. Things had already been getting tense on the streets, and the murder of Pana Suarez guaranteed everything was about to come to a head. This is why, on his way home from the airport, he had hit up some of his associates and suggested a meeting of the minds. For as long as these rogue killers were on the loose, none of them would be truly safe.

After setting the bags down, Knowledge accompanied Big Stone as they made their customary rounds around the house to check in on the family. They found Sandra lying on the couch, knocked out, a half-empty cup of tea on the end table. On the television, the closing credits were rolling on *The Ten Commandments*. Big Stone didn't want to disturb Sandra by waking her up, so he covered her with a blanket, and he and Knowledge made their way upstairs.

Stoney was fast sleep in his bed. Nestled deep under his New York Knicks comforter, he looked more like the innocent little boy who he was supposed to be, rather than the terror that he was. Big Stone leaned to kiss his son on the head and paused, sniffing the air. For a moment Knowledge thought he was going to comment on the lingering smell of weed smoke, but he didn't.

They left Stoney's room and headed down the hall to Pearl's. Big Stone tapped softly on the door but got no answer. When his hand came to rest on the knob, Knowledge couldn't repress the smile that had formed on his face, because he knew what they would find when they opened it. He wasn't happy about the fact that Pearl was about to be in a world of trouble, but he wasn't angry over it either. There was nothing that Knowledge or anyone else could tell Big Stone about his daughter. He placed her on a pedestal and in his eyes she could do no wrong, no matter how foul she moved. It was about time that the blinders were snatched off and he could see for himself that she was no angel.

Knowledge stood back, arms folded and smirking, while Big Stone pushed the door open. "What the fuck?" he heard Big Stone curse under his breath. Knowledge peered over his shoulder, expecting to see an empty bed, but instead they found Pearl fast sleep. It was impossible!

"I keep telling this girl about keeping her room clean." Big Stone huffed, picking up a T-shirt and a discarded pair of socks from the floor and tossing them into Pearl's hamper. "Let's go downstairs. I need a drink," he said, and left the room.

Knowledge lingered in the doorway for a while, his eyes wide with shock. Not ten minutes earlier he had spotted her outside cowering behind a car. There was no way she could've made it into the house and up to her room without them seeing her.

"You gonna keep standing there and gawking at my kid or join me?" Big Stone called from down the hall.

"Sorry, Stone. I'll be right there," Knowledge called back. He spared one last glance at Pearl before closing the door behind him. He wasn't sure how Pearl had pulled off her little miracle, but in the morning he would have a chat with her about what an underage girl was doing in a bar full of gangsters.

Pearl waited until she heard her bedroom door click shut before popping her eyes open. She waited for a few more seconds until she was sure they were gone, and then she threw the blanket back and got out of bed. Through the grace of God, her ruse had worked.

She looked like a hot mess: scuffed, bleeding, and it was a wrap for her outfit. Pearl walked on tender feet over to the vanity and plopped down on the padded stool. She found leaves and pieces of twigs in her hair from the spill she'd taken when she'd climbed the fence to get into her backyard. When Knowledge had cut her off from the front door, she'd thrown a Hail Mary, better known as Nathaniel. Nathaniel was one of three college guys who lived in the brownstone on the next block over, directly behind Pearl's. He and his roommates were pussy hounds, and pressed her and her friends every chance they got. Pearl had no interests in Nathaniel, but promised to go on a date with him if he let her climb his fence so she could get into her yard. He would've probably done it without her offering the date, just for the chance to look up her short skirt as she went over the fence.

While Stone was in the living room checking on Sandra, Pearl crept in through the back door and slipped up the kitchen stairs to her bedroom. She made it into bed and covered up a split second before her dad came into her room to check on her. It had been an extremely close call, so close that that was the last time Pearl planned to try sneaking out at least until the next party.

Pearl pulled off her ruined club clothes and hid them in the back of her closet until she would have a chance to dispose of them properly the next day, and then she jumped into bed. She was a bit on the filthy side from her adventure, but she was too tired and too sore to do anything about it until morning. As she drifted off to sleep, the last thing she thought of was how she wished she could've seen the look on Knowledge's face when he realized she had beat him at his own game.

CHAPTER TWENTY-TWO

It was well past midnight when TJ finally showed up at the bar, and he didn't look like he'd come to have a good time. He was dressed in black from head to toe, with the only splash of color being the canary-yellow diamond pendant hanging from his chain. Normally when he stepped out, he was dressed to the nines and wearing heavy jewelry, but this wasn't a social call. The bar was the last place he wanted to be, but the call he'd gotten said it was a matter of life and death, which he was inclined to believe, considering who had called him. He had been getting a lot of late-night phone calls since his cousin Diamonds had blown into town, and he wasn't yet sure how he felt about it.

All it took was one person to spot TJ, and it gave way to at least a half dozen hands within his first two minutes of being there. TJ was from the neighborhood, and everybody knew him as a cat who was about his money and they respected that. The fact that he was so well-known in the area made the game he was being roped into an extremely dangerous one. TJ didn't have the luxury of being able to live like a nomad. His bread and butter was in Harlem.

When he'd shaken his last hand, he made a beeline to the end of the bar where Diamonds had told him he'd be waiting. He spotted him sitting on a stool in a dark corner, Vita perched on his lap. He whispered softly in her ear while running his finger along the nape of her neck. They had one of the strangest relationships TJ had ever seen, with neither claiming the other and both secretly throwing salt in each other's chances to move on whenever opportunities arose. It was a toxic union at best, but TJ hadn't broken bread with them to judge; he was in it for the potential to make some paper.

When he made to approach Diamonds, Buda's lumbering form stepped into his path. His eyes were red and glassy, and he reeked of whatever he had been drinking. TJ could tell by his posture that liquor had him feeling aggressive, which seemed like a reoccurring theme with him whenever TJ was around. It was always a pissing contest between them over Diamonds's favor.

"State your business, gangster," Buda demanded in his deep, scratchy voice. He was acting like he didn't know TJ or his connection to their crew.

TJ, who was a full head taller than Buda, looked down at him. "Man, why we always gotta play this game?" he asked in a tone that said he didn't have time for the bullshit.

"We gonna play it until I'm sure of what you represent, *outsider*," Buda replied. It was his favorite insult for TJ and a constant reminder that he hadn't come up through the mud with the rest of them.

"Buda, sit your drunk ass down somewhere and get out of the man's way. Ain't nobody got time to be fooling with you," Hank interjected. It was as if he could read Buda's mind and was trying to prevent him from acting on what he was thinking.

Buda continued to eyeball TJ for a time longer before giving the man some space. "Hank, why you always gotta make a big deal out of shit? TJ know I'm just fucking with him. Ain't that right, TJ?"

"Sometimes it don't sound like you playing, Buda." TJ brushed past him.

"Sensitive-ass nigga," Buda mumbled before bellying back up to the bar.

"What's good, cousins?" TJ nodded in greeting to Goldie and Diamonds.

"Considering I've wasted half my night and a few dollars in this joint and ain't made no progress, I'd say nothing is good," Goldie grumbled. He had long ago run out of patience and wanted to either handle business or be free to get on with his night.

"Tone down, sourpuss. Ain't like you've got nowhere better to be." Diamonds eased Vita off his lap and stood. "Apologize for dragging you out of your warm bed and from up under that fine woman of yours on this late night. How is cousin Teisha, by the way?"

"Pissed the fuck off," TJ told him. "Do you know what kind of hell a man has to go through when he leaves his pregnant fiancé in the middle of the night, talking about *I gotta handle something of Diamonds's*?"

"Thankfully no." Diamonds laughed. "Please extend my apologies to your lady, and my new little cousin growing in her stomach."

"This might require a little more than one of your empty apologies. You better show up at the shower with a bomb-ass gift. Y'all still coming, right?"

"You know I wouldn't miss it," Diamonds lied. He'd had so much going on that he'd forgotten TJ had invited them to the baby shower. "I hope you don't mind, but I think I'm gonna have Vita invite them two niggas from Newark who put in that little piece of work for us earlier. I hear they handled themselves like some real gangsters and held Vita down when shit got crazy. Still, I wanna feel them out for myself before I decide how close I wanna let them get."

"I been knowing LA for a while. He's kinda on the wild side, but he handles his business when it comes down to it. Domo is younger, so I don't really know him like that, but I hear he's solid."

"I'll be the judge of that."

"It's cool by me so long as niggas don't show up empty-handed. And if you're going to bring the *entire* Get Along Gang, make sure you keep them dogs on a leash, especially Buda." TJ cast a wicked glance in Buda's direction and found him staring at him and Diamonds, likely trying to eavesdrop on what they were talking about.

"No worries on that front. Anybody I bring into your home will respect it as if it were mine," Diamonds promised.

"I'm gonna hold you to that. Now, on to the matter at hand. What the fuck are we doing here, Diamonds?"

"It's like I told you on the phone: I come attempting to do business but seem to keep getting stonewalled. I'm starting to feel slighted, and we both know how I react to slights."

TJ knew far too well how Diamonds reacted to slights. "Diamonds, this is New York, not the South. You can't just roll into a made man's establishment and demand a meeting, especially when they don't know you. There're protocols that have to be observed with these kinds of things."

"Like when you had to get the blessings of that spic Eddie before I laid Pana to rest?" Diamonds smirked. "Man, I swear New York gotta be the only place I've ever been where you gotta file paperwork to kill a nigga," he said, and chuckled.

"Make jokes all you want, but I'm serious. Muscling Pana out of his territory is something that can be easily overlooked by anybody who matters. He was a savage who had crossed so many different people that it wasn't a matter of if someone was going to cap him, but when. So long as there's someone out there to keep moving them packages, nobody is gonna give a shit which crew it is. Pops Brown is a different situation entirely. He doesn't have major muscle on the streets to speak of, but he is very well liked and highly respected. If he vanishes, somebody is gonna definitely notice."

"Jesus, you act like I'm some kind of monster. I know Pops Brown is a respected man, and I'd never come at him sideways unprovoked. This is a legit visit. You know I been trying to break real ground and get my nightclub thing up and popping."

"You still chasing Purple City?" TJ asked. Other than killing and money, Purple City was all Diamonds ever talked about. It was his brainchild, a franchise of over-the-top strip clubs that catered to exclusive clientele.

"Can't blame a man for having a dream, TJ. Some niggas look to have the best strip club in the city, but I wanna have the best strip club in *every* city. It'll be like McDonald's, only we got Happy Hos on the menu instead of Happy Meals. Pops Brown been doing his thing a long time on the nightclub circuit, and I just wanna see if we can make something happen together. This spot would be a fine location for Purple City New York."

"I know Pops, and he ain't the kind of man who is gonna be open to converting his bar into no whorehouse," TJ told him.

"You never know what a man might be persuaded to do when placed under the right amount of pressure. All I need you to do is get me in so I can make my pitch."

"Diamonds, I really don't wanna get in the middle of this shit . . . at least not like this. Tell you what: I'll make some calls tomorrow and see about getting you a meeting," TJ offered, hoping it would deter Diamonds.

Diamonds looked at TJ like parents would look at their child who had just tried to lie to them. "Who's to say that by morning the secret of *us* killing Pana won't be exposed and this opportunity missed?" He'd stressed *us* to let TJ know that if the shit hit the fan, he'd burn with the rest of them. "Now, I could always have Buda and Goldie drag him out of his office like some savages, or you could smooth things over for us and we can speak like gentlemen. I'm cool with either route."

TJ looked to Goldie and Buda, who looked like they were spoiling for a good fight anyhow. He didn't want to do what Diamonds was asking of him, but he knew what would happen if he didn't. His cousin was someone who did not take rejection well. "A'ight, man," he relented. "Diamonds, I need you to be on your best behavior. Pops Brown is old-school and may not react well to your *eccentricities*."

Diamonds flashed a broad smile. "I promise, all we gonna do is talk."

Moving down the hall that led to the back offices made TJ feel like he was walking the green mile. Diamonds trailed him, followed by Goldie and Vita. He had only agreed to take Diamonds in the back if he left Buda outside. He didn't trust him to mind his manners if the meeting didn't go as expected. Of course Buda wasn't feeling being left out and he threw a fit, so Hank stayed behind to keep an eye on him until they returned.

At the end of the hall he spotted a thickly built man, hunched over and whispering into the ear of a girl. This was Rob, Pop Brown's eldest son and the manager of the bar. When he spotted TJ and company coming in his direction, he shooed the girl away and stood at attention.

"What's good, Rob," TJ slapped his palm in greeting. He and TJ had never been friends, but they knew each other from the street and their days of playing basketball in the New York City summer leagues.

"Ain't nothing. Been a minute since I seen you around here," Rob said.

"Chasing this paper don't leave me with a lot of free time to be sociable," TJ replied. He noticed that Rob kept looking over his shoulder at Diamonds and the others. "This is my cousin Diamonds."

"Yeah, we've met," Diamonds said, remembering Rob as the man who kept telling them Pops wasn't in.

"Is your dad in? I need to talk to him about something."

"Yeah, he's here, but he ain't seeing nobody right now, especially without an appointment, and I don't remember seeing your name on the calendar," Rob said defiantly.

TJ had heard that since Rob had started working for his father, he fancied himself a tough guy. "C'mon, Rob. Stop acting like you don't know me, man."

Rob looked TJ up and down. "Nigga, stop acting like because we played ball together we best friends. I know you out here trying to make a name for yourself and shit, but that don't hold no weight with me, TJ. To me, you still the skinny kid from back in the day who couldn't fight. Now, if you wanna sit with my father, make a fucking appointment like everyone else."

Rob's belittlement of TJ took him back to a place in his childhood where he was a scared kid who was afraid to take a punch. His fists trembled with rage, and he wanted to show Rob just how far he had come over the years and what he was now about, but if he popped, so would Diamonds, and the situation would become lethal. They too much on the ball, so TJ would have to suck it up and deal with Rob another day. "You got it, tough guy," TJ said, slowly backing down the hall. He smirked at Rob, letting him know that it wasn't over. He expected Diamonds and the others to follow, but they didn't. Diamonds continued to stand there.

"What, you hard of hearing or something?" Rob moved closer to Diamonds. As if by magic, a blackjack had appeared in his hand.

Diamonds weighed the question before answering. "Nah, I hear just fine, boss. I just ain't too good of a listener."

"Then maybe I need to knock that Tootsie Roll out ya ear." Rob slapped the blackjack against his palm threateningly. Diamonds was taller, but Rob outweighed him by quite a bit.

When Diamonds smiled, the light caught his teeth, casting golden shadows against his lips. "I welcome you to try it, if you got a mind to, but I'd hate to have to put you down on your father's property. *Souple,* why don't you just go in the back and tell Daddy there's a man out here with a nice business proposition for him? Then you can get out of the way and let the adults talk."

Rob's eyes flashed anger. "I can see I need to teach you a lesson about respect." He moved on Diamonds. Rob was quick, but not quick enough. By the time he'd completed his swing of the blackjack, Diamonds had ducked under it and replied with a vicious uppercut. The sound of Rob's jaw breaking echoed off the hallway walls like a tree branch being snapped in half. He was fast asleep long before he hit the ground.

"Night, night, bigmouth," Diamonds said to the prone man.

"What the fuck, Diamonds? Was that really necessary?" TJ snapped. For a minute he thought Rob was dead until he heard him snoring.

"Quit crying, nigga! You need to be glad I didn't kill him for the way he disrespected my blood," Diamonds said in disgust.

"I was going to address it at a more appropriate time," TJ insisted.

"Disrespect should be addressed immediately so the offender doesn't think to try it again. I love you, cousin, but the next time you let a nigga talk to you like that in front of me, I'm gonna put my hands on you," Diamonds promised before pushing open the door and inviting himself into the office.

CHAPTER TWENTY-THREE

After dropping Big Stone off at his crib and making a few last-minute runs, Knowledge was finally able to call it a night. It felt like all that day the weight of the world had been resting on his shoulders, and he was happy to be able to put the burden down . . . if even only for a little while.

Pana's murder had been on his mind ever since Big Stone had broken the news to him. The fact that he hadn't heard about it first bothered him, but not more than Big Stone's reaction. In his years of service to the Stone family, he had seen death one thousand times over, mostly foes, but there was a fair share of friends, too. Never once had Big Stone so much as batted an eye. That changed when Pana got dropped. Big Stone was a man who had nerves of steel, and during that ride from the airport, Knowledge had seen those nerves waver, and it worried him. If not for Big Stone, than for his own piece of mind, Knowledge was going to making finding out who did it a priority.

Something else that had been troubling him was the situation earlier with Pearl. He thought for sure he had finally caught her ass dead to rights and Big Stone would finally see what everyone else was seeing, but once again she had managed to beat him. Knowledge wasn't someone who took defeat well, especially with someone who he had schooled to the game.

Big Stone was very adamant that street shit should be kept away from his children at all costs, and in the beginning Knowledge respected it, but Pearl made it hard for him to turn a blind eye to her shenanigans. Unbeknownst to her father, she was out and about in a quest to grow up way faster than she needed to, and she was going about it the wrong way. No matter how many times Knowledge chased her off random blocks or threatened her, Pearl always found her way back into harm's way. So Knowledge found himself faced with two choices: stand idle and hope nothing happened to her, or pull her coat and make sure of it. He went with the latter. Knowledge never went as far as putting Pearl in harm's way, but he didn't censor his lessons like her father did. He didn't teach her enough about the streets to turn her into a criminal, but enough to ensure she knew how to survive in the jungle. At the time he thought he was doing a noble thing, but looking back in hindsight, he had helped to create a monster. Lately Pearl had been flying less and less under the radar, and it was time to clip the wings of Daddy's little angel, even if it meant exposing her to her father.

After leaving Big Stone, Knowledge switched back to his own car and headed home. He pulled the Acura into the twenty-four-hour garage, which was two blocks away from where he lived. They had an underground parking garage in his building, but he didn't mind walking the few blocks as an added precaution. Everybody in the hood knew his car, and all it would take was the wrong person to recognize it and it would leave a trail of bread crumbs right to where he rested his head. That wasn't a chance he was willing to take.

On his walk to his building, he stopped at the corner deli to grab a box of cigars and a six-pack. He wasn't really a beer drinker, but after the day he'd had, a cold one seemed like the order of business. There was hardly anyone out at that hour, not that there was really ever anybody hugging the streets in that neighborhood. The quiet was one of the things that always reminded him that he wasn't in Harlem anymore. In the distance, his building loomed, a twenty-something-story high-rise on the Upper West Side. It was a far cry from the rat-infested tenement he had grown up in, but it was still close enough to where he could get to the action when he needed to. Some criticized him for shelling out the money for the two-bedroom apartment. They invested in money, cars, and clothes; he invested in peace of mind.

As he was going into the building, a girl named Laura was coming out. She was a short, thick Dominican girl who lived in the apartment next to his. Her parents had left it to her when they'd bought a house upstate. She played the bourgie role, but Knowledge had heard stories about the things she could do with a dick in her mouth.

"Hey, Mr. Man," Laura greeted him.

"Sup?" Knowledge replied.

"How come I always catch you creeping in and out of the building in the middle of the night?" she asked playfully.

"Same reason I always catch you creeping in and out in the middle of the night," Knowledge shot back.

Her eyes landed on the cigars in his hand. "When are you gonna invite me by for a smoke session? I know you be smoking that fire, because I be smelling it through the walls."

Knowledge cracked a half smile. "Nah, I don't think that be in either of our best interests."

"Why? I don't bite."

"Who says I'm worried about *you* biting *me*? I'm gonna catch you on the rebound, Laura." Knowledge wisely excused himself and went into the lobby.

"One of these days, Mr. Man," she called after him. "One of these days."

Knowledge waited until he was out of her line of vision before letting a sneaky smile form on his lips. Laura had been trying to throw the pussy on him since he'd moved into the building. It was tempting, but Knowledge was no fool. For as bad as Laura was, he knew shitting where he lived would complicate things. He had enough as it was going on in the streets and didn't want any drama in his building.

When he entered the apartment, the first thing he noticed was that it was dark. He usually left the light on over his stove, but the kitchen was pitch-black. The switch in his brain flipped, and the next thing he knew, he was creeping down his hallway, his gun drawn. His heart thudded in his chest as he neared his bedroom. There was a slither of light coming from the partially open door. This was his home . . . his sanctuary, and the fact that someone had violated it infuriated him. He only hoped that they were still in the apartment so that his pistol could properly articulate his displeasure.

He sat his six-pack down so that he could wrap both hands around the handle of his gun. He needed his aim to be steady and true. With his foot braced against the door, he took a deep breath to settle the butterflies in his stomach. No matter how many times he busted out his gun, it always felt like the first time. With murder in his heart, he pushed the door open and stepped into the room, prepared to dispatch the intruder, but his finger stopped short of depressing the trigger when he looked to his bed and found it occupied.

A dime piece of a rich caramel complexion lay nestled under the fluffy brown comforter. A scarf was tied around her head, preserving whatever style she was wearing her thick black hair in that week. She was so engrossed in the novel that she was reading that she didn't even notice him standing there. Knowledge decided to take the opportunity to have a little fun.

"You know what it is, run everything!" he barked. He intended it as a joke, but the joke quickly went sour when the woman dropped the book and produced a small .25. "Asia! Asia! Asia!" he spat her

...e in repetition while waving his hands in surrender, hoping she ...ecognized him before accidentally ending him.

The panicked look she'd been wearing when she drew down on him was replaced by one of relief, then anger. "What the fuck, Knowledge?" She lowered her gun. "You know better than to be sneaking up on me like that. I could've capped you by accident."

"I didn't know walking into my own pad could be considered sneaking up on someone, especially when I wasn't expecting them," Knowledge said.

Asia cocked her head as if she hadn't heard him correctly. "Well, excuse me for intruding. When you gave me a key to your apartment, I assumed that meant we were past the point of me having to call before I came over. My bad—let me get out of your way." She slid from beneath the comforter, wearing only his Patrick Ewing jersey.

Knowledge's eyes drank in her curvaceous figure and tender flesh. A tattoo of a dragon started just above her knee and disappeared somewhere up under the jersey. He knew where the tattoo ended and, with that in mind, moved to stop her. "Hold on, baby." He took her by the wrist. "You know I didn't mean it like that."

"All I know is what you put in front of me." Asia jerked loose. She plucked her blue slacks from their resting place at the foot of the bed, but Knowledge snatched them away.

"Stop acting like that, Asia." He held the pants just out of her arm's reach. "You know damn well I don't have a problem with you being here, and no, you don't have to call. I just meant that . . . fuck what I meant. I'm genuinely happy to see you, ma."

Asia folded her arms, pretending to be angrier than she was. "Umm-hmm." She looked him over. "You're probably really just happy I didn't bust you rolling up in here with one of them hood rats you love to keep company with."

Knowledge moved behind Asia and draped his arms over her.

"You know better than that, baby. Only the queen is fit to grace the palace. I take the hood rats downtown to the Liberty Inn." He planted a kiss on her cheek playfully.

Asia hit him with a sharp elbow to the ribs, knocking him off-balance and then following up with a judo flip onto the bed. While he was still disorientated, she straddled his chest and gave him a little slap across the face. "What did I tell you about playing with me, George?" she said, calling him by his government name.

Knowledge threw his weight to dislodge her and used the momentum to roll on top of her. The tables had now been turned. "And I told you about all this black super-ninja shit. Now stop bugging—you know I only got eyes for you." He leaned in to kiss her, and when he did, she nicked his lip with her teeth. "Ouch! What the fuck, Asia?" He jumped back.

"That old-ass pimp game you keeping picking up from Big Stone only works on women under twenty-three. Had you answered your phone, I could've told you that I wanted to crash here tonight. I've been calling you for the last three hours, but you ain't picking up. This raises the question: What or who you been doing that's kept you too busy to pick up for me?"

"My phone died." The lie rolled off Knowledge's tongue before he even had a chance to think about it.

"Bullshit!" she spat. "Even if it were true, how come you didn't pick up your trap phone? I called that, too, and got the voice mail, and we both know you don't never let the money line go dead."

Knowledge hated the fact that she knew him so well. Without even trying, he could've spun a million different half truths, but he didn't have it in him to get into it with her. "My fault, Asia. I just had a real hard day at work, so I was trying to stay focused on business. There's some shit going down that I need to try to put into perspective," he admitted.

Based on the weary look on his face, Asia knew Knowledge had some heavy shit weighing on him, so she went from shrew back to caring-girlfriend mode. "You know I'm here for you if you need me," she said, rubbing his back.

Knowledge smiled, knowing that his chick had his back. "I know you do, Asia. Honestly, the less you know about what I do in them streets, the better off you are."

Asia frowned. "Here you go, treating me like some little square bitch who don't know what time it is. Knowledge, I knew who you were and what you were about before I decided to get into this relationship. Don't treat me like I'm some broad who's still trying to figure you out. Talk to me."

Knowledge could tell by the intense look in her eyes she wasn't going to let it rest unless he told her something. "Look, I ain't about to get all into detail, but some real bad shit went down in the hood and everybody is just a little on edge."

"All your people good?" Asia asked, genuinely concerned.

"Yeah, as far as I know. We know the dude who got killed, but he wasn't a friend of ours. His name carried a lot of weight, though. When a man of a certain caliber gets clipped and nobody knows jack shit about how or why it happened, it's a sign that everybody with a hand in the pot should grow eyes in the backs of their heads."

Asia wasn't the sharpest knife in the drawer, but she wasn't slow, either. It didn't take her long to figure out that whatever Knowledge was telling her related to what she had seen on the news earlier about an explosion in Washington Heights. She never turned Knowledge onto the fact that she was hip, though. "Should we be worried?"

"No, *we* don't have anything to worry about. I told you when we started messing around that I would never allow what I do to poison what we got going on, and I meant that shit. I just gotta figure a few things out, that's all."

"Maybe now would be a good time we took that vacation we've been talking about for the last six months. Nowhere too far—maybe hit Atlantic City for a week," she suggested.

"And abandon my duties in a time of crisis? You know I can't do that. Big Stone needs me."

"I need you too," Asia countered.

Knowledge ran his hand over his head. "Asia, you said yourself that you knew who I was and what I was about before you got into this relationship, so you should know better than to try to make me choose between my duty and my heart. Let's not go there."

Asia sat up, folding her legs under herself. "Knowledge, I know in the love department I'll always come in third behind the streets and Big Stone. That just is what it is. All I'm suggesting is that you ease back off the front line for a second, at least until you're sure where this is going. You're Big Stone's right hand and have command over his army, so let your soldiers do what you pay them to do."

"I would love to, but you know it ain't in my character to ask another nigga to do anything I wouldn't. A good leader leads by example," he told her. When he saw the troubled look on her face, he softened his tone. "Baby, I know you're worried, and even if I tell you not to be, that won't change. Just know that your man ain't no fool, and I promise I won't be take any unnecessary chances. Now, enough about all this street shit. How was your day?"

"Stressful." She fell across his lap dramatically. "We got called into a meeting this morning so they could announce more budget cuts. In the last month in a half they've already fired four people, and more are sure to follow. Everybody is walking on eggshells, hoping that they're not the next ones banished to the unemployment line."

"Well, you know if things fuck up at your gig, I'll look out for you," Knowledge said sincerely.

"You know I ain't never been one to look for no handouts, but thank you. I got a few things lined up in case the bottom falls out of this. To be honest, I wouldn't be too broken up if they did fire me. Standing on my feet for all those hours during the day and then having to stand up at night while I'm in school is breaking me down."

"Worse case, fuck that job and focus all your attentions on school. How else are you gonna become a head chef in some world-famous restaurant?" Knowledge teased her.

"Fuck being the chef—I wanna be the owner!" she said seriously. "Don't get me wrong—I love cooking. Outside of you, it's one of the few joys in my life. It's my passion, but I've got no plans to be a laborer all my life. I don't mind starting in the kitchen, taking orders, but I wanna end it in the big chair upstairs, taking meetings."

"You know you turn me on when you start talking that boss shit." He leaned over and kissed her on the lips. "If you feel like that, then why don't you quit that pain-in-the-ass job and find something else to hold you down until you finish culinary school?"

"Don't think I haven't thought about it. Getting fired is one thing, but if I quit the job, I'll feel like I'm quitting on the girls I look after all day. There are some bad apples, as with anywhere, but for the most part, I get along with the girls at St. Francis. A lot of these girls come from families that substitute money for love, and these girls are running around, broken inside with nobody to talk to about it, except their shrinks and Officer Jones. To a lot of them, I'm more like a big sister rather than a jailer; they open up to me in ways they can't open up to their parents. It makes me feel good to be able to help them when I can. I'm paying my blessings forward."

"Then maybe you should become a shrink instead of a restaurant owner?" Knowledge joked.

"Laugh all you want, but it's people like me who keep kids like your precious Ms. Pearl out of harm's way. Why is it that every time I turn around, she's into something?"

Knowledge shrugged. "Asia, I'd be lying if I told you I knew. That girl loves trouble."

"Well, she's gonna end up finding out the hard way that trouble don't love nobody," Asia capped.

"By the way, good looking out on helping to squash that thing earlier. Pearl could've gotten into a lot of trouble for that," Knowledge said.

"Trouble is an understatement. From what she did to that girl's face, she's lucky the parents didn't try to press charges; though I hear they're quietly discussing whether or not to sue the school, since it was their lapse in security that allowed someone to come in from the outside and kick the shit out of their daughter." Asia gave him a look.

"Sorry about that, ma. Seriously, you know I'd never intentionally jeopardize your job like that."

"Knowledge, you're my man and Pearl is your family, so whenever I'm in a position to help, I don't have a problem with it. My thing is that it's happening too frequently. That girl runs around like she's Michael Corleone, and I can't keep creeping around, trying to clean up her messes! Maybe if we finally come out of the closet and let Big Stone know we're dating, Pearl would tone it down, knowing she had an extra set of eyes on her."

"Knowing Pearl, it'd probably only get worse if she knew she had someone on the inside," he said honestly. "I'll let Big Stone know what time it is with us when the moment presents itself."

"What, are you ashamed of me or something?" Asia's eyes flashed hurt.

"Not at all, love. Making you wifey was the smartest thing I've ever done in my life, and if I could, I'd shout it from the heavens, but I'm a man who believes in safeguarding what he cherishes, so as not to feed temptation. I'd never want someone to use that which gives me so much joy to try to bring me pain. Does that make sense to you?"

"More than you know," Asia replied. Moments like those allowed her to see Knowledge for the first time all over again and remember all the reasons she fell in love with him. He wasn't perfect, but he was hers.

"So, Madam Chef. I'm sure you didn't come over here and invade my space without at least bringing a sample of your wares," Knowledge said, changing the subject to lighten the mood.

"But of course." She sat up off his lap and propped herself against the cushioned headboard. "There's a plate of beef ribs and macaroni and cheese with collard greens in the microwave, waiting on you, and before you ask, I used turkey not pork neck bones. If you look in the fridge, you'll find the bowl with the potato salad in it. I was pressed for time, so I had to keep it simple." She brushed imaginary dirt off her shoulder.

"Damn, you trying to make a nigga give you his last name." Knowledge pressed his lips against hers.

"The blueprint every girl should follow." She patted him on the cheek softly.

"I'm about to see what this shit hitting for." Knowledge slid off the bed.

"Hold on, baby," she called after him. She pulled the Knick jersey up over her hips and revealed the rest of the dragon tattoo. Its horned head was depicted across the soft flesh just below her bikini line, its gaping maw thrown wide open around the opening to her freshly shaved pussy. The tattoo had been painful, but worth it for the shock value of those who were fortunate enough to ever see it. "Before you get to your main course, come take care of this appetizer."

CHAPTER TWENTY-FOUR

When Diamonds entered the office, the first thing he noticed was a tender little beauty lounging on a cracked brown love seat. She had one thick leg thrown over the arm of the chair, showing off her shaved vagina. She absently ran her fingers back and forth across her bare slit. Her glazed-over eyes drifted toward the new faces in the room, but she looked too stoned off whatever she was on to care.

Sitting behind a desk across the room, enjoying the show, was Pops Brown. He was a balding man with skin the color of scorched earth. His red-rimmed eyes were fixed hungrily on the girl, while his hand was just out of sight under the desk, doing God only knew what. When he noticed that he had company, he reflexively sprang to his feet, forgetting to tuck his squat black cock back into his pants. "Fuck is this?"

"A shame." Vita covered her mouth to hide her snicker. She couldn't help but think how much Pops's dick resembled a breakfast sausage.

Pops composed himself enough to stuff his half-hard cock back into his pants. "TJ, what the hell you doing, busting up in my office like this?"

"Pops, excuse my intrusion—" TJ began respectfully, but Pops cut him off.

"Intrusion is an understatement. Since when do you show such little respect?" Pops was furious. "And where the fuck is Rob? I told him I wasn't seeing anybody."

"I'm afraid I'm the answer to both of your questions, Mr. Brown." Diamonds stepped forward. "I've been passively trying to get an audience with you all night, so when that didn't work, I had to take a bit more of an aggressive approach, which included sending your unruly-ass kid off on a little smoke break." He smirked.

"You hurt my boy?" Pops asked, moving closer to the desk drawer that held his revolver.

"Only his pride. He'll be on a liquid diet for a few weeks, but he's still amongst the land of the living . . . at least for the time being," Diamonds assured him. "You don't mind if I sit, do you?" He motioned toward an empty chair near the desk. He didn't wait for a response before helping himself to the seat.

"Sugar," Pops addressed the girl, "go on and wait for me by the bar. This shouldn't take but a few minutes."

The girl didn't look thrilled to be getting the boot, but she knew better than to argue. She pulled her dress down, rolled her eyes, and left the office.

"Didn't mean to bust up your little party, old-timer," Goldie said from his position near the door.

"I don't recall addressing you, so why don't you keep your mouth shut until I do?" Pops said angrily.

Goldie made to step forward, but a look from his brother stopped him.

"You know all the hostility isn't necessary," Diamonds said in an easy tone.

"And who are you to come into my spot and tell me what is or isn't necessary?" Pops questioned. "And, TJ, I'm surprised at you for pulling this bullshit. I know for a fact these streets raised you better than that, or maybe they didn't?"

While Pops continued to rip into TJ, he looked to his cousin Diamonds, who was shaking his head in disgust. Before coming to New York, TJ had regaled Diamonds with exaggerated stories of his standing in the criminal underworld, and Pops was punching holes in his façade. The conversation was not going the way TJ had planned, and he needed to get a handle on it before his credibility was completely shot in front of his cousin. "Look," TJ said, cutting Pops off. "We came here to speak to you like gentleman and submit a business proposal, so why don't you show a little respect?" he demanded.

"Respect?" Pops laughed as if this were the funniest thing he'd ever heard. "What the fuck have you done in the street that commands respect? You think because you shot a few niggas and moved a little weight, you big-time now? You can lie to people who don't know you, but not with me. You small-time, TJ, and considering the way you handled this tonight, you always will be."

"I was big enough to have Pana Suarez put on his back!" TJ blurted out to everyone's surprise, including Diamonds. The minute the words had left TJ's mouth, he regretted them. He hadn't intended to spill the beans, but Pops had him so flustered, he had to say something to save face.

Pops's face went slack. "Bullshit."

"Afraid it isn't," Diamonds reluctantly confirmed. "I can attest to it because I'm the one who cut his heart out."

Pops suddenly felt his legs get weak, and he leaned against his desk for support. The fact that Pana's heart had been cut out was a piece of information that hadn't been made public. The only reason Pops knew was because of his contacts within the department. "Well, I'll be damned. I have to admit, when I heard Pana got touched, a lot of names popped into my head and yours certainly wasn't one of them, TJ. I never figured you to have the brains or the muscle to make it happen."

"As you can see, I have both," TJ said cockily, motioning toward Diamonds and Goldie. "But like I was saying earlier, we ain't here on bullshit. We here on business."

Pops shook his head. "You think killing Pana is supposed to all of a sudden put us on the same level to where we can break bread? Little boy, you're out of your league and out of your mind if you think you're gonna get me tied to you by association. You're a dead man walking behind what you done . . . all of you."

Diamonds chuckled. "If it were the first time I'd heard that, I might have a mind to be nervous, but men been trying to kill me for years, and as you can see I'm still here to pop shit about it. I'd be more worried about my own mortality than the next man's if I were you."

Pops gave Diamonds a hard look. "You talk a good game, friend, but Pops Brown don't scare that easy. You know I ain't never been no big fan of Pana, but I know some people who ain't happy about his untimely passing. What's to stop me from blowing the lid on this sneaky shit and making you the most hunted man in the city?"

Diamonds's eyes hardened. "I've been hunted all my life, so what's a few more people who want me dead gonna matter? And I know for a fact you ain't gonna open your dick suckers, because you ain't no fool, old head. Let's stop this dance and speak frankly between us." He spread his hands. "I didn't come here intending any disrespect, and I sure as shit didn't mean to lay something on your plate that could put you in a compromising position, but my bigmouthed-ass cousin dragged it to the table, and for this I apologize. Now, based on my body of work, you already know how I play, but what you may not know is that I am a man of reason and vision. As a man of vision, I would never come to a potential ally, or enemy for that matter, unless

I had done my due diligence first. You can act like you're sour over Pana's death, but you and I both know you're really relieved he's gone. You and Pana share neighboring territories, and he had been stepping on your toes for years by letting his bullshit spill over into your yard. Had it been anybody else, you'd have probably rousted what troops you could and rode on him, but you didn't have the muscle to dance with Pana. No slight—just stating what I know. If you look at it, I really did you a favor, whether it was intentional or not.

"No, sir, all I'm asking you to do is to put your assumptions about me aside so you can see the bigger picture. Now, you may not agree with my methods, but you can't deny their effectiveness. With Pana out of your hair, this whole side of Harlem will belong exclusively to the Blacks again, and you finally being able to spread out means an increase in your profits. I'm thinking that maybe this misfortune can turn into a blessing and open up the lane for you and me to get down together on something."

"I can move my drugs well enough on my own. I don't need no partners," Pops told him.

"You got me all wrong, OG. I got no interests in your drug business or any other illegal activities you got going on. I've come to speak to you about your bar."

Pops blinked twice as if he were hearing him wrong. "You went through all this to ask me about my bar?"

"Yes, sir," Diamonds confirmed. I got a million-dollar idea that can turn this hole-in-the-wall—no disrespect—into a cash cow. A franchise of gentleman's clubs called Purple City. It'll boast the baddest bitches and the most exclusive crowd. I'm telling you, old timer, we could make money hand over fist!" he said passionately.

Pops took up a pack of Lucky Strikes from his desk and tapped one of the cigarettes from the pack. He took his time lighting it and exhaling a large cloud of smoke before responding. "Young man, I admire your zeal, and under different circumstances this might be a conversation I'd be willing to explore, but as it stands, I can't do it. And before you ask why, let me offer you a simple explanation. If you and TJ back-doored Pana to take what he had, I'd be a fool to think the same couldn't happen to me if I let you get close enough. A snake don't care who it bites. I'm old, but I ain't no fool. That being said, you can all get the fuck out of my bar."

Diamonds's face saddened. "That's a real shame." He stood and smoothed his shirt. "I'm sure I could've learned a lot about the night-club business from an OG like you."

"Sorry to have to disappoint," Pops replied in a most insincere tone. As he watched Diamonds make his way to the door, Pops felt a sense of relief. The young man who had introduced himself as Diamonds made the old man uncomfortable, and he would be glad when he was out of his office. When he was rid of him, the first thing Pops planned on doing was firing his entire security staff for letting them get so close, including his son Rob.

Diamonds stopped short of the door and turned back to Pops. "I wouldn't say it was a completely uninformative trip, though. Tonight I learned that you can put a suit on a monkey, but it'll still be a monkey."

Quite unexpectedly, Goldie landed a crushing blow on the old man's chin that sent him spilling to the floor. While Pops was trying to push back to himself back to his feet, Vita leaped onto his back and slipped a clear plastic bag over his head. She wrapped her legs firmly around his waist to keep him from getting up while she suffocated him.

"Diamonds, what the fuck are you doing?" TJ sprang to his feet. He was all for roughing Pops up, especially after how he had talked to him, but killing him wasn't part of the plan.

Diamonds spun on TJ with so much hostility in his eyes that for a minute it looked like he would attack. "You don't say another fucking word!" his voice boomed. "You made it like this when you decided to give a full confession and damn the rest of us with it!"

"But, Diamonds—"

"Leave it alone, TJ." Goldie stepped between them. There was something in Goldie's eyes that told TJ it was in his best interest to listen.

Pops was on the floor, kicking and flapping around like a fish out of water. He clawed at Vita, but she was hunkered down tight, limbs bound around him like a human coil. The more Pops fought, the harder it was for him to breathe.

Diamonds knelt beside him, brandishing his dagger so that Pops could see his reflection in the black blade. "You hear that, old man, that thumping in your ears? It ain't your heart; it's hooves. The horseman is on his way to snatch your ass, and I'm the only person short of God who can convince him to make a detour. You ready to have a civilized conversation?"

Pops nodded frantically, trying his best not to black out. Using the blade, Diamonds sliced open the bag, nicking Pops's cheek in the process. The old man watched in astonishment as blood on the tip of the blade sizzled before being drunk into the black steel. He looked into Diamonds's eyes and, for the first time in a very long time, knew real fear. "What kind of devil are you?"

"The kind who won't take no for an answer." Diamonds laughed demonically. "I came here in friendship, offering you an opportunity to turn this shit hole into something special, and you spit in my face. That was a bad move." He grabbed Pops by his jowls and squeezed so tight that Pops's teeth cut into the soft flesh of his inner cheeks. The black dagger glistened menacingly, thirsty for another helping of the old man's blood. "Now you will watch me build on its ashes."

Fifteen minutes later Diamonds was pushing his SUV at a moderate speed down Seventh Avenue. Black smudge marks stained his steering wheel from where his fingers had rested. He'd have to run it through the car wash at some point that day. When he noticed a procession of fire trucks and emergency service vehicles speeding north on the other side of the street, he couldn't stop the thin smile that crept across his lips.

He headed to the East Side, where he kept one of his many emergency storage units. Diamonds and his companions were nearly out on their feet after all that had gone on, but there was one more piece of business that needed attending to before any of them could go to sleep.

It took the combined efforts of Diamonds and Goldie to off-load the rolled-up carpet from the back of the SUV and onto a flatbed. The manager hardly gave them a second look when they passed the small booth, where he spent most of his nights on Myspace or watching porn. Diamonds gave him a thick envelope once a week for the privilege of being invisible when he came and went.

The hallway leading to the unit was quiet, save for the footfalls of the brothers and the squeaky wheels of the flatbed. Diamonds busied himself unlocking the unit while Goldie struggled to drag the rolled carpet from the flatbed. "Shit," he cursed when he lost his grip and the carpet hit the floor with a heavy thud.

"Ain't gonna be much good to us if you damage it, little brother," Diamonds told him, lifting the gate to the unit.

"Like I give a shit. I'm with Buda on this one; you should've tied up all loose ends," Goldie told him.

"Good thing you and Buda ain't running this crew." Diamonds

lifted the carpet and slung it over his shoulder. He carried it inside the unit and dumped it on a pile of laundry in the corner. Diamonds ignored the fact that the carpet started wriggling, and locked the unit up.

In silence, Diamonds and Goldie made their way back down the hall. Diamonds was deep in his thoughts when he heard his little brother start giggling unexpectedly. "What's so funny?"

"Nothing, bro. I'm just wondering how much air is in that thing," Goldie told him.

Diamonds thought on it. "Probably not much. For his sake, he better hope his people move expeditiously to honor our request."

CHAPTER TWENTY-FIVE

After their night's business was concluded, Diamonds drove his crew back to his place. During their reign of terror up the East Coast, they had always found a house or flat to share, but since arriving in New York, they'd all moved into separate apartments throughout the city. TJ and Buda cut, but Diamonds was able to convince Hank, Goldie, and Vita to crash at his place for the night. It had been a long time since they'd all slept under the same roof. Normally Diamonds appreciated his newfound solitude, and their group sleepovers of old didn't come very frequently, but that night he wanted his family around him. He would need to draw strength from them to face what was to come.

Since arriving in New York, Diamonds had managed to land himself a nice three-bedroom apartment in an upscale Manhattan neighborhood that overlooked Central Park. It was located in a swanky building with a doorman and neighbors who looked nothing like him. He'd gotten into the building through a crooked member of the management. They allowed him to make a no-questions-asked cash payment so long as he took out a five-year lease and greased their palms for the hookup.

They pulled the car into the underground garage and filed out, looking every bit of the weary desperados they were. They had dropped TJ off first, a few blocks away from Pops's bar, where he had parked his car. He was clearly still freaked out by everything that had gone down. Trying to muscle the old man out of his place was one thing, but burning it to the ground was something else altogether. It was a bit over-the-top, especially because it had still been crowded with people when Diamonds had lit the blaze. Diamonds had taken the liberty of pulling the fire alarms to give the drunks a sporting chance to make it out safely. The ones who hadn't would be written off as casualties of the war Diamonds was waging in New York. It was a cruel and ruthless thing for him to do, but after the lack of respect Pops had shown, Diamonds needed to make sure he and everyone else had a clear understanding of what type of monster they were dealing with.

To say that TJ was rattled by what had gone down would've been an understatement. At one point Diamonds thought TJ was going to shit his pants. He wanted to feel sympathy for his cousin, but he couldn't find it in his black heart to do so. He'd known from the beginning that TJ didn't have it in him to play at Diamonds's level. He was about his paper, and hardly a punk, but wholesale murder wasn't for him. Still, he was insistent that he was worthy of a seat at the bigboy table, so Diamonds pulled out a chair and let him eat. What his wayward mother's only nephew didn't count on was having trouble digesting the meal. Before parting company, Diamonds reminded TJ of the oath he'd taken when he was inducted into their circle. Each member of their squad was bound by their words and their deeds to the pirate code Diamonds had written and, as such, had an obligation to their crew above all others, even family.

Buda got dropped off next. They left him on 125th Street and St. Nicholas, where the taxis were lined up outside the train station. He didn't bother to say where he was going, and by that point he had

gotten so far under Diamonds's skin that he didn't care to ask. Since
they had left the club, he had been mouthing off over his displeasure
for being left out of the action that had gone on in Pops's office, and
a multitude of other things that had made him feel slighted over the
last few months. Every so often Hank would cut Diamonds a look.
He was no doubt thinking the same thing that Diamonds was: Buda
was getting out of control.

When they got to the apartment, everyone fanned out, Hank and
Goldie going into the living room to raid the liquor cabinet and Vita
disappearing into the kitchen to whip up some breakfast. From the
way she was slamming pots and pans, Diamonds knew she was still
angry about earlier, and he couldn't really say that he blamed her. Diamonds could only imagine how he looked, standing there and grinning at Pearl like a lovestruck teenager. His reaction to her was so far
out of his character that the whole crew had noticed, including Vita.

While his crew had the run of his apartment, Diamonds retreated
to the guest bedroom that doubled as his office/war room. Besides
the bathroom, it was the only room in the apartment where he could
really gather his thoughts. It was sparsely decorated with only a bed,
a recliner, a mini-fridge, a small card table in the corner, and a tall
wooden wardrobe with double doors. His first stop was the refrigerator, where he retrieved a beer and something thick wrapped in
newspaper. Next he moved to the wardrobe and opened it.

There were several odds and ends on the shelves that he had collected in his travels, but he was focused on the floor of the wardrobe.
It was a silver serving tray that was stained with something dark. On
each end sat a candle, one white and one black. Between them was a
withered picture. He gently picked it up and gazed at it fondly. The
picture was faded, but you could still see the images of him and Buda
clearly. They had taken it at Mardi Gras a few years prior. They were
just two punk kids with dreams of taking over the world. Back then

it had seemed far fetched, but at the rate they were going their dream could very well become a reality unless Buda managed to fuck it up. He placed the picture back onto the serving tray before retrieving a book of matches from his pocket. Chanting under his breath, he lit the black candle, then the white. Using the black dagger he'd stolen, Diamonds sliced open one of his fingers and let the blood drop onto the silver platter. The droplets congealed like mercury and separated into two streams that were drawn into the candles. Their flames danced back and forth on phantom winds, whipping across the picture. The image of Buda faded a bit more, as it always did when he performed the dark ritual. Soon there would likely be nothing left but the lone image of Diamonds in the photo, but desperate times called for desperate measures. After it was done, Diamonds closed the cabinet and retired to the recliner with his beer and the parcel he'd gotten out of the mini-fridge. It had been a long night, and the day promised to be even longer.

Auntie was probably frowning on Diamonds from the grave. Not because he murdered in cold blood one of the few people who'd ever shown him love, but because he was corrupting everything she had ever taught him. *"You can't keep taking from the cycle without giving something back."* He could hear her warning as clear as if she had been sitting next to him in that rickety old wheelchair. To her credit, she was right. He had seen plenty of blood and misery over the last couple of years. The cycle he had broken was definitely swinging back around to claim its due, but Diamonds was willing to feed it as many souls as it could digest if it put him closer to his dream. Most men were content to be dubbed kings, but Diamonds wanted to be a god.

For all the bullshit unfolding around Diamonds, there was a bright spot . . . Pearl. She'd been on his mind heavily since their chance meeting at the bar. From what he had seen, she was the perfect package: young, fine, and feisty as hell. Had he not been there on business, he could've spent hours picking her brain to see where her head was at, but his paper trumped his curiosity. He was digging her, but he wasn't ready to go all in and anoint her, especially without knowing if her neck was strong enough to carry a crown on her head. Intense feelings aside, Diamonds was focused enough to know that fast women with pretty faces were a hustler's kryptonite. Pearl didn't strike him as the type, though. Not saying he wouldn't put it past her, but from the clarity of the diamonds in her ears and the quality of the Rolex on her wrist, he suspected she came from money. Not street-corner-hustler money, but old money.

There was a soft knock on the door. Diamonds bid them to enter. *"Vini non nan."*

The door creaked open and Vita crept into the room. She had changed out of her dress and was now wearing a pair of Diamonds's Nike sweat pants and a puke-green T-shirt with the Statue of Liberty on the front. Diamonds had bought it for her at one of those tourist shops in Times Square. It had only cost him five bucks, but she treasured it the same as if he'd paid a grip for it at Nordstrom. "You hungry?" She patted the top of her head with the palm of her hand. She'd ditched the wig and was rocking her natural hair, braided into neat cornrows. "I got some eggs and sausage on the stove. Get it while it's hot or before them greedy niggas out there hog it up."

"I don't have too much of an appetite right this second, but thank you." Diamonds took a sip of his beer. "Did you extend that invitation to your people like I asked?"

"Yeah, I spoke to LA and he's all in. I haven't been able to reach Domo, though," Vita told him.

A disapproving look crossed Diamonds's face. "You think he gone rabbit?"

"I doubt it. The shock of what he did has probably set in, and it's gonna take him a minute to process," Vita reasoned. "You remember what it was like the first time."

"Truthfully I don't. Feels like I've been putting in work as far back as I can remember," Diamonds said. "I want you to make sure them niggas come through so I can size them up. We'll be meeting with a new supplier in a few days, and I wanna make sure everybody flying under this flag is built properly for what's to come."

This came as a surprise to Vita, as he had never mentioned it to her before then. "So we're gonna break the deal we made with Eddie?"

"Nah, at least not yet. We'll keep our arrangement with Eddie and let him supply us with cocaine, but I'm looking into a dope plug. Them jokers from Queens I was telling you about are hooking me into some Haitians from out of Brooklyn who're holding a big bag and are willing to cut us in if we step with the right deal."

"Do you trust these guys who are hooking us in with the Haitians?" Vita asked.

"Not particularly, but it's a calculated risk. We gonna need friends on the inside if we're to rule this city."

"Be mindful when dealing with these up-North niggas, Diamonds. They don't play by the same set of rules," Vita warned.

"There's only one rule in this game, and that's *survival*," Diamonds told her. "Since when you been so concerned with tactical operations? What, you don't trust my judgment no more?"

"Never that!" She sat on the arm of the recliner opposite the wrapped parcel. "You know I will. I have followed you into the deepest parts of hell and never once complained, so the fact that you even asked is a little offensive. You been on a real head trip lately. Maybe the Big Apple is fucking with your head and you're forgetting who's with you for a reason and who's with you for a season."

Diamonds knew what she was hinting at and didn't feel like

getting into a jealous argument with her. "Cut that shit out, V. I'm in here stressing over some real shit, and you coming at me cross. *Tonbe tounen.*" He made a dismissive gesture.

" 'Fall back,' my ass!" she translated. "Diamonds, don't get to trying to dismiss me like I'm one of these random bitches you keep sticking your dick in from state to state. I don't see none of them hos out here on the front line, dumping when the shit gets thick!"

"Vita, make no mistake that I realize you're the backbone of this crew, and that's why I fuck with you like I fuck with you. I'll take one of you versus any five seasoned niggas into battle and feel confident in my chances of coming up on top."

Hearing that made Vita feel good but still not special. "That means a lot to me coming from you. If only your actions still matched your words, I might not be standing here, looking at you sideways. Something ain't right with you, and I can feel it."

"Girl, you talking crazy. I'm still the same nigga I always been." He tried to turn away, but she straddled his lap, cupping his face in her hands and making him look at her. Worry danced in her brown eyes.

"You can't fool somebody who knows you better than she knows herself. Baby, since we left New Orleans, there's been a darkness clinging to you like a second skin, and for the last two years I've been watching it spread and eat away at the man I used to know. I want to help, but I can't if you don't tell me what's going on."

Diamonds closed his eyes and shook his head. "It's nothing, Vita. I just got a lot on my mind. This crown I've chosen to wear seems to get heavier by the day," he said honestly.

"Then stop trying to carry it on your own." She ran her hands over his shoulders and brought them to rest on his chest. Vita stared into his black eyes, feeling the familiar beat of his heart in her palm. She tried to convey just how much she loved him and how far she was willing to go if he would only let her. Diamonds had made it clear to her long ago that what they had could never be more than what it was, but she couldn't help how she felt. He was her first love. With this in mind, she leaned in and kissed him.

Intimacy had been the furthest thing from Diamonds's mind when Vita had come into the room, but when she started, he didn't stop her. The heat from her body against him pulled his busy mind from the million things he was trying to sort out and made him focus on the beautiful woman on his lap. He cupped her face in his hands and kissed her back. His tongue explored her mouth and found it fresh and clean like she had just brushed her teeth. He felt his cock swell in his jeans, and from the way Vita's eyes popped open, she must've felt it too.

"I see at least part of you still recognizes who the fuck I am." Vita smiled devilishly, sliding off his lap and onto her knees. "Don't worry about nothing, baby." She undid his belt. "Mama gonna get all that evil up out you."

While he watched Vita tug his thick, throbbing cock from his jeans, he heard Hank's warning in the back of his mind. For a moment guilt tried to set in, and he thought about telling her to stop, but when he felt Vita's hot mouth wrap around his dick, the guilt faded into euphoria. She took him into her mouth a little at a time, every so often popping his penis out and running her tongue around the head. When she had his member good and slick, she opened the secret compartment in the back of her throat and took him in balls deep. Diamonds wanted to squeal like a schoolgirl, but he couldn't lose his cool in front of her. One thing Diamonds always appreciated about Vita was how seriously she took whatever she set out to do. Whether it was busting her gun in a firefight or sucking cock, she gave it her all. She was sucking him off so good that her mouth started to feel like a pussy.

Vita took his cock like a champ as Diamonds plowed his huge cock into her throat. Between pumps, she would grab him by the hips and force him to the back of her throat while running her tongue over his balls. Diamonds had gripped the sides of her head and was pumping into her mouth so furiously that she couldn't come up for air. Vita felt like she was coming close to blacking out, but she wouldn't stop him. Her need to please the man she loved took precedence over everything, including her own well-being. She was determined to remind Diamonds why he had chosen her in the first place. When she ran her hands down his stomach and felt the muscles tighten, she knew he was about to blow his load, but she wasn't done with him yet. With a popping sound, she pulled his dick from her mouth and squeezed the top of it hard enough to make him wince. "If you think you're gonna get yours before I get mine, you've got another think coming." She climbed back onto his lap.

Diamonds's eyes rolled to the back of his head when he felt Vita's warm box settle over his penis. She was tight, but not tight enough to where he had to force it. Her pussy fit over his dick like a glove. He wrapped one arm around her small waist and leaned forward, her hanging slightly off him, so he could dictate the pace. He jammed himself into her slow and steady, savoring her. He smiled inwardly when he looked down and saw the white buildup of foam that had formed around his cock, knowing she was reaching her happy place.

All Vita could do was bite down on her lips and curse under her breath as Diamonds stabbed into her womb over and over. He was fucking her so good that she was torn between kissing him and killing him. She had been with other men over the course of their on-again-off-again relationship, but none of them slung pipe quite like Diamonds. She thought of the girl at the bar she'd caught him talking to and the way his face had lit up in her presence, and it made her angry all over again. Sharing his dick, no matter how painful, she could deal with. But the thought of him taking it away from her altogether brought on a temporary moment of insanity.

Diamonds was just getting into his groove when Vita popped off his lap unexpectedly, leaving his dick bobbing back and forth like a spring. When he saw the crazed look in her eyes, he was taken aback—for a minute he thought she might attack him. Instead Vita turned her back to him, planted her hands on the ground, and placed her legs on the arms of the chair. Stretched out like the letter *Y,* she lowered herself back onto him and showed him a side of her he hadn't seen in a long time.

Vita felt his hands trying to grab onto her ass to get her to slow down, which only made her throw it harder. Diamonds prided himself on always being in control, and she intended to strip him of that. She bounced on his lap ferociously, not caring if she broke his dick off while trying to get hers. "I'm 'bout to nut. . . . I'm 'bout to nut," she heard him say, panting breathlessly behind her. But when he tried to push her off to release himself, Vita put all her weight on Diamonds and made him explode inside her. She continued to grind back and forth on his lap until she felt his dick start to go soft and was sure she got every drop of his joy juice.

"What the fuck, Vita?" Diamonds cursed, and shoved her off him. He jumped to his feet, dick swinging and dripping.

Vita rolled onto her back and gave him a lazy smile. "What you tripping off? Ain't like this is the first time you nutted in me, and I ain't popped up pregnant yet."

"Spiteful bitch!" he growled. He knew Vita making him bust inside her was payback for him being all up on Pearl. She could be vindictive as hell when she set her mind to it. He cursed himself for not heeding Hank's warning and keeping his dick out of her. Needing to put some distance between himself and Vita before he was tempted to slap the shit out of her, Diamonds grabbed the parcel from the arm of the recliner and retreated to the card table on the other side of the room.

"What you doing?" Vita strolled over as if she hadn't done anything wrong. She was still naked, sashaying to try to entice him, but he was too mad to bite . . . at least not again.

"Trying to keep from kicking your ass." He was rummaging through the drawers of the card table, looking for something. "You know I ain't trying to bring no babies into this fucked-up life."

"Neither am I, so don't flatter yourself, nigga!" she spat. "You know, for as much as you talk shit about not wanting to bring babies into this, it don't seem to stop you from running up in me raw or dumping off inside me when your ass is too drunk to pull out. You kill me with your double standards."

Diamonds brandished the hammer he had found in the drawer. "I'm gonna kill you with this if you keep testing me."

"The day you raise your hand to me will be the day when you had better learn to sleep with one eye open," Vita warned. "The reason you think you can do and say what the fuck you want to me is because I let you. Your ass done got comfortable, thinking I ain't going nowhere, but one day I'm going to surprise you."

"Do whatever you gotta do, Vita. I ain't gonna lose no sleep," Diamonds told her, giving a dismissive shrug. This only made her angrier.

"You know, I don't even know why I'm surprised at how shitty you're acting toward me, since you do it every time we get to a new city. Vita's pussy is good enough for you to pound on whenever you're horny, until you get to sniffing around a new bitch," Vita accused.

"Go ahead with that shit." He made a dismissive gesture. He didn't want to admit it, but Vita knew him better than he thought.

"Do you love her?" Vita asked unexpectedly.

The question caught Diamonds off guard. "Who?"

"You know who: little Ms. Fine I caught you with at the bar."

Diamonds gave her a dumbfounded look. "I ain't about to answer that shit," he said.

"You ain't denying it either," she shot back.

"Vita, you don't even know that girl. What's your problem with her?"

"My problem is, tonight I saw you look at a total stranger the way I've always prayed you'd look at me," she said emotionally.

Hearing the hurt in her voice stung Diamonds, and he felt low. Not because he had hurt her feelings, but because she was so dangerously close to the truth. For as foolish as it was, all he had been able to think about since their meeting was Pearl, a girl he barely knew. To spare his pride and Vita's feelings, he opened his mouth to spin a lie, but his ringing cell phone saved him the trouble. "Talk," he answered the call. "Can it wait? I ain't been to sleep yet." He listened for a while longer before his face soured at whatever was being said on the other end. "A'ight, I'll be there." He ended the call and placed the cell phone on the table, next to the parcel.

"Everything cool?" Vita asked, momentarily forgetting about the argument. When Diamonds got off the phone, he appeared to be in an even fouler mood than he had already been in.

"Yeah, I gotta go handle some shit. It seems King Wetback wants to meet the man responsible for handling his little problem," Diamonds told her.

"About fucking time. If you ask me, we should've met the nigga before we did the job. I'll round up the troops," Vita said, and headed for the door.

"Don't bother. He wants to meet me alone."

Vita's head whipped around. "Alone? What for?"

Diamonds shrugged. "You know these old-school niggas are hella suspicious of new faces, even ones who commit murder for them."

A worried expression crossed Vita's face. "I don't like this, Diamonds. We don't know these Spanish niggas like that. You could be walking into a setup."

"It's possible, but I doubt it. Eddie ain't no fool. After what we did to Pana and his whole team, he knows that if anything were to happen to me, you and the boys would rain hell down on his bean-eating ass. And I won't be alone; TJ will be there too."

Vita snorted. "Shit, if he's who you're taking with you for backup, then you might as well be alone. He ain't the most useful muthafucka I've met."

"Cut the boy some slack, Vita. Not everybody got the stomach for what we do. TJ may have his faults, but if it hadn't been for him, we wouldn't have been able to get into position so quickly when we rolled into town."

"Yeah, he's good at making deals. I'll give him that. But the boy needs to stay in his lane. That shit he pulled earlier could've compromised us."

"But it didn't," Diamonds countered. "In any event, I don't think it's a mistake TJ will be making again anytime soon," he added, to assure her.

"You better hope not, because blood or not, I'll take that big-mouthed nigga out the game myself," Vita promised. "And, speaking of mistakes, what's with you showing mercy earlier? I think you leaving that old man and his brat alive are invitations to disaster. We should've let both of their asses burn along with the bar instead of pulling them out. If they're dead, then they ain't liabilities."

"And if they're dead, Pops can't sign over the deed to what's left of that property," Diamonds said, enlightening her. "The lawyer is gonna pay a call on him this morning, and I want you to go with him. The fact that we're holding his kid hostage at the storage unit should be enough insurance for Pops to keep up his end of the bargain, but seeing you will remind him of what will happen if he doesn't."

"Sounds like you've pretty much got it mapped out, but there's one thing you haven't considered. Even if Pops does sign over his property, what's to stop him from blowing the whistle on us after he gets his kid back, bringing the wrath of every boss in New York down on our heads?"

Diamonds laughed. "V, you of all people should know me better than that." He unwrapped the newspaper he'd taken from the refrigerator. Lying in the center of the bloodstained wrapping was a cow's tongue. "When I'm done, the last thing you'll have to worry about is a nigga speaking ill of this crew."

CHAPTER TWENTY-SIX

Long after Diamonds had dropped Buda off, anger still burned in Buda's chest. The only reason he had gone along with Diamonds to that shit hole bar was because he knew it would present him the opportunity to bust some heads. Diamonds had claimed they were only going to try to negotiate with Pops, but because Buda knew Diamonds, he also knew it would turn physical. Diamonds dealt with people who didn't submit to his will by putting his hands on them or making them disappear. This was the reason he and Buda had been clashing so often lately. Buda was no yes-man, and Diamonds couldn't deal with that.

Back in the day, Buda and Diamonds had been more like brothers than he and John-Boy. They could come to each other in times of trouble, love or war, but it seemed like their relationship had changed since they'd left New Orleans. Diamonds had become distant and had started treating him more like one of the other soldiers rather than the man he had trusted enough to appoint his second-in-command. Buda had been ten toes down since the beginning and was always the first to step up when the situation called for it. Diamonds had a knack for overlooking the good things he did and focusing on the bad. Granted, Buda knew his drinking was becoming an issue, but none of them were without their vices, including Diamonds.

With all the pent-up aggression he had going on, there was no way Buda was going home. His first mind was to take a taxi to his car and hit different strip clubs until he got lucky, but he'd been drinking and had a pistol on him. He'd be ripe for the plucking for some overzealous cop. It was best that he took a cab to wherever he planned on going rather than risk spending the weekend in lockup.

It was then that he remembered he had a chick who didn't live too far from where Diamonds had dropped him off. Of all the women he had spread out all over the city, she was the one he could call anytime of the day or night, and she'd be down for whatever he wanted to do and then some. He'd been knocking the bottom out of her for a few weeks and couldn't get enough of what she had between her legs. He whipped out his phone and scrolled until he saw the name GOOD PUSSY and hit send. She picked up on the second ring, and a sultry voice came over the line.

"Well, hello, stranger. I haven't heard from you in a while. I was beginning to think you stopped fucking with me."

"Never that, sweetheart. Shit, just been hectic, so I ain't had a lot of playtime, ya know?"

"Sho ya right. Get that money, big daddy," she said, stroking his ego.

Buda got to the point. "So what's up? You home? I got an itch I need scratched."

"No, I'm not home, but I'm not far, either. I'm out having drinks with some people. You remember the place you met me at, right?"

"Yeah." He recalled the after-hours gambling spot where he'd first laid eyes on the object of his affection. "What are the chances that if I swing through there, you'll cut your company loose and we can get into some grown folk's action?"

"Slide through and find out," she teased, and ended the call.

Eight minutes later Buda was climbing out of a taxi on 118th and Lexington. At that hour of the night there weren't many people out, except drug addicts and people looking to gain entrance to Hades. Hades was located in the back of a storefront that doubled as a small bakery during the day. It was a spot where you could go when the regular clubs had closed down but you wanted to keep the party going. Buda had discovered the dive through a pill dealer he knew, during one of his all-night benders. To that day it was still the most fun he'd ever had in New York City.

Buda knew he would be subjected to getting searched like everyone else, so he stashed his pistol under a trash can on the corner. He hated moving around without his gun, especially when he was alone. That was all the more reason for him to get in and get out. Outside there were a couple of girls standing around, waiting their turn to be allowed inside and trying not to look suspicious. It was kind of hard to do, considering they were hanging out on a known drug block, wearing heels and short skirts. Anyone who saw them knew that they were either looking for a good time or selling pussy. Their thirsty eyes latched onto Buda as he bypassed the line and marched through the small entrance.

Before he could cross the threshold, he was greeted by a monstrosity of a man who stood at least six foot five and had a large block head and a scar that resembled a lightning bolt across his forehead. He bore a striking resemblance to the Mary Shelley character he had been nicknamed after, Frankenstein. He stood between Buda and the rear door that led to the lounge and scowled at him from under thick bushy eyebrows.

"Sup? I was here the other night with Boogie," Buda said in an attempt to jog Frankenstein's memory.

"Boogie ain't here," Frankenstein told him in a voice that sounded like two stones grinding together. "If you plan on going inside, it'll be a fifty-dollar cover."

When Buda had first come there with Boogie, they were whisked inside with no hassle, but now Frankenstein was acting like he didn't know him. Buda didn't want to seem like a petty nigga for arguing with him, so he dug into his pocket and paid the cover. Frankenstein gave him a thorough searching before standing aside and allowing him to pass through the back door.

Hades wasn't a lounge, a club, or a bar. It was a storeroom that had been gutted and filled with some small tables, a few chairs, a sectional couch, and a bar that looked like someone had ordered it from a Fingerhut catalog. Though it might not have been much to look at, it had a reputation amongst underworld circles. For all intents and purposes, Hades was pretty much just what the name described it to be: a place where you could entertain your vices. Girls, gambling, cheap liquor . . . they had it all.

Buda scanned the faces inside Hades, looking for the one he felt was the most beautiful in the room. He found her on the second sweep. The moment Buda spotted Mercedes, he felt the familiar tightness around his heart that crept in every time he'd seen her since the first time he'd laid eyes on her. She was a thick Latina with long legs and a head full of thick black hair that hung down to her pumpkin-sized ass. Mercedes was sitting at a table in the back with some corny-looking dude invading her space and whispering in her ear. Buda knew he and Mercedes weren't exclusive, but it didn't stop his heart from filling with jealous rage at seeing another man sniff around what he had tasted.

He moved through the room at a tipsy lumber, with little care or concern for those he bumped passed or flat-out knocked over. Mercedes spotted him first, nostrils flaring and eyes flashing anger. She never even had a chance to warn her companion before one of Buda's meaty fingers jabbed him in the shoulder. The companion turned, lips pursed to bark at whoever was intruding on what he had going on, but seeing the bearded Mack truck hovering over him, he cowered against his chair

"Take a powder," Buda ordered.

The companion looked back and forth between Buda and Mercedes, not entirely sure what was going on.

"Fuck you, looking at her for when it's me who's talking to you," Buda snapped.

"Check this out. I don't know what's going on, but—" the companion began, but his words were cut off when Buda grabbed the back of his chair and pulled it out from the table. The companion's heart leaped into his throat when the brute grabbed a fistful of his shirt and yanked him to his feet.

"Let me see if I can say this in a language you understand." Buda rained spittle down onto the man's face. "I said get the fuck out of here!" He shoved the companion away with so much force that he tripped over his feet and landed on his ass. He looked up at Buda as if he were thinking about mounting some sort of defense, but he thought better of it and scampered away. "Pussy." Buda laughed and took the seat the man had just vacated.

"You know you just cost me some money, don't you?" Mercedes coolly tapped a cigarette from her pack and placed it between her crimson-painted lips.

"Fuck that nigga." Buda pulled out a lighter, reached over, and lit her cigarette for her. "Whatever that clown was spending tonight, I'll double it. I don't see why you're still hustling in this dive anyway when I told you I'd take care of you."

"Is that right? And what do you think my girlfriend is going to say about you trying to snatch me from her?" Mercedes asked playfully.

"If her pussy is as good as yours, then I might have to see if we can swing a two for one. Y'all can be sister wives and shit," Buda half joked. He'd never met her, but he had seen pictures of the girl Mercedes was seeing. She had a thick, yellow bone structure and perfect dick-sucking lips. He'd been pressing Mercedes for a threesome, but she had yet to cave to his request.

When Mercedes laughed, it sounded like sweet music to him. "Honey, I'm flattered, but I'm incredibly high-maintenance, and don't even get me started on Zonnie's saditty ass."

"You trying to say that my pockets ain't deep enough to keep y'all laced in whatever you need?" Buda was offended.

"Calm down, lover. I ain't trying to insult you—just keeping it honest. You're a loads of fun, but I been around long enough to know that street-corner hustlers have short expiration dates. The day I stop hustling to get my own, it'll be for a man who owns some shit, and I don't mean cars or whips. I mean someone who really has it together."

"What if I told you that I was about to be one of the richest niggas in this city?" Buda challenged.

"Then I'd say you've got my attention."

Buda looked around to make sure no one was listening before leaning in to whisper. "Listen, baby, I'm about to run some shit down to you, but it's gotta stay between us."

"Honey, most people I deal with are more interested in what's going in my mouth than what's coming out of it," she told him.

"I got some big shit lined up, and when it goes down, I'm going to run this city," Buda told her.

"You think you're the first man to whisper those same words in my ear, daddy? No disrespect, but what makes you any different than the rest of these jokers who come in here kicking that 'I'm taking over' shit?"

"Because the rest of these jokers didn't kill Pana Suarez," Buda boasted.

Mercedes couldn't hide her shock at Buda's admission. Everybody with an ear to the streets had heard about the assassination of one of Harlem's biggest dealers. There was much speculation as to what had had happened to Pana and why, but no one could say for sure what the real story was, though there were quite a few people anxious to find out. Mercedes had even overheard a guy her girl was dealing with say there was a price on the heads of anyone involved. The wheels in Mercedes's head immediately started spinning. "You're shitting me."

"Do I look like a man who would bullshit such a pretty lady?" he asked seriously. "Pana was the first of the dominos to fall, but they'll be others. When it's all said and done, these niggas are all going to line up to kiss the ring of New York's new king."

"Wow, that's some heavy shit."

"Because I'm a heavy nigga," he capped. "I'm telling you, baby, all you gotta do is have a little faith in a nigga, and within six months I'm gonna be sitting on enough cake to take care of you, your girl, and three more bitches. Picture it, all of us set up in a big-ass house, some Hugh Hefner shit."

Mercedes was about to respond when her eyes darted to something just over Buda's shoulder. "Damn."

Buda turned and saw the companion headed his way, but he wasn't alone. There were two large men with him in black T-shirts that read SECURITY in white letters across the chests. Leading the march was Christian Knight. Christian was a pimp and a pill pusher, but more important, he was the owner of Hades as well as the building above it. As usual he was in all his splendor, wearing large fish-bowl sunglasses, a pair of tight leather pants, no shirt, and a coat that looked like it was made from canary feathers. His normally smiling face was now twisted into a mask of irritation.

"Is there a problem?" Buda rose to his feet. Christian stood several inches taller than Buda, but he was at least fifty pounds lighter.

"That's what I'm trying to figure out," Christian replied in his silky voice. "I understand that there was some kind of discrepancy between you and this man over one of our girls?" He motioned toward the companion.

"Nah, wasn't no discrepancy. The lady is with me tonight," Buda said as if that should've been the end of it.

"That's not how it works here, friend. The lady is property of the club, so she belongs to whoever's money is in my pocket, and I can't seem to remember you greasing my palm when you came in here," Christian told him.

"Baby, it's cool. We can hook up later," Mercedes said, trying to defuse the situation. She got up and attempted to go around the table, but Buda jerked her back by the arm.

"Nah, fuck that. If this is about money . . ." Buda dug into his pocket and flashed his bankroll.

Christian shook his head. "This isn't about money; it's about etiquette. If I let you abscond with Mercedes, after she and this man already came to an arrangement, it would reflect poorly on me. But look: just to prove I'm not an unreasonable dude, how about you grab any other girl in the joint and take her for a test drive? On me, of course."

"I already got the girl I want." Buda pulled Mercedes closer.

Christian sighed. "I'm trying really hard to be a gentleman about this, but I'm afraid you're pulling the gangster out of me."

"Gangster?" Buda looked over his outfit and laughed. "Go ahead with that bullshit, man. Why don't you and your boys take a walk before your pretty ass makes me do something one of us will regret?"

"Well, like the commercial says, *At Burger King, you can have it your way.* The same rule applies in Hades." Christian motioned security forward.

Buda could tell from the mean scowls on their faces that security had no intention of letting him leave quietly. This was going to get messy, and that was just how he liked it. The first member of security who stepped within his arm's reach caught it the worse. Buda's fist slammed into his chin with so much force that it took him clean out of one of his shoes. He was asleep long before he hit the floor. The second bouncer would be no such fool. He whipped out a metal baton across Buda's forearm. He attempted to swing a second time, but Buda caught his wrist midair and delivered a crushing blow to his midsection. The second bouncer went down, clutching his broken ribs and gasping for air.

The two downed bouncers brought out more, and before Buda knew it, he was in the middle of an all-out brawl. For every one punch he threw, he was hit with three more, but he kept swinging. The fight carried across the floor and spilled out into the bakery area. Buda was giving as good as he got, but the tide turned when a pair of massive hands wrapped around the back of his neck. Buda clawed futilely at the hands as he was lifted off his feet. He was as strong as an ox, but whoever had him had superhuman strength.

"I knew your ass was going to be trouble when you walked in here." Frankenstein shook him like a rag doll.

"I'm gonna show you trouble if you don't turn me loose," Buda threatened.

Christian came strolling out of the back, a triumphant grin plastered across his face. "I tried to warn you, didn't I?" he said, taunting the restrained Buda.

"Shut your mouth, sissy, before I come over there and fuck you in the ass!" Buda spat.

"Quiet." Frankenstein gave Buda another shake. "Christian, you want me to break this clown's neck?"

Christian thought on it for a long moment. "No, murders are too expensive to clean up these days. Make sure he leaves my establishment, but don't bother using the door."

"You got it." Frankenstein began dragging Buda away.

"Fuck you doing?" Buda struggled against Frankenstein.

"Giving you your walking papers," he told Buda before hurling him through the bakery window.

Buda skidded across the hard concrete like a stone skipping over a calm lake. The world spun as he rolled across the ground. Stars danced before his eyes when his back slammed into a car idling at the curb. When his vision cleared, he saw NYPD stenciled along the side of the car, and the scowling face of a policeman glaring down at him from the passenger window.

PART

DAMAGE CONTROL

CHAPTER TWENTY-SEVEN

One of the hardest things Knowledge ever had to do was pull himself away from the crook of Asia's arm that morning. After he'd gorged on her pussy, she'd fucked him damn near into a coma. After their round of lovemaking, Asia heated his food up, fed it to him, and then fucked him again. This went on until the first rays of sun finally peeked through the windows and both of them were too spent to do much other than lie there and listen to each other's breathing.

Knowledge propped himself up onto his elbow and watched Asia as she slept. His eyes were fixed on the slow rise and fall of her chest, and his ears honed in on her soft snoring. They were little things to most, but to him they were anchors to his sanity. Having a good woman like Asia by his side was a constant reminder to him that there was more to life than the way he was living it.

On the nightstand, his digital watch chirped, letting him know it was time to start his day. Gently, he slid out of the bed. Asia stirred, but didn't wake. On the balls of his feet he crept to the bathroom and stealthily closed the door. After taking a quick shower, he came out into the bedroom and started getting dressed.

"Where are you going?" Asia asked, startling him as he slipped one leg into a pair of crisp blue jeans.

"I gotta go out and handle some business right quick. Go back to sleep," Knowledge told her.

Asia pushed herself up into a sitting position. "Damn, it seems like you just got here, and now you're rushing off already?" she pouted. "I was hoping we could at least do breakfast before you get to running the streets."

Knowledge popped a fresh white T-shirt from a new pack and slipped it over his head. "I'll only be gone a couple of hours, and I promise when I get back, I'll take you out on a proper date."

"A *proper* date." Asia snorted. "I can't think of the last time we went on one of those. Lately it seems like all you have time to do is fuck me silly and then fall asleep while we're watching TV, or run right back out onto the streets. I'm starting to feel more like your jump-off than your girl."

Knowledge paused his dressing and turned his attention to Asia, who was glaring at him with a sour look on her face. He crawled across the bed and planted a reassuring kiss on her lips. "Ma, I know shit been crazy lately, and I'm sorry if you feel like I'm neglecting you. I promise, once we get this shit sorted out, I'm gonna put in some quality time with you."

"I hear you talking. . . ." Asia rolled her eyes.

"Real shit, baby." He eased off the bed and walked back to the dresser to retrieve his jewelry and car keys. "You gonna be here when I get back?"

"I might be, or maybe I'll decide I'm tired of you always running and find me a square nigga," Asia teased him.

"Don't get fucked up," he warned her.

"Shut up and go do what you gotta do so you can come back and knock me off again." She tossed a pillow at him.

"Yeah, Imma beat that shit up proper later on." Knowledge tucked his gun into his waistband and headed for the door.

"Knowledge," Asia called after him. "Be careful out there."

"I got you, baby. No unnecessary chances," he promised, and headed out.

It was still a while before Knowledge was to meet up with Big Stone, but he wanted to get an early start so he could handle some other business, namely getting a lead on Pana's killers. He knew it would only be a matter of time before the streets started talking and his network of spies started relaying information. There were different accounts, ranging from the plausible to the outrageous. One old wine head who claimed to have seen the whole thing said that a demon with teeth that sparkled like glass had come up through a hole in the ground from the explosion and dragged Pana back to hell with him.

Knowledge disregarded the tall tales and focused on the facts. Though there were conflicting versions of what had happened, the common factor was that there had been several men, all wearing masks, all striking with military precision. He reached out to several brokers he knew in and around the city, but none of them claimed to have brokered the contract. Of course, they could've been lying, but he doubted it. For the most part, they were all familiar enough with Knowledge to know that getting caught lying to him could prove to be a fatal mistake.

This brought his thoughts back to Eddie. No one had seen much of him in the last twenty-four hours, which was strange. Men like Eddie were creatures of habit who generally didn't venture too far from their comfort zone, but there was no sign of him anywhere in Washington Heights. His sudden disappearance told Knowledge that it was either one of two reasons: hearing what happened to Pana spooked him and he'd gotten out of Dodge for fear of his life, or he was lying low until he saw what kind of fallout there would be behind the assassination. Big Stone didn't seem totally convinced that Eddie had a hand in it, but Knowledge wasn't ready to write him off as a suspect just yet.

Trying to unravel the mystery, with minimal results, was stressing out Knowledge to the point where he felt like his head was going to explode. He needed something to sooth his nerves before going to deal with Big Stone, and he knew just the place to get it.

Knowledge pushed the Acura up Central Park West, heading north to Harlem. Along the way he caught a red light on Ninety-Sixth Street. As he sat there, waiting for it to turn green, he drummed his fingers on the steering wheel and looked around casually at the people who were out and about. A man chatting on his cell phone crossed the street directly in front of his car, and he caught Knowledge's attention. He was tall and well built, with long dreadlocks that hung down his back. Through the partially open window Knowledge could hear him barking something in what sounded like French. Knowledge wasn't sure why, but something about the stranger put him on edge. From the big chain around his neck to his sagging jeans, he looked totally out of place in the predominantly white neighborhood. The stranger must've felt Knowledge staring at him, because he turned to meet his gaze. There was a brief exchange of eye contact before the stranger drew back his lips into a threatening sneer, and when he did, the morning sun cast a glare off his diamond-plated teeth, making them sparkle like *glass*.

Behind him a car horn blared, drawing Knowledge's attention to the traffic light, which was now green. Sparing one last glance at the dread, Knowledge pulled through the intersection and continued on his way.

Knowledge couldn't say he was surprised to see Power already up and outside. He had been an early riser for as long as they had known each other. The barbershop wouldn't be open for a few hours yet, so Power was putting in work at his second job as the weed man.

Idling at the cub, a few car lengths from where Knowledge had pulled up, a shiny black BMW X5 idled. From the dealer plate in the back window he knew the car had to be new. He sat and watched for a few seconds as Power exchanged pleasant words with a pregnant girl who looked slightly familiar. He waited until she had conducted her business and gotten back into the X5 before getting out of the Acura and approaching Power.

"Peace, God." Power stood to greet his friend.

"Peace." Knowledge gave him dap. "Ain't that what's-her-face from the St. Nick projects?" He looked at the BMW as it pulled away from the curb.

"Yeah, that was Teisha, but she don't live in the projects no more. I hear she's in the Bronx or some shit now. Man, I used to wanna fuck her bad as hell in high school, but she wouldn't give me the time of day," Power said, reflecting on his days as a pussy-hungry teen.

"Be glad you didn't. That broad is so fertile, if you sneeze on her, she might get pregnant." Knowledge chuckled. He'd never smashed her personally, but he knew a few cats who had, and they all swore her pussy was lined with gold. I guess that explained why she was twenty-five with three kids by three different niggas and, from the looks of things, one more on the way. "What you doing out here, making sales to pregnant women?"

Power shot his friend a look. "C'mon, God. You know I ain't a complete savage. She needed the bud for a get-together she's having."

"Bullshit—she's probably selling it," Knowledge said.

"Considering she bought a half pound, I wouldn't doubt it. But so long as she's not stepping on my toes, I don't care."

"A half pound?" Knowledge asked in surprise. "Now where does a broke-ass hood rat who ain't never worked a day in her life suddenly come up with the cash to buy a half pound of weed and a new BMW?" His wheels started spinning.

"I wondered the same thing," Power admitted. "You know her man been running around for the last few weeks on some bossed-up shit. You remember the skinny dude TJ, right?"

"The guy she was messing with in high school?" Knowledge searched his mental Rolodex to put a face to the name.

"Yeah, that's him. I was at the spot a few nights ago when he pulled up, flossing in the new Benz truck. My mans and them was plotting on sticking him up, but he was rolling with some new faces, some real hard-looking cats. Nobody was really sure what time it was with them, so they let TJ breathe. But if I were him, I'd slow down with all that fronting."

Knowledge processed what Power was telling him. From what he recalled, TJ had always been one of those dudes who danced on the fringes of the game but had never gone all in. Knowledge had heard chatter over the last few months that TJ had been trying to step his game up, but he had never been big enough to really be on Knowledge's radar. Now all of a sudden he was throwing bread around and flossing new whips.

"Everything good?" Power asked as if he were able read his friend's face.

"Nothing, just trying to sort some shit out," Knowledge told him. More pieces of the puzzle were being dumped onto the table, but he still wasn't certain *how,* or even *if,* they fit. "So, you cutting today or you thinking about becoming a full-time hustler again?" Knowledge said, changing the subject.

"I never stopped being a full-time hustler; I just switched the product. On some G shit, I'm good with cutting hair. Selling this weed helps me make ends meet and have a little extra to play with, but ain't no way I'm throwing my hat back into the arena with y'all cats unless it's for a damn good reason."

"I guess prison does reform some people."

"Not everybody—just the smart ones. See, you ain't never been locked down for no long period of time, so you don't know how that shit is. Bulls barking at you twenty-four-seven and dictating when you eat, sleep, and shit like you're some damn dog." He shook his head as some of the memories came flooding back. "Living in captivity is enough to make you lose your shit. The most valuable lesson I learned in prison was that it ain't for me. Some cats go back and forth like a revolving door, but bet I won't be one of them. When I say they'd have to lay me in the streets before I ever allowed myself to be caged again, I mean it!"

"But fuck all that jail talk. I'm trying to get blazed. What you got for me?" Knowledge inquired.

Power's face lit up. Weed and cutting hair were his passions. "I got the usual suspects, Haze, Dro, and a real mellow strain of chocolate. But if you really wanna go to the moon, I got some new shit in from Portland that's supposed to be hitting. I call it the Electric Boogie."

Knowledge was curious. "Why you call it that?"

"Because after you hit that shit, you'll be so high that you might find yourself break-dancing!" He burst out laughing.

"If that's the case, give me an eighth of that shit!" Knowledge began fishing around in his pocket, but Power placed a hand on his wrist.

"Don't insult me like that. Your money ain't no good here. Go see my man in the building and tell him I set to set you out."

Knowledge walked into the building and, less than thirty seconds later, was coming back out, a huge smile on his face. "This shit must be superpotent, because you can smell it through the bags."

"C'mon, sun. You know I don't deal in no bullshit," Power said proudly.

"You trying to blaze one right quick before I dip off?" Knowledge offered.

"Nah, I'm gonna pass on that. I gotta work at the shop today, and I don't like cutting heads when I'm high. Besides, my PO is gonna piss test me this week when I go check in."

"How the fuck do you know that? I thought the urine tests were always random?"

"Not when you're knocking the lining out of your parole officer's pussy." Power smiled slyly.

Knowledge gave his friend dap. "I'm glad to know some things haven't changed."

"Oh shit," Power blurted out. "I meant to ask you: What you make of that fire last night?"

"What fire?" Knowledge asked.

"Pops Brown's bar burned down last night," Power told him.

Knowledge was stunned. Pops Brown's place had been around for longer than Knowledge could remember. It had started out as an arcade and candy store where all the kids had gone to play video games, but about ten years ago Pops had gotten a liquor license and turned it into a bar. It became a wateringhole for gangsters throughout the city and was considered neutral territory. More important, it was the same place he had seen Pearl the night before.

"What happened?" Knowledge pressed.

"There're a few different versions of the story. The *official* word is that it was some kind of electrical fire."

"What are the streets saying?"

"The streets are saying Pops Brown pissed the wrong people off, and they expressed their displeasure with a Molotov cocktail. Most of the people inside made it out, but not all of them," Power said sadly.

"And Pops? He good?"

"He's alive, but in bad shape at Harlem Hospital. They say he'll make it, but losing that place will likely take him out of the game," Power said, stating the obvious. Pops had a few operations going on in the streets, but the bar and the things that went on there were his bread and butter.

All Knowledge could do was shake his head as he processed everything he'd learned in the last twenty-four hours. First Pana gets knocked off, and then someone firebombs Pops Brown into retirement. Had these two events occurred individually, they could've been shrugged off as rotten luck, but their happening back to back meant something bigger. There was a power move being made. "I need to go see Big Stone. I'll get with you later, P." He gave his friend dap and then started for his car.

"You watch your ass out here, Knowledge!" Power called after him. "I got a bad feeling that it's cats out here who ain't moving correct, and I'd hate to have to lay somebody for coming at my brother," Power said seriously.

Knowledge stopped, raising an eyebrow. "I thought you said you'd never throw your hat back into the arena?"

"I said it'd have to be for a *good reason*, and somebody trying to hurt you justifies breaking that oath," Power said seriously.

This brought a smile to Knowledge's lips. "Glad to know there're still a few of my day-one niggas who're still down for me."

"No question, God. From the cradle to the grave, baby. We all we got."

CHAPTER TWENTY-EIGHT

When Pearl awoke the next day, she was sore as hell. It felt like somebody had whipped her ass in her sleep. She guessed that was what happened when you tried to play Spider-Woman. The night before had proven to be both eventful and informative.

She reached for her phone and saw she had several missed calls, most of them from Marisa. Pearl started to dial her back, but then she remembered she wasn't fucking with her like that again just yet. She was mad at Marisa for disappearing on her, and would surely give her the cold shoulder for a while before making up. Sheila, on the other hand, she wasn't sure if she could ever be friends with again. None of them were angels—they had all engaged in some grimy shit—but Sheila walking them into a den of prostitutes and not letting them know ahead of time was low. There were a million things that could've gone wrong in that situation, and Pearl shuddered to think what would've happened had she had to call on one of her father's people to get her out of a jam. Somebody would've likely gotten killed, and Big Stone would've hung his foot off in all three of their asses for being fast.

Though she was angry with Sheila, she was also concerned. Pearl knew Sheila's family wasn't as well-to-do as hers or Marisa's, so she always had to have a side hustle to keep up, but selling pussy? At one point or another, they had all slept with someone in exchange for gifts, but that was the game. Outright slapping a price tag on her ass was something Pearl would never do. For Sheila to go that far, something had to have been going on at home that she hadn't told them about. Maybe when Pearl calmed down, she would investigate, but right then she didn't give a fuck.

Pushing thoughts of other people's problems from her mind, Pearl focused on her own . . . namely, the homeless-looking condition she was in. She was still filthy from the night before and felt like she had slept in the streets. She hopped into the shower and let the scalding-hot water run over her body. As she shampooed the grass out of her hair, her thoughts went back to the previous night's event. She had to admit, before Zonnie had come at her with bullshit, Pearl had been having a good time. Doodles and his people partied like bosses, which is the only way Pearl knew how to do it. She couldn't have seen herself getting with any of them, except maybe Franz, but now that she knew how his team got down, that was off the table. At least now she knew why he had looked at her as if she was shit on a shoe when she tried to push up.

Her thoughts then shifted to the drink she'd shared with the man whose mother had named him Diamonds. Out-of-town guys usually weren't Pearl's speed, especially country niggas, but there was just something about Diamonds that made her itch in places she'd be ashamed to scratch . . . at least in public. He had a presence about him that made Pearl feel like the walls were closing in on her. From the moment she'd looked into his inky-black eyes, she'd known he was dangerous, and that was part of what attracted her to him. It was true what they said: little girls grew up and looked for men who reminded them of their fathers. Diamonds definitely embodied that. Pearl had never been in love, so she had no clue what it felt like, but she imagined it to resemble the growing tightness she felt in her chest when visions of Diamonds danced in her head.

Until she felt the wave of pleasure roll up through her thighs, Pearl hadn't even realized she had been touching herself. She blushed, thinking how a man who had never laid hands on her could take her mind so far into the gutter. Pearl felt ashamed, but not so ashamed that she wasn't going to finish herself off before she got out of the shower.

Feeling fresh, and relieved, Pearl strolled into her bedroom to dress for the day. She threw on a pair of fitted blue jeans, a cute top, and her vintage white Reebok 54-11s. Thankfully she didn't have school, so she could spend her day doing more important things, like shopping. She scooped up her phone and saw that she had had another missed call while she'd been in the shower. This one was from an unknown number. Before she had time to even ponder it, the phone rang in her hand. Again the call was from an unknown number. Normally Pearl would've let it go to voice mail, but her curiosity got the best of her so she answered it.

"So what, you ducking my calls now?" Devonte's voice boomed over the phone before she could even say hello.

Pearl pulled the phone away from her ear and looked at it to make sure she wasn't bugging, before going back to the call. "Nigga, you need to slow your fucking roll. Ain't nobody gotta be ducking you. I didn't know you called. I'm just waking up. And why are you calling me from a blocked number?"

"Because you weren't answering when I called you from my cell. Now, don't change the subject. Where you been?"

"I told you—I'm just waking up," Pearl repeated.

"Must've been a rough night for you, huh?" he asked accusingly.

"It was . . . interesting enough." Pearl smiled, thinking of Diamonds.

"I'll bet it was, since you was in the back of Pops's bar, selling pussy with the rest of them bitches!" Devonte raged. "Don't try to deny it either. One of my boys was in there, and he told me that you and your girls were getting busy with them nasty-ass Jamaican niggas! How you gonna do me like that, Pearl?" he said, his voice trembling.

"Devonte, on my mama, don't ever disrespect me by insinuating some I'd stoop to doing some ho shit. You know my name and my fucking pedigree, so don't play yourself!" she spat. "Now, if you'd asked me instead of shooting off at the mouth like you somebody's daddy, I'd have told you that I was in the bar with some friends last night. I'd have also told you that once I realized what the fuck was going on, I got the hell out of there. Not that it's any of your fucking business," she added.

"I don't even know why Pops let you in there. Your ass isn't even old enough to drink!"

"I'm not old enough to be fucking a nigga seven years older than me either, but it don't stop you from sniffing around this pussy!" she shot back. "You know what? I don't even know why I'm on the phone, explaining this shit to you like you're my man, when you're really just a slide. As a matter of fact, you ain't even a slide. You're just some nigga I let get me off on them days when my dick reservoir is running low."

Devonte was silent for a long moment. For what seemed like a minute Pearl thought he might've hung up the phone until she heard his cracking voice come back on the line. "You're a heartless bitch, Pearl."

Was he crying?

"I tried to show you love," he continued, "but what I should've done was treated you like the low-life cunt I knew you were."

Pearl's eyes flashed rage. Had Devonte been standing in front of her, she would have laid hands on him, but she had to let her words do what her fists couldn't. "You listen to me, and you listen good, you half-ass fucking hustler." Her words dripped venom. "You a weak nigga, Devonte. More important, you're insignificant. You're so low on the totem pole that I could get you erased with a phone call and nobody would miss your hand-to-hand, crack-slinging ass. Your saving grace is that on this side, we only dispatch hitters for real threats and you ain't no threat. You're a side bitch who didn't know how to stay in his lane, so consider the road closed."

"So I'm supposed to let you go, just like that?" Devonte choked up.

"Nigga, whatever you do or don't do ain't my concern. I thought you was cool, but you turned out to be a real cornball. Lesson learned. Now lose my fucking number, clown!" She ended the call.

Pearl was in such a rage that she nearly threw her phone, until she remembered how much her father had paid for it. It would've been her second phone in two months, and he had made it clear she wouldn't be getting another one. Devonte had played himself, which he'd been doing a lot of lately. She could overlook the clinginess she'd started to notice in him, but disrespect was something she wouldn't tolerate from him or any other man. Part of her was sad she had to cut him from the team, because Devonte ate pussy better than any nigga she had ever laid with, but bomb head be damned, he couldn't stay in his lane so he was gone.

The smell of something tasty being cooked tickled her nose. Her stomach churned, reminding her that she hadn't eaten anything since dinner the previous evening. Sandra must've awoke from her drug-induced stupor and was getting busy in the kitchen. It was only right, seeing how her unofficial man was back from vacation and no doubt craving some home-cooked food. If Pearl knew Sandra the way she thought, Big Stone would be eating more than just bacon and eggs for the rest of the weekend. A well-fed and well-fucked man was a happy one, so Pearl decided to make her way downstairs to crack on her father for some mall money while he was in a good mood.

CHAPTER TWENTY-NINE

The smell of fried bacon filled the upstairs hallway of the house, causing Pearl's nose to twitch like Elizabeth Montgomery's in *Bewitched*. It was like the closer she got to the kitchen, the hungrier she became. Her mouth watered at the thought of tasting some of Sandra's homemade banana pancakes.

When she reached the bottom of the stairs, the first person she ran into was her brother Stoney. He had a shit-eating grin plastered across his face and a new gold chain hanging from around his neck.

"You see what Dad brought me back?" He brandished the round medallion hanging from the end of the chain.

"That's nice, little bro." She leaned in closer to inspect it and saw that it bore his initials. "You better make sure you don't let one of these jack boys snatch it from you out in these streets." She faked like she was going to grab the chain, but her little brother didn't even flinch.

"These muthafuckas ain't crazy enough to try me out here. They know who my daddy be," Stoney said confidently.

"Stuff like that sounds cool when they say it in the movies, but that ain't how the real world works. Daddy has a lot of respect in the streets, so it does provide us a veil of protection, but never fool yourself into thinking any man is untouchable. For as many people there are that love Daddy, there are probably twice as many who hate him and would happily get at one of us to get to him," she warned. "This is why I always be on your back about hanging with them thug-ass niggas Raheem and Domo."

Stoney rolled his eyes, not really wanting to hear Pearl's speech. "Why you always sweating me about my friends?"

"Because your friends are baby criminals," Pearl shot back. "Don't act like I don't know what time it is with them and that Blood shit they rep. They can do what they want, but if I ever find out either of them ever tried to recruit you into a gang, they're going to have a problem they don't want."

"Nah, I ain't with that gang shit, Pearl. Domo and Rah my boys, but that ain't my style," he said honestly.

"Better not be. Now, where's Daddy?"

"Last I checked, he was in the kitchen with Sandra."

"Good." She brushed past him. "If he brought your nappy-headed ass a chain, I can't wait to see what he's got for me."

As soon as Pearl walked into the kitchen, she could pick up on the fact that something was wrong. Sandra was floating around, finishing up breakfast, but instead of her usual smile, she wore a look of great worry on her face.

Big Stone sat at the breakfast table, hunched over a half-eaten plate of bacon and eggs. His thick brows were knitted and his face sour as he spoke with someone on his cell phone. To his right sat his shadow, Knowledge. He had his cell phone in his hand too, thumbs moving frantically, composing a text or an e-mail. When they made eye contact, Pearl flashed him a smile, but he went right back to his typing. Something was up, and she had a feeling it was about her. Suddenly she was tempted to slip back out the way she had come in.

As if reading her mind, Big Stone raised his finger, motioning for her to give him a second while he finished his phone call. "Okay, I'll get there as soon as I can," he said to whoever he was talking to. He listened for a few more seconds before ending the call. Placing the phone on the table, he turned his attention to Pearl.

"Hey, Daddy, how was your trip?" Pearl asked innocently.

"Stressful." Big Stone huffed. "Take a seat. I need to talk to you about something." He motioned to the empty chair opposite him.

Pearl sat in the chair with all the enthusiasm of a woman about to be interrogated by the police. "What's going on?"

"That's what I'm trying to figure out. I need to ask you something and I want an honest answer."

"Um . . . okay."

"Did you go out with your friends last night?" he asked.

Pearl's eyes immediately went to Knowledge, who just sat there, staring at her, waiting to hear her answer. She thought he had given her a chance the night before, but he must've ratted her out to her dad that morning. She didn't know why she was surprised. He was the guardian of the Stone family, but his loyalty was to Big Stone above all others.

"I . . . um . . ."

Sandra spoke up, to the surprise of both Pearl and Knowledge. "Pearl was home all night. We stayed up watching *The Ten Commandments*. I dozed off halfway through, but when I got up at about eleven thirty, she was in her bedroom, asleep."

It was a lie, and both Pearl and Knowledge knew it, but Pearl wasn't about to question why Sandra was saving her ass. "Yeah, I was tired so I crashed early," she continued the story. "Is something wrong?"

"There was an accident last night. A fire broke out at Pops's Bar on a Hundred and Forty-Fifth Street, and some people got hurt," Big Stone said with a heavy heart.

This came as a surprise to Pearl. Things had been fine when she'd been there, so it must've happened after she'd left. Her thoughts immediately went to Marisa and Sheila. Even before he said it, she knew what would come next.

"The reason I asked you about it is because two of your people were there, the Haitian girl Sheila and T's little girl Marisa," he informed her.

"Oh my God." She slapped her hand over her mouth. "Are they . . . ?"

"Calm down, honey. Marisa wasn't amongst the casualties," Big Stone told her. "I just got off the phone with Tito, and he told me that the girls were rushed to Harlem Hospital. Marisa is being treated for some minor injuries, smoke inhalation and a sprained ankle. She'll be fine."

"And Sheila?" Pearl asked, with hope in her heart. That hope died when Big Stone lowered his head.

"I'm sorry, honey."

Pearl felt like someone had just slapped the taste out of her mouth. She was pissed off at Sheila for what she did, but not to the point where she would wish something like this on her. Guilt gripped her heart as she thought about her fight with Sheila and the nasty words they'd exchanged before she'd left. If only she hadn't been so quick to abandon her friends, Sheila might still be alive. When she thought of how horribly she must've died—trapped, alone, and burned alive—it made Pearl feel ill.

"You okay?" Sandra asked, noticing the color drain from Pearl's face.

"Yeah." Pearl swallowed back the bile that was trying to escape her throat. "Could somebody give me a ride to the hospital?"

CHAPTER THIRTY

Domo awoke with a start and sat bolt upright. He couldn't remember what it was he had been dreaming about, but it had been troubling enough to startle him awake. It was funny, because he hadn't even recalled going to sleep.

After completing the job, Vita had dropped him and LA off in their hood. LA was still supercharged about what had happened and wanted to pop a few bottles in celebration of Domo catching his first homicide. Domo didn't think death was something that should be celebrated, but he agreed just to shut him up. He left LA in front of the liquor store and went home to change out of the no-name-brand shit Vita had given them to change into after the heist. He had only planned on being home for a few minutes at most, but at some point he had dozed off. When he woke up, it was the next day.

Swinging his long legs over the edge of his bed, he stretched his weary bones. He had been asleep for at least ten hours, but he was still tired. He plucked his phone from the floor and saw that he had 30 percent left on his battery and ten missed calls. The call log revealed that most of the calls had come from LA, Raheem, and his mother, but there was also a text from Vita. Curious, he opened the text and found only an address, date, and time. He guessed that was her way of requesting an audience with him, but he was still unsure how or if he would respond.

Rolling into that apartment with Vita was both the most terrifying and exciting thing he had ever experienced in his life. Domo had run up in spots before, but never for that big of a take and certainly never for a job that organized. Vita was meticulous in her planning and moved like a seasoned general in her execution. Domo had encountered some broads on the set who were down to let it go, but never one who had just the right balance of toughness and sex appeal to turn him more on than off.

Grabbing the charger wire hanging from the wall, Domo went to plug his phone in, but nothing happened. It was then that he remembered the reason he had taken LA up on his offer in the first place: their electricity had been shut off. Cursing under his breath, he shuffled into the kitchen and found a note pinned to the microwave.

> Hey, Domonique,
> Sorry about the electricity situation. Plan on handling it when
> I get in. I got two early hair appointments that should be able
> to cover what we owe. Can you throw out all the food that
> went bad? I'll restock the fridge when I get back. Left you
> some McDonald's in the microwave.
> Love,
> Mom

She must've come and gone while he was sleeping it off. Domo plucked the McDonald's from the microwave and then tossed the spoiled food from the refrigerator into the trash. The whole time he was reading her note, he could almost feel the shame in her words. For as long as he could remember, she had been the sole provider for their little family. Even when his brother was out hustling, it was still his mother who made sure they kept a roof over their heads. Domo knew that his mom busted her ass to make the best out of what little they had, and he wished she wouldn't get so down on herself when things didn't go right.

After chomping down the two double cheeseburgers his mom had left, Domo showered, got dressed, and prepared to hit the streets. He was going to grab some weed and a bottle of Hennessey. It was a little early to be sipping, but he was in good spirits. Before heading out, he peeled five hundred dollars off the money he had made with Vita and put it in his mother's stash spot, in the shoe box under her bed. He wanted to give her more, but it would be hard enough as it was to explain where he'd gotten the five hundred he'd left for her. He'd tell her he won it in a dice game. His mother frowned on him gambling, but it would be easier to get her to accept that rather than telling the truth: that he had earned it by helping to kill an apartment full of people.

As he was sitting on the couch, tying his shoe, he heard a familiar *Soooowooo* outside his living room window. He crept over, carefully peeling the curtain back, and saw Raheem standing on his stoop. Raheem usually didn't get out of bed before noon on weekends, so the fact that he was on his doorstep so early meant that he had either gotten into it with his stepdad again and gotten put out or had some neighborhood gossip that couldn't wait.

"Fuck is you doing out here so early?" Domo asked, bouncing down the steps of his building.

"Came to check my best friend and the hood's newest celebrity." Raheem beamed. He had a lit blunt pinched between his lips. He took a deep pull and then passed it to Domo.

"What you talking about, Rah?" Domo accepted the blunt.

"C'mon, Domo. How long we known each other? Ain't no

secrets between us, so you ain't gotta act like that. LA been telling everybody on the block how you held it down like a real gangster last night!" Raheem said proudly.

Domo choked on the smoke and damn near dropped the weed. "What? What did he say?"

Raheem snatched the blunt back. "Told me y'all hooked into a serious crew for a caper, and when shit went sour, you saved everybody's ass. He said when you backed out the hammer, all them niggas turned cold pussy and gave up their shit! Word to mine, y'all lucky I wasn't there, because nobody would've left out that bitch alive!" he boasted, shaping his fingers in the form of a gun.

Domo let out a small sigh of relief that LA had omitted the more sensitive parts of the story, but he was still angry. They had all agreed to keep what had gone down a secret, because of the harsh ramifications that could come of it. Murder was nothing to play with, and neither were Vita and her crew. The right words whispered into the wrong ears could land Domo in the morgue or in prison, and neither prospect appealed to him. Domo and LA were definitely going to have a conversation when he saw him.

"Yo, niggas been buzzing about that shit all night," Raheem continued, exhaling a cloud of smoke. "Talking about that they didn't know you had it in you. Shit, I told them muthafuckas my right-hand man Domo is quiet, but he about that life; they just don't know you like I do." He extended the blunt again.

"Right." Domo took a toke. His mind had gone back to the cryptic text he'd gotten from Vita in the middle of the night. Had LA's bragging gotten back to her and her people? For all he knew, the address she wanted him to come to might very well end up being his final resting place.

"Damn, you just hit a big score and instead of you being happy about it, you standing around, looking like somebody kicked your dog," Raheem observed. "If anything, I should be the one wearing the sour grill."

"How you figure?" Domo didn't understand what he was getting at.

"Man, me and you go back to free lunch, and you didn't even call me when somebody came along and offered you a chance to make some chips," Raheem complained.

"Rah, it wasn't even like that. This whole thing popped up on some random shit, and I went with it. I don't even know the people like that who set it up," Domo said honestly.

Raheem gave him a disbelieving look. "LA says they're making major moves over in New York and are looking for stand-up niggas to get money with."

"Man, you need to stop listening to LA's high ass. It was one job, Rah. We don't even know the people who set it up like that—at least, I don't. For all we know, they could just be blowing smoke," Domo said, downplaying it.

Raheem sucked his teeth. "Domo, this is me. How long we been sniffing around Stoney's people, trying to get plugged into a real crew, and now that the door is open, you ain't gonna pull ya man in with you? That's fucked up. I thought we were better than that."

"Rah—" Domo began, but Raheem cut him off.

"Blood, you know I pull my own weight, so I'm not coming at you for a handout. All I need is an introduction, and I can create my own opportunities from there."

Domo looked at his friend, wishing he could break it down to him in a way he could understand without incriminating himself. Raheem was looking at it as Domo not wanting to put him on, but he was actually trying to keep his friend from getting tied up in some shit he wasn't sure if either of them were truly prepared to handle. He hadn't even known Vita for twenty-four hours, but she had already shown him that she and her people were playing at a level that wasn't for the faint of heart. But he knew that Raheem wasn't going to let it go, and if Domo denied him, he'd just turn to LA and try to get plugged in.

"Okay," Domo relented. "I'll take you to New York with me tonight and introduce you."

"That's what I'm talking about, my nigga!" Raheem said happily.

"Look, I'm gonna let you know ahead of time: I don't know too much about these cats, but I do know that they don't fuck around. So when we roll up in there, you mind your manners and don't do nothing stupid. We'll be too far from home for a lifeline, though I doubt there'd be too much anyone could do if we end up on the wrong side of these people anyhow," Domo warned.

Raheem gave him a look. "C'mon, man. Stop treating me like I'm some square-ass nigga. I'm gonna go in there and let my gangster speak for itself."

"And that's exactly what I'm afraid of."

CHAPTER THIRTY-ONE

Knowledge, Big Stone, and the ladies climbed int the SUV and headed out. Normally Big Stone would've let Sandra take Pearl to the hospital to see her friend so he and Knowledge could handle street business, but since everyone who needed to be seen was in the same hospital, they could kill two birds with one stone.

The ride was an eerily quiet one, everyone lost in their own thoughts. Pearl was visibly shaken up by receiving the news about her friends, and Knowledge couldn't say he blamed her. He had lost his fair share of people over the years, but it never got easier, especially when they were that young. He knew from the look on Big Stone's face when he was on the phone with Tito that it tore his heart out to hear his friend weeping over almost losing his baby girl. No one had spoken to Sheila's parents yet, but he could only imagine what they were going through. No parent should have to bury their child. This made Knowledge glad that he didn't have kids, because he wasn't sure if his heart could take that kind of loss.

The parking situation was suspect, meaning they would have to drive around and look for a spot, which would eat into precious time that they didn't really have to spare that day. Big Stone suggested that they drop the women off while they looked for a parking spot, but

Sandra volunteered to do it. Pearl looked like she could use an extra few minutes to get her nerves together before going up to see her friend. Big Stone wasn't keen on the idea, but it would give him a few extra minutes to handle his other business before he joined them on their visit to Marisa and her family.

Knowledge led the way to the nurse's station, where they revealed that Lance "Pops" Brown was in a private room on the fifth floor, but only family was allowed in to see him. This came as a bit of surprise to Knowledge, considering he wasn't in intensive care or recovering from a major surgery. What were all the extra precautions about? A few well-spread bills and the nurses looked the other way while Cousin Knowledge and Uncle Stone went to check on their ailing relative.

Pops's room was at the end of the hall. The door was slightly ajar, and they could see that he wasn't alone. Knowledge gave a quick tap on the door before pushing it open and inviting himself in. Pops was propped up on a stack of pillows, signing some papers that were on his lap. At his bedside, overseeing the signatures, were two people: a tall white man wearing a suit, and a young black woman. Dark sunglasses and her long red wig obscured most of her face, and a long overcoat hugged her body, despite the warm weather. Something about her presence raised a red flag with Knowledge, but before he could ponder it further, Big Stone announced their presence.

Big Stone's voice filled the room. "Sorry, didn't mean to interrupt."

The pen dropped from Pops's hand like a hot coal when he noticed Big Stone standing in his room. "Oh . . . hey, Big Stone. Didn't hear you come in." He tried to muster a grin but then winced in pain.

"If this is a bad time, I can come back," Big Stone offered in a less-than-sincere tone.

"Nah, they were just leaving," Pops said, cutting his eyes at the man in the suit.

"Right." The man in the suit took the hint. He gathered the papers from Pops and stuffed them hastily into his briefcase. "Thank you again for your time, Mr. Brown. If there's anything else, someone from my office will give you a call." He gathered his things and hustled out the door.

The girl wasn't so quick to move. She lingered in the chair for a moment longer, regarding Knowledge and Big Stone from behind her sunglasses. She nodded as if she had just completed some assessment of them, before rising from the chair. "Nice doing business with you," she told Pops slyly before sauntering out the door.

"What was that all about?" Big Stone asked, his eyebrow raised.

"Nothing man, just wrapping up some business. C'mon in and have a seat." Pops motioned toward the chair the girl had just vacated.

"Nah, I'll stand. I don't plan on being here that long. I gotta go see somebody else who's up in here," Big Stone told him.

"So, is that what brings you this way?" Pops asked.

"Came to check on an old friend. I hear you ran into a bit of misfortune last night."

Pops snorted. "More like my whole world came crumbling down around my ears. That bar was the only thing I had left to hold on to."

"A real tragedy, and I was sorry to hear about it," Big Stone said sincerely. "How are you fixed for bread until you get back on your feet?"

"I got some moves in the works. They won't put me back where I was, but hopefully they'll pull me out of where I am," Pops said sadly.

"Well, you know if there's anything I can do to help, all you have to do is reach out," Big Stone told him.

"You know I ain't never been one to walk around, hat in hand," Pops said proudly.

"Cut that, Pops. What's a few dollars between friends? You just tell me what you need, and I'll make sure you get it," Big Stone assured him.

"You're a good man, Big Stone . . . a damn good man."

"That I am, but don't let it get out. Might fuck up my reputation." Big Stone chuckled.

"And the insurance money?" Knowledge plucked the chart from the foot of Pops's bed and gave it the once-over.

"Huh?" Pops was caught off guard by the question.

"They say it was an electrical fire that took your place down, so I'm guessing you'll be able to file an insurance claim on it, right?" Knowledge pressed.

"Right, right . . . the insurance will kick out something, but it probably won't match up against what I invested. Besides, it'll probably take them forever to pay it off."

"If that bullshit claim holds up," Knowledge challenged.

"What are you trying to say?" Pops asked defensively.

"I think you know what I'm trying to say." Knowledge touched the purple bruise on the side of Pops face, causing him to flinch. "Did you get that when you *narrowly escaped* that fire?" His voice dripped sarcasm.

Pops's eyes darted to Big Stone, pleading for him to interject, but he remained silent. Knowledge had already brought him up to speed on his suspicions, and he had agreed to let him handle it and watch it play out.

Knowledge snapped his fingers to draw Pops's attention back. "Why are you looking at him when I'm the one asking the questions?"

"Now, hold on, Knowledge. I got a lot of respect for you on account of Big Stone, but I don't think I appreciate how you're speaking to me." Pops puffed up.

"And I don't appreciate you trying to play us for some fucking chumps." Knowledge drew his gun and put it to Pops's head. "I'm not

the smartest man in the world, but I don't believe that fire at your place
was an accident, nor am I buying that you got all them lumps and
bruises during your great escape. Somebody worked you over, and I
want to know who it was and how it ties into what happened to Pana."

"Kid, you're crazy. I don't know shit about what happened, don't
know nothing about what happened to Pana except what everybody
else does: some young niggas killed him!" Pops babbled.

Knowledge cocked the hammer and pressed the barrel deeper
into Pops's temple. When he spoke, his voice was a low hiss. "According to everyone else, they were wearing masks, so how would
you know they were young niggas?"

Pops's mouth suddenly became as dry as a desert. He cut his eyes
back to Big Stone, again hoping to get some sympathy, but all he saw
in the face of the man he'd once called a friend was contempt. "Big
Stone, how far we go back, man? You gonna let your boy do me dirty
like this?"

"Only thing gonna be dirty is that wall when your brains hit it if
you don't cut the bullshit and come correct," Big Stone spat. "Now, I
was genuine when I said I would help you out, but not if you keep
pissing on my head and trying to tell me that it's raining. Somebody
has been making unauthorized moves on this chessboard, and I need
to know who it is. Tell us what really went down at your bar, Pops."

The old man remained silent.

"Fuck it. Shoot this chump and let's go," Big Stone ordered.

"Okay, okay, okay! Don't shoot! I'll talk!" Pops said frantically.

Big Stone waved Knowledge off and motioned for Pops to continue.

"Listen, Stone, you known me twenty-something years . . . ,"
Pops began. "I ain't never took a dime that didn't belong to me or
step on a toe that wasn't over my side of the line. I been around since
a time when the game had rules, before these disrespectful lil niggas

started stepping on the backs of old-timers like me to get where they gotta go."

"I'm well aware of your résumé, Pops. I need to know who torched your place and how they got to Pana," Big Stone told him.

Pops went on to tell him the short version of the young desperados who bragged about murdering the crime boss Pana, before whipping his ass and burning his bar to the ground. "They not only made me watch while they set fire to twenty years of my hard work, but they made me sign over what was left of it to them. Took my boy Rob hostage to make sure I went through with it."

Knowledge shook his head sadly at the end of the old man's tale. "I knew all this shit happening wasn't a coincidence. This is bad . . . real bad."

"Bad is an understatement," Pops added. "These fuckers are predators and don't too much care who they feed on. First Pana, then my spot. Hell, ain't no telling who they could go after next."

"Including us." Big Stone had said what everyone in the room was thinking. "We gotta get out ahead of this thing. Is there anything else you can tell us that might help, Pops? A name or anything?"

Pops thought on it. "As a matter of fact, yeah. The ring leader of the crew had a real girlie-sounding name. If I recall correctly, it was D . . . Dia . . ." Pops suddenly broke into a fit of coughing.

"You okay?" Big Stone asked nervously, watching the old man choke. He grabbed the pitcher of ice water from the nightstand and filled a plastic cup. When he tried to tip it to Pops's lips to get him to take a sip, the old man let out a hard cough followed by a spray of blood. "Jesus!" Big Stone jumped back. "Get some help!" he ordered Knowledge.

Knowledge came back a few seconds later with several nurses and a doctor in tow. He and Big Stone stood off to the side and watched as they tried to resuscitate the old man, but it was no use. He lay there, eyes staring vacantly into space, his tongue lolling out of his mouth. It was swollen and had turned a sickly shade of purple. It was the first time any of them had ever seen a man literally choke on his own words.

CHAPTER THIRTY-TWO

The ride around the block to search for parking was a quiet one. Pearl was lost in her own thoughts while Sandra kept her eyes peeled for an empty space. The young girl just couldn't wrap her mind around the idea that one of her best friends was gone and she felt partially to blame.

"You know this ain't on you," Sandra said as if she could read her mind.

"Huh?"

"What happened to that girl," she explained. "It's not your fault, even though I *know* y'all were there together."

"What gave me away?" Pearl asked.

"C'mon, Pearl. I might be old, but I ain't no fool. I got up early this morning to collect everyone's laundry to put in the wash, and I found your outfit stashed in the back of your closet. You know it was stupid of you to sneak out, knowing your father was coming home last night."

"I know, but I just wanted to have a little fun," Pearl told her.

"A little fun can lead to big trouble, as I'm sure you've figured out by what happened to your friends."

"If you knew, how come you didn't tell Daddy on me?" she asked curiously.

"Because he's got enough on him as it is without you adding to it with your foolishness. I spared your ass this time, but don't let it happen again. Are we clear?"

"Yes, ma'am," Pearl said sheepishly.

On the second loop of the block, the parking gods decided to be kind, and somebody vacated a spot across the street from the hospital. After parking, the two women strode inside the hospital. They stopped at the information desk to find out Marisa's room number before riding the elevator to the third floor. Pearl's legs felt like noodles as she moved down the white hallway. It was like walking the green mile, and she was going to the electric chair instead of to visit her friend.

Standing vigil outside the door was Knowledge. There was a troubled expression on his face, but he wiped it away when he spotted the two women coming in his direction. He gave a curt nod before stepping to the side and allowing them access. As Pearl passed him, she could feel his accusing eyes on her. Normally she would've made a smart remark about it, but it was neither the time nor the place.

Big Stone and Tito stood off near the bathroom, speaking amongst themselves. Marisa's father's normally youthful face now seemed aged and etched with worry. Pearl's dad gave his shoulder a reassuring squeeze, telling him everything would be okay. It was obvious Tito was hurting, but he put up a good front. Evelyn, on the other hand, was in bad shape.

Marisa's mother looked like a slightly older version of her daughter, except she had alabaster skin and her hair was dyed a deep shade of plum. She was a beautiful woman who was always immaculately dressed, her face perfectly beat, but that day she looked like a train wreck. Her clothes looked they had been slept in, while her eyes were red and weighed down with heavy bags. Pearl couldn't ever remember seeing Marisa's mom without her makeup and her hair done, so seeing this woman in front of her felt like looking at a stranger. She sat on the edge of the bed, stroking her daughter's hand lovingly.

Marisa's eyes lit up when she spotted Pearl, and she motioned that it was okay to approach. Pearl took timid steps to the bedside, eyes wandering over her injured friend. She lay with her head propped up, a gas mask covering her nose and mouth. From the streaks cutting through the soot on her cheeks, Pearl could tell that Evelyn wasn't the only one who had been crying that morning. She couldn't say that she blamed her. Marisa had no doubt gone through a tragic experience, and she was lucky to have survived. Seeing her best friend like that threatened to break Pearl down, but she held it together so as not to add to the sadness that was already filling the room to capacity.

"Hey," Pearl offered when she had finally found her voice.

"What's up, *chica*?" Marisa tried to push herself into a sitting position but broke into a fit of coughing.

"You have to take it easy. Remember what the doctor said about overexerting yourself," Evelyn gently pushed Marisa back down and fixed her pillows.

"I'm fine, Mom. Would you cut it out?" Marisa swatted at her hands.

"How you holding up, Miss Evelyn?" Pearl asked.

"As well as can be expected, mami. When I got that call in the wee hours of the morning, my heart literally stopped." Evelyn sighed. "That's every parent's nightmare, to hear a stranger's voice on the other end of the line telling you something has happened to your kid. I'm not letting this one out of my sight again until she leaves for college."

"Ma, I think you're overreacting," Marisa said, trying to downplay it.

"Overreacting?" Evelyn's neck snapped back. "Can you imagine my surprise when I found out that instead of being at a friend's house, watching movies, like she told me, my *teenage* daughter was in a bar full of *grown-ass men,* doing God knows what? You had no business being in that freaking *fiesta del gamberro* in the first place!"

Marisa sighed behind the oxygen mask. "It wasn't a thug party. I was there with some friends," she argued.

"What friends? Were you there too, Pearl?" Evenly turned her angry eyes on her.

Pearl looked to Marisa, not quite sure what she had or hadn't said.

"No, she wasn't there." Marisa saved her the trouble of having to answer. "I got other friends in school besides Pearl."

"See, that's the problem right there. You keep throwing the word *friend* around, and I don't think you have the slightest clue what it means. A real friend wouldn't have given underage girls alcohol in a place where just about anything could go down. Look, I get it. I'd be lying if I said me and my friends had never snuck a bottle into the house or had a few drinks at a house party, but you were way out of your depth by being in that place."

"C'mon, Mom. Stop acting like you know what time it is on the streets. This ain't the eighties," Marisa quipped.

"Same game, different players, baby girl," Evelyn shot back. "Don't act like we raised you with rose-colored glasses. Me and your dad have been through some shit that would've broken your pampered-ass back, and we did it all to make sure you would never need, want, or suffer. Now, you can keep letting this nice life we've provided you and your sister go to your head, or you can get it through that thick-ass skull of yours that it ain't nothing new under the sun. Everything you're trying to do, I've already done ten times over. Before I was a wife or a mother, I was a survivor!" she said heatedly.

"E, how about you and me go get some coffee and give the girls a few minutes?" Sandra walked up and placed a hand on Evelyn's shoulder.

Evelyn looked up at Sandra, and there was a silent exchange that bled away some of her anger. "We're gonna go to the store. Do you guys need anything?" she asked sweetly, as if she hadn't just been about to go postal.

"I'm good. Thanks," Pearl said.

Marisa simply folded her arms.

Sandra and Evelyn headed over to Tito and Big Stone, where they exchanged a few words before the four of them left the room together to give the girls some privacy. Knowledge, of course, stayed at his post outside the door. With all the adults finally gone, the two teenage girls were able to speak freely.

"How are you feeling?" Pearl sat at the foot of the bed.

"To be honest with you, I'm fucked up," Marisa said, removing the mask. She inhaled and exhaled slowly as if she were testing the recycled air of the hospital. "My whole body is sore, and my lungs feel like I've been smoking cigarettes the last five years. It's gonna take me a second to recover, and I'll probably be grounded until menopause, but at least I'm still here. That shit with Sheila . . ." She choked up.

"What the hell happened?" Pearl asked the million-dollar question.

"Honestly? I'm still not entirely sure." Marisa placed the mask back over her face and sucked in some much needed air before continuing. "One minute I'm in the bathroom with Doodles eating my pussy like it was the last supper, and the next all hell is breaking loose. When we came out of the bathroom, the alarms were blaring and the whole bar was filling up with smoke. The first thing I did was try to go back to the VIP to check for you and Sheila. Shit was crazy with all those people trying to bum-rush their way out. I ended up coming

across that nigga Boom, and he told me y'all were already outside. It
wasn't until I got out there and couldn't find either of you that I realized he was full of shit. By then the roof had caved in, and it was
over for whoever had been trapped inside." Tears welled up in her
eyes.

Pearl hadn't realized that she was crying too until a tear splashed
the back of her hand. "Do they know how it happened? How she
got trapped?" She didn't know why she had asked or why it even
mattered, other than there being part of her that needed to piece
together the last moments of her friend's life.

"When I was riding in the back of the ambulance, I heard the
paramedics talking about two guys and a girl who had gotten trapped
in a supply closet when the place went up." Marisa wept.

Pearl thought of the two guys who had been trying to slide off
with Sheila before she had intervened. "Damn" was all she could
manage to say. She imagined that Sheila had died a horrible death in
that supply closet. She just hoped it had been quick.

Marisa read Pearl's face. "Our girl never had a chance."

Raised voices in the hall drew both of the girl's attention to the
room door. Knowledge was outside, explaining to someone why he
couldn't allow them into the room. Pearl craned her neck to see who
it was, and spotted Sheila's parents. A lump jumped into her throat,
as she had been hoping to avoid them, at least until the loss wasn't so
fresh in everyone's hearts. She looked to Marisa for direction as to
what to do next, but her friend just shrugged. Pearl told Knowledge
it was okay, and he reluctantly let them pass him and go into the room.

Sheila's parents, Mr. and Mrs. Dubois, came in dressed every bit
of the conservative parents they were, in shades of brown and black.
Looking through their wardrobes, you'd have thought vibrant colors
were a sin. Mrs. Dubois continued on to Marisa's beside, a tattered
brown leather-covered bible tucked to her chest. Mr. Dubois hovered

near the door, glaring over the rim of his glasses at Pearl and Marisa like he'd caught them staggering out of a whorehouse.

"How are you girls?" Mrs. Dubois asked in a thick accent, managing to muster what passed for a smile under the circumstances.

"Fine. How are you, Mrs. Dubois?" Pearl stood and gave her a hug.

Mrs. Dubois pulled her in tight and inhaled deeply as if she were looking for traces of her daughter in those closest to her. "I've been better, but the good news is that it can't get any worse."

"We are truly sorry for your loss," Pearl said sincerely. It took everything she had to keep from crying.

"Mesi." Mrs. Dubois clasped Pearl's hands between hers. "May neither of your parents ever know the grief that fills our home on this day."

The statement stung Pearl and stirred her earlier guilt. "My condolences to you, too, Mr. Dubois." She changed her focus so she wouldn't have to look into Mrs. Dubois's heartbroken eyes any longer.

"I appreciate your condolences, but I'd rather one of you told me who had my daughter in that bar." Mr. Dubois stepped forward. His broken eyes swept back and forth between Marisa and Pearl.

"Mr. Dubois—" Pearl began, but was cut off.

"Please, before you refer to this *street code* of see no evil, hear no evil and tell me you don't know what happened to my daughter, even though there is no doubt in my mind that the three of you were together last night, I would like you to consider this: not only did we lose our child, but a university lost a future scholar. Did Sheila ever share her good news with you?"

"Good news?" Pearl was out of the loop.

Mr. Dubois looked at Mrs. Dubois, who gave him the approving nod that it was okay to continue. "Sheila got into Rutgers University," he confessed, to both Pearl's and Marisa's surprise. "It was only a partial scholarship, so everybody in the family had started taking on extra work so that we could make up the difference by the time she had to leave for New Jersey at the end of the school year."

Pearl couldn't hide the shock on her face. She knew that Sheila wasn't a dummy—all the girls in the crew got good grades—but Rutgers? All Sheila had ever talked about was partying, boys, and money. Whenever the subject of college had come up, Sheila had always laughed it off as if college was a big waste of time. Pearl guessed she kept it to herself so as not to be ribbed by the cool kids about wanting to make something of herself. Now it made sense why Sheila was willing to go as far as she had for extra money. This made Pearl feel even worse for the way she had judged her.

"I had no idea," Pearl said just above a whisper.

"She was very secretive about it," Mrs. Dubois spoke up softly. "We tried to tell Sheila that it was an accomplishment she should be proud of, but she was worried about people making fun of her for it. These are sad times we live in when children are ridiculed for wanting to better themselves," she said. "If there's anything at all either of you can offer to help us understand what really happened, we would deeply appreciate it."

Pearl looked to Marisa, who was trying hard to maintain her poker face, but she could tell she was moments from breaking down. Pearl was about to tell Sheila's parents everything she knew about the party and the guys when Marisa leaned forward and spoke.

"We snuck in on our own. Nobody took us there," she lied.

Mr. Dubois looked like he didn't buy it, but he left the subject alone. "Come. There's nothing else to be learned here." He helped his wife to her feet. "Ladies, if you'll excuse us, we have to go home and tell Sheila's siblings that their sister is dead."

Mrs. Dubois allowed her husband to lead her toward the door.

Her shoulders were hunched like she was carrying the weight of the world on her shoulders. Before leaving, she looked back at the girls and mustered a weak smile. "If nothing else, I'm glad to know that my daughter had good friends like you in her life, no matter how short it was."

"This is so fucked up." Marisa flopped onto her pillows and released a heavy sigh after the Duboises had gone.

"Tell me about it. I feel horrible about lying to them. Maybe we should've told Sheila's parents what really went down," Pearl suggested.

"Maybe, but what good what it have done? Sheila would still be dead, and we'd be branded snitches if it ever got out that we told on Doodles and his crew. Nah, telling them would've created more problems and still no resolution."

Marisa had a point, but it still didn't make Pearl feel any better about it.

Just then the nurse came into the room, holding a clipboard. "I need to check on the patient,. You're going to have to step out for a few minutes," she told Pearl.

"It's cool. I should get going anyway." Pearl leaned in and hugged her friend. "You make sure you call me when they discharge you."

"Pearl," Marisa called after her as she headed for the door. "What happened last night that made you just cut out like that without saying anything? Did something go down?"

Pearl considered telling her what had happened with Zonnie and the fight she and Sheila had had outside, but what would be the point? "Nah, just trying to get home before my dad did. That's all."

By the time Pearl staggered out of Marisa's hospital room, she felt dizzy. It was like the weight of everything that had happened in the last twenty-four hours was finally settling in on. No matter how much she tried to block them out she kept seeing Mrs. Dubois's pain-filled eyes pleading with them or the truth and the lie she had allowed Marisa to feed them. She felt ill and need to brace herself against the wall to keep from falling.

"You good?" Knowledge reached to help steady her, but Pearl pulled away.

"I'm fine," Pearl pushed off the wall and kept moving. She went from staggering, to hurried steps, and finally jogged down the hall toward the stairs.

"Wait! Where are you going?"

Pearl heard Knowledge calling after her, but didn't stop to reply. Honestly, she had no clue where she was going. She just knew she had to get out of that place.

CHAPTER THIRTY-THREE

The meeting with Eddie had been confirmed and was set to take place at a restaurant in Washington Heights, Eddie's home turf. This was where he felt most comfortable, which was why Diamonds changed the location at the last minute. What he had said to Vita about not being worried about Eddie trying anything was true, but he also wasn't foolish enough to tempt fate. Having them meet somewhere both public and neutral would keep everyone honest.

It was really a twofold precaution. Diamonds wanted to assure that there were no surprises in store for him, but more important, he was testing his sponsor's sincerity about backing their plans for New York. He had fully expected Eddie to balk at the unexpected change and possibly insist that they stick to the original plan, so when Eddie agreed with minimal fuss, it raised a red flag. Diamonds had yet to meet Eddie personally, but he knew his type. Men in positions of power didn't defer to those who they saw as beneath them, and the fact that he had done so meant that there was more to this meeting than Diamonds was being told.

When Diamonds arrived at the Columbus Circle subway station, he wasn't surprised to see Eddie and Blanco already there, waiting. What did throw him was the fact that TJ was also there. He and TJ were supposed to hook up and attend the meeting together, but he hadn't been able to get him on the phone since the initial call to set everything up. For a minute Diamonds had thought his cousin was going to leave him hanging, but there he was, snickering and grinning all in Eddie's face. Diamonds made a mental note to himself about how cozy TJ and Eddie seemed to be as of late.

"*Bonjou,* gentlemen," Diamonds greeted them.

"Sup, cuz?" TJ embraced him.

"You tell me. I've been trying to get you on the phone but kept getting your voice mail," Diamonds told him.

"My fault. My phone is dead and Teisha has had me running around all day with this baby shower shit and I haven't had a chance to charge it," TJ said smoothly.

"Is that right?" Diamonds glanced at the cell phone clamped to TJ's belt. "Don't worry about it, cousin. Let's go ahead and get this meeting started."

"Right," TJ said, seeming relieved that Diamonds had let the subject of his phone go. "Eddie," he called to the older Hispanic man, who had been eyeing the exchange, "this is my cousin Diamonds. Diamonds, this is Eddie."

"So, this is the guy who levels an entire city block to take the life of one man?" Eddie regarded Diamonds.

Diamonds shrugged as if it were nothing. "Sometimes making a mess is the best way to really drive your point home. Before we get to discussing sensitive topics, might I suggest we do it away from prying ears?"

A few minutes later they were all standing on the platform of the uptown-bound A train. It was crowded with people hustling back and forth, and it seemed like there was a train pulling in and out of the station every few minutes, creating quite a bit of noise.

"Tell me why you wanted to have this meeting in a subway station again? We can barely hear ourselves over the noise!" Eddie shouted over the squealing breaks of a train that had just pulled in.

"That's the exact reason I picked this place. If we can't hear ourselves, neither can anyone else," Diamonds explained.

"What, did you think we'd come to this meeting wearing wires?" Blanco asked defensively.

"I'd never disrespect a man of Eddie's caliber by suggesting something like that. My words are not for everyone's ears," Diamonds told him.

"Sounds like bullshit to me!" Blanco spat.

"And I can respect your opinion, but seeing how you ain't the head nigga in charge, it holds no weight in this dialogue," Diamonds capped.

Blanco took a menacing step toward Diamonds, but Eddie waved him off. "Everybody, relax. We're all friends here, aren't we?"

"That's exactly what I'm trying to figure out. My cousin said you wanted to meet me, so here I am," Diamonds said, getting right to it.

"First and foremost I want to commend you on that piece of work you handled for us yesterday . . . ," Eddie began. "I have to admit, when TJ came to me and said you could succeed where others had failed, I was skeptical. Pana had a small army behind him, and you were but a handful."

"Sometimes a handful is all it takes, especially when everybody is dedicated to a common goal," Diamonds said proudly.

"And what is your *goal* here, in New York?" Eddie asked him.

"It's like we told you from the beginning: all we're looking for is to carve out a little niche to call our own. With your blessing of course," TJ answered, which got him a sharp look from Diamonds.

"My *blessing,* huh?" Eddie repeated TJ's words, but studied Diamonds's face, which was unreadable. "Well, my friends, a nice *little* niche you shall have. As per our agreement, all Pana's territories are now yours. Of course, it'll be up to you and your people to stomp out any wayward roaches you might've missed during your initial extermination. There are still some who are loyal to Pana's cause."

"And they will stand with him again soon enough," Diamonds assured him.

"After seeing your body of work so far, there's no doubt in my mind about that," Eddie agreed. "Now that we've got the official business out of the way, let's get into something *unofficial*. I hear you and Pops Brown had a conversation that went south."

Diamonds cut his eyes at TJ, who lowered his gaze. "I don't know if I'd call it that. More like a tough negotiation, but in the end we were able to come to terms we both deemed fair."

"I guess that all depends on which end of the negotiations you're on, considering Pops's bar is now a pile of sticks and ash on the corner of a Hundred and Forty-Fifth Street," Eddie said.

"An unfortunate accident, but from the rubble of something new will sprout something bigger and better. You have my word on it," Diamonds promised.

"That old bar was an eyesore, but it don't change the fact that nobody authorized you to move on it. That wasn't part of our initial agreement," Eddie told him.

Diamonds's nose scrunched. "Eddie, maybe there was a miscommunication somewhere. Our initial agreement was just that: *initial*. You and your uncle Michael looked the other way when we greased Pana, and now we have free rein to flood his territory with coke so long as we buy from you. With all due respect, I don't see how what we do outside of that arrangement is any of your business."

"It becomes *my* business when you go and do something that can bring heat down on *my* head!" Eddie shot back.

"Eddie, it isn't as bad as it seems. This is an easy fix," TJ interjected.

"An easy fix?" Eddie's angry eyes turned to TJ. "How is potentially starting a war because you and your little friends got overambitious an easy fix? TJ, you're local, so I shouldn't have to tell you how much love the streets had for that old man and how closely people are gonna look at this. How long do you think it'll take for them to make the connection between Pana getting killed and Pops getting muscled out?"

"Not long at all, I suppose," Diamonds spoke up. "And when that time comes, you'll have no cause to worry, because all eyes will turn to us."

"That'd be a hell of a lot of eyes. You think you and your little crew can handle that type of heat?" Eddie asked.

"Let's just say I'm more than confident in our resourcefulness. Just know that regardless of how it plays out, I'd never compromise your or your uncle's positions. I'd gladly fall on the sword before I let that happen," Diamonds assured him. "Not to be rude, but if we're done here, I've got shit to do."

Eddie slapped his palms together as if he were dusting something from between them. "I guess you got it all figured out, big man. Enjoy the rest of your day," he said dismissively.

Diamonds caught the slight, but he let it go and simply walked off. TJ gave Eddie an apologetic shrug before following his cousin.

"I don't like that arrogant son of a bitch," Blanco said once Diamonds was out of earshot.

"Not arrogant—ambitious," Eddie corrected him. "Maybe too ambitious for his own good. I fear we may have invited a weasel into our henhouse."

"You want me to put a bullet in him, boss?" Blanco asked, hoping he'd get the green light.

Eddie pondered it. "No, you're far too valuable to me to lose. Put a set of eyes on him. I want to know his comings and goings at all times. Also, have some of our people downtown dig up whatever they can on our mysterious friend from New Orleans. If Diamonds has a weakness, we need to find it. We may end up having to euthanize that rabid dog."

"I don't know if it was such a good idea for you to speak to Eddie the way you did," TJ griped when they came out of the subway station.

"What you talking, TJ? All I did was let him know what it's hitting for."

"No, you told him to go fuck himself," TJ countered. "Eddie is trying to look out for us, so maybe we need to show a little more gratitude."

"How, by choking on a yard of his dick and asking him to go deeper?" Diamonds spat. "Sorry, T. Blow jobs are your thing, not mine."

"And what the fuck is that supposed to mean?" TJ asked.

"It means, you need to learn to shut that fucking mouth of yours when grown folks are talking," Diamonds spat.

"I've got just as much at stake in this as anybody, Diamonds. Or did you forget who it was who stuck their neck out to get you on your feet in New York?" TJ reminded him.

"Nah, I ain't forgettin' what you done, T. It's because of that and the fact that you're my mama's nephew that I didn't slap the dog shit out of you the first time you drifted out of your lane. You're treading on thin ice, so I suggest you get your ass back on solid grown before you fall in."

"Diamonds, I'm a little tired of you talking to me like I'm Buda or one of them niggas. We're supposed to be partners in this, and you need to start showing me a little respect," TJ demanded.

"Whatever." Diamonds made to walk away, but TJ refused to let it go.

"Don't walk away from me when I'm talking to you!" TJ grabbed Diamonds's arm and quickly learned the error of his ways.

Faster than the naked eye could follow, Diamonds whipped out the black dagger and pressed it to TJ's throat. His other hand grabbed a handful of TJ's shirt. "Tenderhearted nigga, how dare you call your-self stepping to me over how I run *my* crew?" he hissed. "I put you in position, TJ, and I can take you out of position. The only reason my people ain't gobbled your slick-talking ass up is because you're my family, but don't let the blood we share fool you into thinking I won't feed your ass to the great beyond if you open your mouth one more damn time without me telling you to. Do we understand each other?"

"Yeah, man . . . you got it," TJ said nervously.

"Good." Diamonds lowered the blade and smoothed the wrin-kles he'd created in TJ's shirt. "Now you go and finish helping that pretty girlfriend of yours prepare for the baby shower. I've got a new property I need to inspect."

CHAPTER THIRTY-FOUR

Whenever Pearl was stressed-out, she ran to blow off steam, so run she did when she came bursting out on the lobby of Harlem Hospital like the devil was on her heels. The blocks fell behind her at a steady pace as she jogged north up Lenox Avenue. She had no idea where she going and honestly didn't care; she just needed her legs to carry her to a place where it didn't hurt anymore.

Seeing Marisa laid up had done a number on her, but sending Sheila's parents away, still with lingering questions about what had happened to their little girl, fucked her up. Was Marisa right that telling them about Doodle's party would've brought about more problems than closure, or had she just convinced herself that it was the right thing because the lie was easier than the truth?

Pearl continued her run until her lungs began to pulse and the smell of charred wood slipped into her flared nostrils. She was hunkered down so deep in the recesses of her mind that she hadn't even realized where she was going until she saw what remained of Pops's bar looming just ahead of her. The once jumping night spot was now little more than a smoldering husk. A small crowd of people were gathered behind the yellow police tape that roped the place off, speculating about what had happened and mourning the loss of what had been considered a landmark to the locals. Pearl was also mourning a loss, but not for the bar. She couldn't help but wonder what Sheila's last moments must've been like, and prayed that her death came quickly.

"They say that if you love something, you should let it go. If it was meant to be, it'll come back. So I guess this was meant to be." A voice came from behind Pearl, startling her. She turned to see the jeweled smile of the man she had shared a drink with in that very same bar the night before. "Sorry, didn't mean to scare you."

"You didn't scare me—just caught me off guard." Pearl wiped beneath her eyes with the backs of her hands.

Diamonds's smile faded when he noticed she had been crying. "Why the long face? It's just a bar. In six months I'm sure they'll be another wateringhole to take its place. Let's just hope the next one is built sturdier than a tinderbox." He joked in an attempt to make her laugh, but her face darkened.

"I lost one of my best friends when this place went up, so you'll have to excuse me if I don't find that shit funny," Pearl snapped.

Diamonds suddenly felt very foolish. "My apologies. I meant no offense with my tasteless joke. Please accept my condolences for the loss of your friend."

"Thank you, and I'm sorry I bit your head off. This wasn't your fault," she told him, not realizing the irony in her words.

"It's fine, love. Losses tend to bring out the worst in us, even more so when it's someone close to us," Diamonds said with a tinge of sadness to his tone.

"Spoken like someone who has gone through it," Pearl observed.

"More times than I care to count." Diamonds thought back on John-Boy and Auntie.

"Were you here? I mean, when the fire started?" Pearl asked.

"No, thankfully me and mine left before it happened. I ain't much for late nights," he lied.

"Me either," Pearl said while looking out at the remains of Pops's bar.

"I guess we should count ourselves amongst the fortunate." He moved to stand beside her, wondering if she, too, saw the things that he did dancing in the wisps of smoke still coming off the rubble.

"I guess, but it sure doesn't feel like it."

"Enough talk about death. It's far too nice of a day to dwell on things we can't change. Let's go somewhere that'll make us both smile?"

"And where would that be? A hotel?" Pearl asked sarcastically. The last thing on her mind was sex, though with a man as fine as Diamonds, it was hard not to think about it.

Diamonds shook his head in disappointment. "Again you misinterpret my intentions. I was thinking more of us grabbing a bite to eat, since I left without having breakfast this morning. No offense, but I can only imagine the types of niggas you attract if the only thing they're focused on getting from you is pussy when you clearly have so much more to offer."

"And how would you know what I have to offer when you just met me last night?" Pearl challenged.

"I might've only known you a little while, but I've been dreaming of you all my life," Diamonds said with such sincerity in his voice that she felt it in her chest.

"You claim you ain't trying to get into my pants, but those sweet words are sure trying to woo these panties off," Pearl joked to try to hide how hot and bothered he was making her.

"To say that every fiber of my being isn't raging to make love to you would be a lie, but that's not how I want to start this. I'd rather take some time getting into your head first before I make my way further south," Diamonds told her.

Pearl studied his face. "I like you, Diamonds. You're a little on the cocky side, but you're honest."

Diamonds laughed. "Don't go convincing yourself that I'm no choirboy, Ms. Pearl. I got plenty of sin in me, but I'm hoping you can help me wash it away."

"Maybe you've got it wrong and I'm the one who needs her sins washed away," Pearl challenged.

"Then I would gladly bathe you from the soles of your feet to the crown of your head in the waters of salvation."

Pearl hadn't even realized he'd moved until she found herself wrapped in his arms. Her mind told her to pull away, but her body wouldn't let her. She looked into those same black eyes that had seemed so cold and commanding at the bar and found longing and compassion. It was like she was drifting through a beautiful dream she had no desire to wake up from. "Diamonds, you make it real hard for a girl to say no to you." She lolled in his arms.

"Then don't," he countered. "One date . . . one chance. That's all I ask," he said, breathing over her parted lips. "Come, have lunch with me and see for yourself what kind of man I am."

"Jesus, Pearl! I've been trying to catch up with you for blocks!" Knowledge appeared and ruined their perfect moment.

"Sorry, I just needed to clear my head." Pearl pushed herself away from Diamonds.

"Who the fuck is this?" Knowledge's eyes fell on Diamonds, who was regarding him curiously. Something about Diamonds tugged at Knowledge's brain, but he couldn't put his finger on it.

"A friend of mine. Why are you being all aggressive?" Pearl asked with attitude.

"Because that seems to be the only way to get through to your ass!" he shot back.

"Listen, friend," Diamonds interjected, "if this is your lady, then you have my apologies. But if you got no legitimate claim to her, then I'd appreciate it if you took some of that bass out of your voice."

"Do you know who the fuck you're talking to?" Knowledge let his hand drop to where his gun was tucked.

Diamonds spared a glance at the bulge beneath Knowledge's shirt. He recognized the threat but was unmoved by it. "I got no clue who you are, but if your hand moves another inch, you're likely to find out just who *I am*."

An oppressive tension imposed itself between the two men, and for the briefest of moments the threat of violence hung in the air like the smell of salt water coming off the beach at high tide. It wasn't until Pearl stepped between them that the coming storm finally receded. "Normally I'd be flattered over two men about to go head up over me, but this isn't the time, and my nerves can't take any more drama today. Neither one of you are my man or my daddy, so knock it off!"

"You're right, and you need to be thankful that it's me catching you all up on this nigga instead of your dad, because he'd probably have air-holed this dreadlocked muthafucka by now!" Knowledge spat.

"Boy, you ain't too fond of living, is you?" Diamonds took a step forward, but Pearl placed a hand on his chest.

"Don't."

Diamonds gave Knowledge one last defiant look before stepping back. "You got it, Ms. Pearl. I ain't looking to upset you further. You've already been through enough."

"Thank you. I appreciate that. Knowledge"—she turned to her guardian—"could you give us a minute?"

Knowledge looked at her as if she had taken leave of her senses. "Please," she added.

Knowledge grumbled something inaudible before giving them their space, but not much. He leaned against a parked car and glared at them the whole time.

"Sorry about that," Pearl told Diamonds. "Shit is kinda crazy around my house after what happened to Sheila. I'd love to see where this moment would've gone, but right now isn't a good time for me to be chasing romance. I gotta get back to my house and wait until everything settles, but maybe we could hook up later tonight?"

"I think I can find a hole in my schedule later on," he joked.

"Whatever, nigga. I may give you a play tonight, but if we do go out, I have some conditions," Pearl informed him.

"This is supposed to be a date, not a negotiation."

"Everything is a negotiation with me, baby," Pearl capped. "You wanna hear them or not?"

"Fine, I'll humor you."

"First, you can't come to my house. We don't know each other well enough for me to trust you with where I live. We can meet somewhere and go from there."

"Sounds fair enough. Is that all?"

"No, my girl Ruby has to come with us."

Diamonds frowned. "You wanna bring a third wheel on our first date?"

"I told you, we don't know each other like that. For all I know, you could be some kind of killer. And Ruby won't be a third wheel because you're going to bring somebody for her, too, and they better not be ugly."

Diamonds shook his head. "For all the shit you're putting me through, this better be worth it."

"Trust me, love, my company is well worth the effort."

"And you called me cocky." Diamonds laughed.

"Pearl!" Knowledge yelled far louder than he needed to. He was getting tired of waiting.

Diamonds glanced over at Knowledge and gave him an amused smirk. "Pearl, let me let you go before I have to fuck this nigga up. Hopefully I'll see you later on." He pinched her cheek and spun off. Diamonds made it a point to pass Knowledge on his way back to his car. "Our paths will cross again soon and under far different circumstances," Diamonds said as he flashed a smile and kept it moving.

When Knowledge got a glimpse of the grills in his mouth, it suddenly occurred to him why he looked familiar. It was the same guy who had mean-mugged him at the traffic light. " 'Teeth that sparkled like glass,' " Knowledge mumbled, recalling the old wine head's account of Pana's killer.

"What did you say?" Pearl asked.

"Nothing," Knowledge lied. "What's up with you and the dude?"

"Oh, he's just a friend."

"You've said as much already. I meant, what's his name?"

"Damn, you nosey." Pearl sucked her teeth. "His name is Diamonds. Why, do you know him?"

Knowledge looked in the direction Diamonds had gone. "I'm not sure yet, but I'm going to find out."

CHAPTER THIRTY-FIVE

Diamonds was proud of himself. The whole time Knowledge had been bumping his gums, he had wanted nothing more than to reach out and snatch his lips off, so he could have Vita sauté them over rice later on, but he didn't. Two things stayed his hand: one, it was far too early for Pearl to see that side of him, and two, the identity of her guardian angel.

He'd heard the name Knowledge early in his residency in New York, when he was doing reconnaissance for his invasion. For the most part, he knew who old the old-timer players were, but Diamonds was more focused on who their number-two men were, as they represented the next generation and his eyes were on the future. It would be the young ones who he inspired to break their chains of servitude and stand with him in the coming war. The neglected and underappreciated would help him build his foundation, or it would be their blood he used as mortar to hold the stones together.

Knowledge had been mentioned as being a strong ally or dangerous enemy. Diamonds had expected their paths to cross eventually. That was inevitable. He'd just never expected Pearl to be the thing that brought them together. Even though Pearl had insinuated their relationship wasn't an intimate one, Diamonds suspected different. The way Knowledge had thrust himself between her and unknown danger without a second thought was an act of love. If it hadn't gone down between them yet, it wasn't for a lack of want. Something else that Diamonds had caught was the mention of Pearl's father. Diamonds knew that Knowledge was the right arm of an old-school gangster named Big Stone, but how was Pearl connected? The more he thought about it, a theory began to form in his head that didn't quite make sense to him. For all intents and purposes, Pearl seemed like a square broad from a good family who got her kicks dancing on the wild side, but what if there was more to her than that? Could she, like Diamonds, be wearing a mask to hide what she really was? And if so, what did that mean to his plans for the city?

Before he could ponder it further, his cell phone rang. "What?" he answered a little harsher than he'd meant to. When he heard who was on the other end, his tone immediately softened. "Sorry about that. Been one of those days, ya know? So, to what do I owe the pleasure of this call? I ain't due to see you for another two weeks." He listened intently as the caller on the other end delivered a piece of information that only further darkened his mood. "You've got to be shitting me." He shook his head. "Thanks for calling. I'll be there to fetch him personally." After ending the call, Diamonds hit speed dial and placed another one. "Hank, it's me."

"That's funny, because I was just going to call you. Your boys from Queens been blowing my line up all day. We need to—"

Diamonds cut him off. "Whatever them niggas want can wait, I need you to meet me at the twenty-sixth precinct and bring some cash. This nigga Buda done got himself pinched last night."

By the time Hank arrived at the precinct, Diamonds was already there. He was outside, pacing, and he looked like he was trying his best not to explode.

"What the hell happened?" Hank offered by way of a greeting.

"This fucking idiot has gone and gotten himself arrested over some dumb shit," Diamonds fumed. "It's just dumb luck that they brought him to the precinct a friend of ours in blue works out of."

"What's the charge?"

"They wanted to hit him with assault and destruction of property, but a few coins placed in the right hands brought it down to drunk and disorderly. They're going to release him with a desk appearance ticket. So long as we take care of the fine, it'll get swept under the rug."

"This ain't good." Hank shook his head. "In every city we've swarmed, anonymity has always been our greatest asset. By the time anybody even notices we're in town, we've already infested their hoods. We invade, we feast, and we move on. Landing on the police radar, even for something as petty as this, can crack the whole foundation of we've taken all these years to lay."

"Thanks for pointing out the fucking obvious, old man!" Diamonds snapped.

"This old man can still kick your ass, so you might wanna watch that mouth of yours," Hank warned. "Look, kid. I know you're frustrated, but I ain't the one you need to be sore with. Buda ain't been right since he lost John-Boy, and that bottle ain't helping him none. My heart goes out to the boy, but I ain't trying to die or go to prison because he can't let go of them demons. Bottom line: Buda is going to bring this whole operation down unless we do something about him."

"So what you saying? You suggesting I clip my best friend?" Diamonds asked defensively.

"No, I'm suggesting you put that dog on a leash before he winds up biting you next."

Diamonds didn't want to admit it, but he knew Hank was right.

He wished could've said he hadn't seen it coming, but he had. The tea leaves had told him as much. Each time he gazed into the remains of the brew that Auntie had taught him to make when he was a kid, he hoped for a different outcome, but the story in the leaves never changed. In his arrogance he had thought he was skilled enough in the dark workings of the here and there that he could intervene on what fate had already predetermined, but he had only made things worse. *The same power you crave so desperately is going to rise up and swallow everything you hold dear to your heart*: the curse Auntie had laid on him right before he'd stolen her life. Her power rang in his head. The old witch was probably sitting somewhere in the pits of hell, cackling her ass off at him.

"Did you hear what I said?" Hank snapped Diamonds out of his daze.

"Huh?" Diamonds hadn't even realized Hank was still talking.

"I said your boys from Queens called again about the meeting," Hank repeated.

"How many fucking times do they need to go over this shit? Three days from now we sit down with their people and negotiate terms," Diamonds said in frustration. The two guys who were supposed to introduce them to the heroin supplier had been on his back about the deal since he agreed to do business with them. They had to be two of the most paranoid fuckers he had ever met, but considering the audacity of the double cross they were pulling, he was having a hard time blaming them.

"That's the thing: the plans have changed. They need to meet today," Hank told him. "Apparently, the leader of the crew had some kind of family emergency. Appears a friend of his got himself cooked in that mysterious fire that broke out uptown last night."

He now had Diamonds's full attention. "You've got to be shitting me."

"I wish I were."

"They know how the fire got started?" Diamonds asked.

"Nah, they got the same story everyone else did that it was an electrical fire. I guess they got some family coming into town to take care of the arrangements, so he'll have his hands full with that and wants to sit with you beforehand. He just wants certain assurances that we'll be able to handle the arrangement."

"Assurances?" Diamonds made a face as if this were laughable. "They only thing they need to be assured of is that when they open the pipeline, I'm gonna flood this city with dope!"

"You know it and I know it, but with the tense nature of everything in the streets lately, they want to make sure their investments are protected."

"Hit them back and tell them today is no good. We got TJ's shower, and I don't wanna hear him crying about us missing it. If my word that I can do what I say ain't good enough, then they can go fuck themselves. I ain't got time to be keep explaining myself to these New York niggas. I'm a gangster, not a politician."

"That's the cost to be the boss," Hank reminded him. "Now, if you wanna blow these jokers off, that's up to you, but you might wanna take into consideration what it could do to the deal. You said yourself that hooking into these Haitians niggas is the power play we need to really establish ourselves in New York. Now only that, but think about all the money we stand to make by pumping heroin into other cities we got business in, like Miami and Dallas. You slight these boys all because you feel like being petty, they could snatch the deal off the table. Now, I'm pretty sure we could find another dope plug, but it'll take time, and there's no guarantee the next connection will have access to the kind of weight we'll need to really step it up. So you need to ask yourself: Is your ego worth more than this paper?"

Before Diamonds could answer, Buda came walking out of the precinct. His shirt was torn, and there was some slight bruising under his eye. When he saw Diamonds and Hank standing at the curb, waiting, a look of shame crossed his face. He knew he had fucked up.

A second or two after Buda, another man came out. He was tall, with brown skin and an angular face, and dark keen eyes that seemed to look everywhere at once. He had thick sideburns and a deeply cleft upper lip that gave him an almost canine appearance. With his hair in cornrows and his baggy jeans cuffed over his Timberlands, he looked like your everyday corner boy, but the badge hanging from around his neck said he played for the other side. He paused just long enough to look at the trio like they were shit on a shoe before ambling across the street to the bodega.

"Diamonds," Buda began, "before you start in, let me explain. It wasn't my fault."

"It never is, Buda," Diamonds said sarcastically.

"Don't you even wanna hear my side of the story?" Buda asked, not feeling the way Diamonds was looking at him.

"Ain't no need, because whatever you got to say is likely only gonna make my mood worse. This shit is a never-ending saga with you, Buda. Go with Hank and wait by the car while I finish cleaning up your fucking mess!" Diamonds spat.

"So you're just gonna dismiss me like I'm some kid?" Buda asked angrily.

"Buda, with the shit you been pulling lately, you need to consider yourself lucky that all I'm asking for is your absence and not your life," Diamonds growled. The minute the words crossed his lips, he knew he had crossed the line, but it was too late to take it back so he stood on it.

There was a tense moment between them. Both men locked eyes, ready to react to whatever the other was contemplating.

"Buda," Hank called out. He felt a storm coming and wanted to defuse it before the situation exploded. "Take a walk with me."

Buda gave Diamonds one last hard look. "A'ight." He backed away, keeping his eyes on Diamonds.

When Buda was out of sight, Diamonds let out a long, fatigued sigh. He and Buda both knew how close they had just come to throwing blows. It wouldn't have been the first time since they had known each other, but this time it was different. The stakes were higher, and a simple fight amongst friends could affect the balance of power. Buda had been his right hand for a great many years, but there was only room enough for one ass to sit on the throne. Putting his frustration with Buda to the side, Diamonds got back to focusing on business.

He ambled across the street and entered the bodega. In back, near the deli section, the detective who'd come out behind Buda stood, ordering a sandwich. He spared Diamonds a brief glance before turning back to the man behind the counter and commanding that he put more mayonnaise on his hero. Diamonds stopped short of him and began perusing the rack of potato chips as if he were having trouble making a selection.

"If your friend is any indication of the kind of dysfunctional niggas you've recruited into your little army, you ain't gonna last long in this city," the detective said over his shoulder, keeping his eyes on the man making his sandwich.

"Your counsel is always appreciated, Detective Wolf, but who I keep company with is my business," Diamonds said.

"Your business becomes my business when I have to convince my watch commander to give a pass to a guy who put two people in the hospital," Wolf retorted.

"What the fuck happened?" Diamonds asked.

"According to the uniforms who brought him in, he got into a head-busting contest at this spot uptown. The unofficial word is that there was some kind of dispute between him and another dude over some broad, and your boy went postal and started busting the place up. He sent two of the bouncers to the hospital. The only reason your friend is getting just a slap on the wrist instead of charged with something heavy is because the place he trashed ain't exactly legit, and the owner pays the cops handsomely to look the other way when shit like this occurs. I know the owner personally, and despite his flamboyant appearance, he's an extremely dangerous man. It's a wonder Buda ended up in the tank instead of the morgue. But Christian ain't gonna let this rest without some type of compensation. I can squash it for you, but it ain't gonna be cheap."

Diamonds cut his eyes at Wolf. "I see that badge ain't took none of the larceny out of your heart."

"It's the larceny that keeps me from digging into my pocket to pay for a bridge every time somebody like you comes along, trying to sell one," Detective Wolf capped, accepting his sandwich and making his way to the register to pay for it.

Diamonds followed, carrying a bag of onion-and-garlic chips and a soda. "Your envelope will be in its usual place, waiting for you," he said to the detective's back while he waited his turn in line. "When you come up with a number to squash my boy's mishap, just push it through to my people and I'll make sure you're taken care of."

The detective nodded. "That's why I like you, Diamonds. You and your crew are about as big of hillbillies as I've ever met in my life, but you pay like you weigh when you want shit done. I don't have to haggle over paper with you like I do with some of these local shitbirds."

"Chalk it up to my Southern charm," Diamonds said.

"Whatever, nigga." Wolf laughed and walked out of the bodega. He stopped on the sidewalk to take a bite of his sandwich and allow Diamonds to catch up with him. "I'm usually not in the goodwill business, but I kinda like you, kid. If you don't fuck around and get your head blown off before you can complete your hostile take-over, you might wind up being somebody in the world. That being said, does the name Eddie Costas mean anything to you?"

"I've heard the name, but can't say I've ever met the man personally," Diamonds lied.

"So then I guess there's no cause for concern that his people have been asking a whole lot of questions about you?"

Diamonds shrugged. "People are curious about the unknown. I suspect that before long, I'll be the topic of more than a few conversations."

Detective Wolf nodded. "Just be sure they're the right kinds of conversations. There's a condo in Miami that I've had my eye on, and at the rate I'm cleaning your messes up, I'll have the down payment in no time, provided you don't get yourself whacked or locked up first."

"Spoken like a true pig," Diamonds capped. "In any event, thanks for the solid you did for Buda."

"No problem." Wolf took another bite of his sandwich. "One day I may call on you for a favor, and I trust you'll pay me the same courtesy," he said suggestively.

Diamonds read between the lines. Thanks to Buda, he was now in the detective's debt. "You got that," Diamonds assured him before walking off.

As usual, Diamonds's chat with Detective Wolf proved to be both informative and frustrating. He hated the way the narcotics detective spoke in riddles. It was like you could never get a straight answer from him unless he was telling you how much you owed for whatever nasty little deed he'd taken care of for you.

The news about Eddie digging into Diamonds's past was

something he had expected to happen, but not quite so soon. He was content to bide his time and let Eddie continue to think he was just a country-ass nigga who was happy to be eating, until the time came to show his true hand. But once again TJ had altered his plans by running his mouth. He'd allowed his anger at his cousin to cause him to give Eddie a glimpse of the monster beneath the mask. Unlike TJ and the others who Eddie could twist to his will, Diamonds's spine was made of steel and would not bend. Eddie was a lot of things, but you didn't make it to his status by being a fool. He'd be paying closer attention now, so Diamonds had to move wisely going forward.

Then there was the issue of Diamonds's latest business partners, or at least that was what he allowed them to think of themselves as. They were really just stepping stones to the next level of his dastardly plan. Had they been just any random New York cats who'd pitched him about the heroin deal, he'd have told them to fuck off, but their affiliation gave them credibility. If they could deliver half of what they had promised, then they'd indeed prove valuable.

As he approached the car where Buda and Hank were waiting, his cell phone rang. A cold chill settled in his belly, and he was hesitant to answer it. With the mood he was in, if he got one more piece of bad news, he was going to lose it. "What now?" he answered angrily.

Goldie's voice came over the line. "Sounds like someone is having a shitty day."

"Little brother, you don't know the half." Diamonds sighed.

"Well, I got a bit of news that might perk you up. That science experiment in your office fridge has taken a turn for the worse. Last I checked, it looked like it was rotting," Goldie told him.

Diamonds knew he was speaking of the tongue. He smiled, as it was the first piece of good news he'd gotten all day. "The little birdie tried to sing but couldn't finish the song. I guess that means we don't need that insurance policy anymore either."

"You want me to take care of it?" Goldie asked.

Diamonds thought on it briefly. "Nah, I got a better idea. Grab my gear and meet me at the storage unit. I think I just figured out a way to kill two birds with one stone."

PART

V

LOVE AND CONSEQUENCES

CHAPTER THIRTY-SIX

Up until the point Domo arrived at the address, he had been suspicious of Vita's intentions for him. The fact that LA had gone on ahead of him and Raheem didn't do anything to assuage his nerves. The whole ride on the train into New York, his mind played more than a hundred different scenarios, and he started to consider turning back, but reasoned he didn't want Vita hunting him down if he blew her off. Against his better judgment, he answered the summons, preparing for himself for whatever she would throw at him. Of all the things he expected to find at the end of his journey, a party wasn't one of them.

The address brought them to a two-story house in a part of the Bronx that Domo had never ventured to. It was on a quiet, tree-lined street with manicured lawns. Most of the houses were almost identical in make and color, but Domo had no trouble picking out the one they were looking for. It was the only one with colorful balloons tied to the fence, and men who didn't look like they belonged in the sleepy neighborhood loitered in the front yard. Several sets of eyes turned to the approaching strangers.

"You sure we good out here?" Raheem asked, inching his hand toward the .38 in his back pocket.

"Honestly? Nope, but I ain't about to turn back like some pussy." Domo continued toward the house.

One of the men peeled himself from the group. "You boys lost?" He was a tall brown-skinned fellow with thick lips that currently held a smoldering blunt between them. Tied snugly around his neck was a black bandanna.

Domo stood there for a few ticks, not really sure how to reply. It wasn't like he had a formal invitation to whatever they were celebrating—he only had the text message.

"Goldie, stop being a dick and let them boys pass," a feminine voice called from somewhere in the front yard. Vita muscled her way through the cluster of men. Her eyes were glassed over, and a blunt bobbed between her lips. She was wearing a short denim skirt and a tight T-shirt that showed off erect nipples.

The man she had called Goldie cracked a sly smile. "Sorry, V. Didn't know these pups belonged to you, seeing as how they ain't wearing collars."

Vita exhaled a cloud of smoke into Goldie's face. "Collars are for dogs, and this here is a pure-bred wolf cub." She draped her arm around Domo.

"We'll see about that." Goldie turned and walked around the side of the house to the backyard.

"Pay Goldie no mind. He'll warm up to you eventually—or try to kill you," Vita said half jokingly. "Glad you made it out, even though you brought company." She eyed Raheem.

"Rah, is cool." Domo assured her.

"I wasn't sure you were going to come."

"I wasn't sure I was going to come either," Domo confessed. "I wasn't really sure what to expect, especially not a party."

"Well, what did you expect? That I'd bring you all the way out here to whack you?" Vita said as if she could read his mind. "Lighten up, pretty boy" She patted his cheek. "Of all the things I might take from you before this night is said and done, your life isn't one of them . . . provided you know how to play your position. Now, stop standing there, looking like a tourist, and come on in the back so I can introduce you to the rest of the crew."

As it turned out, the party wasn't a party after all. It was a baby shower thrown for a guy Vita introduced as TJ and the mother of his pending child. The backyard was laid out with tables full of food and a fully stocked bar in the corner. Boxes and bags of gifts seemed to take up every bit of available space, with a revolving door of people dropping more off every time Domo looked up. TJ was cool, but Domo wasn't sure how he felt about Teisha just yet. It was obvious she was a hood chick, but she went out of her way to play the role of ghetto fabulous. She sat perched on a wicker throne in the corner, receiving guests and giving orders like she was the Queen of Sheba. When Domo and Raheem had first come in, she assumed they were the help and tried to send them to take out the trash, but Vita set Teisha straight. She let her and anyone else wondering that Domo was family.

Vita made sure Domo and Raheem were situated with plates of food and drinks before heading back out to make her rounds through the shower. Teisha was the one having the baby, but it was Vita who moved amongst the guests, making sure everyone had what they needed and that the event proceeded smoothly. She had a way about her that put people at ease, and had Domo not seen firsthand the murderous fury bottled up inside that small frame, he, too, might've believed her façade.

Domo played the background, picking at his plate and sipping a plastic cup full of Hennessey. They had been there for nearly an hour, but there was still no sign of the mysterious Diamonds, or LA either for that matter. Vita had stressed how bad Diamonds wanted to meet Domo, but he wasn't about to wait around all night for him to make his grand appearance. He would give him a few minutes more, and then he was heading back to Jersey.

Raheem clung to Domo like a shadow. His friend was trying to play it cool, but Raheem couldn't hide the nervousness in his eyes. They were out of their depth and they both knew it, but they were playing the roles anyhow. Raheem gabbed into Domo's ear constantly, and every few minutes Domo would nod as if he were really listening, but he was more focused on the cast of characters surrounding him. He hardly knew anyone there besides Vita, but he did recognize a few faces from being around Stoney's family. One in particular was a dealer named Born. He had seen him at the house once with Knowledge. He didn't know much about Born, except that he was one of the men Big Stone supplied. With him was another man who Domo wasn't familiar with. He was slightly older than Born, but he dressed like a man half his age, in baggy clothes and rocking a do-rag. Studying his face, Knowledge couldn't help but to notice how much he resembled Big Stone. The older man looked uneasy being there, but Born had made himself right at home. Domo watched as he shook hands with and hugged TJ as if they were old friends. As far as Domo knew, Vita and her crew were new to town, so he wondered what Born's affiliation was.

"You good?" Vita startled him. She moved so quietly, he hadn't heard her approach.

"Yeah, I'm straight. Thanks," Domo replied.

"Well, if you're done stuffing your face, come with me inside so I can introduce you to the rest of the boys."

Domo and Raheem followed Vita through the back door and into the house and found it almost as crowded as the backyard. Children were ripping and running all through the house, laughing and knocking things over, while their parents acted like they didn't see them. Sitting around the table were four older women engaged in a card game. Domo had to do a double take when he saw the silver-haired old broad sitting at the head of the table, peeking at him over the rim of her violet bifocals.

"Well, well," she said, plucking a cigarette from behind her ear and tapping it on the back of her hand, "ain't this a small world."

"How you doing, Ms. Sweets?" Domo greeted her respectfully.

"You two know each other?" Vita asked in surprise.

"Shit, everybody in Essex County knows Carolina Sweets!" Raheem added.

It was true. On the other side of the Hudson, Carolina Sweets was something like a living legend. She had a track record of putting in work that went back to the sixties and consisted of everything from armed robbery to selling pussy. She was an OG for real. Domo knew her because she was sort of like a godmother to his mom, and she had looked out for them a few times. It had been a minute since he had seen Sweets, but last he heard, she was working as the madam at a cathouse in East Orange.

"How's Lisa?" Sweets asked after his mother.

"She's good," Domo replied.

"When you see her, tell her I'm gonna come by for a touch-up next week." Sweets fluffed her curls.

"Yes, ma'am."

Sweets eyeballed the two boys suspiciously. "What y'all two young-ass niggas doing this far from home?"

"They're here with me," Vita answered.

"Damn, V. I enjoy a young piece of meat from time to time, but these boys still got titty milk on their breath," Sweets joked.

"I don't know about the chubby one, but from what I can tell so far, Domo is man enough," Vita said suggestively.

"Ha!" Sweets slapped the table hard enough to rattle the glasses on it. "You just be mindful not to break your new toy, because he's kinda on the scrawny side. I'd hate to have his mama come 'round, looking for you."

Vita sucked her teeth. "Sweets, why you acting like you don't know my résumé?"

"Oh, I know you're thorough, Vita. In fact, I'd put money on you against most men, but Domo's mama ain't no slouch. Back in the day, she did her share of slaning and banging. You kinda remind me of her, which is probably what got Domo sniffing around you. You know they say every boy wants a woman who reminds him of his mama."

"Whatever." Vita laughed it off. "Where're the boys?"

"Them hooligans down in the basement, probably tearing up some more of my niece's shit. Them fools are like bulls in a china shop. I swear, Vita, I never understood how such a sweet young thing like you hooked into such a group of classless men."

Vita shrugged. "They ain't the most prized bunch, but they're all I have. Catch you later, Sweets." She started toward the door to the basement, Domo and Raheem following.

"Vita, be mindful when you go down there. That fool-ass Buda is drunk and on one," Sweets warned.

Vita shook her head sadly. "When the hell is he not?"

CHAPTER THIRTY-SEVEN

"So, how y'all know Sweets?" Domo asked Vita as they descended the stairs to the basement.

"She's Teisha's aunt. She and I got close, because when we first arrived in New York, the boys were always running to Jersey to party with her girls, and I always ended up sitting out front with Sweets until they were done being nasty. The stories that old broad can tell." Vita chuckled.

"You ain't got to tell Domo, since he's lived through half of them," Raheem joked, drawing a dirty look from Domo.

Domo's mother was a good woman, but she hadn't always been. In Domo's younger days, she was kind of on the wild side and spent a lot of time in the streets. He never asked his mother about her life prior to slowing down to raise him, but he had heard the rumors. Still, he liked to keep his family business close to his chest. Raheem was out of line, and the only reason Domo didn't check him was because they were in front of Vita.

As soon as Vita opened the second door at the foot of the stairs, they were nearly overcome by a thick cloud of smoke. From somewhere in the basement he could hear raised voices. Domo wasn't sure why, but his heart suddenly started thudding in his chest. When they rounded the corner that lead into the main area of the basement, there was a group of men huddled around a pool table, engaged in a dice game. LA was one of them. He had a fistful of cash in one hand and was shaking the dice in the other. Also present were Goldie and a brutishly built cat who they had yet to be introduced to. From the sour expression on his face, Domo reasoned it must've been his money clutched in LA's mitt.

"There're my niggas!" LA shouted when he spotted Domo and Raheem. He raised a cash-stuffed hand and waved them over. "Glad you're here. I was starting to think you were gonna miss this little event." He embraced Domo.

Domo ignored the pungent stench of alcohol, and something that wasn't weed, coming off LA. "If you were that concerned, how come you didn't wait for us since we were all coming to the same place any-way?"

"Aw, man. I had some shit I needed to do in New York, so I came over a little early," LA said, downplaying it. "But fuck it—we're all here now, and that's what's important. Welcome to the big-time, baby!"

"Jersey nigga, you gonna shoot the dice or keep making goo-goo eyes with your girlfriend?" the brute with the beard asked sarcasti-cally. His face reflected that of a man who had already lost a few dol-lars to LA, and the half-empty whiskey bottle in his hand said he was just tipsy enough to make a big deal of it. That had to be the Buda who Sweets was speaking of.

"Slow your roll, Buda. I can take your money with or without the disrespect." LA tossed the dice. "Up, bitches!" He snapped his fingers. They danced across the pool table, and four was his point.

"All that just to throw a weak-ass four." Buda snatched the dice. "I'm sending this nigga home in his socks tonight," he boasted, and tossed the dice. All the bravado left him when he rolled a three and lost again. "Damn it!" He slammed one of his fists on the edge of the pool table, cracking the wood.

"Damn, Buda. Why you gotta be on some gorilla shit? You know TJ is gonna be pissed about you messing up his pool table," Goldie said.

"Fuck TJ, and fuck this table!" Buda spat. "I blame these bad luck–ass niggas for this. I was about to come back up before they rolled in here. Who the fuck are y'all anyway?" He looked Domo and Raheem up and down.

Domo looked into Buda's glassy eyes and could tell the liquor had him spoiling for a fight. Vita slipped closer to Domo, as if anticipating something about to go down. Whether it was for his or Buda's benefit, he wasn't sure.

"Ah, these must be more of Vita's new little friends," a voice called from somewhere behind Domo. Domo spun and found himself staring into a pair of inky-black eyes partially obscured by the long locks that hung down over his face. He seemed to have appeared as if by magic, because Domo certainly hadn't seen him in the basement when they'd first come down. He didn't need an introduction. The air of menace coming off him could only be produced by a man fit to command such a dangerous crew. It had to be Diamonds.

"This is the young boy I was telling you about," Vita told him, shoving Domo forward.

Standing there under Diamonds's inquisitive gaze made Domo uncomfortable. He tried to keep his poker face, but he had a feeling the taller man saw right through it. "Domo." He extended his hand. It hung in the air for what felt like an eternity before Diamonds finally shook it.

"Diamonds," he said. "I hear y'all ran into some trouble yesterday and you handled yours like a G."

"I wasn't trying to be a hero. It was more moving on instincts than anything," Domo admitted.

"Then you've got good instincts, especially when them instincts allowed my lil gangsta bitch to be returned to me in one piece." Diamonds pulled Vita to him and cupped her ass. A look of embarrassment crossed her face, but she didn't pull away. Diamonds was making a point, and Domo got it. "I trust y'all been having a good time at my cousin's baby shower?"

"Yeah, ya peeps been showing mad love," Raheem spoke up.

"That's Vita for you—a regular welcome wagon." Diamonds gave Vita a hard squeeze before releasing her. "I hate to talk business at a party, but I need to bend your ear right quick. Got another piece of business for you if you're interested?"

"Yeah, we down for whatever," Raheem said eagerly.

Diamonds looked at him. "No disrespect to you, lil homie, but I don't know you from a can of paint. Why don't you hang back with the rest of the fellas while we talk shop?"

Raheem looked at Domo.

"It's cool. I'll get back with you in a second." Domo let him know he was good.

"A'ight, I'm about to go over here and see if I can get some of this money." Raheem excused himself and joined the dice game.

"That your man?" Diamonds asked Domo, watching Raheem amble over to the pool table to join the game. He wasn't sure if he liked him, and made no attempt to hide it.

"Nah, that's my *brother*," Domo replied, letting Diamonds know they were more than just friends.

"Right, my brother's keeper, huh?" Diamonds eyed Domo. "Judas was his brother's keeper too, but I don't recall him helping Jesus drag that cross through the streets. Still, I can respect a loyal man, even if those loyalties may be misplaced. But enough about relationships; let's talk business. I know Vita broke bread with you from that thing last night, so how does it feel having some of them holes in your pocket filled?"

"It was a decent lick," Domo said coolly.

"Decent?" Diamonds cocked his head. "Soft words for a young man on hard times."

"So now you got X-ray vision into my pockets?" Domo asked sharply. He hadn't meant to give an attitude, but he felt slighted by Diamonds's assumption.

"I meant no disrespect," Diamonds clarified. "It's just that you wore a hoodie to an invitation-only event and you took public transportation here from Newark."

Domo flashed a glare at Vita, assuming she had been pillow talking his business to Diamonds.

"I spotted you walking down the block when there's plenty of parking out front. That's how I knew you didn't drive—or get a ride," Diamonds explained. "No need to be cross with Vita; she didn't spill whatever secrets y'all got between you . . . at least not yet. But let me not stray from the point I was attempting to make. I like the way you handled yourself last night. Not just because you saved Vita's ass, but because you showed you can think on your feet. Being a quick thinker is an excellent trait when you're involved in a lifestyle that moves at a million miles per minute and never slows down. Some people have a problem keeping up when they're forced to move at a pace they ain't used to. Are you one of those people?"

Domo laughed. "Man, if the bread is right, I'll be Carl Lewis."

Diamonds patted Domo on the shoulder reassuringly and smiled. "Spoken like a man who only sees one side of the coin. Let me paint a naked picture for you, so there's no mistake about where I'm at with it and what comes with being part of this crew. It'd be an insult to your intelligence for me to feed you some bullshit movie script about:

I'm going to take care of you because a boss takes care of his family.
Fuck that—I ain't running no soup kitchen. With us, you'll have to
sweat, and sometimes even bleed, for every dollar you touch. There
are only three possible outcomes of this game we've decided to play:
prison, death, or becoming so rich that the first two are worth the
risks. That being said, you need to ask yourself how much paradise
on earth is worth to you, because you'll be held accountable for that
decision."

Just then three more people lumbered down into the basement.
One was an older gentleman with a hard face. Diamonds was the
leader of the crew, but from the way all eyes turned to the old-timer
when he entered the room, Domo knew he was also a man whose
words carried weight in the crew. Behind the man were Born and the
Big Stone look-alike.

"Damn, Diamonds. That was a long-ass five minutes. I thought
you were coming right back?" Born asked, clearly not feeling being
left waiting.

"My fault, Born. I was just down here having a little chat with
one of my boys," Diamonds said.

"You recruiting them kinda young, ain't you?" Born gave Domo
an unimpressed look.

"Don't let the baby face fool you. Anybody fucking with my team
is more than qualified to do whatever needs to be done," Diamonds
said confidently.

Born studied Domo's face. "Shorty, don't I know you from somewhere?"

"Nah, man," Domo lied.

"You sure? You look familiar as hell," Born insisted. "Where you
from?"

"Who's your friend? I don't think we've met yet." Vita took the
attention off Domo. Her eyes were fixed on the Big Stone look-alike.

"Oh, this is my boy Rolling," Born said. "He's the main reason we were able to broker this little situation; they're his people."

"Yeah, V. Rolling is the man with the golden ticket," Diamonds said sarcastically.

Rolling smiled sheepishly. "I don't know if I'd call it all that. Sometimes it's just good to know people."

"And is everything all set with your people?" Diamonds asked.

"Oh yeah, I spoke to my man before we came here. They should be by in a little while," Rolling assured him.

"Good, because I hate mixing business with family. The sooner we get this over with, the sooner I can get back to my family and finish celebrating this blessing," Diamonds said.

"I was hoping we could get a word in before they got here. Maybe in private." Rolling glanced at Domo.

"I'll go watch the dice game," Domo said, knowing how to take a hint.

"So, what's on your mind?" Diamonds asked after Domo was out of earshot.

"First," Rolling said, "let me start by saying I appreciate y'all for everything you've done. I—"

Diamonds cut him off. "A man who begins a statement with a compliment usually ends it with an insult. This is our first time meeting, so you may be unfamiliar, but I'm sure Born can tell you that when speaking to me, you should choose your words very wisely."

Rolling looked over at Born, who wore a worried expression on his face. He swallowed hard before continuing. "Look, I don't mean any disrespect. I'm just trying to make sure we all understand what's at stake here. We're sticking our necks out just by making the introduction."

"And you're being well compensated for your roles in this, or have you forgotten our agreement? You guys are plugging us with your Haitian friends, and in return I'm going to make you lord over all you survey, by giving you domain in my new kingdom. I think that's a sweet-ass deal, unless you boys are content to be workers and have no desire to stand as bosses."

"No, it's nothing like that, man. We just wanna make sure you guys are prepared to handle what could potentially be behind this," Born explained.

"I think we've proven that we can be quite resourceful when we get a mind to be. Or ain't you been reading the papers the last few days?" Diamonds boasted. "Why don't you boys cut the shit and tell me what's really got you all rattled?"

"My brother," Rolling finally admitted. "Him and those other greedy fucks who call themselves kings of the city don't want nobody else to be able to get a crumb out here, unless it comes off their cookies. Shit, I'm his blood, and he ran me out of New York like I was some kinda stray dog. It's bad enough that this little venture may encroach on his territory, but the fact that me and Born are going behind his back could get us both killed."

"Then why even bother trying to branch out in the first place?" Diamonds asked.

Born and Rolling exchanged nervous glances, neither really sure how to answer, but it was Born who spoke up. "To be honest with you, because I'm tired of eating shit and being asked to like it. Real talk, I've given up years out of my life in the penitentiary and spilled blood in the streets . . . and I'm rewarded for it by watching niggas who ain't got half my stripes get bumped up the ladder, while I'm still moving crack in the projects. I didn't sign up to be no yes-man."

"And, you?" Diamonds turned to Rolling. "What would make a man stick a knife in the back of his own brother?"

"Because it's the only play he left me," Rolling said honestly.

Diamonds didn't miss the edge of hurt in Rolling's voice. Whatever his reasons for crossing his brother, they were personal and had nothing to do with money or status. "Listen, boys, I can assure you that you have nothing to fear. If this deal goes through as promised, you will both be under the protection of this crew and no one will be able to touch you."

Rolling looked around the room at the hard faces assembled in the garage. "No disrespect, but you're talking like a nigga who's got an army, and all I see is a handful of people here with you."

"It doesn't always take an army. Sometimes all you need are a few dedicated souls who are willing to go further than their opponents in order to win. You boys worry about making sure your people come through with the heroin, and I'll worry about any fallout that may come of it. When the time is right, I'm going to approach all these so-called kings and make my position clear. The wise ones who understand the need for change will stand behind the alpha and join the pack." He pounded his chest. "The foolish will feed us through the long winter to come."

Diamonds was about to continue his speech when a disturbance broke out by the pool table.

"C'mon, Buda. Don't start this shit." Goldie sighed.

"Nah, fuck that. This lil nigga been humping his gums since he got here," Buda snarled while staring daggers at Raheem.

"Fuck is going on here?" Diamonds walked up.

"What's going on is these young pussies need to learn to respect their elders. Lil nigga fixed his mouth to call me a cheat," Buda spat.

"I didn't call you no cheat; I just said your roll wasn't no good because all three dice didn't hit the bumper," Raheem tried to explain, as he had several times prior, but Buda wasn't trying to hear him.

"Buda, let that shit go and just roll the dice again," Goldie urged him, trying to defuse the situation.

"I ain't rolling shit again. Lil nigga lost—simple as that." Buda snatched the money off the pool table and started tauntingly counting it in Raheem's face. "Yeah, I'm gonna get good and fucked up tonight on you, fat boy."

"I ain't letting you take my money." Raheem puffed up, much to everyone's surprise. He was only trying to stand up for himself and not look like a punk in front of the others, but Buda took it as an invitation to do battle.

"Oh, you trying to play tough now, lil nigga?" A sinister smile crossed Buda's big lips. Everyone knew what would come next. "What you gonna do if I don't kick it back? You got some frog in you, then jump, pussy."

LA took a step, but Hank cocking a gun behind him gave him pause. "I kinda like you, youngster, but I like TJ more, and I'd hate to blow your brains all over his basement floor when he just got the carpet laid."

"So this is how y'all do? Invite niggas to break bread then pull pistols on them?" LA fumed.

"He's got a point," Diamonds finally interjected. "We invited these young men here on good faith, and I'd be an ungracious host if I let you plug him, Hank." He gave him a look and Hank lowered the gun. "Still, this does leave us with a bit of a dilemma." He approached Raheem. "Let a man take from you once, and he'll never stop taking from you. In this crew, there are no weak links. So my question to you is: What do you intend to do about it? Fade or flight?"

Domo, along with everyone else, watched Raheem to see how he would respond. Buda stood a few feet away, cracking his knuckles in preparation of testing the younger man's chin. Raheem was by no means a coward, but Domo knew he wasn't a fighter, either. He didn't stand a snowball's chance in hell against Buda, but if he backed down, it would make all of them look bad. Before Domo could stop himself, he opened his mouth and said something that took the attention off Raheem and turned it to him. "I'll take his fade."

CHAPTER THIRTY-EIGHT

"Diamonds, are you seriously going to let this go down?" Vita asked as they all marched out into the front yard.

"It ain't about what I'm *letting* go down; it's about what *needs* to happen. You know the rules better than anybody: if you can't settle with words, you settle it in combat. I didn't see you pleading Goldie's case last summer in Miami when him and Hank squared off over that misunderstanding they had," Diamonds reminded her.

"That was different. Goldie is trained; he could handle himself. But Buda is a killer and Domo is just a kid!" Vita argued. She had seen what Buda could do with those battering rams he called fists, and it wasn't pretty.

"That *kid* became a man the minute he picked up that strap and decided to throw in with this bunch. You're awful damn concerned for a nigga you ain't known for a full forty-eight hours yet. What's the matter, V? You think I'm gonna let Buda break your little boy toy?" He smirked.

Vita bristled. "No, just think it'd be a shame to waste a good soldier over some bullshit."

"If all he is to you is a solider, then you should understand why this is baptism by fire." Diamonds walked off to join the festivities.

Both men had stripped down to their bare chests. Buda's thick chest and arms were covered in tattoos he had collected over the years, while Domo's skin was still smooth and unblemished. Standing beside Buda, the wiry teen looked every bit the child he actually was. Still, child or not, he had wanted to play grown men's games and was therefore subject to the rules.

"Diamonds, is this really necessary? I've got guests in the backyard for Christ's sake!" TJ protested. He had not been happy when one of Teisha's aunts had told him how some of his guests had decided to turn his front yard into a UFC arena.

Diamonds ignored him and continued toward the two men. "Okay, boys, you all know how we handle family disputes, and for those of you who don't, here's a quick rundown: first man on his back is the loser of the dispute. Simple." He stepped back.

"Go easy on the boy, Buda," Hank urged.

"Don't you worry, Hank. I ain't trying to hurt him. I'm just gonna rough him up. Y'all said he's family, so I'm gonna treat him the same way Diamonds treats the rest of us," Buda said slyly. He turned to Domo and extended his hand. "Don't take this ass whipping personally." When Domo went to shake his hand, Buda sucker-punched him.

Domo felt his whole jaw shift when Buda's fist met it. The world swam in bright, beautiful colors, and Domo could feel himself drifting into a peaceful, worriless sleep, until Buda slugged him in the stomach, and he threw up the barbecue he'd eaten all over the front yard.

Buda danced around Domo, who was doubled over on his hands and knees, thumbing his nose mockingly. "Man, when this punk volunteered to take his man's ass whipping, he might've been about something. Yo, LA, he got y'all Jersey niggas looking bad out here."

"Fuck you!" LA spat while trying to will Domo with his mind to get up.

There was a feral growling coming from somewhere behind Buda. He turned just in time to see that not only had Domo gotten to his feet, but he was rushing at him like a speeding bullet. Buda instinctively covered his face, leaving his soft gut wide open. Domo's hands moved like the wind as he fired punch after punch into Buda's stomach. Buda threw a wild overhand, which Domo easily side-stepped and replied with a hook to the jaw. Much to everyone's surprise, including Buda's, it stumbled him.

The unexpected turn of the tide drew a round of *oooh*s from those who were watching, and this seemed to only infuriate Buda. He rushed Domo, swinging haymakers in an attempt to knock his head from his shoulders. Domo mounted a defense by raising his forearms so they took the brunt of the blows. Every time Buda struck him, he felt like a bone was fractured. One wayward blow managed to make it pass and clip Domo's ear. Bells rang in his head, and the next thing he knew, he was down on one knee. Buda swooped in behind him and put Domo in a reverse chokehold, applying enough pressure to where Domo knew he intended to snap his neck. Things had gone from bad to worse.

"Stop it! He's going to kill him!" Vita surged forward, but Diamonds snatched her back and grabbed her in a bear hug.

"Ah, ah . . . not until one of them is on their backs," Diamonds whispered mockingly in her ear.

Domo clawed at Buda's forearms, but he wouldn't release his grip. Spots began to dance before him, and he could feel himself trying to go out. With hazy eyes, he looked around at the faces of his comrades. LA had to be restrained by Hank and Goldie to keep him from jumping in while Raheem stood there with a grim expression on his face. He knew what Domo's brain refused to accept: that he was about to die. In desperation, Domo made one last-ditch attempt to save his life, and grabbed a handful of Buda's nuts.

"Muthafucka!" Buda roared as his testicles were being crushed. He was in so much pain that he immediately released Domo's neck, but the youngster maintained his grip on Buda's balls. "Get that nigga off me!" he demanded. His face was now a deep shade of red.

"You know the rules; it ain't over until someone is on his back!" Diamonds taunted from the sidelines. "You gonna concede or let this little nigga make you sterile?"

Buda turned his rage-filled eyes to Diamonds. "On my baby brother's soul, if this little nigga don't let me go, he better hold on to my dick forever, because when I do finally get loose, it's over for him."

Diamonds knew Buda well enough to tell that the joke was almost to the point of having gone too far, and there was a strong possibility that he would keep true to his word. "A'ight, that's enough." Diamonds gave Goldie and Hank the nod, and they pried the combatants apart. As soon as Buda had gotten his nuts free of Domo's hand, he tried to rush him, but Diamonds stepped between them. "Don't make this more than it is. Let it go," he warned.

Buda locked eyes with Diamonds, still clearly mad as hell. "So you gonna side with these out-of-town niggas over your own kin?"

"Never that. I'm just siding with what's right in this. Ain't no need to take this to the next level. We're all family here."

"Family?" Buda snorted. "I'm starting to wonder how much weight that word still holds these days."

"And what you mean by that, Buda?"

"Nothing. I don't mean shit. I'm going for a walk." Buda turned to leave, but Diamonds stopped him.

"Ain't you forgetting something?" Diamonds extended his hand.

Buda gave Diamonds a stunned look. "Are you fucking serious?"

"Don't be like that. The little nigga earned it."

Buda looked like he was ready to blow a gasket, but he wisely held his tongue. "This is some bullshit, but I'm gonna let you have that, boss man." He tossed a few bills onto the ground and stormed out of the front yard.

"You think it was wise to embarrass Buda like that in front of all these people?" Hank eased up beside Diamonds, who was kneeling down to pick up the bills Buda had dropped.

"Ain't nothing but a case of bruised ego. Buda been on some other shit lately, and maybe this little spectacle will slow him down a taste."

"Or make an already bad situation that much worse," Hank retorted. "Diamonds, you can keep ignoring our little problem, but that ain't gonna make it go away. Buda's drunken antics are getting out of hand. I know you keep saying you'll talk to him, but I think we may be past the point of talking. It's time to take action."

"I done already told you about that shit," Diamonds reminded him.

"The boy is becoming a danger to himself and us, Diamonds, and we ain't no real friends if we continue letting this go on. If not for the sake of all we got riding on this, but to save his own fool life, maybe we should bench him for a while . . . maybe even see about getting him some professional help. I know a place that's right outside the city."

Diamonds waved him off. "Man, that's white people shit. I don't care what Buda's hang-ups are; he's still our brother. Family takes care of family; they don't turn them over to some muthafuckas in white coats, prodding us to tell them how fucked up our childhoods were. Whatever is ailing Buda, we'll handle it as a family."

"Well, what if we ain't equipped to handle it?" Hank questioned.

"I said Buda is fine, and I'll have no more talk about sending him away." Diamonds walked off before Hank could protest.

It took Domo quite a few minutes before he could catch his breath. The fight between him and Buda had only lasted a minute or two, but it felt like he had gone for several rounds. When he was finally able to will his tired legs to move again, he began the task of collecting his hoodie and T-shirt from the front lawn, where he had tossed them before the fight. He used his T-shirt to blot his throbbing lip, and it came away bloody. He could only imagine what his face must've looked like. When he lifted his arms to slip his hoodie over his head, he winced in pain. He'd never had a broken rib, but he imagined that was what it must feel like. Nameless faces patted him on the back, congratulating him on his win, but he didn't feel like a winner. He felt like a man who had just been hit by a tuck.

"That's my boy! You showed that nigga!" Raheem said proudly, draping his arm around Domo's shoulder.

"Fuck off me." Domo shrugged him off.

"Damn, what's your problem?" Raheem asked, as if he didn't know why Domo was angry.

"What do you think my problem is?" Domo snapped. "You couldn't just fall back and be quiet, could you? You just had to get us into some shit, like you always do! I brought you here to see about getting this money, not for you to join in some stupid-ass dice game that could've gotten both of us killed!"

"Domo, you saw what happened. He started it!" Raheem argued.

"Right, and *I* had to finish it! This shit is getting real old, real fast, Rah," Domo fumed.

"So what you saying?"

"I'm saying, I'm getting tired of cleaning up your fucking messes," Domo told him, and walked off.

"C'mon, don't act like that! Your face don't even look that bad!" Raheem called after him, but Domo never stopped.

"Where you off to in such a rush?" Diamonds fell into step beside Domo.

"I gotta get going," Domo said in a clipped tone. He was angry

and didn't feel like talking, but Diamonds either didn't get the hint
or didn't care.

"C'mon, shorty. Don't be salty about that whole business with
Buda. He gets into it with everybody. Slugging it out with that mean
old bear at least once has become a rite of passage in this crew," Diamonds joked, but it didn't do anything to lighten Domo's mood.

"If that's the case, then it's no wonder your numbers look so thin,"
Domo said over his shoulder.

Diamonds stepped out in front of Domo and stopped his exit.
"How about you hold your ass still for a second? I ain't in the business
of chasing niggas." He waited until he made sure Domo understood
his meaning before continuing. "I know my homeboy was on some
bullshit, and I apologize for that. On the upside, you handled yourself like a G. Not too many can take a punch from Buda and still
walk away on their own two feet. For that alone I think you've earned
the respect of everyone who saw it. Here you go." He attempted to
hand him the bills he'd collected from Buda.

"What the fuck is that?" Domo eyed the money suspiciously.

"It's what you bled for and what Buda owed," Diamonds told him.

"If you think I did it for the money, then you've got a lot to learn
about me." Domo chuckled.

"So you just got the shit kicked out of you for free?" Diamonds
cocked his head, trying to understand.

"Where I'm from, we protect those we call family—not bully
them or make sport of them, beating the hell out of each other for
other people's amusement. Thanks for the food and the drinks, but
I'm gone." He brushed passed Diamonds, who was standing there,
an amused smirk on his face.

"I'll talk to him," Vita offered, and went off after Domo. She
caught up with him about a half block away. "Slow down, pretty boy."

"My name is Domonique, or *Domo* if that's too hard for you to remember," he corrected her, but didn't break his stride.

"Okay, *Domonique.* Slow your ass down." Vita grabbed his arm and spun him around. Standing in the light, she could see clearly what Buda had done to him. Surprisingly, it wasn't as bad as she had expected it to be. He had a bruise under his eye, and his bloody lip had doubled in size, but considering it had been Buda who hit him, she knew it could've been far worse. "You okay?"

"Does it look like I'm okay?" he snapped.

"No, it looks like you just got your ass whipped." Vita laughed, but he didn't. "Okay, maybe it was too soon for that," she said, realizing her mistake. "Honestly, your face doesn't even look that bad. A little ice, and the swelling will be down by morning. I'd say you got off lucky, considering what I've seen Buda do to other people with those jackhammers he calls fists."

"He's the lucky one, because I almost started to pull out and blast his ass." Domo brandished his .22.

"First of all, I done already told you about pulling that starter pistol out. It's embarrassing. I gotta get you a real gun. And second of all, had you drawn down on Buda, you and your whole little posse would've gotten wiped the fuck out, so I'm glad you exercised common sense. It'd have been a shame to waste you before we've had a chance to taste this money you're about to make fucking with my crew."

"And who says I still wanna fuck with your crew?" Domo challenged.

"You ain't gotta say it, because I know you're smart enough not to let a little scuffle get in the way of this paper," she told him. "The worse of it is over. You tangled with Buda and lived to tell about it, and ain't nobody in the crew gonna challenge you again. Diamonds will see to that."

"Oh, so your boyfriend is gonna look out for me now?" Domo asked sarcastically.

"It ain't about nobody needing to look out for you—you've already proven you can look out for yourself. And Diamonds isn't my boyfriend; he's just someone I have history with," Vita explained.

"So you say, but from the way he was cuffing you, it seems like a little more than history. I'd say it looked pretty present."

"Domonique, is that jealousy I smell coming off you?" She smiled. It had been a long time since a man had taken enough of an interest in her to get jealous.

"Shorty, you bugging. Ain't nobody stunting what you got going on." Domo turned his face so she couldn't see him blush.

Vita realized she was embarrassing the young boy, so she didn't press it. "You gonna come back to the house or keep standing out here, pouting? Though I can't front, you're kinda cute when you pout."

"Ha, tell me anything." He smiled at her. "Nah, I think I've had my fill of your people for the night. I'm going to the hood."

"Well, give me a few minutes to grab my purse, and I'll take you back to Jersey," Vita offered.

"You don't have to go through all that. I can get home the same way I got here: on public transportation."

"I ain't gonna let you do that. I brought you all the way out here for this bullshit to happen, so I kinda feel like it's my fault. Giving you a ride home is the least I can do," Vita said sincerely.

Domo wanted to stick to his guns and refuse the ride, but he couldn't front like he was really up to taking the train back to Newark. He was tired, sore, and probably looked like shit after the fight. The confines of a car on his long journey would be far more comfortable than the PATH. "A'ight, I'll take the ride back to New Jersey, but that don't mean I'm fucking with you like that," he told her.

"Whatever, nigga." Vita smiled knowingly. "Wait right here while I get my keys and see if your people are ready to go."

"Nah, I took this ass whipping by myself so I'll take ride alone too. They'll be okay."

"Never took you for the petty type, but the color looks good on you, Domonique." Vita winked and went off to fetch the car.

CHAPTER THIRTY-NINE

Looking at herself in the mirror, Pearl couldn't help but smile at the young woman staring back at her. It was a far cry from that train wreck that had staggered out of Harlem Hospital a few hours prior.

Knowledge was pissed for her running off like that, and made sure to let her know just how angry he was the entire walk back to the hospital. During his tirade, she had expected him to mention their run-in outside Pops's bar, but surprisingly it never came up. He seemed more concerned about Diamonds and her relationship with him. Had it been just his usual badgering of her about staying away from older men, she wouldn't have given it a second thought, but Knowledge seemed to have a special interest in him. He never said why, but from the way he was acting, Pearl deduced that Diamonds was either very important or very dangerous. Both possibilities intrigued Pearl and made her anticipate their date that night even more.

Diamonds had insisted that she didn't have to get all dolled up for whatever it was he had planned for them, but there was no way Pearl was going to half step. It wasn't her style. She didn't have a lot of time to get ready, and there was no way she could get an appointment with her regular beautician on such short notice, so she took a gamble with a new spot that had opened up in the neighborhood called Rouge, which was a full-service salon. She remembered Sandra taking her there one day and introducing her to the owner, Elaine, who was a *friend from the old neighborhood,* as she put it.

Pearl was skeptical, but to their credit, they hooked her up. Elaine attended to her hair personally, while two of her most skilled technicians took care of her manicure and pedicure. Two hours later Pearl walked out looking like a million bucks. She tried to pay Elaine for the stellar job, but she wouldn't take the money. All she asked in return was that Pearl spread the word about the shop to her friends and mention to her father that the girls at Rouge had looked out for her. It hardly seemed like a fair trade for the work they had put in, but she wasn't about to argue. It was just another one of the perks that came with being a Stone.

"Somebody is getting awful snazzy for a night at the movies." Sandra snapped Pearl out of her daze. She was leaning against the doorway of the bathroom, eyeing her suspiciously.

"A lady never steps out looking anything but her best. You taught me that." Pearl smiled. "Looks like I'm not the only one getting dolled up." She gave Sandra a once-over. She was wearing a nice green dress and high heels, her hair pulled into a tight bun.

"Believe it or not, but your daddy is taking me out tonight," Sandra told her.

"Really?" Pearl asked, surprised, because she knew her dad wasn't the dating type. "What brought that on?"

"Me telling his ass that while he's busy watering them weeds in the streets, the flowers under his roof are starting to dry out and I'm thinking about calling in a *real* gardener." She rolled her hips seductively. "We've got dinner reservations in an hour."

"Y'all make such an adorable couple. I don't know why Daddy doesn't stop playing and put a ring on your finger already."

"You know your father isn't the marrying kind, and to be honest with you, I'm not so sure I am either. Some people might not understand this strange arrangement of ours, but what we've got works for us. Life is too short not to squeeze every bit of happiness out of it that we can, while we can."

Sandra's words about the shortness of life struck a chord in Pearl. Her mind went to Sheila and what almost was. "Well, even if my fool-ass daddy never recognizes what he has, we do. Sandra, you're the closest thing to a mother Stoney and me ever had or will have, and though we probably don't say it enough, we love and appreciate you." She hugged Sandra quite unexpectedly.

Sandra's eyes misted, but she wouldn't let the tears fall, for fear of smearing her makeup before her date. "Well, what's gotten into you?" She held Pearl at arm's length and studied her face to see if she was high.

"Nothing, just putting things into perspective," Pearl told her.

"That's good to hear, Pearl, and I hope you mean it. Don't think just because I talked your father into letting you go out tonight that I've forgotten that bullshit you pulled by sneaking out. I know you were with those girls last night, and it was only through the grace of God that you left before the fire broke out. You had no business being in that bar, and had it not burned to the ground, I'd have sent a few of the boys over there to have a talk with Pops about serving alcohol to minors. Who were y'all in there with? And don't lie. Tell it straight."

Pearl fidgeted like a child being scolded. "Just some guys. One of them was having a birthday party there."

"Anybody having a birthday party in that shit hole is obviously playing on the wrong side of the law," Sandra scoffed. "Pearl, I don't know what your fascination with gangsters is, but you're going to get enough of being fast."

"Sandra, it wasn't like that. I was just chilling, not doing anything crazy," Pearl said honestly.

"You ain't gotta be the one acting crazy to get caught up in the craziness," Sandra shot back. "Pearl, being around certain types of people invites certain types of energies. When you keep company with men who do dirt, you can't expect not to get dirty. A split-second decision can change the course of your entire life. If you don't believe me, go on down to the city morgue and ask Sheila."

"Gosh, why you gotta take it there?" Pearl rolled her eyes.

Sandra placed her hands on her hips. "Chile, I wish you would roll them eyes at me again so I can snatch them out. This is me you're talking to, not one of your damn friends!"

"Sorry," Pearl mumbled.

"Don't be sorry; be more mindful of how you're moving and who you're moving with. This is the last pass you're going to get from me, Pearl Stone. The next time I catch you wrong, you won't have to worry about what your father might do to you, because I'm going to handle you personally. I might be getting on in years, but I'm not too old to put my sneakers on and drag your young ass up and down through that backyard. Stop being in such a rush to grow up, and stay in a child's place. Are we clear on that?"

"Yes, ma'am."

From downstairs they could hear the chime of the doorbell.

"That's probably, Ruby," Pearl said, glad to have a distraction from Sandra's grilling. She gave herself one last look in the mirror before heading out of the bathroom.

"Pearl," Sandra called after her. "Your father has got enough on his plate as it is without having to worry about his baby girl putting herself in harm's way. You keep that in the back of your mind while you're out at your *movie*. I've given you the rope, but that doesn't mean you need to hang yourself."

"I won't," Pearl promised, and headed down the stairs to greet Ruby.

The conversation with Sandra went far smoother than it could have. Sandra was cool, but when you got on her bad side, she'd jump in your ass. Pearl knew she was still pissed about the lie from earlier, so it was surprising that she'd vouched for her to go out that night. After what had happened with Marisa and Sheila at the bar, Big Stone was adamant about not wanting to let Pearl out of his sight. When she mentioned going out that night, he initially shot it down, but after some coaxing from Sandra, he agreed to it.

Sandra cosigning Pearl's outing helped, but who she was going out with played a large part in it too. Big Stone was old-school in his thinking and was under the misconception that because Ruby was white that she didn't get into *hood shit*, which he couldn't have been more wrong about. Ruby, being under lock and key all the time, was one of the wildest of the bunch when she did get to taste freedom. Still, Pearl was content to let her father's backward thinking work in her favor so she could get out of the house.

Pearl arrived at the top of the stairs to find Stoney leaning against the doorframe and whispering only God knew what in Ruby's ear. He had been trying to get in her pants ever since he discovered his dick, and from the way she was gazing at him and grinning, he appeared to be making progress. Pearl cleared her throat to announce her presence, and both of them jumped like they had just been caught fucking.

"Stoney, why don't get your ass out of that girl's face?" Pearl descended the stairs.

"I don't hear her complaining," Stoney capped.

"Well, I'm complaining for her." Pearl shoved him aside. "What's up, girl? You ready to go?"

"Yeah, but I gotta be back by ten," Ruby told her.

"What the fuck? It's not even a school night!"

"Pearl, you know how my parents are. I'm lucky to have gotten out at all, but they're feeling sorry for me over what happened to Sheila. We went by her parents' house to pay our respects today, but they weren't really in the mood to receive guests."

Pearl shook her head. "Tell me about it. I saw them at the hospital this morning, and they were in pretty bad shape." She went on to tell Ruby the short version of their encounter, omitting the part about lying to them about how they ended up at the party.

"My heart goes out to them," Ruby said sincerely. "The crew isn't going to be the same without Sheila."

"I know," Pearl said sadly. "This will be the first birthday I'll be celebrating without Sheila since we've known each other."

"So what's the plan for your birthday? Did you hear anything from your dad about a party yet?" Ruby asked.

"Not yet. I feel kinda fucked up about even thinking about a party with one friend in the hospital and another in the morgue," Pearl said.

"I know what you mean. But whether he throws you a party or not, we still need to do something special. Sheila wouldn't want us sitting around like some grieving widows. She'd want us out there, doing us."

"You're right about that. Sheila loved a good time more than anyone I know," Pearl said, reflecting on her friend.

"Then that's what we need to do. Let's not only celebrate your birthday, but Sheila's life as well. Lets do it for our girl!" Ruby declared, louder than she needed to.

"What's all this noise out here?" Big Stone came out of the kitchen. He was wearing dark slacks, a white shirt, and red suspenders hanging off his hips. Clutched in his hand was a turkey sandwich. His ever-present shadow, Knowledge, trailed him.

"Oh, nothing, Dad. We're just about to head out and catch our movie," Pearl told him.

"Which theater did you say y'all are going to again?" Knowledge asked suspiciously.

"I never did, but if you must know, we're going to the one near Times Square," Pearl said with attitude. "Why are you asking? You plan on paying for our tickets?"

"Slow your roll, Pearl. I'm just trying to make sure y'all don't end up at none of them ghetto-ass theaters uptown. The streets of Harlem are real tense right now, and niggas are acting a fool. I'm pretty sure your dad don't want you hanging around no *undesirables*."

"Sure as hell don't!" Big Stone chimed in. "These lil niggas running around these days calling themselves players have turned the damn streets into a shooting gallery. Use to be a man could walk through Harlem without having to worry about some young punk with a pistol and a dream trying to take what they want instead of working for it!" he fumed.

"Dad, is everything okay?" Pearl asked, picking up on his mood.

Seeing the look of concern in his daughter's eyes, Big Stone's face softened. "Yeah, everything is cool. I'm sorry, baby girl. Yo daddy is just venting. You got money to move around with?" he asked, changing the subject.

"Yeah, I got a few dollars, but I'll take whatever you were planning to give me too." Pearl batted her lashes at her father.

Big Stone shook his head in amusement before digging into his pocket for bankroll. "I swear, when you do that, you remind me of your mama. She was the only female I'd ever met in my life who could get me to break bread with just a look. But if you ever tell Sandra I said it, I'll deny it." He held out some bills.

"Don't worry—your secret is safe with me." Pearl took the money and shoved it into her purse. "Let's get going, Ruby." She pulled her friend by the hand toward the door. She wanted to get out of there before she was subjected to another round of Twenty Questions.

"Pearl," Knowledge called after her. "You be sure to stay out of Harlem tonight, okay?"

"Oh, don't worry. I have no plans to hang out in Harlem this evening," Pearl assured him before she and Ruby disappeared out the front door.

By the time Pearl and Ruby got to the corner, a cab was waiting for them. Pearl had called a Harlem car service and requested a driver she was familiar with to come to pick them up. She didn't have him pull up in front of the house because she'd told her father they were taking the bus downtown. Once inside, they were whisked toward their destination. Part of her felt guilty for lying about going to the movies, but at least she would keep her word about staying out of Harlem. She was meeting Diamonds in the Bronx.

"That Knowledge gives me the creeps," Ruby admitted once they'd left the block. "The way he's always watching us and asking questions, you'd think he was psychic or something."

"That nigga ain't psychic; he's just nosey as hell." Pearl waved her off. "Knowledge gets on my damn nerves the way he's always spying for Daddy, but he ain't all bad. He could've blown my spot when he saw me at the bar, but as far as I know, he still hasn't dropped a dime on me."

"Really? What do you think his angle is for keeping his mouth shut?" Ruby asked.

Pearl shrugged. "Beats the hell out of me. Trying to read Knowledge is like trying to guess which way the wind is gonna blow. But to hell with him. We're about to have a good time, and I brought something to get us in the mood!" She pulled a joint out of her purse.

"Pearl, you can't light that in a taxi!"

"Why the hell not? This ain't no regular taxi. Me and Nine-Five got an understanding, don't we, Nine-Five?" Pearl addressed the cab driver by his car number instead of the name she never bothered to find out.

The African cab driver spared a glance over his shoulder. "Get as high as y'all want, ma. As long as you pass that shit this way."

"See, I told you're we're good. Now, stop whining and let's get loose." Pearl lit the joint.

It was a smooth ride from Manhattan to the Bronx, and the bomb-ass weed Pearl had scored from one of the white hippies who lived on her street made it smoother. Nine-Five had his system tuned to Hot 97, and the girls jammed and sang along. Pearl's cell phone rang in her purse. She looked at the caller ID and shook her head before tossing it back down. Less than a minute later it rang again, and knowing it would only continue, she just shut it off.

"Who's blowing up your phone like that? Your dad?" Ruby asked.

"No, pain in the ass Devonte." Pearl huffed.

"What happened? I thought you guys were good?"

"We were until he started getting all clingy. I told him it was over, but he's acting like he's got wax in his ears. He keeps calling my phone, and I could've sworn I saw him when I was leaving the salon earlier. Good pussy will turn a man into a love-sick puppy."

"Or a stalker," Ruby countered. "Don't take this lightly. My mom had a friend who broke it off with a guy she was seeing, but somebody must've forgotten to tell him that. It started with him blowing up her phone and stalking her house. It was only a matter of time before he really jumped out the window and did something horrible."

Pearl sucked her teeth. "Devonte's ass ain't that crazy."

"That's the same thing my mother's friend said, right before the guy showed up at her job one morning and threw acid in her face."

"Damn!" Pearl said in disgust.

"This is something you might want to tell your dad about, or maybe even Knowledge," Ruby suggested.

"Maybe you're right," Pearl said, suddenly not so confident in knowing what to expect from her scorned lover. Until her conversation with Ruby, she had never considered that Devonte could possibly try to harm her. Granted, his constant calling and pleading was starting to creep her out, but violence had never crossed her mind. Devonte couldn't possibly be that crazy . . . could he?

Twenty minutes later Nine Five had crossed into the neighborhood of the address Pearl had given him. As they neared the house, Pearl spotted Diamonds standing on the curb. There were several men standing behind him while he exchanged words with a tall dread outside a black SUV. She watched curiously as Diamonds and the dread shook hands. The dread waved the men with him back to the car, and they began to pile in. When Pearl spotted the familiar face standing beside the dread, she had to do a double take.

"Stop the car!" Pearl ordered, causing Nine-Five to slam on the brakes.

"Everything good, shorty?" Nine-Five asked, pulling a gun from the hidden compartment under the glove box. He wasn't a gangster by any stretch, but he liked Pearl and was well aware of who her father was and what he could benefit from if he held his little girl down in a time of trouble.

Pearl's eyes zeroed in on the men climbing into the SUV. "I think I know those guys."

CHAPTER FORTY

"Nigga, I can't believe you just orchestrated a fight in the middle of a baby shower," Goldie said, still in disbelief.

"That wasn't no fight, lil bro. Nothing more than a scuffle," Diamonds said, downplaying it.

"Still, at a baby shower?" Goldie questioned, as if his older brother should've known better. "TJ is pissed, and ain't no words for what Teisha is right now."

"I'll go in and make my apologies soon," Diamonds said. "It was fucked up on my part to let that go on here, but you gotta admit that it was funny as hell. You see Buda's face when the young boy grabbed his nuts?"

Goldie didn't want to laugh, but he couldn't help it. " 'Get this little nigga off me!' " he imitated Buda. "Yo, I dead thought his eyes were gonna pop out of his head. Where did you find that crazy-ass young dude?"

"Vita recruited him. He came over with your boy LA to handle that piece of business with Pana's other spot," Diamonds told him.

"He looks a little on the young side, but his boy LA seems to be solid enough, and he speaks highly of the kid. Heard he dropped some bodies uptown, so I guess he can hold his weight around here."

"Vita sure as hell seems to think so," Diamonds said in a less-than-thrilled tone.

"If I didn't know any better, I'd say you were jealous," Goldie teased him.

"Of that lil nigga? Fuck outta here! That meat way too tender. Vita likes a tougher cut," Diamonds said. "Anybody see where Buda got off to?" he said, changing the subject.

"I seen him jump in a cab a while ago. He's probably headed over to see that broad he's been keeping time with," Goldie said.

"One of his jump-offs?" Diamonds asked.

"Nah, for as much time as he spends with this chick, I think it's a little more than that. He's been spending a lot of time with her. If you ask me, I think that boy is sprung."

"How long this been going on?"

"I ain't for sure, but I'd say a little while. When he ain't getting on our nerves, he's out chasing her."

"What we know about this chick?" Diamonds asked.

Goldie shrugged. "Not too much. Buda been real secretive about her, like he's worried about one of us trying to steal her. I haven't officially met her yet, but I've seen her before. Nice-looking Spanish broad."

Something about it didn't sit right with Diamonds. For as long as he had known him, Buda had always been a notorious woman-izer, so hearing some mysterious chippie had his attention raised a red flag in his head. "I think at some point we gonna need to meet this mystery woman just to make sure everything is on the up-and-up."

"You know Buda ain't gonna be feeling you digging into his personal business like that," Goldie warned.

"I don't care what Buda is or isn't feeling. As captain of this crew, it's my job to make sure everybody we come into contact with is who they're supposed to be. That reminds me: I need you to do something for me tonight."

"What?" Goldie asked suspiciously.

"Don't look at me like that. You act like I'm walking you into some bullshit," Diamonds assured him.

"Like the time when we were little and you sent me into the candy store with that note without telling me you and Buda were going to rob the joint?"

"Man, that was different." Diamonds waved him off. "This will require minimal work, and you might end up getting a treat at the end of the night."

"Then tell me what it is," Goldie demanded.

Before Diamonds could answer, Hank walked up. He looked tired and aggravated, which was nothing new. "Fuck y'all out here doing, yanking each other's dicks?"

"Don't be the next one to get dropped out here." Goldie launched fake punches at Hank's midsection.

"I'll whip your little young ass later. Right now we've got business to handle." Hank nodded toward the black SUV that had just pulled up at the curb. From the way Rolling and Born were climbing over each other to be the first ones to greet the vehicle, Diamonds knew it had to be the connect. The moment of truth had arrived.

"Goldie, do me a solid. In the house, amongst the rest of the gifts, you'll find a bag with a gold-wrapped box in it. Why don't you go fetch it for me?"

"C'mon, bro. You acting like I don't wanna meet the connect too," Goldie complained. He hated when Diamonds put him in the *little brother* zone.

"You'll get your introduction *after* you bring me the bag," Diamonds told him.

"A'ight," Goldie pouted like a child, and sulked off.

"Showtime." Diamonds started toward the SUV.

When Rolling spotted him coming, he said something to someone on the passenger side, which prompted all four of the vehicle's doors to open at once. Two hard-looking characters wearing black sunglasses jumped out and gave a quick look around before taking up positions at either end of the truck. Next out was a young dude who looked to be not long out of high school. His scowl was hard, but his face was still tender and innocent. The last man to climb out of the SUV was surprisingly familiar to Diamonds. He was the dread with all the jewelry who he had seen with Pearl and her friends at the bar. That night, he was laughing and having a good time, but tonight his face was hard and serious. His keen eyes locked onto Diamonds, who was coming out the front gate to meet him.

"Bon Mesye aswe," Diamonds greeted them.

"A good evening indeed," the dread replied, letting Diamonds know that he, too, spoke Creole.

Rolling made the nervous introduction. "Doodles, this is the guy Diamonds who I was telling you about." He was standing between two of the most dangerous men he had ever met, outside out of his brother.

"It's good to finally meet." Diamonds shook Doodles's hand, and it seemed to ease some of the tension between their two caps. "I appreciate you coming all this way, especially with all you have going on. My condolences on your loss, by the way."

"It was actually a friend of my son's." Doodles pointed to the young kid with him.

Diamonds didn't see it at first, but now that he mentioned it, there was a resemblance between him and the scowling kid. They had the same eyes and thick lips. "Sorry for your loss."

The kid just nodded.

"One of Franz's friends caught a bad break last night in that bar

fire on a Hundred and Forty-Fifth. You hear anything about that?"
Doodles asked.

It seemed like an innocent enough question, but there was something behind it. Diamonds thought about playing dumb, but the direct approach had always been more his style. "Actually I was there," he admitted. "Thankfully me and my friends left long before the fire started."

Doodles nodded as if Diamonds had passed whatever test he'd just been given. "Some of Ricky's family are in town, and I need to attend to them. So you'll excuse me if I insist we make this brief."

"I wouldn't have it any other way," Diamonds agreed. "As far as I knew, we were good, but now I'm hearing you got some concerns about the deal."

"I wouldn't call them concerns, more like reservations," Doodles corrected him. "I did my homework on you, Diamonds. Your work in Miami and Texas tells me that you're a man who knows how to flip a coin, but you also tend to leave big messes behind in every city you visit."

Diamonds shrugged. "In this life people, die every day. It's simply part of who we are."

"I'm a man who understands that, but I'm also a man who understands that we have to pick our battles, not go out and invite them."

"Trust me: I can handle anything I invite to my house," Diamonds capped.

"Like you did Pana Suarez?" Doodles asked. When he saw the tick in Diamonds's eye, he knew the information he'd received had been accurate. "Don't look so surprised. I told you: I did my homework. Now, I didn't know that man and don't care why you did what you did to him, but I'm pretty sure there are people who do care and who are going to be looking for someone to lynch behind this. I just wanna make sure that the bullshit you're up here kicking don't splash on my side of the grass."

"I feel you on that, and I can assure you the two won't cross. One thing doesn't have anything to do with the other," Diamonds assured him.

"You and I both feel that way, but who's to say that all parties involved will agree?" Doodles questioned. "People could look at me supplying you with heroin during your coup as picking a side. This could potentially turn your enemies into my enemies."

"Well, under such unfortunate circumstances, that would make you my friend."

As if on cue, Goldie came walking out with the bag Diamonds had sent him for, and he handed it to him. Diamonds took a peek inside and smiled before extended the bag to Doodles.

"What the fuck is that?" Doodles eyed the bag suspiciously.

"One thing you'll learn about me is that I take good care of my friends, but better care of my enemies." Diamonds placed the bag on the floor and stepped back.

Doodles waved one of his men forward to open the package. They all watched in anticipation as he carefully tore off the wrapping paper. It was expensive-looking hatbox tied off with a satin ribbon. He looked up at Doodles, who motioned for him open it. When his bodyguard removed the lid, he recoiled at the sight of the severed head inside. Men on both sides drew their pistols, and Diamonds and Doodles found themselves in the middle of a standoff.

"What's the meaning of this fuckery?" Doodles snapped. His head whipped around toward Born and Rolling. "I come here to do business, and he lays a threat at my feet? I should kill the both of you for this disrespect."

"D-doodles . . . I . . . I . . ." Rolling stuttered.

"Everybody, calm the fuck down." Diamonds stepped up. He

waved to his men to lower their guns, and they reluctantly complied. Doodles's people kept their guns raised. "You got it wrong, friend. This here ain't no threat; it's me reassuring you that I take care of my own."

"Fuck are you talking about?" Doodles's eyes kept going from the head in the hatbox to Diamonds.

Diamonds picked the box up and peered inside before tilting it so that Doodles could see the petrified death mask on the head's face. "This here isn't just any old head. It's the head of the man who's responsible for the loss of your son's friend . . . well, one of the men, at least."

Doodles motioned for his men to lower their weapons, now interested in what Diamonds had to say.

"Like you already know, I was at that club last night, and could've bit it behind that bogus-ass fire too. I had some of my people do some digging, and as it turned out, it wasn't an accident at all. Pops was drowning in debt, so he and his boy here got it in their heads to burn the place down to collect on the insurance money," Diamonds said as if it were gospel.

"And how exactly do you know all this?" Franz questioned. It was clear from his look and his tone that he wasn't buying into Diamonds's story.

"Because I wanted to buy the place from him." Diamonds revealed the sliver of truth in his story. "I been on the old man for a time for the property, and I finally got him to cave. It was a cash deal, so we could leave the liquor license in his name and not have to bother with transferring it over. Old Pops thought he was going to beat me and the system, but he never counted on that fire spinning out of control. I hear he barely made it out."

Doodles studied Diamonds's face for signs that he was lying, but he found the young man unreadable. "So did you kill him because the fire took the life of one of mine or because his father tried to rob you?"

Diamonds pondered the question. "I killed because they tried to steal from me, but I cut his head off to earn the favor of a new friend. Will you be my new friend?" He extended his hand.

Doodles looked at the hand for a long while. The man was either shit-house crazy or more cunning than Doodles had expected. Either way, Doodles had decided at the moment that hatbox had come open and he saw the head, he'd much rather have Diamonds as an ally than an enemy. "Yes, I think I'd like that very much." He shook Diamonds's hand and sealed the bargain.

Doodles had barely cleared the block before men came spilling from the front yard and surrounded Diamonds. They were whooping and patting him on the back like he had just hit the game-winning shot in the playoffs. They all knew what time it was with the meeting and what the deal would mean for their crew. Shit was about to change. TJ was in his ear, going ballistic over the fact that he'd hidden a human head amongst the baby shower gifts. It wasn't the smartest idea he'd ever had, but it beat toting the damn thing around all night. TJ was mad, but he'd get over it when he saw what his end would be from the heroin deal Diamonds had just secured. It was truly a good night to be a bad guy.

"You sure about being more gangster than politician?" Hank approached Diamonds after the crowd had dispersed. "That was a load of bullshit worthy of Washington."

"Bullshit is in the eye of the beholder, old-timer. I'd have convinced that muthafucka that the sky was purple if it meant getting to that heroin," Diamonds said.

"I still can't believe you pulled that shit off," Goldie said.

Diamonds grabbed him in a playful headlock and rubbed his knuckles across the top of his head. "Have I ever promised you anything I couldn't deliver?"

"I gotta hand it to you, kid. When you set your mind to something, you don't stop until you get it," Hank said proudly.

"This is only the beginning." Diamonds released Goldie. "Having this heroin-rolling plug is gonna open a lot of doors for us, boys. Before you know it, we'll be rolling in dough."

"So long as we ain't rolling in bullets first," TJ said, adding his two cents. "What about Eddie? Man, he gave us a shot and we're burning him."

"Calm your nervous ass down. Nobody is getting burned. We just ain't putting all our eggs in one basket," Diamonds explained.

"Yeah, unlike some of us, we ain't quite so trusting of Eddie yet," Hank added. He hadn't missed out on the fact that TJ had seemed to be entirely too pro-Eddie throughout the whole ordeal.

"Stop coming at me like that, old man, because you know I'm just as down for this team as anybody!" TJ declared. "All I'm saying is, I'm about to have a new baby, so unlike y'all, I don't have the luxury of picking up and moving from place to place like a damn gypsy."

"Relax, cousin. Nobody is going to have to move. New York is home to all of us right now, but when and if that happens to change, I'll make sure you and your family got no worries. Now, why don't you go attend to your woman and let the grown folks talk?" Diamonds made a dismissive gesture. TJ was blowing his moment.

"What the fuck?" they heard Hank blurt out. All eyes turned to see what he was looking at.

"Who is that?" Goldie squinted to get a better look at the young ladies coming across the street.

"That, little brother, is the favor I need from you." Diam
smiled.

Directly across the street from TJ's house, a man sat hunkered down
behind the wheel of a beat-up Ford Explorer. He'd been parked there
for over an hour, surveying everything that was going on. The fight
that had broken out on the front lawn provided him a good laugh. He
would've bet money on the brute, but David ended up triumphing over
Goliath.

Not too long after the scuffle, the two combatants went their separate ways. The big man jumped in a taxi, and the young guy cut out
with the girl who'd hung around the crew. He already knew where
the big guy was off to, and he had one of his boys follow the girl. A
black SUV pulled up, and several men jumped out. Diamonds and a
few of his boys came out of the front yard to greet them. He recognized the man in the SUV, who was leading the group. He had seen
him around a couple of times, but he knew him more by reputation
than personally. Him being there was a bad sign, but the handshake
he and Diamonds shared before parting company was even more dis-
turbing.

The man surveying the scene was just reaching for his burner
phone to report his findings when things took yet another twist. In
his rearview mirror, he spotted two girls crossing the street from
behind his truck. One was a chubby white girl, the other a shapely
black chick. He adjusted his mirror to get a better look and realized
he had seen the black girl before. If the girl was who he thought she
was, then the situation had taken a turn toward the truly bizarre.
Once he had seen enough, he picked up the burner phone and dialed
the only number in the call log.

"Yeah, it's me. I think you boys have got a bigger problem than
you thought."

CHAPTER FORTY-ONE

"So glad you could make it." Diamonds pulled Pearl in for a warm hug. "I trust you didn't have a problem finding this place."

"It'd have been kind of hard to miss." Pearl looked over the sea of men who were staring at her and Ruby like hungry dogs. "I feel kind of overdressed for a barbecue." She motioned over her cute skirt set and heels.

"Don't worry, baby. I'd never have you waste such a nice fit on these hard legs. This is just a pit stop before we push off to our next destination."

Behind them, Ruby cleared her throat.

"Oh, sorry," Pearl said as if she were just remembering her friend was there. "Diamonds, this is my girl Ruby."

"Nice to meet you, Ruby." Diamonds shook her hand. "I'd like to introduce you to—"

"His brother, Goldie," the younger sibling cut in. He took Ruby's hand and kissed it. "Charmed."

From the way the two of them were gazing at each other, there was no question as to whether they would get along or not.

"And, Pearl, I think you remember Hank from the bar." Diamonds motioned to his OG, who was standing off to the side, looking at both of them as if they had sprouted additional heads. She waved to Hank, and he responded by shaking his head before storming back toward the house. "Pay him no mind; he's on the rag today," he joked. "So long as you're here, let me introduce you to the rest of the family. I trust you'll be seeing a lot of them in the near future, so might as well get familiar."

"Who says I'm going to be around long enough to get to know them?" Pearl asked playfully.

"Sweetie, now that I've got you, you'd be a fool to think I was ever gonna let you go." Diamonds looped his arm through hers. "Now, let's go get my new lady acquainted."

They were only supposed to be at the barbecue for a few minutes, but it had been over two hours and they hadn't left yet. Initially Pearl was upset because she had gotten all dolled up for a date, not to spend her night in a backyard, but after a while she settled in and actually started enjoying herself. The music was rocking, the drinks were flowing, and there was a spread of delicious food that looked like it had been professionally catered. As far as baby showers went, it was one of the best she had ever attended.

Diamonds had strutted her proudly around the backyard, introducing her to what he referred to as his *family*. They were really a ragtag bunch comprised of soldiers he had recruited from different cities during his push to New York. From the way the men embraced her, you'd have thought Diamonds was the president of the United States and she was the First Lady. The same couldn't be said for the women. Some of them were cool, but most of them were shooting her shady looks. Pearl knew what that was all about. She was young, fine, and a new face, and the eyes of their men followed her everywhere she went. Pearl couldn't blame them for feeling threatened, but they had nothing to worry about. She only had eyes for Diamonds.

After he was done introducing his cabinet to his new first lady, Diamonds got Pearl a plate and helped her to a chair in a quiet corner of the backyard. He excused himself momentarily while he handled something in the house. Goldie had taken that opportunity to go show his new redheaded toy off to his friends near the make-shift bar. They had hit it off right away, which was surprising to Pearl, because he wasn't her type. Goldie was handsome to the point of almost being pretty, and Ruby usually went in for a rougher-looking sort. She was glad to see her friend having a good time and hoped that whatever seed had been planted between Ruby and Goldie blossomed. She and Pearl would be the envy of every girl in school if they showed up at prom with the brothers as their dates.

"Mind if I sit?" Hank spooked her when he pulled out the chair next to hers. He didn't wait for her to reply before sitting down. "It's Pearl, right?"

"Yes," she answered uneasily. There was something about how he was looking at her that she didn't like.

"You know, it ain't hard to see why Diamonds is so smitten with you. You're a fine piece of woman." His eyes roamed over her. "A little young, but fine. So tell me, what's a square broad like you doing in the company of gangsters?"

"And how you figure I'm a square?" Pearl snaked her neck, offended by the assumption.

"It ain't too hard to tell. The way you dress, the way you talk, the way your eyes lit up like you had just walked into a circus when he brought you back here." Hank snickered. "You might get your kicks hanging out in the slums, but you ain't from 'em. What's your angle here, baby?"

"Excuse me?" Pearl was confused.

"I mean, what are you *really* doing with Diamonds?" Hank asked flatly.

"I don't know what you're hinting at, and frankly I'm starting to get a little bit offended." Pearl stood to leave, and was surprised when Hank grabbed her by her wrist and yanked her back down into the seat. Pearl's eyes rolled up the length of Hank's arm, and when she looked at his eyes, they were hard and serious. "Nigga, you got exactly three seconds to get your slimy-ass hand off me, or I promise you that you'll live just long enough to regret it."

"What you gonna do, call your daddy and have him send some of his shooters at me?" Hank asked slyly. The look of shock in the girl's eyes made him smile. "Oh, you surprised I know who you really are, *Pearl Stone*? Little girl, I've been guarding Diamonds's back and his heart since long before you sniffed your first dick. The minute I saw how wide open his nose was over you, I started doing some digging into your backyard."

Pearl snatched her hand away. "So what? My daddy's a gangster. That doesn't have anything to do with what me and Diamonds got going on."

"Foolish child, that has everything to do with what you and Diamonds got going. You might play naïve, but I know good and well you ain't, so you already know what time it is with us. How do you think your father would react if he found out a hooligan like Diamonds was deflowering his one and only daughter?"

Pearl sucked her teeth. "You're taking this way too serious. Me and Diamonds just met, and though I admit I'm feeling him, it's way too early to be talking about taking him home to meet my dad."

Hank shook his head sadly. "You just don't get it, do you? Diamonds doesn't have to say it for me to know he's fallen for you; I can see it in his eyes. When he gets it in his mind that he wants something, there ain't gonna be nobody short of God who can change his mind about it, and that includes your daddy."

"Well, maybe we'll end up falling for each other," Pearl challenged.

Hank sighed. "You can try to trade words with me until the sun goes up, but it don't change what is and what will be if you keep entertaining this puppy love shit. I know the way I'm giving it to you is harsh, but I'm only trying to help. You and Diamonds hooking up is something that won't be good for any of us."

"Well, I appreciate your concern, but I think I'll take my chances." Pearl flipped her hair and gave him her back. If the sour old man thought he was going to scare Pearl off, he had another think coming. The fact that he was so against their relationship only made her want Diamonds more.

"Everything cool over here?" Diamonds walked up. He could sense the tension between Pearl and Hank.

"Yeah, everything is cool, but I think it's about time for us to get going." Pearl got up from her chair.

"What's the matter, baby? I thought you were having a good time?" Diamonds was confused by her sudden change of mood. "Look, I know I promised you a night on the town, so if you want, we can get out of here and go somewhere a little more upscale."

"No, it's not that. I've had a wonderful time tonight, but Ruby has a curfew, so I gotta get her home," Pearl half lied.

Diamonds didn't totally buy her excuse, but he didn't press her further. "Okay, love. Whatever you want."

"I'll wait for you out front," Pearl said, and left without bothering to say good-bye to Hank.

Diamonds looked from Perl back to Hank. "What the fuck was that all about?"

"Nothing, man. Was getting to know your new friends. Do you have any idea who the fuck that little girl really is?" Hank asked.

"Yeah, Pearl Stone. Big Stone's daughter," Diamonds replied, much to Hank's surprise.

"You mean to tell me that you already knew who that broad was and you still pursued her?"

"I didn't know at first, but I eventually put the pieces together. I don't see what the big deal is," Diamonds said as if it were nothing.

"The big deal is one of these days during the course of our little hostile take-over, you may have to put a bullet in her father!" Hank reminded him.

"Nah, that's where you're wrong, Hank. I got no interest in killing Big Stone. He's one of the few I respect out of all these so-called kings of the city. I plan to try to woo him to our side, and I'm going to use his little princess to do it. Now, before you open your mouth to shoot my plan down, let me stop you. I ain't fool enough to think me and shorty can keep creeping around forever, so I'm going to use honesty as my shield, and approach Big Stone like a respectable young man, but it'll be on my time and my terms. He might not like it, but when he sees all the work I'm going to put into the courtship of his daughter, it's going to make me real hard to hate. At the very least, he'll hear me out when I lay it on the table for him. By then we'll be so strong out here that he'll see why partnering with us is more profitable than going against us. Besides, how would it look to his little girl if he killed his future son-in-law?" Diamonds smiled.

"So you're saying this whole thing between you two is just a business move?" Hank didn't believe it.

"Hank, you know you're one of the few people I'd never try to run game on. I don't know what to make of these feelings of mine, but whatever they are, they're genuine. Still, I've never been one to let my heart get in the way of a business opportunity."

Hank wanted to argue all the things that could go wrong with

Diamonds's plan, but he knew there would be no changing Diamonds's mind. "You're going to get us killed."

"Or make us rich," Diamonds countered. "Either way, it'll be a story for the history books." He smiled and jogged off to catch up with Pearl.

As usual, Diamonds had successfully managed to frustrate Hank. He loved the young man and would follow him to the ends of the earth, but sometimes Diamonds danced too close to the edge for his tastes. This thing between him and Pearl was a disaster waiting to happen. He knew it, and the others would know it too. It wouldn't go over with the crew, especially Vita.

CHAPTER FORTY-TWO

Domo didn't have too much to say on the ride to New Jersey. He was slumped deep in the passenger seat, pretending to still be angry and giving Vita the silent treatment, but in truth he wasn't talking because he wasn't sure what to say. It was the first time he and Vita had ever been alone in close quarters.

For the most part, Vita left him to stew and lick his wounds, only asking for the occasional direction to his house. Every so often he would catch her watching him from the corners of her eyes. If he didn't know any better, he'd have said she was concerned. Of all his new friends, she was the hardest to read, going from sweet to sour as the moods struck her. There was chemistry between them; he felt it and was pretty sure she felt it too, but he wasn't sure how to react to it. What if he pushed up on her only to find that he had misread the signs and ended up embarrassing himself? A better question was: How would Diamonds take him encroaching on his territory? Vita claimed there was nothing between her and Diamonds but history, but Domo knew better. He seemed to have some type of hold on her that Domo couldn't quite figure out.

"You gonna keep staring at me or speak your mind?" Vita asked without taking her eyes off the road.

"I wasn't staring," Domo lied.

"Sure you weren't. It must be someone else's eyes I feel burning a hole in the side of my face," she said sarcastically. "I know you ain't still sitting there mad at them love taps you caught?"

"Nah, shit don't even hurt no more," Domo lied. He jaw actually felt like it was hanging off the hinges, and it pained him to talk. "So what's good with you and Diamonds?" he said, changing the subject.

Vita cut her eyes at him. "You still on that? I told you, me and him got history, nothing more. Why are you so stuck on Diamonds? It ain't like you're checking for me."

"Who says I'm not?" Domo wasn't sure why he had said it, other than it was the first thing that popped into his head. Her lack of an immediate reaction made him feel like he had played himself. He wished he could have the words back, but then a thin smile creased her lips.

"Domonique, your young ass ain't ready for what I got cooking between these thighs. This"—she grabbed his hand placed it up her skirt—"is grown woman pussy, not little girl snatch. I'd fuck around and have you sprung."

"Or it could play out the other way around." Domo let his hand linger on her crotch, appreciating the heat coming through her panties. Once the ice was broken, the liquor and weed he'd consumed that night took over and he was feeling himself. He was contemplating testing his luck and trying to slip a finger inside her, but she must've been reading his mind because she moved his hand.

"Don't start something you aren't prepared to finish, little boy," Vita warned.

"Stop shooting me mixed signals and I will, *old head,*" he capped back.

There was an awkward silence between them for the next few miles on the Turnpike. They had opened a door they'd both been looking at but neither of them had planned on unlocking, and it raised the question as to whether to step through it or not.

"How do you think your boys are gonna take you leaving them like that?" Vita broke the silence.

"Like I give a shit. LA didn't ride with me in the first place, and Raheem is lucky all I did was leave him instead of fucking his ass up!" Domo fumed. He was angry with Raheem for getting them into the situation, but angrier with himself for not letting him handle it on his own.

"Can I say something without you getting all in your feelings about it?" Vita questioned.

"I got a feeling you're going to say whatever it is regardless of how I might react to it."

"I know that's your boy, but that kid is deadweight," Vita said flatly. "LA is a fucking head case who's likely to get murdered before he gets rich, but he'll stand up and do what needs to be done when the time comes. Your other friend . . ." She shook her head.

"How about you let me worry about Rah?"

"C'mon, kid. You know that ain't how this works. I told you from the beginning what you were getting into and what was at stake. Each of us is responsible for the lives of the others. I wouldn't trust Raheem with my car, let alone my life. Letting that kid in on what we're bringing you into is likely going to get you killed, and I can't have that. I'm sorry, kid, but if you want in, then he's out."

Domo didn't want to admit it, but Vita was right. He wished he could say that what Raheem had done at the baby shower was a random occurrence, but it wasn't. It had been the story of his life since he'd met Raheem. Rah would always start some shit and leave it to Domo to clean up. Even his brother, Understanding, had warned him against playing Raheem so close, but Rah was one of the only real friends Domo had. Still, maybe it was time to put a little space between them. Maybe once Domo got established, he would be able to pull Raheem in, but while he was on the come-up, it was best if his friend played the background.

Ten minutes later they turned down Domo's block. Vita was surprised at how quiet the street he lived on appeared to be in contrast to the dangerous-looking neighborhoods they'd crossed through to get there. It was almost as if the tree-lined streets and the quaint two-family houses didn't belong. She pulled up in front of the house he'd directed her to and put the car in park.

"This your place?" Vita looked over the two-story house, with its cut grass and recycling bins propped neatly at the curb.

"Me and my mom," Domo told her. He looked to their second-floor window. The lights were on, which meant his mother had found the money and taken care of the bill. It made him feel good to know that he had been able to help, but she was sure to have questions about the money. When she saw his lip, it would open up an entirely different can of worms.

"Everything cool?" Vita noticed his reluctance to exit the car.

"My mom is still up," Domo confessed. "I can't go home with my face looking like this."

"Then don't."

"What am I supposed to do, sleep in the car?" Domo laughed. His laugher died when Vita's hand landed on his lap.

"Or we don't have to sleep at all."

CHAPTER FORTY-THREE

Eddie sat in his office, drumming his fingers on the desk and trying his best to hide his irritation. He hated last-minute meetings, especially when the person he was supposed to be meeting kept him waiting. Just when he was about to pick up the phone and tell them to forget it, there was a knock at the door.

Blanco looked to Eddie, who gave him the nod before getting up and opening the office door and letting Knowledge in. Eddie had heard that Big Stone's second-in-command had been asking around about him all day, so he wasn't surprised when he had gotten the call to request a sit-down. With the way Diamonds was laying siege to the city, it was only a matter of time before people started putting their heads together to try to identify the new threat. The fact that Knowledge was there meant that there was suspicion, but the absence of Big Stone meant there was no proof . . . at least not yet.

"When you called about a meeting, I had assumed it would be Big Stone who I was actually talking to," Eddie said, reminding Knowledge that the two of them weren't of the same social status.

"My big homie is attending to some other business, but I'm here on his authority. I won't take up too much of your precious time," Knowledge assured him.

"Fine then, what I can I do for you in the name of Big Stone?"

Knowledge got right to it. "I'm sure by now you've heard about the death of Pana Suarez and Pops's joint burning down."

"Yeah, a shame about the old man. I kinda liked him, but I can't say I'll lose any sleep over Pana," Eddie said sarcastically.

"Yeah, what happened to Pops is fucked up."

"Any idea who torched his joint?"

"See, that's the thing. Right before he told us, Pops mysteriously passed away. The doctors said he choked on his own tongue," Knowledge revealed.

Eddie was shocked but did his best to hide it. "Wow, now that's a fucked-up way to die."

"Sure is. I'm not really here to talk about Pops though. I'm more interested in what happened to Pana. A man that heavy getting greased without putting up so much as a fight has raised quite a few eyebrows," Knowledge said.

"Knowledge, let me save you some time and trouble. Tell Big Stone me nor any of my people killed Pana," Eddie said flatly.

"Oh, we already know that your hands are clean of this. Whoever took Pana out was definitely not local," Knowledge informed him.

"Then why come see me?" Eddie questioned.

"For the same reason whoever blew into town and whacked Pana might've," Knowledge replied. "If I were new to the city and planned on making a big play, you'd probably be the first person I'd come to see to get my feet wet. I'd be itching to see what I could do to get into your good graces, so I could tap into that primo coke you're sitting on."

"You flatter me, kid, but I'm not the only one moving weight in the city. What makes me so special that these people would come to me instead of going to one of my competitors?"

"Because of everyone holding enough weight to mean something, you're the only one who ain't got no hang-ups about who you'll do business with. You don't care whether they're black, white, brown, or polka dot. So long as the money is green, you'll take it."

Eddie had to admit, Knowledge was a sharp one, but it'd take more than speculation to trip him up. "So Big Stone sent you here to insult me?"

Knowledge raised his hands in surrender. "I meant no disrespect, Eddie. I'm just saying what everyone, including yourself, knows to be true. Now, nobody is saying you're out here moving foul, Eddie. We just know that your path crosses with a lot of people from different places and spaces. Maybe one of those people went by the name Diamonds?"

"Sorry, doesn't ring a bell." The lie rolled off Eddie's tongue far too smoothly. "Is that who did the Suarez hit?"

"Maybe . . . maybe not," Knowledge said coyly. "We're still investigating the situation, but we're getting close . . . real close."

"Out of curiosity, why the hell do you guys even care?" Eddie asked. "Big Stone, nor any of his associates, had business with Pana. Why not charge this shit to the game and let it go?"

"Because maybe whoever went at Pana won't be content to stop there. If they got away with knocking one boss off, maybe they'll get the balls to go at another one. Could be Big Stone, maybe Pharaoh. Hell, they might even try to make a move on you."

Eddie laughed. "They'd be crazy to move against me. I'm connected from on high."

"I'll bet that's the same thing Pana thought before he got his heart cut out," Knowledge said.

"Well, I thank you and Big Stone for your concern, but we're good over here." Eddie stood. "If I happen to hear anything, I'll be sure to let you know. Blanco will see you out."

Knowledge glanced over his shoulder at Blanco, who was

hovering behind him. "I can see myself out." He ambled pass the
bodyguard and toward the door. But before he left, he had some
parting words for Eddie. "Eventually we will find out who was
behind Pana's murder and deal with them and everyone else involved
accordingly," he assured him before he left.

"You believe the nerve of that *shine* coming in here talking like
he's somebody?" Blanco asked after Knowledge had gone.

"Yeah, that little shit is getting beside himself," Eddie agreed. "I
can remember when he was a dirty little fucker running around stealing packages, but now he's walking and talking like he's a fucking
boss. If it weren't for Big Stone, someone would've put a bullet in his
head a long time ago."

"But Knowledge ain't the problem here, Eddie. Diamonds is,"
Blanco reminded him.

"What did your people say on the phone?"

"Our friend has been pretty busy. He just took a meeting with
those Haitian smack dealers from Brooklyn. Looks like they've
thrown in their lot with Diamonds."

Though Eddie tried not to show it, this troubled him. Doodles
was a big-time heroin importer, and if he had opened up his network
to Diamonds to flood the streets of Harlem, it could cause a shift in
power. He had underestimated Diamonds's resourcefulness, and it
was coming back to bite him. "That overly ambitious hillbilly is becoming more of a headache than he's worth."

"I told you from the beginning that I thought it was a bad idea
to do business with anybody TJ brought to the table. He's a piece
of shit, and you know what they say about birds of a feather. The
way Diamonds is moving, he's going to end up drawing a lot of
unwanted attention. Nobody can tie us to him or his bullshit right
now, but who's to say what'll happen later? You see the way Knowledge came in here asking a bunch of questions, and I'm sure he's

not alone in this. All it'll take is for Big Stone to start whispering in the right ears, and people are gonna start looking at us funny . . . real funny."

"Tell me something I don't know." Eddie flopped back into his chair.

"Eddie." Blanco sat in the chair across from him. "I hope I'm not being out of line, but I gotta be honest about this. Individually, I'll go toe-to-toe with any of these muthafuckas in the streets and me and my boys will hold our own, but if these old-timers think we're playing foul and decide to declare us the common enemy, we're gonna have a serious problem on our hands. Under that kind of pressure, I doubt even think Michael will be able to do anything for us, short of going to war with the other bosses."

"And we both know my uncle ain't gonna do that. Michael loves his family, but he loves his money more. War is bad for business."

"Here's where the situation gets more interesting, though. After the Haitians left, Diamonds had another visitor. Care to take a guess who it was?"

"Blanco, do I look like I'm in the fucking mood to play guessing games?" Eddie snapped. "Spit it out."

"Pearl Stone."

"Who?" The name didn't sound familiar to Eddie.

"Big Stone's kid," Blanco said, enlightening him.

"Now, that is interesting. I know for a fact that Big Stone keeps his kids away from anything street related, so this raises the question as to what the fuck Pearl Stone was doing slumming with a piece of shit like Diamonds?"

"Taking it up the ass maybe?" Blanco laughed.

Eddie ignored the tasteless joke and rolled the information over in his head. It now made sense where Knowledge had gotten the name from. He'd likely seen him sniffing around Pearl, but that still didn't explain why he thought Eddie would know him. Maybe he was just fishing, or maybe he knew more than he let on. Either way, Big Stone's people were getting too close to the truth, and that didn't sit well with him. It was time to take drastic measures, and Pearl's secret relationship with Diamonds might be the additional edge he needed.

"Maybe it's time for us to cut our losses," Blanco said as if he were reading Eddie's mind. "The only ones who can tie us to any of this are Diamonds and his crew. I say we take them down and bury the secret with their corpses."

"I couldn't agree with you more. Diamonds has definitely got to go, but it has to be done in a way where it doesn't lead to us having to answer a whole bunch of uncomfortable questions. This is why the I took the liberty of looking into an insurance policy. When I set my plan in motion, this mess will clean itself up."

"How do you mean?" Blanco asked.

"Let's just say that there are people out there who want to see Diamonds dead worse than we do, and some of them are willing to pay big bucks for the pleasure. I expect that very shortly Diamonds won't be our problem anymore."

CHAPTER FORTY-FOUR

Since Ruby lived in Hell's Kitchen and Pearl lived uptown, they deci
ded to take two separate cars. Goldie would take Ruby back to her
place, and Diamonds would drop Pearl off. The brothers said it was
for convenience, but it was really so each of them could spend some
alone time with their respective ladies.

Pearl was still acting a little stiff after whatever exchange between
her and Hank had occurred at the baby shower. Diamonds prodded
her as to what had been said, but she remained tight-lipped about it.
Diamonds, knowing Hank the way he did, figured he'd probably said
something out of pocket, as he tended to do sometimes. He couldn't
figure out who was a bigger cock-blocker: Hank or Vita. He understood the OG's concerns, considering who Pearl's father was and
what was at stake, but it was a calculated risk that Diamonds was
willing to take. He genuinely believed that Pearl had come into his
life for a reason, and in time his crew would all see it too.

Diamonds picked up his cell phone from the center console when
he heard it vibrating against the plastic. He checked the caller ID and
set it back down, only for it to ring again a few seconds later. Most
were calls from different people he had working for him, but there
was a number that had popped up three times already that he didn't

recognize. He started to answer it just out of curiosity, but decided against it. When time allowed, he would have to go and pick up a second cell phone, because taking business and personal calls all on the same line didn't provide him much peace, nor was it the smartest thing for him to be doing.

"Does that thing ever stop ringing?" Pearl asked with an attitude.

"My bad." He picked it up again and powered it off.

"Why'd you cut it off? Your girlfriend, Vita, blowing your line up?" Pearl asked sarcastically.

"I thought I told you that Vita wasn't my girlfriend."

"Girlfriend, fuck buddy, whatever you wanna call her."

"What the hell is eating you? You've been acting funny since we left the baby shower."

"I'm not acting funny. I'm good," she said, and busied herself looking out the window.

"Pearl, if I did or said something to offend you, I apologize."

"No, you've been a perfect gentleman. Sorry I can't say the same for the rest of your friends," Pearl said.

"What happened back there between you and Hank?" Diamonds asked.

"Nothing, we were just having a little chitchat about life and relationships. I don't think he likes me very much."

"Don't pay Hank's sour ass no mind. He's distrustful of new people and can be a bit overprotective when it comes to me."

"Have you guys known each other a long time?" Pearl asked.

"Shit, me and Hank go back damn near as far as I can remember. Back in the day, he owned a grocery store in the little town I grew up outside. Back then I wasn't this refined piece of man you see sitting next to you. I was a skinny, barefoot kid who didn't speak a lot of English and had to either hunt or steal my for my supper. Whenever Hank would see me skulking about town, he'd bless me with food or whatever else I needed from his store. Some nights I would've probably starved to death if it hadn't been for he mercies of that man. Hank is the closest thing to a daddy me and Goldie ever had. I'd kill or die for that man."

"Have you?"

"Have I what?" Diamonds didn't understand the question.

"Ever killed anyone," she elaborated.

Diamonds cut her a look. "You wound me, Pearl. Do I strike you as the murderous type?"

"That's not what I asked you."

"Sweetie, don't ask questions you really don't want to know the answers to."

"I wouldn't ask if I didn't want to know."

When Diamonds looked at her and saw the seriousness in her eyes, he pulled over. "What's all this all about? You wired or something?"

"No, just trying to get a feel for who you *really* are," Pearl told him.

"I've already laid my cards on the table, which is why I'm trying to figure out what the Twenty Questions is about all of a sudden."

"Truths," she said flatly. "All bullshit aside, I know you're in the life. I was raised by and around hustlers, so I know my own kind. I'm not judging you for it. I just want to know how deep the rabbit hole goes before I decide if I wanna crawl into it with you, feel me?"

"Okay, you want some truth? Fine. I came up a dirt poor kid in the sticks and promised myself that if I ever got out, I'd never know the taste of a fucking possum or rat ever again in my life. Am I a saint? Absolutely not, but I'm not no demon either. I do whatever I gotta do to feed me and my people and I make no apologies for it. That truthful enough for you?" he snapped.

"Diamonds, I didn't mean to offend you," Pearl said, picking up on his irritation.

"I'm not offended, Pearl, just confused. You know, one minute it's like we're on the same page and everything is good, and the next it's like you're pulling away. I'm feeling you and I thought you were feeling me, but maybe I was wrong."

"The fact that I wore a five-hundred-dollar pair of heels to hang out with you in a backyard in the Bronx should tell you that the feeling is mutual."

"Then what's the problem?"

"I dunno," she said hesitantly. "I guess I'm just afraid that our pasts could interfere with our futures."

"And what's that supposed to mean?"

Pearl looked into his eyes and saw pleading in them. Diamonds had bared his soul to her, and she hadn't shown him the same courtesy. It wasn't because she intentionally wanted to mislead him, but because she was afraid of it changing the dynamics of what was going on with them. Though their relationship was still very fresh, it felt so right, and she didn't want to do anything to ruin it. Hank's warning played on repeat in her head. She really liked Diamonds and wanted to see where things would go, but what if the old man was right and they were courting disaster by being together? After some great debate, Pearl decided to lay all her cards on the table and let fate handle the rest. "Diamonds, there's something I think you should know before we go any further."

"I sure as hell hope this ain't the part of the story where you tell me you were born a boy," Diamonds joked.

"Could you just be serious for minute? I need to say something to you, and after I do, there's a strong possibility you may feel differently about being with me."

"How about you let me be the judge of that."

Pearl was hesitant, but the longer she waited, the harder it would be. "Are you familiar with the name Big Stone?"

Diamonds shrugged. "Who isn't? He's one of the biggest dealers in the city."

"He's also my father."

The car became deathly silent. Pearl watched in anticipation as Diamonds processed what she had just revealed to him. Her family name was both a gift and a curse, closing as many doors to her as it opened. When most guys found out who her father was, they either took off running or tried to get her to put them on. Either way, it always changed things. She had hoped Diamonds would be different.

"Aren't you going to say anything?" she asked after a full minute had gone by without him responding.

"What's there to say? Some kid's daddies' are garbagemen or doctors, and yours just happens to be a gangster," he said as if it were that simple.

"Big Stone isn't just a gangster; he's *the* gangster," Pearl corrected him.

Diamonds shrugged. "You know what I do for a living, so I'm hardly in any position to judge what the next man does to put food in his babies' mouths. The dirt under your daddy's fingernails ain't got nothing to do with what's going on between us."

"So knowing who my father is and what he could do to you, you still want to see me?" She was surprised.

"Why wouldn't I?" He took her hands in his and looked Pearl directly in the eyes. "Let me make something clear to you, doll. I wasn't bullshitting you earlier when I said I had been waiting for you my entire life, and what you just told me lets me know I'm not crazy to feel that way. I know what you're risking by sharing that, and I'm

honored that it was me you chose to share it with. I know all too well
how heavy secrets can get when you carry them long enough, and
that's why I don't ever want anything but honesty between us. As long
as you down for me, I'll down for you, and that's all we need to keep
this thing strong."

"You mean that?" Pearl's eyes misted.

"On my life." He leaned in and kissed her.

The moment Diamonds's lips touched hers, Pearl felt that familiar spark again. This time she was prepared for it and embraced it.
She grabbed a fistful of his long hair with one hand; she ran the other
down the length of his body and traced a line over the top of his pants,
tickling the hairs on his stomach. She slipped her hand in a little far-
ther and felt the beginnings of his penis. It was thick and hard. Her
hand continued its descent, tracing the vein along the shaft of his dick,
and she was pleasantly surprised by how long it was. Her pussy
throbbed, imagining him penetrating her. Throwing caution to the
wind, she began trying to free his dick from his pants, but Diamonds
stopped her.

"What's wrong?" Pearl asked.

"Not like this," Diamonds told her. "When I make love to you
for the first time, it won't be in the backseat of no ride. I got too much
respect for you for that."

"Now there's something you don't hear every day." Pearl sat back
in her seat, a disappointed look on her face.

"I keep trying to tell you: I'm not your average dude. Don't fret
over it, Pearl. I'm gonna hit you with this pipe soon enough, and when
I do, I promise you it'll be worth the wait."

A few minutes later they were pulling up at the corner of Pearl's block.

"You sure I can't drop you off at your door? I feel kinda like a
creep for kicking you out on the curb like this," Diamonds said.

"Its all good. I gotta stop at the store anyhow. Don't worry about it. I'll be okay," she assured him.

"A'ight, but you better make sure you call me as soon as you're in the house. And remember what I said earlier: as long as you got me, I got you," Diamonds promised before pulling away.

Pearl waited until Diamonds was out of sight before allowing a smile to creep across her face that was so big they could probably see it at the other end of the block. The talk she'd had with Diamonds had lifted a weight off her shoulders. Normally she didn't care what guys thought about her or her family's affiliation, but with Diamonds, it was different. She couldn't quite understand why, but his opinion mattered to her.

When she got to the bodega she placed her order through the small window: two Philly Blunts and a bottle of water. When she went to pay for her purchases she realized that she had left her car purse in Diamonds's truck. The money wasn't a big deal because she knew the guy at the store and it was nothing for him to give her the items on the arm until she was able to swing back the following day, but she had also left her keys in the bag. This meant she would have to ring the doorbell instead of creeping in, which would lead to Sandra asking her a million questions as to where she had been. As she thought on it that might not have been such a bad thing because she needed to talk to her anyhow.

She knew when she broke the news to her father about the new guy she was seeing, he would likely be against it. No man would ever be good enough for his little girl, especially one cut from the same end of the cloth as he was. Even getting him to be open-minded about the idea of her seeing Diamonds would be a struggle, because Big Stone didn't know what it felt like to love someone on the wrong side of the law. Fortunately for her, Sandra did. If she could get her to like Diamonds, it'd be easier to convince Big Stone to give

him a chance. She felt good about the budding relationship between her and Diamonds. It was as if for once, the universe had
finally decided to send her a good man, even if he was a criminal.

As Pearl was walking towards her home she was so caught up in
thoughts of teenage love that she hadn't even realized someone was
behind her until the street overhead street lamp cast an extra shadow
on the ground. Her hand instinctively went for her purse, and the gun
inside, then she remembered she didn't have either. She was just about
to breakout into a dead sprint when a familiar voice called out.

"Pearl, its me!"

Pearl turned and squinted against the darkness and was able to
make out a man walking towards her with his hands up to show they
were empty. When her eyes landed on his face her mood went from
sugar to shit. "No the fuck this nigga didn't."

"Now hold on. Before you say anything, just let me explain."
Devonte pleaded.

"You ain't got to explain shit but why your ass creeping on my
block like some nut-ass stalker!" Pearl barked.

"Well you wouldn't talk to me on the phone." Devonte tried to
reason.

"So you pop up in my hood?" Pearl looked at him as if he had
lost his mind.

"I know I'm out of order, and I apologize for that but I needed to
talk to you, baby." Devonte said in an almost whining tone.

"Fuck outta here," Pearl spat. "I said everything I had to say on
the phone. What part of its over didn't you understand?"

Devonte took a step forward and reached for her hand, but she
jerked it back. "Don't do me like that, Pearl. I know I fucked up, but
I love you. Why can't you just give me the chance to show you that?"

"I can do you one better. I'll give you a chance to get your silly ass
off this block before something bad happens to you." Pearl capped and

turned to walk away, but to much to her surprise Devonte grabbed her arm. When she looked into his eyes, she didn't see the smooth talking young dude she had been fucking and bleeding for the last few month. She saw someone she had never met before and it made her nervous.

"See, I came over here to try and talk to you like an adult, but I see you wanna be a child about it. You want to make a nigga beg and shit!" Devonte rambled.

"Devonte, you're hurting me." Pearl said as calmly as she could. She didn't want to do anything that could potentially set him off.

"Kinda like you hurt me, huh?" he smiled sinisterly. "See, I thought you was different . . . tried to treat you different, but you're just like the rest of these scandalous ass bitches! You take what you want and give nothing in return!"

"Baby just calm down and we can talk about this." Pearl tried to sooth him.

"Oh, so now you wanna talk?" Devonte chuckled. "Sure, lets go talk," he began dragging her by the arm across the street. She hadn't noticed before, but his car was parked in front of a hydrant a few houses down.

"Devonte, where are you taking me?" Pearl struggled against him, but he had a death grip on her arm.

"You said you wanted to talk, so we're gonna go someplace quiet and have a nice chat." He pressed a button on the remote and released the automatic locks.

By then Pearl had gone from just being nervous to about ready to shit herself. Of all the times not to have her gun, she picked the night Devonte decided to whip out his bag of crazy. She looked up and down the block frantically for signs of someone . . . anyone, who might be able to derail what was about to happen to her, but the street was naked. As Devonte began forcing her inside the car, she sent out one last-ditch prayer and thankfully it was answered.

"Fuck is you doing?" Stoney's high pitched voice cut through the night. Pearl had no idea where he had come from, but she had never been so happy to see her little brother.

"Stay outta grown folk's business, shorty." Devonte growled.

"My sister is my business, muthafucka!" Stoney barked back. It was then that they noticed the small gun in his hand.

Devonte shoved Pearl away and turned his attention to Stoney. He could tell by the way that his hand shook and his eyes couldn't seem to rest that he was nervous. "Shorty, why don't you give me that gun before I fuck your little ass up?" He took a step towards him.

Without missing a beat Stoney fired a shot into the ground just between Devonte's feet. "Next one is in your dome." He raised the gun. "Now try me like you don't know what my last name is."

Devonte weighed his chances and reasoned that a good run was better than a bad stand. "A'ight," he began backing away. "You got that." He eased into his car under the watchful eyes of Pearl and Stoney. "This conversation ain't over, ma. Believe that," he promised her and pulled off.

Devonte hadn't even cleared the block before Pearl rushed to Stoney and wrapped him in a loving hug. As she held him she couldn't tell which one of them were trembling more. Stoney talked tough, but he was no killer. Her little brother was a good boy, but he proved that he would stand tall when it came to protecting his family.

"You okay?" Stoney asked Pearl.

"I am now," Pearl released him.

"Who was that dude?" Stoney asked.

"Just some thirsty nigga I was dumb enough to give my time to." Pearl told him. "If you hadn't shown up when you did there's no telling what that nut would've done."

"This is Stone hood and niggas can't come through here without a pass." Stoney boasted.

"Shut up, Super Thug." Pearl teased him. Now that the immediate threat had passed they were both calmer. "Where the hell did you get that?"

"This?" Stoney raised the small pistol. It was a two shot derringer. "Daddy got at least a half dozen guns stashed around the house. I doubt if he even noticed this one was missing."

"Well guns are not toys and your young ass shouldn't have one," Pearl snatched the gun from him and stuffed it into her bra. "Now let's get inside before somebody calls the police about that gunshot."

By the time Pearl and Stoney reached their brownstone, Sandra was coming out the front gate. She was wearing a bathrobe and had her hair wrapped in a scarf. In her hand was a .357 with a barrel so long that it looked like something you'd see in a cartoon. No doubt she'd heard the shots and like any good queen she was ready to protect her kingdom. When she saw the kids, she tucked the gun behind her back.

"What the hell is going on out here in the middle of the night like two crack heads? I thought I heard shooting." Sandra's eyes darted up and down the block, searching for signs of danger.

"We didn't hear anything." Stoney lied.

"Pearl, I know you were out with your friends but you're cutting it kind of close on the time. And you," she turned to Stoney, "I thought your daddy said to keep your ass in the house? Last I checked you were upstairs playing video games; so how did you manage to make it out here?"

Stoney had snuck out earlier that night to go and see a girl, with the intention of being back before anyone knew he was missing. He was already grounded for getting suspended from school, and the new offense was sure to have him bound to the house for the rest of the summer.

"I'm sorry, it was my fault Sandra." Pearl spoke up. "I took a cab home and didn't realize that I was out of cash. I called Stoney to meet me outside with a twenty."

The story smelled like bullshit, but Sandra was too tired to care. She would revisit it in the morning, but that night she was just glad they were both safe. "Well y'all come on in the house. This ain't a good night to be wander about. There's evil in the air tonight." She pulled her robe tighter. "I can feel it in my bones."

CHAPTER FORTY-FIVE

What had started off being a shitty night for Buda had thankfully started to turn around. Everyone had assumed he had stormed off because of his scuffle with Domo, but it was only half true. He had planned to make an example of Domo in order to send a message to all the new guys Diamonds was recruiting that he was still top dog. It was supposed to be quick and very painful, but Domo had surprised him when he fought back. The kid was obviously no match for Buda, but he had to give him credit for being resourceful. After the pain of having his nuts damn near pulverized had worn off, he was able to find a newfound respect for Domo. He still didn't too much care for him, or any of his people, but Domo had proven he was no punk, which was more than he could say for most of the new faces that had been around lately.

Thinking about the direction their crew was going in made his blood boil. When they had learned of Dip's betrayal, when he'd stolen the drugs and the money, the remaining crew members had made a pact on the soul of his deceased little brother: no outsider would ever be able to move amongst them again. But lately that's all Buda ever saw around them . . . outsiders. Of course, he knew that the five of them would never be able to accomplish what they had set out to do alone, so he understood recruiting extra muscle from the cities they pillaged, but they were supposed to be little more than soldiers. Diamonds had changed the rules when he started giving them seats at their table, the same table John-Boy had given his life for.

Regardless of how angry Buda got at Diamonds, he still loved him like a brother, which was why what was happening between them hurt so much. He'd been noticing a gradual change in his friend as they hit more cities and made more money, but the changes had started to become more apparent when they were in Miami. It was supposed to be them against everybody else, but the more money they made, the more Diamonds became like the people they fed on. He was more enamored with the flash and the power than with the cash. No longer was it good enough to play the shadows, feasting on cities from the inside out until they were fat with cash. Diamonds was determined to make a name for himself, and he didn't care who or what he put at risk to do it. The others might've been content to sit by silently while Diamonds and his ever-growing ego pissed away everything they had built, but not Buda. He was loyal to Diamonds, but if he was unfit to lead them, Buda wouldn't hesitate to step up. Some might've called Buda's train of thought jealousy, but the way he saw it, he was protecting the interests of the crew.

After he left TJ's baby shower, Buda hopped in a taxi and headed back to Harlem. Mercedes had hit him up and told him to come by her place because she had a surprise for him. As they were talking, he could hear the muffled giggles of another female in the background. His heart filled with the hope that he might be finally going to get the threesome he had been practically begging her for.

Before going upstairs to her apartment, he stopped at the corner liquor store and grabbed a bottle of whiskey for himself and vodka for her. He was too anxious to wait for the elevator, so he bounded the stairs three at a time, all the way up to the sixth floor. With a trembling hand, he knocked on the door and waited. A few seconds later the door opened, and Buda found his breath stolen.

Mercedes opened the door, wearing nothing more than a sheer robe and red pumps. Her face was flawlessly made-up, her lips painted a bright shade of crimson. Dark silver-dollar-sized nipples stood hard and erect behind the thin fabric, causing a stir in his crotch. "So, you gonna stand there gawking or come inside?"

Less than a minute later, Buda and Mercedes were in her bedroom going at it. His hands explored her body, paying special attention to her breasts. Using his thumbs, he flicked her nipples, making them stiffer than they already were. He grabbed a fistful of her hair and kissed her passionately on the lips. Mercedes's mouth tasted of cigarettes, liquor, and something else he wasn't familiar with, but he ignored it and kept letting his tongue explore her mouth. He had almost sucked all the breath from her lungs when Mercedes pulled away.

"Calm down, boo. We got all night." Mercedes backed toward the bed.

"Fuck that. I been dreaming about this pussy all day." Buda panted, following her as if he were hypnotized. He took his gun from his pants and set it on her dresser while he tried to get his belt undone.

"Is that right?" She slid back on the bed.

"Better believe it." He finally got the belt loose.

"Then prove it." She spread her legs and showed him her shaved nest.

Buda didn't even bother to take his pants all the way off. He pushed them down around her ankles and crawled up onto the bed.

His thick, veiny, cock felt heavy in his hand as he guided it toward her pussy. When the tip touched her lips, he could feel that she was already soaking wet. He was about to take the plunge when she placed her hands on his chest to stop him.

"You know the rules." Mercedes reached over to the nightstand and retrieved a condom.

"C'mon, baby. Let me feel that raw," Buda pleaded.

"Nah, papi. You know I ain't going out like that. Either put the condom on or leave with blue balls," she told him in the tone that said it wasn't up for negotiation.

"Fuck it," Buda said angrily, and snatched the condom and rolled it on. Once she was satisfied, she allowed him to enter her pearly gates. The moment Buda slipped inside her, he let out a high-pitched sigh. Even with the condom standing between them, Mercedes's pussy felt like a warm summer day.

Mercedes placed her legs on Buda's shoulders and grabbed him around the wrists. She hiked her ass up and began sliding herself ever so slowly back and forth on his dick. From the way he was biting his lip, she knew it felt good to him, but little did he knew it was about to get even better.

Buda was hunched over Mercedes, just getting into his groove, when he felt the presence of someone behind him. He jumped out of the pussy and spun, dick swinging and fists drawn back, ready to strike. His hand immediately dropped to his side when he saw who it was.

The pictures he had seen of Zonnie hardly did her justice. She was wearing nothing more than a T-shirt and a pair of furry slippers, so he was able to really appreciate her curves. She had wide hips and thick thighs, but her stomach was as flat as a board. Her skin was the color of honeysuckle melon, her lips the color of rose petals.

Alluring hazel eyes traveled the length of Buda's body and came to rest on his dick. She nodded in approval.

"What's this?" Buda asked, already knowing the answer and praying he was right.

"It's like I told you: I had a surprise for you," Mercedes said with a mischievous smirk.

Zonnie stepped up and took his thick manhood in her hand. "So what's up? Is this a private party or can I join in?"

Buda lay back on the bed and prepared himself for the wild ride he was sure was coming. Mercedes lay across Buda, her ass hiked high in the air, while Zonnie positioned herself behind her. She buried her face in the crack of Mercedes's ass and began dragging her tongue from clit to booty.

The sight of Mercedes's eyes rolling into the back of her head as she was carted off into the throes of passion turned Buda the fuck on. He leaned up to try to kiss Mercedes, but she shoved him back down. He had been reduced to the role of spectator, at least for the moment.

When Zonnie was sated on Mercedes's juices, she gave her a playful slap on the ass, letting her know it was time to switch positions. Zonnie went high while Mercedes elected to go low. Zonnie pressed her lips over Buda's, allowing him to taste the woman they had been sharing. He wasn't sure which was sweeter, Mercedes's pussy or Zonnie's lips.

Feeling a pair of hot lips wrap around his dick jerked Buda up so fast that he and Zonnie almost butted heads. Mercedes was effortlessly taking him from tip to balls in and out of her throat, drooling down his shaft and inner thighs. Not to be outdone, Zonnie abandoned Buda's lips and moved south. As he lay, his head propped on a pillow, watching the two beautiful women fight over his cock, his chest swelled with pride. For the first time since he'd been in New York, he felt like a boss.

About an hour after the marathon sex session, Buda was snatched from his peaceful sleep by a sudden feeling of dread. He looked around the room and everything appeared normal, but there was no sign of either of the girls. When he ran his hand over the bedsheet next to him, the spot was still warm, meaning they hadn't been gone long.

He got up and started making his way toward the living room. As he drew closer to the living room, he could hear the soft sounds of voices and he smelled weed. It appeared the girls were trying to keep the partying going without him. They were probably talking shit about having fucked him into a coma. If they thought they were off the hook that easily, they were going to be surprised as shit when he popped up ass naked with a rock-hard dick, ready for round two. But when Buda rounded the corner, it was he who was in for a surprise.

He found the two girls sitting on the couch, passing a joint back and forth and drinking up the liquor he had brought, but they weren't alone. Wedged between them was a man Buda had become recently familiar with because of his dealings with Diamonds, but he looked nothing like the clown he seen earlier. He'd traded in his baggy jeans and do-rag for a pair of slacks and a cashmere sweater. Aside from his new clothes, there was something else different about him that Buda couldn't quite put his finger on.

"I'm surprised that thing still works, considering that young boy almost ripped it off," Rolling said, looking at Buda's dick.

Buda turned to make a run for his gun, which he had left in the bedroom, and he ran smack into Born coming out of the bathroom. He was leveling a 9mm at Buda's face. "Good to see you again, playa." He motioned for him to move back into the living room.

"I trust you remember Born, and I see you've already met my ladies." He threw his arms around Zonnie and Mercedes. "Why don't you have a seat so we can chat for a minute?"

"Fuck you, nigga!" Buda spat.

Rolling gave Born a nod, and he cracked Buda upside the head with his gun so hard that it dropped him onto all fours.

"You know, it really doesn't have to be like this," Rolling said coolly. "I was hoping we could chat without all the theatrics."

Buda gave him an amused look. "Fuck we got to talk about? You think a new set of clothes makes you somebody? You still ain't shit but a yes-man!"

"Coming from a man who'd rather carry Diamonds's dirty laundry than try to go out and get his own, I know how much stock to put in your opinion, Buda," Rolling mocked him.

Buda made an attempt to get up, but Born's gun at the back of his head reminded him of his current situation.

"I provided your boy Diamonds with a great opportunity," Rolling continued, "and instead of showing a little appreciation, he treats me like some dog to kick around."

"All you did was make the introduction. Doodles is the man holding the bag."

"And who do you think it was that gave Doodles the bag in the first place?" Rolling questioned.

Buda gave a hearty laugh as if this were the funniest thing he'd ever heard. "So you expect me to believe that Doodles really works for you?"

Rolling laughed. " 'The greatest trick the devil ever pulled was convincing the world he didn't exist.' People tend to focus so much on my baby brother that they overlook the monster hiding in plain sight." He got off the couch and came to stand before Buda, brandishing a large .357. "One of two things will go into your ear tonight,

my friend. My proposal"—he put the gun to the side of Buda's head—
"or a bullet."

When Buda looked into Rolling's eyes, he realized what had been
different about him other than his clothes. The ever-present fear normally in his eyes was now nowhere to be found. It was replaced by
something darker and more sinister. He knew without question that
Rolling had played them all.

"Don't look so surprised, Buda." Rolling got up and began pacing in a tight circle around Buda. "You aren't the only one to fall for
this sniveling middle-man routine. Goodness knows, I've had years
to practice it while living in the exile my little brother imposed on
me. What I learned during my time away is a man who is always
taken as a joke is never seen as a threat until it's too late. You and
your boys were proof of that."

"So you did this deal with us just to pull this shit?" Buda motioned toward Born, who was still holding his gun to the back of
Buda's head.

Rolling stopped his pacing and stood before Buda. "Just because
I'm a snake doesn't mean I'm not a wise businessman. Doodles has
been bringing in some nice change off the dope I've been having
smuggled into Brooklyn, but his reach is . . . *local,* for lack of a better word. You boys haven't got those kids of hang-ups. I knew that if
I brought your crew in at the rate you gobble up territory, and competition, it'd only be a matter of time before you bumped heads with
Big Stone and did what I couldn't, and that's remove him from the
equation so I can take back what he stole from me. Then your boy
Diamonds had to go and fall for my niece and fucked everything up."
He extended his hand, and Born placed his 9mm in it.

"You mean the little brown-skinned thing he's been sniffing
around is Big Stone's kid?" Buda was shocked. He'd known something was up with that girl from the moment he'd laid eyes on her.

"And now you understand why you find yourself ass naked and confused. See, with Diamonds seeing my niece, that kills any hopes I had on him going at my brother, at least so long as he's leading the crew. And that fucks up everything I was planning." He placed his gun next to Buda's head. "The way I see it, I'm faced with two options: whack all you little muthafuckas for all the time and money I've already wasted"—he lowered the gun—"or me and you can come to some type of understanding."

The sounds of WBLS hummed softly through the speakers of the SUV as Diamonds navigated his way south through Harlem. The quiet storm was jamming some of his favorite old-school cuts, and most of them all fit his mood.

The talk he'd had with Pearl had done wonders for his soul. He had known already who her father was, but he had no plans to tell her that. The fact that she had been up front with him about it said a lot about how she was built. His people might've felt like he was speeding by getting so caught up with her so quick, but Diamonds knew what he was doing. She was beautiful, intelligent, loyal, and connected. You didn't leave a woman like that blowing in the wind; you made her yours.

By the time Diamonds pulled into the garage of his building, he was so tired that he could barely keep his eyes open. He had been going for days on little to no sleep, and couldn't wait to get upstairs and crash on his featherbed mattress. As he was waiting for the elevator that would take him up to his floor, he remembered that he'd never turned his phone back on from when he'd left Pearl. As soon as he did, he was immediately bombarded with alerts. He had five voice mails and a few text messages, most from Goldie and Hank wondering where the hell he was. He'd follow up with them in the morning. He was just about to slip the phone back into his pocket when he saw a text message from Wolf pop up. They always spoke on the phone or in person, never via text message. Curious, Diamonds opened the message. It only contained six words: DON'T GO HOME UNTIL WE TALK.

"What the fuck?" Diamonds was still trying to make heads or tails of the message when the elevator door opened. When he looked up, he caught a flash of a two men wearing stocking caps over their faces, before something slammed into the back of his head and everything went black.

CHAPTER FORTY-SIX

Vita's eyelids felt like they had sandbags in them. Every so often they would try to droop and pull her into the ever tempting sleep she so badly needed, but she had to stay awake. She was coming across the George Washington bridge, so it would only be a short while longer before she was back at her apartment and in her bed.

Her night with Domo had proved to be far more eventful, and taxing, than she had anticipated. From the moment she had laid eyes on the quiet young man from Newark she knew there was something special about him. He was cute, but a little young for her tastes. Vita usually went for older guys. Seeing the way he had handled himself in the shootout made her look at him in a different light, and how he handled himself against Buda was the cherry on top.

Diamonds had peeped her openly flirting with Domo at the house and tried to act like it was no big deal, but she could tell it was eating him up. That's what she had intended, to show him how it felt when the shoe was on the other foot. Jealous tactics aside, it did feel good to be wanted for once. When Diamonds looked at her, all he saw was a crime partner, and an occasional warm hole to take his frustrations out on, but it was different with Domo. He saw her for what she was, a woman.

She hadn't meant to sleep with him, at least that night and especially not in the backseat of her car like some whore, but she couldn't help herself. Between the liquor and all the sexual tension that had been built up throughout the night, Vita started feeling some type of way, and obviously the feeling was mutual for Domo. She tried being aggressive, hoping it would scare him off and bring her back to her senses, but he called her bluff and they ended up going at it like two jackrabbits at a truck stop off the New Jersey Turnpike. Domo might've been slight of build, but he was heavy of cock. God have given that boy a gift and he put it on Vita, over, and over all through the night and well into the morning. He was still somewhat inexperienced, more thrust than technique, but in time she would train him properly in the art of pleasing a woman. Diamonds had had been accurate when he kept referring to Domo as Vita's boy-toy, because that's exactly what she had planned on making him. She was sure that Diamonds wouldn't be happy when he found out Vita and Domo were fucking, but she didn't care. She'd waited for him to come around and claim her long enough, and not it was time she starting doing her.

"Fuck him," Vita mumbled as she paid the toll and came across the bridge into New York.

The last thing Vita expected to see when she arrived at her apartment building was her whole crew huddled up on the front stoop. She saw the dark expressions on their faces and knew immediately that something was wrong. When she noticed that everyone was there except Diamonds a cold chill gripped her heart.

"What's the hell is going on?" Vita asked jumping out of the car.

"Where you been, V? We been trying to hit you all night." Hank told her.

"I was out and my phone was dead. What's happened?" Vita looked over the sea of faces.

"What's happened is, while your ass has been MIA our whole operation has been falling apart!" Buda snarled. His face was bruised and one of his arms was in a sling.

"Buda, what are you talking about? And what happened to your arm?" Vita was confused.

"Big Stone happened to my arm." Buda replied. "Apparently he found out what we were up to and didn't like it. A few of his boys came to pay a call on me in the wee hours. As you can see, I almost didn't make it." He pointed to the sling. "When you went missing we thought they might've come at you too."

"Where's Diamonds?" Vita asked. At the mention of his name everyone got quiet. "Somebody talk to me!" she demanded. When she looked at Goldie's face, the tears dancing in his eyes told her all she need to know. "No." her legs suddenly got weak, and she would've fallen to the ground had Hank not moved to steady her.

"Easy, baby girl. We don't know if he's dead, but we haven't been able to reach him." Hank told her.

"Seeing how Big Stone and his boys move, the chances of him still being alive are slim to none," Buda said.

"Watch yo mouth, nigga! That's still my brother," Goldie warned.

"Goldie, you know I didn't mean it like it sounded." Buda's voice softened. "Diamonds is my brother too and I'm just as worried as the rest of you. I'm just speaking facts. Everybody knows that if you wanna kill a monster, you cut off the head and the body will follow. Diamonds was our leader, so what better way to cripple us than to take him out?"

"I ain't letting this shit ride," Vita said, just above a whisper. She was so overcome with emotion that she could barely speak.

"None of us are. Diamonds has been there for me, for all of us, more times than I can count. Whoever is responsible for this is gonna

K'WAN

feel us!" Buda promised. "I say we hit that nigga Big Stone and every-one close to him."

"Calm your ass down Buda. We can't go to war with an orga-nization of that size without finding out all the facts first." Hank told him.

"They touched our family, what the fuck else is there to know?" Buda shot back. "Look, I ain't trying to throw my weight around or nothing, but Diamonds made me second in command because he knew if something ever happened to him, I'd step up and do what needed to be done. Now y'all can stand here and jaw about it like some bitches, or strap up and do what we do. With or without you, in a few hours the sun won't be the only thing going down." He stormed off.

"I'll go talk to him." Hank offered. "Goldie, you stay here with Vita. I don't think it's a good idea for her to be alone right now. I'll hit you in a little while when I find out more about all this."

"I got you, OG." Goldie said.

"I still can't believe he's dead," Vita said, after Hank and Buda had gone.

"Neither can I, nor will I until I see a body. Something ain't right with this," Goldie told her.

"What you saying, Goldie?"

"I'm saying this this whole situation stinks of something foul. My brother is way too paranoid to let an outsider get the drop on him, so I figure whoever did this had help from someone close. You love him too much to let anything happen to him unless it was by your own hand, so that leaves Hank and Buda."

Vita frowned. "Hank loves Diamonds like kin, and Buda is a snake but I don't think he'd stoop that low."

"Maybe . . . maybe not, but I'm not willing to bet my brother's life or mine on it." Goldie said seriously. "My brother ain't dead."

"I don't know, Goldie. Maybe we just don't want to accept the obvious, so we're holding onto hunches."

"Ain't no hunch, V. I'm telling you what I know," Goldie said seriously. "I know sometimes its easier to turn a blind eye rather than to acknowledge the unexplainable, but I think you all know what Auntie was teaching my brother and me out in that swamp and it wasn't our ABCs. Diamonds and me are tethered by more than genetics, and there's no way he could've passed on without me knowing."

Though Vita would never admit it, she knew there was truth to Goldie's words. Diamonds trafficked in things that were better left undiscussed in public. "So if you're right and Diamonds is still alive, where the hell is he?"

"I don't know, but I think you and me owe it to him to find out."

EPILOGUE

Diamonds was stirred by a sharp pain on his cheek. The fog was still heavily wrapped around his brain, but a second slap across the face woke him up fully. His hands were suspended over his head and cuffed around a metal pipe. He was hanging just high enough to where his bare toes could touch the ground but he couldn't plant his feet. It took a few seconds for his eyes to adjust to the darkness of the room he was in, but when he was able to focus he realized he wasn't alone. Standing in front of him was a light-skinned man wearing a New Orleans Saint's cap. His cat-green eyes stared at Diamonds quizzically.

"Glad to see you're awake. For a minute I thought I had hit you too hard with that pipe and put you in a coma." The light-skinned man said with a smirk.

"Tariq, get your ass from over there and quit fucking with him. I don't want you damaging the merchandise before we get paid." A second man appeared. He was older than the first and sported a full beard. The black suit jacket he wore struggled to contain his mountain-like shoulders.

"Chill out Blue, I'm just having a little fun," he said, and turned back to Diamonds. "You know, when I heard how much was offered up on his head I was expecting more. They talk about you like you're some kind of monster, but you don't look like much. Hardly worth fifty grand." Tariq gave him a nudge and caused him to sway.

"Why don't you come a little closer and I'll see if I can change your mind." Diamonds challenged. The one called Tariq looked like he was about to test his luck until the other man stepped in.

"I said knock it off." Blue shoved Tariq away from Diamonds.

"Since you seem to be the man in charge, I'll see if I can appeal to your sensibility," Diamonds addressed Blue. "If you boys cut me loose now I'll make it so there's enough left of you for your mamas to have open casket funerals."

Blue laughed. "I don't think you're in a position to negotiate. Besides, I ain't the one in charge. I'm just hired muscle."

"Then why don't you get whoever is running this circus out here so we can speak like bosses," Diamonds said.

"A boss? Is that what you think you are now? You always did have an inflated sense of self-importance," a familiar voice called from somewhere behind Diamonds.

Diamonds couldn't turn to see who was speaking to him, but he could hear them approaching: clip-clop . . . clip-clop. It sounded like a limping horse, and was drawing ever nearer. When the speaker stepped from the shadows, Diamonds's breath caught in his throat. He had seen a great many unexplainable things in his life, but never a resurrection. Standing there, leaning on a walking stick, in all his blubbery glory, was the last man Diamonds had ever expected to see again.

"Considering the money and dope you took from me helped to finance your new lifestyle, I'd have thought you'd be a little happier to see me." Big Slim limped closer to Diamonds. He had lost some weight since Diamonds had tried to blow his head off, but he was still fat as hell. "I once told a friend of yours that I didn't care how long it took, but I would track you down and settle our debt." He pulled the walking stick apart and exposed the blade hidden inside. "It's taken me some money and some years, but at long last I have come to collect."

ABOUT THE AUTHOR

K'WAN is a multiple literary award winner and bestselling author of more than twenty titles, including *Gangsta, Road Dawgz, Street Dreams, Hoodlum, Eve, Hood Rat, Blow, Still Hood, Gutter, Section 8, From Harlem with Love, The Leak, Welfare Wifeys, Eviction Notice, Love & Gunplay, Animal, The Life & Times of Slim Goodie, Purple Reign, Little Nikki Grind, Animal II, The Fix, Black Lotus, First & Fifteenth, Ghetto Bastard, Animal 3, The Fix 2, The Fix 3,* and *Animal 4.* He is also the author of several dark fantasy novels written under a pseudonym.

K'wan currently resides in New Jersey, where he is working on his next novel.